Faye Kellerman was born in St Louis, Missouri, and graduated in Mathematics and Dentistry at UCLA. She began her career as a dentist but turned to writing after the birth of her first child in 1978. She has now published thirteen hugely successful novels featuring Peter Decker and Rina Lazarus, as well as a non-series thriller, MOON MUSIC, and a historical novel, THE QUALITY OF MERCY. She lives in Los Angeles with her husband, Jonathan Kellerman, also a bestselling thriller writer, as well as a psychologist, and their children.

Also by Faye Kellerman

Stalker
Jupiter's Bones
Moon Music
Serpent's Tooth
Prayers for the Dead
Justice
Sanctuary
Grievous Sin
False Prophet
Day of Atonement
Milk and Honey
The Quality of Mercy
Sacred and Profane
The Ritual Bath

The Forgotten

Faye Kellerman

headline

First published in Great Britain in 2001
by HEADLINE BOOK PUBLISHING

First published in Great Britain in paperback in 2002
by HEADLINE BOOK PUBLISHING

10 9 8 7 6 5 4 3 2 1

ISBN 0 7472 5924 0

Typeset by Letterpart Ltd
Reigate, Surrey

Printed and bound in Great Britain by
Mackays of Chatham plc, Chatham, Kent

HEADLINE BOOK PUBLISHING
A division of Hodder Headline
338 Euston Road
London NW1 3BH

www.headline.co.uk
www.hodderheadline.com

For Andy, Joanne and Miriam
In memory of Shira – *aleha ha'shalom*.

Acknowledgements

Special thanks to Malka Hier and the staff at the Museum of Tolerance in Los Angeles. May you go from strength to strength.

1

The call was from the police. Not from Rina's lieutenant husband, but from the *police* police. She listened as the man spoke, and when she heard that it had nothing to do with Peter or the children, she felt a 'thank you, God' wave of instant relief. After discovering the reason behind the contact, Rina wasn't as shocked as she should have been.

The Jewish population of L.A.'s West Valley had been rocked by hate crimes in the past, culminating in that hideous ordeal a couple of years ago when a subspecies of human life had gotten off the public bus and had shot up the Jewish Community Center. The Center had been and still was a refuge for all people, offering everything from toddler day camps to dance movements to exercise classes for the elderly. Miraculously, no one had been killed – *there*. But the monster – who had later in the day committed the atrocious act of murder – had injured several children and had left the entire area with numbing fears that maybe it could happen again. Since then, many of the L.A. Jews took special precautions to safeguard their people and their institutions. Extra locks were put on the doors of the centers and synagogues. Rina's *shul*, a small rented storefront, had even gone so far as to padlock the Aron Kodesh – the Holy Ark that housed the sacred Torah scrolls.

The police had phoned Rina because her number was the one left on the *shul*'s answering machine – for emergencies only. She was the synagogue's unofficial caretaker – the buck-stops-here person who called the contractors when a pipe burst or when the roof leaked. Because it was a new congregation, its members could only afford a part-time rabbi. The constituents often pitched in by delivering a Shabbos sermon or sponsoring an after-prayer *kiddush*. People were always more social when food was served. The tiny house of worship had lots of mettle, and that made the dreadful news even harder to digest.

Driving to the destination, Rina was a mass of anxiety and apprehension. Nine in the morning and her stomach was knotted and burning. The police hadn't described the damage, other than to use the word 'vandalize' over and over. From what she could gather, it sounded like more cosmetic mischief than actual constructional harm, but maybe that was wishful thinking.

She passed homes, stores, and strip malls, barely glancing at the scenery. She straightened the black tam perched atop her head, tucking in a few dangling locks of ebony hair. Even under ordinary circumstances, she rarely spent time in front of the mirror. This morning, she had rushed out as soon as she hung up the phone, wearing the most basic of clothing – a black skirt, a white long-sleeved shirt, slip-on shoes, a head covering. At least her blue eyes were clear. There had been no time for her makeup; the cops were going to see the uncensored Rina Decker. The red traffic lights seemed overly long, because she was so antsy to get there.

The *shul* meant so much to her. It had been the motivating factor behind selling Peter's old ranch and buying their new house. Because hers was a Sabbath-observant Jewish home, she had wanted a place of worship that was within walking distance – real walking distance, not something two and a half miles away as Peter's ranch had been. It wasn't that she minded the walk to her previous *shul*, Yeshivat Ohavei Torah, and the boys certainly could make the jaunt, but Hannah, at the time, had been five. The new house was perfect for Hannah, a fifteen-minute walk, plus there were plenty of little children for her to play with. Not many older children, but that didn't matter, since her older sons were nearly grown. Shmueli had packed out for Israel, and Yonkie, though only in eleventh grade, would probably spend his senior year back east, finishing yeshiva high school while simultaneously attending university. Peter's daughter, Cindy, was now a veteran cop, having survived a wholly traumatic year. Occasionally, she'd eat Shabbat dinner with them, visiting her little sister – a thrill since Cindy had grown up an only child. Rina was the mother of a genuine blended family, though sometimes it felt more like genuine chaos.

Her heartbeat quickened as she approached the storefront. The tiny house of worship was in a building that also rented space to a real estate office, a dry cleaners, a nail salon, and a take-out Thai café. Upstairs were a travel agency and an attorney who advertised on late-night cable with happy testimonials from former clients. Two black and white cruisers had parked askew, taking up most of the space in the minuscule lot, their light bars alternately blinking out red and blue beams. A small crowd had gathered in front of the synagogue, but through them, Rina could see hints of a freshly painted black swastika.

Her heart sank.

She inched her Volvo into the lot and parked adjacent to a cruiser. Before she even got out of the car, a uniform was waving her off. He was a thick block of a man in his thirties. Rina didn't recognize him, but that didn't mean anything because she didn't know most of the uniformed officers in the Devonshire station. Peter had transferred there as a detective, not a patrol cop.

The officer was saying, 'You can't park here, ma'am.'

Rina rolled down the window. 'The police called me down. I have the keys to the synagogue.'

The officer waited; she waited.

Rina said, 'I'm Rina Decker, Lieutenant Decker's wife . . .'

Instant recognition. The uniformed officer nodded by way of an apology, then muttered, 'Kids!'

'Then you know who did it?' Rina got out of the car.

The officer's cheeks took on color. 'No, not yet. But we'll find whoever did this.'

Another cop walked up to her, this one a sergeant by his uniform stripes, with *Shearing* printed on his nametag. He was stocky with wavy, dishwater-colored hair and a ruddy complexion. Older: mid to late fifties. She had a vague sense of having met him at a picnic or some social gathering. The name Mike came to mind.

He held out his hand. 'Mickey Shearing, Mrs Decker. I'm awfully sorry to bring you down like this.' He led her through the small gathering of onlookers, irritated by the interference. 'Everybody . . . a couple of steps back . . . Better yet, go home.' Shouting to his men, 'Someone rope off the area, now!'

As the lookie-loos thinned, Rina could see the exterior wall – one big swastika, a couple of baby ones on either side. Someone had spray-painted *Death to the Inferior, Gutter Races*. Angry moisture filled her eyes. 'Is the door lock broken?' she asked the sergeant.

' 'Fraid so.'

'You've been inside?'

'Unfortunately, I have. It's . . .' He shook his head. 'It's pretty strong.'

'My parents were concentration camp survivors. I know this kind of thing.'

He raised his eyebrow. 'Watch your step. We don't want to mess up anything for the detectives.'

'Who's being brought in?' Rina said. 'Who investigates Hate Crimes?' But she didn't wait for an answer. As she stepped across the threshold, she felt her muscles tighten, and her jaw clenched so hard it was a wonder that her teeth didn't crack.

All the walls had been tattooed with one vicious slogan after another, each derogatory, each advocating different ways to exterminate Jews. So many swastikas, it could have been a wallpaper pattern. Eggs and ketchup had been thrown against the plaster, leaving behind vitreous splotches. But the walls weren't the worst part, minor compared to the holy books that had been torn and shredded and strewn across the floor. And even the sacrilege of the religious tomes and prayer books wasn't as bad as the horrific photographs of concentration camp victims that lay atop the ruined Hebrew texts. She averted her eyes but had already seen too much – ghastly black and white snapshots depicting individual bodies with tortured faces and gaping mouths. Some were clothed, some nude.

Shearing was staring, too, shaking his head back and forth, while uttering 'Oh man, oh man' under his breath. He seemed to have forgotten about her. Rina cleared her throat, partially to break Mickey's trance, but also to stave back tears. 'I suppose I should look around to see if anything valuable is missing.'

Mickey looked at Rina's face. 'Uh, yeah. Sure. Did the place have anything valuable . . . ? I mean, I know the books are valuable, but like flashy valuable things. Like silver ecumenical things . . . is "ecumenical" the right word?'

'I know what you mean.'

'I'm so sorry, Mrs Decker.'

The apology was stated with such clear sincerity that

it brought down the tears. 'No one died, no one got hurt. It helps to get perspective.' Rina wiped her eyes. 'Most of our silver and gold objects are locked up in that cabinet . . . the one with the grates. That's our Holy Ark.'

'Lucky that you had the grates installed.'

'We did that after the Jewish Community Center shootings.' She walked over to the Aron Kodesh.

Shearing said, 'Don't touch the lock, Mrs Decker.'

Rina stopped.

He tried out a tired smile. 'Fingerprints.'

Rina regarded the lock with her hands behind her back. 'Someone tried to break inside. There are fresh scratch marks.'

'Yeah, I noticed. Because you have the lock, they musta figured that's where you keep all your valuables.'

'They would have been right.' A pause. 'You said "they". More than one?'

'With this much damage, I'd say yeah, but I'm not a detective. I leave that up to pros like your husband.'

Abruptly, she was seized with vertigo and leaned against the grate for support. Mickey was at her side.

'Are you all right, Mrs Decker?'

Her voice came out as a whisper. 'Fine.' She straightened up, surveying the room like a contractor. 'Most of the damage seems superficial. Nothing a good bucket of soapy water and a paintbrush can't take care of. The books, of course, are another story.' Replacing them would put them back at least a thousand dollars, money that they had been saving for a part-time youth director. Like most labors of love, the *shul* operated on a shoestring budget. A tear leaked down her cheek.

'At least no one tried to burn it down.' She bit her lip. 'We have to be positive, right?'

'Absolutely!' Mickey joined in. 'You're a real trooper.'

Again, Rina's eyes skittered across the floor. Among the photos were Xeroxed ink drawings of Jews sporting exaggerated hooked noses. They probably had been copied out of the old *Der Stuermer* or the *Protocol of the Elders of Zion*. Again, she glanced at the grainy photographs. Upon inspection, she realized that the black and whites did not look like copies. They looked like genuine snapshots taken by someone who had been there. The thought – someone visually recording dead people – sickened her. Now someone was leaving them around as a frightful reminder – or a threat.

Again, her eyes filled with furious tears. She was so angry, so desolate, that she wanted to scream at the world. Instead, she took out her cell phone and paged her husband.

Decker had many thoughts rattling through his brain, most of them having to do with how Rina was coping. Still, there was some space left over for his own feelings. Anger? No. Way beyond anger, and that wasn't good. Such blinding rage caused people to make mistakes, and Decker couldn't afford them right now. So instead of mulling over a crime he had yet to see, he looked out the window and tried to get distracted by the scenery. By the rows of houses that had once been citrus orchards, by the warehouses and strip malls that lined Devonshire Boulevard. He tried not to think about his stepson in Israel or his other stepson at a Jewish high school. Or Hannah, who was currently in second grade – young and trusting and as innocent as those rows of pre-schoolers led out of the JCC a couple of years ago after that god-awful shooting.

He realized he was sweating. Though it was the usual overcast May in L.A. – the air cool and a bit moldy – he turned the air conditioner on full blast. Someone had given him the address as a formality, but even if he hadn't known the locale, the cruisers would have been a tip-off.

He parked his car in a red zone, got out, and told himself to take a deep breath. He'd need to be calm, not to deal with the crime but to deal with Rina. A quartet of uniforms was buzzing around the space like flies. Decker hadn't taken more than a couple of steps when Mickey Shearing caught him.

'Where is she?' Decker's voice was a growl.

'Inside the synagogue,' Shearing answered. 'You want the details?'

'You have details?'

'I have . . .' Mickey flipped through his book '. . . that the first report came in at eight-thirty in the morning from the guy who operates the dry cleaning. I arrived about ten minutes later, found the door lock broken. I called up the synagogue to find out if there was a rabbi or someone in charge. I got a machine with a phone number on it. Turned out to be your wife.'

'And you didn't think to call *me* before you called *her*?' Decker's glare was harsh.

'There was just a phone number on it, Lieutenant. I didn't realize it was your wife until afterward.'

Decker broke eye contact and rubbed his forehead. 'S'right. Maybe it's better coming from you. Anyone been interviewed?'

'We're making the rounds.'

'Nothing?'

'Nothing. Probably done in the wee hours of the morning.' Shearing slid his toe against the ground. 'Probably by kids.'

'Kids as in more than one?'

'A lot of damage. I think so.'

'Tell me about the guy in the dry cleaners.'

'Gregory Blansk. Young kid himself. Uh . . . nineteen . . .' He flipped through more pages. 'Yeah, nineteen.'

'Any chance he did it and is sticking around to see people admire his handiwork?'

'I think he's Jewish, sir.'

'You *think*?'

'Uh . . . yeah. Here we go. He is Jewish.' Shearing looked up. 'He seemed appalled and more than a little frightened. He's a Russian import himself. Two strikes against him – Jewish and a foreigner. This has to scare him.'

'Currently, Detective Wanda Bontemps from Juvenile is assigned to Hate Crimes. Make sure she interviews him when she comes out. Keep the area clear. I'll be back.'

Having worked Juvenile for a number of years, Decker was familiar with errant kids and lots of vandalism. He had worked in an area noted for biker bums, white trash, hoodlum Chicanos and teens who just couldn't get behind high school. But this? Too damn close to home. He was so distracted by the surroundings, he didn't even notice Rina until she spoke. It jolted him, and he took a step backward, bumping into her, almost knocking her down.

'I'm sorry.' He grabbed her hand, then clasped her body tightly. 'I'm so sorry. Are you okay?'

'I'm . . .' She shrugged in his arms. *Don't cry!* 'How long before we can start cleaning this up?'

'Not for a while. I'd like to take photographs and comb the area for prints—'

'I can't stand to look at this!' Rina pulled away and turned her eyes away from his. '*How long?*'

'I don't know, Rina. I've got to get the techs out here. It isn't a murder scene, so it isn't top priority.'

'Oh. I see. We have to wait until someone gets shot.'

Decker tried to keep his voice even. 'I'm as anxious as you are to clean this up, but if we want to do this right, we can't rush things. After the crews leave, I will personally come over here with mop and broom in hand and scrub away every inch of this abomination. Okay?'

Rina covered her mouth, then blinked back droplets. She whispered back, 'Okay.'

'Friends?' Decker smiled.

She smiled back with wet eyes.

Decker's smile faded as the horror hit him. 'Good

Lord!' He threw his head back. 'This is . . . awful!'

'They took the *kiddush* cup, Peter.'

'What?'

'The *kiddush* cup is gone. We kept it in the cabinet. It was silver plate with turquoise stones and just the type of item that would get stolen because it was accessible and flashy.'

Decker thought a moment. 'Kids.'

'That's what they're all saying. Why not some evil hate group?'

'Sure, it could be that. One thing I will say on record is it's probably not a hype. If he wanted something to swap for instant drug money, the crime would have been clean theft.'

'Maybe the cup is hidden underneath all this wreckage.' Rina shrugged. 'All I know is the cup isn't in the cabinet.'

Decker took out his notebook. 'Anything else?'

'Fresh scratch marks on the padlock on the Aron – the Holy Ark. They tried to get into it, but weren't successful.'

'Thank goodness.' He folded his notebook and studied her face. 'Are you going to be okay?'

'I'm . . . all right. I'll feel better once this is cleaned up. I suppose I should call Mark Gruman.'

Decker sighed. 'He and I painted the walls the first time. Looks like we're going to paint them again.'

Rina whispered, 'Once word gets out, I'm sure you'll have plenty of willing volunteers.'

'Hope so.' Decker stamped his foot. An infantile gesture but he was so damn angry. 'Man, I am pi— mad.

I'd love to swear except I don't want to further desecrate the place.'

'What's the first step in this kind of investigation?'

'To check out juveniles with past records of vandalism.'

'Aren't records of juveniles sealed?'

'Of course. But that doesn't mean the arresting officers can't talk. A couple of names would be a good start.'

'How about checking out *real* hate groups?'

'Definitely, Rina. We'll work this to the max. Nothing in this geographical area comes to mind. But I remember a group in Foothills – the Ethnic Preservation Society or something like that. It's been a while. I have to check the records, and to do that properly I need to go back to the office.'

'Go on. Go back. I'll be okay.' She turned to face him. 'Who's coming down?'

'Wanda Bontemps. She's from the Hate Crimes Unit. Try not to bite her head off. She had a bad experience with Jews in the past.'

'And this is who they bring down for a Jewish hate crime?'

'She's black—'

'So she's a black, and an anti-Semite. That makes it better?'

'She's not anti-Semitic at all. She's a good woman who was honest enough to admit her issues to me early on. I'm just . . . I shouldn't have even mentioned it.' He looked around and grimaced. 'I should learn to keep my mouth shut. I'll chalk it up to being a little rattled. Wanda's new and has worked hard to get her gold. It hasn't been an easy ride for a black forty-year-old woman.'

'I'm sure that's true,' Rina answered. 'Don't worry about her, Peter. If she just does her job, we'll get along just fine.'

2

The pictures of the concentration camp victims had to have come from somewhere. It was possible that they were downloaded from a neo-Nazi on-line site and enhanced to make them look like real photographs. Still, it was equally likely that they had come from some kind of local organized fascist group. The fringe group that Decker had remembered from his Foothills days had tagged itself the Preservers of Ethnic Integrity. When he had worked Juvenile, it hadn't been much more than a post-office box and a once-every-six-months meeting in the park. A few quick phone calls told him that the group was still in existence and that it had evolved into something with an address on Roscoe Boulevard. Decker wasn't sure what they did or what they espoused, but with that kind of a name, the hidden message had to be white supremacy.

He checked his watch, which now read close to eleven. He got up from his desk and went out into the squad room. There were lots of empty spots, signifying that most of Devonshire's detectives had been called into the field, but luck placed Tom Webster at his desk, and on the phone. The junior homicide detective was blond, blue-eyed, and spoke with a good-ole-boy drawl. If anyone could pose as an Aryan sympathizer, it would be Webster . . . except for the dress. Neo-Nazis didn't usually sport designer suits. Today, Tom had donned a navy suit, white shirt, and a maroon mini-print tie – probably Zegna. Not that Decker wore hundred-dollar ties, but he knew the brand because Rina's father liked Zegna and often gave Sammy and Jake his cast-off cravats.

Webster looked up, and Decker caught his eye, pointing to his office. A minute later, Tom came in and closed the door. His hair had been recently shorn, but several locks still brushed his eyebrows, giving him that 'aw shucks' look of a schoolboy.

'Sorry about this morning, Loo.' Webster took a seat across Decker's desk. 'We all heard it was pretty bad.'

'Y'all heard right.' Decker sat at his desk and sifted through his computer until he found what he wanted. Then he pressed the print button. 'What's your schedule like?'

'I was just doing a follow-up on the Gonzalez shooting. Talking to the widow . . .' He sighed. 'The trial's been delayed again. Perez's lawyer quit, and they're assigning him a new PD who is not at all familiar with the case. Poor Mrs Gonzalez wants closure and it isn't going to happen soon.'

'That's too bad,' Decker stated.

'Yeah, it's too bad and all too typical,' Webster answered. 'I have court at one-thirty. I thought I'd go over my notes.'

'You're a college grad, Webster. That shouldn't take you long.' Decker handed him the printout. 'I want you to check this out.'

Webster looked at the sheet. 'Preservers of Ethnic Integrity? What is all this? A Nazi group?'

'That's what you're going to find out.'

'When? Now?'

'Yes.' Decker smiled. 'Right now.'

'What am I inquiring about? The temple vandalism?'

'Yes.'

'Am I supposed to be *sympatico* to the cause?'

'You want information, Tom; do what you need to do. As a matter of fact, take Martinez with you. You're white, he's Hispanic. With racists, you can do good cop, bad cop just by using the color of your skin.'

From the synagogue, Bontemps called Decker and told him about the three kids she had hauled in for prior vandalism. All of them had sealed records.

'How about a couple of names?' Decker asked.

Bontemps said, 'Jerad Benderhurst – a fifteen-year-old white male. Last I heard, he was living with an aunt in Oklahoma. Jamal Williams – a sixteen-year-old African-American male – picked up not only for vandalism, but also petty theft and drug possession. I think he moved back east.'

'That's not promising. Anyone else?'

'Carlos Aguillar. I think he's fourteen, and I think

he's still at Buck's correction center. Those are the ones I remember for vandalism. If you check with Sherri and Ridel, they might have others.' A pause. 'Then again, Lieutenant, you might want to consider the bigger picture when it comes to tagging.'

Decker knew exactly to whom she was referring – a specific group of white, middle-to-upper-class males who were not only testosterone laden, but also terribly bored with life. Recently, after having been caught, the kids had secured their daddies' highly paid lawyers before they had even been booked. The entire bunch had gotten off, the tagging expunged from the records, and in record time. Most of the kids were enrolled in private schools. For them, even drugs and sex had become too commonplace. Crime was the last vestige of rebellion.

'There was a group of them last year,' Wanda said. 'Around twenty of them dressing like Homies and trying to act very *baaaad.* They defaced a lot of property. If I thought about it, I could remember some names.'

'You could also have your ass sued for giving me the names,' Decker said. 'As far as the records are concerned, they don't exist. But I know who you mean.' A glance at the wrist told him it was eleven-twenty. 'How's it going over there?'

'Photographers are almost done. So are the techs. Your wife is waiting with a crew of people – all of them armed with soapy water pails, cleaning solutions, rags and mops. They are ready to start scrubbing, and they are angry. If the police don't hurry up, someone's gonna get impaled on a broomstick.'

'That sounds like Rina's doing,' Decker stated.

'You want to talk to her? She's hanging over my shoulder.'

'I am not hanging,' Rina said, off side. 'I am waiting.'

Wanda handed her the phone. Rina said, 'Detective Bontemps has offered to spend *her* lunch hour helping us clean.'

'Is that a pointed comment?'

'Well, you might want to take a cue.'

Decker smiled. 'I'll be there as soon as I get off work. I will paint and clean the entire night if necessary. How's that?'

'Acceptable, although by the time *you* get here, it may not be necessary.'

'I hear you have quite a gang.'

'Specifically, we've got the entire sisterhood here with brooms and buckets. Someone also made an announcement over at the JCC. Six people came down to clean and paint – one guy actually being a professional painter. Wanda, who's been a doll, actually called up her church and recruited several volunteers. Even the people from the press have offered to help. We'd like to start already.'

'Detective Bontemps told me they're almost done.'

'It's just so . . . ugly, Peter. Every time I look at it, I get sick all over. Everyone feels the same way.'

'Who is down there from the press?'

'*L.A. Times*, *Daily News*, there are some TV cameras, but Wanda isn't letting them in yet.'

'Good for her.'

'Have you narrowed down your suspect list?' Rina asked.

'I'm making a couple of calls. I'll let you know if I have any luck.' He waited a moment. 'I love you, darlin'. I'm glad you have so much support over there.'

'I love you, too. And those *mumzerim* haven't heard the last from me. This *isn't* going to happen again!'

'I admire your commitment.'

'Nothing to admire. This isn't a choice, this is an assignment. Have you checked out the pawnshops?'

'What?'

'For the silver *kiddush* cup. Someone may have tried to pawn it.'

'Actually no, I haven't checked out the pawnshops.'

'You should do that right away. Before the pawnbroker gets wind of the fact that he has something hot.'

'Anything else, General?'

'Nothing for the moment. Someone's calling me, Peter. I'll give you back to Detective Bontemps.'

Wanda said, 'She's quite the organizer.'

'That's certainly true. Thanks for helping out.'

'It's the least I could do.'

Decker said, 'The taggers you were referring to, Wanda. Most of them went to private school.'

'Some of them did – Foreman Prep . . . Beckerman's.'

'That could work in our favor. I'd have a hard time doing search and seizure with kids in public school. But in private school, they are subjected to different rules. Lots of the places have bylaws allowing the administration to open up random lockers to do contraband searches.'

'Why would a private school administrator agree to do that for us, sir?'

'Because it would look bad if they didn't help us out. Like they were hiding something. Chances are I won't find much . . . a secret stash or two.'

'What specific contraband would you be looking for, sir? Anti-Semitic material?'

'A silver wine cup.'

'Aha. That makes sense.'

'It's worth a try,' Decker said.

But one not without controversy or consequences. Because in order to appear objective – and the police needed to appear objective – he'd have to search several of the private schools, including Jacob's Jewish high school. He'd start with that one.

3

'What's the address?' Webster asked.

Martinez gave him the number while taking a big bite out of his turkey, tomato, and mustard sandwich, rye bread crumbs sprinkling his steel-wool mustache. He had been thinking about shaving it off now that it was more gray than black. But his wife told him that after all these years of something draping over his mouth, he probably had no upper lip left. 'Any particular reason why Decker is using Homicide Dees for this?'

'Probably because I was in the squad room.' He looked at his partner's sandwich. 'You carryin' an extra one, Bertie?'

'Oh, sure.' Martinez pulled a second sandwich out of a paper bag. 'You didn't eat lunch?'

'When did I have time?' He attacked the food, wolfing half down in three bites. 'Decker cornered me just as I was hangin' up on the widow Gonzalez. The

Loo has a boner for this one.'

'Yeah, it's personal.'

'It's personal. It's also very ugly, especially after the Furrow shooting at the JCC and the murder of the Filipino mail carrier. I think the Loo wants to show the world that the police are competent beings.'

'Nothing wrong with us bagging a bunch of punks.' Martinez finished his sandwich and washed it down with a Diet Coke. 'You know anything about these jokers?'

'Just what's on the printout. They've been around for a while. A bunch of nutcases.'

Webster slowed in front of a group of businesses dominated by a 99 Cents store advertising things in denominations of – you guessed it – ninety-nine cents. The corner also housed a Payless shoes, a Vitamins-R-Us, and a Taco Tio whose specialty was the Big Bang Burrito. Cosmology with heartburn: that was certainly food for thought. 'I don't see any Preservers of Ethnic Integrity.'

'The address is a half-number,' Martinez said. 'We should try around the side of the building.'

Webster turned the wheel and found a small glass entrance off the 99 Cents store, the door's visibility blocked by a white, gathered curtain. No address, but an intercom box had been set into the plaster. Webster parked, and they both got out. Martinez rang the bell, which turned out to be a buzzer.

The intercom spat back in painful static. 'We're closed for lunch.'

'Police,' Martinez barked. 'Open up!'

A pause, then a long buzzer. Webster pushed the door, which bumped against the wall before it was fully opened. He pushed himself inside. Martinez had to take a deep breath before entering, barely able to squeeze his belly in through the opening. The reception area was as big as a hatchback. There was a scarred bridge table that took up almost the entire floor space, and a folding chair. They stood between the wall and the table, staring at a waif of a girl who sat on the other side of the table. Her face was framed between long strands of ash-colored hair. She wore no makeup, and had a small, pinched nose that barely supported wire-rim glasses.

'Police?' She stood and looked to her left – at an interior door left ajar. 'What's going on?'

Martinez scanned the décor. Two prints without frames – Grant Wood's *American Gothic* and a seascape by Winslow Homer – affixed to the walls by Scotch tape. Atop the table were a phone and piles of different colored flyers. Absently, he picked up a baby blue sheet of paper containing an article. The bottom paragraph, printed in italics, identified the writer as an ex-Marine turned psychologist. Martinez would read the text later.

'A synagogue was vandalized earlier today.' Martinez made eye contact with the young woman. 'We were wondering what you knew about it.'

Her eyes swished like wipers behind the glasses. 'I don't know what you're talking about.'

'It's all over the news,' Webster said.

'I don't watch the news.'

'You've got a radio on. I b'lieve it's tuned to a news station.'

'That's not me, that's Darrell. Why are you here?'

'Because we know what this place is all about,' Martinez said. 'We're just wondering exactly what role you had in the break-in?'

A man suddenly materialized from the partially opened door. He was around six feet and very thin, with coffee-colored frizzy hair and tan eyes. He had a broad nose and wide cheekbones. Martinez wondered how this guy could be an ethnic purist when his physiognomy screamed a mixture of races.

'May I ask who you all are?' he said.

'Police,' Webster said. 'We'd like to ask y'all a few questions, if that's okay.'

'No, it's not okay,' the man said. 'Because no matter what I say, my words will be twisted and distorted. If you have warrants, produce them. If not, you can help yourself to the door.'

'That's downright unneighborly of you,' Webster said.

The man turned his wrath toward the girl. 'How many times do I have to tell you that you don't let anyone in unless you're sure of who they are!'

'They said they were the police, *Darrell*! So what do I do? Just leave them there, knocking?'

'And since when do you believe everything someone says? You know how people are out to get us. Did you even ask for ID?' Darrell turned toward them. 'Can I see some ID?'

Webster pulled out his badge. 'We're not interested in

your philosophy at the moment, although I reckon we're not averse to hearing your ideas. Right now, we want to talk about a temple that was vandalized this morning. Y'all know anything about that?'

'Absolutely not!' Darrell insisted. 'Why should we?'

'Is there anybody who can vouch for your whereabouts last night or early this morning?' Martinez asked.

'I'll have to think about it,' Darrell said. 'If I knew I was going to be raked over the coals, I would have established an alibi.'

''Scuse me?' Webster said. 'This is being raked over the coals?'

'You barge in—'

'She buzzed us in,' Martinez interrupted. 'And you haven't answered the question. Where were you and what were you doing last night?'

'I was home.' Darrell was smoldering. 'In bed. Sleeping.'

'Alone?'

'Yes. Alone. Unless you count my cat. Her name is Shockley.'

'And this morning?' Webster inquired.

'Let's see. I woke up at eight-thirty . . . or thereabouts. I don't want to be held to the exact time.'

'Go on,' Webster pushed.

'I exercised on my treadmill . . . ate breakfast . . . read the paper. I got here at around ten-fifteen, ten-thirty. Erin was already here.' His eyes moved from the cops' faces to the pitchfork of the Grant Wood classic. 'What exactly do you want?'

'How about your complete names for starters.'

'Darrell Holt.'

Martinez looked at the woman. 'You're next, ma'am.'

'Erin Kershan.'

Holt tapped his foot, then released a storage cell of aggression. 'I had nothing to do with the vandalism of a synagogue! That isn't what this group is all about! We don't hate! We don't persecute! And if you were told that, you've been misinformed. We do just the opposite of persecute. We encourage ethnic integrity. I applaud Jews who wish to congregate with one another. Jews should be with other Jews. African-Americans should be with African-Americans, Hispanics with Hispanics, and Caucasians with Caucasians—'

'And what exact ethnicity are you?' Webster asked Holt.

'I'm Acadian, if you must know.'

'You don't sound like any Cajun I ever met,' Webster said.

'The original Acadians came from Canada – Nova Scotia specifically.' Holt gave off a practised smile. It was condescending and ugly. 'I am proud of my heritage, which is why I feel so strong about preserving cultural purity. And it has nothing to do with racism, because as you can see for yourself . . .' He pointed to his hair and nose. 'I have black blood in me.'

'So you admit to being a mutt,' Webster said.

Holt bristled. 'I am not talking about bloodlines, I'm talking ethnicity. My ethnicity is Acadian and it is my wish to preserve my ethnic purity. It is our opinion that the mixing of ethnicities has ruined civilization and certainly the individualization and pride of too many cultures. Immigration has turned everything into one big amorphous blob. Look at cuisine! You go out to a French restaurant when you're in the mood for French food. Or perhaps a Mexican restaurant when you want enchiladas. Or Italian or American or Southern or Tunisian whenever you want the various cuisines. Imagine what it would be like if you mixed up all these nuances, all the flavors. Individually they work; together, they'd make for one horrible stew.'

'We are not beef Stroganoff, sir,' Martinez said. 'Food isn't the issue. Crime is the issue. Vandalism is a crime. What happened today at the synagogue constitutes a *hate crime*. The vandals will be found, and they will be punished. So if you know something, I suggest you get a load off now. Because if we come back, it's going to be bad for you.'

'You have us all wrong.' Holt picked up a handful of leaflets and handed them to Martinez. 'You'll probably throw them away. But should you care to enlighten yourself enough to give us a fair shake, you'll see that what we say makes a lot of sense.'

Erin broke in. 'We have all kinds of members.'

'All kind of ethnicities,' Holt added. 'We cater to the disenfranchised.'

'Like who?' Martinez asked.

'Read our flyers. Our members write the articles.' He plucked a few from the table. 'This one – on the ills of affirmative action – was written by an African-American, Joe Staples. This one is on English as a second language in America, written by an ex-Marine turned psychologist.' He focused in on Martinez. 'Mr

Tarpin is just elucidating a well-known point. That in the United States, we have only one official language and that language is English. If you read it, you'll see that he has nothing against Hispanics. Everyone who lives in the U.S. should speak English.' He smiled. 'Just like you're doing right now.'

'I'm glad Mr . . .' Martinez looked at the flyer. 'Mr Tarpin would approve of my English skills.'

'Which makes sense, being as Detective Martinez is American,' Webster stated. 'Which means, if you're Canadian, Mr Holt, Detective Martinez is more of an American than you are. And if you advocate people staying with their own kind, maybe you should go back to Canada.'

Webster was florid with fury, his hands bunched into fists. Martinez, on the other hand, was completely impassive, glancing at Mr Tarpin's words on why English was such a wonderful, expressive, and large language. That was certainly true enough. Compared to Spanish's blooming buds, English was an entire bouquet of flowers because it used words from a variety of other languages. The irony was lost on the author.

Martinez said, 'Did you print these flyers yourself?'

'The PEI did. Absolutely.'

'Things were left behind in the synagogue,' Martinez said. 'Nazi slogans that were printed on flyers just like these.'

'There's a Kinko's about a mile away from here,' Holt retorted. 'Why don't you ask them about it?'

Webster said, 'And if we were to download your

computer files, we wouldn't find neo-Nazi groups bookmarked on your favorite places?'

'No, you would not,' Holt said confidently. 'But even if you did find anything you deem as offensive, it still proves nothing. *I* did not vandalize anything!'

'There were also photographs left behind at the temple,' Martinez said. 'Horrible pictures of Holocaust victims—'

'That's terrible,' Erin piped in. 'That's not our thing.'

'What is your thing?'

'Erin, I'll handle this,' Holt said.

She ignored him. 'Our thing is keeping ethnic identity pure. Gosh, we do it with animals – purebred this and purebred that. So what's so wrong about wanting people to stay pure? You call it racism, but like Darrell stated we are not racists! We are preservationists. We have nothing against Jews as long as they stick with Jews, and stop controlling the stock market—'

'Erin—'

'I'm just saying what Ricky says. He says the Jews control all the computers. Just look at Microsoft!'

'Erin, the head of Microsoft is William Gates III,' Holt said. 'Does that sound like a Jewish name?'

'No.'

'That's because William Gates III is not Jewish. If Ricky told you that, Ricky is full of shit!'

Erin's mouth formed a soft O.

'Who's Ricky?' Martinez asked.

'Some jerk . . .' Holt made a face at Erin. 'Why do you bring him up?'

'You said he was your friend. Didn't you go to Berkeley together?'

Holt rolled his eyes. To the cops, he said, 'Ricky Moke is to the right of Hitler. Why don't you go hassle him?'

'Where can we find him?'

'That's a good question,' Erin said. 'He hides out a lot.'

'Erin, shut up!'

'Don't yell at me, Darrell. You were the one who gave the cops his last name.'

'Is this Moke a fugitive?'

Erin and Darrell exchanged glances. Holt said, 'Moke tells lots of stories. Among them is this tale about his being a wanted fugitive.'

'What is Moke supposedly wanted for?'

'Bombings.'

The cops exchanged glances.

'Bombing what?' Webster asked. 'Synagogues?'

Holt shook his head. 'Animal laboratories. Not the actual cages, just the data centers. Ricky, by his own admission, is an animal lover.'

4

Torah Academy of West Hills had been molded from an old veterinarian clinic. It must have been a thriving practice, and for big animals, because the examination rooms were extra large though still too small for classrooms. So the majority of actual learning took place in prefab trailers that filled the parking lot, save for a few science classes that were held in the animal morgue. The other clinic rooms had been turned into offices for the administration. Like everything in this community, Decker knew that the school was run on hope, volunteers, and the occasional out-of-the-blue donation.

Rabbi Jeremy Culter was in charge of secular studies. He was in his mid-thirties, and considered very modern for an Orthodox rabbi. In addition to being ordained as a rabbi, he had a Ph.D. in education and, most telling, he didn't have a beard. He was fair complexioned and on the short side – trim with very long and developed arms. His office held a minimal look – a desk, a couple of chairs, and a bookshelf filled with *sepharim* – Jewish books – as well as books on psychology, sociology, and philosophy. The walls were cedar-paneled and still retained a faint antiseptic odor, along with an occasional waft of urine.

Usually, when Decker visited the school, he wore a yarmulke – a skullcap. But today he was there not as a father but in an official capacity. He didn't wear a yarmulke when he worked because he often dealt with people who hated him in particular and cops in general, and he didn't want to give any psycho-felon, anti-Semite any more fodder to use against Jews. Still, sitting in front of Culter, he felt exposed without a head covering. If Culter noticed, he didn't let on.

He said, 'I can't believe you actually think that one of our own boys – your son's classmates – desecrated a *shul* and left concentration camp photos around? Children with grandparents who are survivors!'

Decker looked at him. 'How'd you find out about the specifics of the crime?'

'This is a small community. Do I really have to explain this to you?'

'Did my wife call you?'

Rabbi shook his head.

'Must have been one of the members of the bucket brigade.' Decker smiled at him. 'I've just assigned you the role of my clergyman. Now I have confidentiality. Okay with you?'

Rabbi said, 'Go on.'

'This is the deal. We're calling it a random drug

check for the boys. I'm going to use that ruse with all the schools I'm going to. What I'm looking for is evidence of who might have done this. If you and your school cooperate with me, Rabbi, I'll have muscle when dealing with the other privates.'

Culter nodded. 'The law is an objective animal and so are the police.'

'Exactly,' Decker said. 'If I searched my own son's school, then what excuses can the other principals give me?'

'You're getting resistance.'

'You're the first school, so I'll find out. But I can tell you that no swanky private school will freely admit having vandals in their student body. It doesn't sit well with the parents who pay enormous tuition bills.' He pointed to his chest. 'I can attest to that personally.'

'Are you positive that kids did the crime?'

'No, I'm not. The police are checking out a number of leads. I've assigned myself the role of school snoop. Lucky me. This isn't going to give me status with my stepson – invading the privacy of Jacob and his friends. But it's worth it if I get results. When other principals see a clergyman not attempting to protect his own, what excuse do they have?'

'The parents are not going to be pleased.'

'Rabbi, I want to *nail* these bastards. I know you do, too.'

Culter lifted his brows. 'So I'm supposed to tell everyone that it's just a random drug check.'

'If you could do that, it would be extremely helpful.'

'What if . . .' The rabbi folded his hands over his

desk. 'What if you find something incriminating on your son?'

'Meaning?' Decker kept his face flat.

'I think you know what I mean. Yaakov has given me the impression that you two talk about personal matters.' A very long pause. He rubbed his nose with his index finger. 'Perhaps I just spoke out of turn.'

'You mean drugs?'

Culter shrugged.

Decker said, 'Jake spoke to me about marijuana use. If it's more than that, I don't know about it.'

The rabbi was stoic. 'What are you going to do, Lieutenant, if you find anything in his locker?'

It was a legitimate question, and it churned Decker's stomach. 'I'll decide if and when I have to deal with it. Right now, I'm willing to take a chance. Because I really want these punks behind bars. Please help me out. Help the community out. Not only do we want to find the perpetrators, but we don't want this to happen again.'

'I agree.'

'So you'll help me?'

'With reluctance, but yes, I will help you.'

'Thank you, thank you!' Decker stood. 'All right. Let's get this over with.'

'Are you personally going to do the searches?'

'Yep. If it turns out okay, I'll take the credit. If not, I'll accept the blame. Where do you want to be during this fiasco?'

'By your side,' Culter said. 'You're not the only one who believes in justice.'

★ ★ ★

The contraband consisted of a few dirty magazines, as well as several plastic bags of suspicious-looking dried herbs, enough for Decker to act the bad guy and scare a few kids into behaving better. He used fear rather than actual punishment, effective in getting the point across. Yonkie's locker was literally clean, stacked neatly and free of garbage. The teen's recent behavior had indicated a change for the good, but Decker couldn't deny the relief of just one less thing to worry about. As it was, there were going to be repercussions because the kids didn't understand why Decker – an Orthodox Jewish lieutenant – had singled them out. It played to the boys as the Gestapo sending in Jewish capos to persecute their own. Yonkie did have the sense to keep his mouth shut, but his eyes burned with anger and humiliation.

There'd be trouble at home, but Decker would tolerate it. His strategy had worked. Even before he had cleared out of the yeshiva, Decker had phoned up and received an appointment with Headmaster Keats Williams from the exclusive Foreman Prep boys' school. If the rabbis had agreed to a check, what excuse did the others now have?

Decker was at his car when Yonkie caught up to him. Almost seventeen, the boy had heart-throbbing good looks with piercing ice blue eyes and coal black hair. Even in the school's uniform – white shirt and blue slacks – he was more matinee idol than bumbling teen. The kid was glancing over his shoulder, his body jumping like fat on a griddle.

He said, 'This had nothing to do with my former drug use, right?'

'Right.'

'Because you couldn't have orchestrated all this just to check up on me.'

'Correct.'

'I mean even you don't have that kind of power.'

'No, I don't have that kind of power, and that would be a big abuse of power.'

'Yeah . . . right. So there had to be another reason.'

Decker could have kissed the boy. 'Very good.'

'My friends don't know that, though. They're totally wigged. They think you're pissed at me and taking it out on them.'

'That's ridiculous.'

'I told them that you're not from Narcotics. That this is a separate thing. So this whole drug search is probably a screen for something. Does this have anything to do with the *shul* being vandalized?'

Decker hesitated. 'Who told you about that?'

'Dad, it's all over the school. Everyone knows and is pretty freaked out about it. Now you're here . . . You couldn't think that one of us did it? I can't believe you'd think that. It's ludicrous.'

Decker didn't answer.

'Oh, man!' Yonkie turned away, then faced him again. His face was moist and flushed. 'You know, they're going to talk against you. About how you're picking on your own people because we're easy targets. Eema's going to take a lot of flak. If you had to do this, why did you come personally? To show your bosses that you're not biased? You should be biased. You should have excused yourself. You should be at Beckerman's or Foreman Prep. Or do the rich get special privileges?'

Yonkie was a mass of burning indignation, and Decker tried to take it in his stride. What had to be done, had to be done. But the words hurt more than he'd like to admit. 'I'm not responding to this. You'd better go back to class—'

'It's not enough that they snicker behind your back,' Yonkie shot out. 'You have to make me and Eema and Hannah pariahs as well?'

The barbs cut deep. Such venom from the mouth of a child that he had taken on as his own. 'Jacob, I'm sorry that my position as a cop put you at odds with your friends. But it can't be helped. I really have to go.'

'Where are you going?' Yonkie demanded to know.

'Not that it's any of your business, but I'm going to Foreman Prep.'

The boy was quiet, his mind tumbling for something to say. He had reddened with embarrassment. 'So you're like . . . checking out all the schools?'

Decker offered him a tolerant smile. 'I'm checking out everything. The vandalism was vicious. It qualifies as a hate crime that carries extra weight and extra punishments. I'd like to nab the perps. I assume you'd like that, too. That much we can agree upon. Good-bye.'

Jacob blurted out, 'Did I just put my foot in my mouth?'

'Don't worry about it.'

The boy turned his head away, but didn't move. 'I used to keep my mouth shut. I never spoke my mind no matter what I was thinking.' He scratched his face. Bits of beard stubble were shadowing his cheek and it irritated him. Jacob used to have a stunning complexion. Porcelain smooth with hints of red at the cheekbones. His skin was still blemish free, but coarser now, like that of a young man. 'What the hell happened to me?'

'You had secrets, and were afraid to talk. Now you don't have secrets. The trade-off is a big mouth. It's fine, Jake. I'm a tough guy; I can take a little sassing. I'll see you at home tonight.'

'This whole thing was just a setup.' Jacob was whispering, more to himself than to Decker. 'So you could go to the other places and say, "I'm checking out everyone including my own son's high school." Then they wouldn't have an excuse.' He looked at his stepdad. 'Am I right?'

'Shut up and go back to class.'

'I'm really stupid.'

'More like impulsive.'

'That's true, too.' Instinctively, the kid reached out and hugged him quickly. Then he took off, embarrassed by his sudden display of emotion.

Decker bit his lip and watched him run away. Standing alone, he whispered, 'I love you too.'

5

Driving up to Foreman Prep, Decker was sorely reminded of the difference between parochial private schools and preparatory private schools. The acreage of Foreman was vast and green, shaded by specimen willows and stately sycamores. Behind the layers of arboreal fence were sprawling, Federalist-style, brick buildings. Or probably brick-faced, because architects did not design solid brick structures in earthquake-prone Los Angeles. Whether they were brick or brick-faced, the edifices were impressive and sufficiently ivy-covered to evoke dreams of the eastern universities. Decker didn't care about the form, but he did care about the content. Foreman Prep had a course catalogue that could rival those of most colleges. Both Decker's stepsons could have gotten in, but Rina wouldn't hear of it. Religious education was paramount even if the current yeshiva had minimal grounds and rotating teachers. For her – and for the memory of her late husband – some things were non-negotiable.

The headmaster, Keats Williams, was a double for Basil Rathbone except for the bald head – a topographic map of veins and bumps pressing against shiny skin. His eyes were hazel green, and his speech held a slight British accent. Affected? Probably. But at least he allowed Decker to present his scheme without sneering. As the headmaster lectured back his response, Decker's eyes sneaked glances, trying not to widen at the richness of Williams's office – something that Churchill would have been comfortable in. He wasn't just a headmaster. Nor was he just a doctor of sociology as indicated by his Ivy League diploma. No, Williams was more. Much more. Williams was a friggin' CEO.

'We just had an all-school drug check,' the headmaster informed Decker. 'We have a zero tolerance for drugs at the school. Drugs, weapons and explicitly sexual material. Even the swimsuit edition of *Sports Illustrated* is not to be brought to school, although it isn't grounds for suspension – the first time. It's impossible to keep teenage boys from thinking about sex. It's always there just like a pulse. Still, that doesn't mean it has to be addressed all the time. We're out to train progressive minds.'

Decker said, 'I heard about that. I've also heard that your school offers a very liberal freedom of speech policy, including platforms on abortion, legalization of opiates and prostitution, and euthanasia.'

'You've heard correctly.'

'You don't shy away from controversy.'

'Indeed. But I'm sure I don't have to remind you that

these are but some of the issues that have come before our legislative body. We like to keep our students up to date . . . topical if you will. However, controversial issues do not extend to hate crimes, which are odious and against the law. I know you're using drugs as an entrée to students' lockers, but if you find any . . . and I do mean *any* evidence . . . that any of our boys are behind this heinous event, I want to know about it immediately. Proper remedies will be taken to assure that this issue will be addressed.'

'Doctor, if I find proof that one of your boys was part of this morning's vandalism, he will be arrested.'

Williams was silent. It was one thing for him to reprimand and even to punish the students involved. It was quite another for their felonies to be broadcast over airwaves – not the PR that Foreman Prep liked. 'Exactly how do you determine proof?'

'It varies.'

'If you should find proof . . . or perhaps the correct word might be "evidence"?'

' "Evidence" is fine,' Decker said.

'And if it should be necessary . . . for you to take appropriate action, is there a way that this can be handled . . . without a tremendous amount of fanfare?'

'I have no intention of calling up the press.'

'And if the press should call you?'

Decker was silent.

The headmaster placed his hands, fingers fanned out, on his highly polished walnut desktop. 'Our boys are minors. If their names are released to the press, there will be problems.'

'Dr Williams,' Decker chided. 'Surely you don't advocate suppression of the public's right to know.'

'Innocent until proven guilty,' Williams stated.

Decker smiled. Spoken like a true American with his ass against the wall.

'I'm Dr Jaime Dahl – special services administrator.'

Decker stuck out his hand. 'Thank you for taking the time—'

'I didn't volunteer for this witch-hunt, it was foisted upon me.' A swish of blond hair. 'Let's get that *straight.* I don't approve of any kind of searches. I believe it's a violation of civil rights.'

His day to get grief. Yet it wasn't entirely her fault. At Decker's behest, Dr Williams hadn't informed her or anyone else of the true purpose of the search. She'd probably be appalled by hate crimes, though she'd no doubt retort with, 'One violation doesn't excuse another.'

Through designer eyeglasses, she was slinging wicked looks his way. What made it worse was she was a fox – around twenty-five, with lush lips and knockout legs. She was wearing a black business suit and looked more like an actress playing the part of a school administrator. If this were a Hollywood script, they'd be in bed an hour from now. He must have inadvertently smiled, because her eyes grew angrier. She sneered at him. Too bad. He hated being dissed by anyone, let alone a fox.

She spoke in a clipped cadence. 'Follow me.'

She led him down a flight of stairs, down a long, wide and Berber-carpeted hallway, designated the student locker area. They were waiting for him – rows of adolescent boys standing next to their little bit of privacy, their hands at their sides. Two uniformed guards were watching them. The scene made Decker feel as if he were the aggressor and that didn't sit well with him. He stopped. 'Is there any specific place I should start?'

'One is as good as the next.' Jaime tapped her toe, her left buttock moving with each rhythmical click of the shoe. 'Let's go from freshmen to seniors. They know what to do. They just went through the routine drill a few weeks ago.'

'They may know the drill, but I don't.'

Jaime sighed impatiently. 'One boy at a time will open his locker, swing the door all the way out, then take two steps back. Then you do your search and seizure. When you're done, *you* step away and let the boy close his locker. Give them back a little piece of their stripped dignity.'

'That sounds fine—'

'I'm glad you approve,' Jaime snapped back. 'Shall we get on with it?'

'The quicker I'm out of here, the happier I am.'

'I suppose that about sums it up for me, as well.'

'Why are you so unhappy about this, Dr Dahl? Drug checks are part of standard operation in this school. You had to have known that when you took the job.'

'For the administration to do what's necessary to maintain standards . . . that's one thing. We don't need the gendarmes telling us how to run our school.'

'Ah—'

'Yes, ah!'

Decker's smile was wide. He tried to hold it back and that only made her angrier. She stomped over to the first lad – a fourteen-year-old moonfaced kid with a sprig of freckles across the nose – and asked him to open his locker.

He did, following Jaime Dahl's drill to a tee. Decker was impressed.

Inside were papers, notebooks, pens, a few car magazines, and lots of candy wrappers.

'Thank you,' Decker said, taking a step backward.

The boy closed his locker. Jaime told him that he could go.

The boy left.

One down, about three hundred to go.

The tenth kid had a locker containing two bottles of pills. They looked to be prescription. He asked Dahl about them.

'As long as the medicine is from a doctor, we allow it into the school.'

'Can I pick up the bottles?' Decker asked her.

'Why are you asking me? You're in charge.'

He picked up the bottles. 'It's all the same medicine.'

'I have a note,' the kid said anxiously. 'You can call my mom.'

Decker looked him over. A stick of a kid: he was shaking. 'I'm just wondering why you need sixty pills of any kind *at school* when the dose is one a day . . . *at night*.'

The kid said nothing.

Decker put the bottle back inside his locker.

'Something you might want to think about. Someone could get the wrong idea . . . like you were selling off the excess. Of course, I know that's not the case. But . . . it kinda looks bad.'

The kid mumbled a pathetic 'Yessir'.

'It's all right, Harry,' Jaime comforted him. 'We can talk about this later.'

'Yes, Dr Dahl.'

Decker went on to the next one, then the next. Over the course of the next hour, he found lots of bottles that looked suspect. Either they were genuine pharmaceutical containers with pills that didn't match the prescribed medicine, or they carried counterfeited labels altogether. Since medicine was allowed, Decker left it up to Dahl to discipline. Usually, a stern look from the beautiful doctor was enough to send the boys into paroxysms. Decker felt for the kids, just like he had felt for Jacob after the boy had confessed his drug use. Kids had a way of doing that to him, making him feel bad even when he was just doing his job.

Rooting through the trash of rotting food, old papers, wrappers, and garbage. Not to mention old, wet gym clothes that smelled riper than decayed road kill. Besides the pills, Decker found more than a fair share of cigarette butts – tobacco and otherwise. He pretended not to notice them. He also came upon packages of condoms – most of them unopened. There were also lots of pinups – mostly female, but there were some studly males as well. All of the posers wore smiles and adequate amounts of clothing. He also found several indiscreet Polaroids that he conveniently overlooked. It didn't take long before Jaime Dahl became acutely aware of his omissions. It didn't make her friendlier, but it did make her curious.

She said, 'You're not taking notes.'

'Pardon?'

'I see you're not making note of any of the material you're finding.'

'I haven't found anything significant.'

'What would you consider significant?' The blue eyes narrowed. 'You're obviously not from Narcotics. Why are you here?' Suddenly, she took his arm and pulled him aside, out of earshot of the waiting students. She whispered, 'Surely a police lieutenant has better things to do with himself than to hassle young minds in the throes of experimentation for freedom.'

'Surely.'

'You *didn't* answer my question.'

It was Decker's turn to narrow his eyes. It seemed to unnerve her. 'If we can't be buddies, maybe we can try civility?'

'I know your type. Don't even *think* about asking me out!'

He stared at her, then laughed. *What's on your mind, honey?* He said, 'My wife would have a few choice words to say to me if I did.'

Her eyes went to his hand.

Decker said, 'Not all married men wear wedding rings.'

'Only the ones who don't want women to know they're married.'

'Dr Dahl, I've got a wife, four kids, three stifling

private-school tuitions, a choking home mortgage, and car payments on a Volvo station wagon that's already out of alignment. I've got the whole nine yards of suburbia. And I'm still smiling because deep down inside, despite my cynical view of this entire planet that we call Earth, I am a very happy man. Can we move on, please? I have a schedule and I bet you do as well.'

She regarded his face, but said nothing. Decker took the silence as an invitation to finish up. He was up to the senior class, and had gone halfway through its roster without finding anything incriminating. He was discouraged by his failure, but encouraged by it as well. Maybe the school was really the best and the brightest.

He was almost done, finishing the last row of lockers. One of them belonged to a good-looking boy of seventeen – around six feet tall and muscular. He wore his brown hair in a buzz cut and had storm-colored eyes – electric and very dark blue. His locker was free of contraband and very neat. No pictures, nothing chemical, nothing out of place. Yet there was something on the kid's face, a smirk that spoke of privilege. Decker met the kid's eyes, held them for a moment.

'Let me see your backpack.'

'What?' The boy blinked, then recovered.

'This isn't the procedure,' Jaime stated.

'I know,' Decker said. He turned to the boy. 'Do you object?'

'Yes, I do.' The muscular boy tapped his foot several times. 'I object on principle. It's an invasion of my civil rights.'

Again, Decker met the kid's eyes. 'What's your name?'

'Do I have to answer that?' the boy asked.

Decker smiled, turned to Jaime Dahl. 'What's his name?'

Putting her in a bind. It was beginning to look like the stud was hiding something. If she didn't at least minimally cooperate, she'd look like she was hiding something as well. Reluctantly, she said, 'Answer the question.'

The boy's name was Ernesto Golding.

Decker said, 'Let me make a deal with you, Ernesto. I am not interested in drugs, pills, weapons . . . well, maybe weapons. You have a stash in there, and tell me it's fish food, I'll believe you.'

'Then why do you want to look in his backpack?' Jaime asked.

'I have my reasons.' He smiled. 'What do you say?'

The boy was silent. Jaime looked at him. 'Ernie, it's up to you.'

'This is clearly police abuse.'

Decker shrugged. 'If she won't make you do it, I don't have any choice. But you'll hear from me again, son. Next time, I may not be so generous.'

Ernesto stood on his tiptoes, attempting a pugilistic expression. 'Are you threatening me?'

'Nah, I never threaten—'

'Sounds like a threat to me.'

'Shall we move on, Dr Dahl?'

But Jaime didn't move on. Instead, she said, 'Ernie, give him your backpack.'

'*What?*'

'Do it!'

The boy's face turned an intense red. He dropped the pack at his feet, the storm in his eyes shooting lightning. Decker picked the knapsack up and immediately gave it to Dr Dahl. 'You look through it. I don't want to be accused of planting anything. Tell me if you see anything unusual.'

'What am I looking for?'

'You'll know it when you see it.'

What Decker expected to find were obscene photographs of concentration camp victims. What Jaime Dahl pulled out was a silver *kiddush* cup.

6

It stood out, a surface of metal against books and papers. Decker brought his eyes over to the young man's face. Ernesto Golding was dressed in khakis and a white shirt. Ernesto Golding had intense eyes on a good-looking face, a broad forehead, and weightlifter's arms. Ernesto Golding didn't look like a thug. He looked like a macho teen with better things on his mind than killing Jews. Decker took a handkerchief from his pocket and held up the *kiddush* cup. 'Where'd you get this?'

Ernesto folded his arms across his chest, pushing out his bulging biceps with his fists. 'It's a family heirloom.'

'And why are you bringing a family heirloom to school?'

The boy's face was an odd combination of fear and defiance. 'Show and tell, sir.'

I'll bet you've been doing lots of show and tell, Decker thought. Jaime spoke up. 'What's going on?'

'That's what I'm trying to figure out,' Decker answered. But his eyes remained on his prey. 'The cup has some Hebrew writing on it. See here?' He showed it to Golding. 'It's easy Hebrew. Read this for me.'

'I don't read Hebrew—'

'I thought you said it was a family heirloom.'

'My family's origins are Jewish. But that doesn't mean that I know Hebrew. It's like assuming every Italian knows Latin.'

Decker was taken aback. 'Your family's Jewish?'

'No, my family is not Jewish. We're humanists with ancestry in the Jewish race.'

The Jewish *race* – a Nazi buzz phrase.

'I don't want to repeat myself,' Jaime stated bluntly, 'but what is going on?'

Decker said, 'Did you listen to the news this morning, Dr Dahl?'

'Of course.'

'Then you must know that a local synagogue was broken into and vandalized. I was down there. Most of the damage was ugly, but can be repaired. The one thing that was reported stolen was a silver benediction cup.'

Jaime looked at Ernesto, then at Decker, who held up the cup. 'This *family heirloom* is inscribed with the words "Bet Yosef". That's the name of the vandalized synagogue.'

'It's a family heirloom,' Ernesto insisted. 'We're doing a family history. A family tree for honors civics. Dr Dahl is aware of this assignment. Back me up on this one, Doctor.'

'There is a family-tree assignment in honors civics – Dr Ramparts.'

'Yeah. Third period.' Ernesto rubbed his nose with the back of his hand. 'I brought this in specifically to illustrate my family's past, and to give Dr Ramparts a more . . . genuine feel for where I came from. I'm sure there is more than one Bet Yosef in the world.'

The kid was oh so cool. And he probably thought he was pulling it off. Never mind about the beads of sweat that dotted his upper lip. 'I'm sure there are, Mr Golding. Even so, you're coming with me.'

'I want a lawyer.'

'That can be arranged.'

They took him to Dr Williams's office, Decker standing over Ernesto's shoulder as the kid called his parents – Jill and Carter Golding. Decker could hear outraged voices on the other side of the line. He couldn't discern much, but he did hear them instruct Ernesto to refrain from talking to anyone. From that point on, things moved quickly.

Mom made it down in six minutes. She was a pixie of a thing with pinched features and thin, light brown hair that was long, straight, and parted in the center. She wore rimless glasses and no makeup. Behind the specs, her eyes were smoldering with anger that only a parent knew how to muster. First, there were a few choice glances thrown in Decker's direction. The stronger ones were reserved for her son. Decker knew what that was about.

Dad arrived about ten minutes later. He was short

and thin. The eyes were dark and most of the face was covered with a neatly trimmed brown beard flecked with silver. He appeared more befuddled than angry. He even shook hands with Decker when introduced. Ernesto didn't resemble either of his parents, leaving Decker to wonder if the boy had been adopted.

The last part of the equation came in on Dad's heels. Everett Melrose was an Encino lawyer who had made a name in California Democratic politics. He was well built, well tanned, and had the appropriate amount of sincerity in the eyes and distinction in the curly gray hair. He wore designer suits and dressed with flair. He had a wife, six kids, and was active in his church. He had defended some very big and bad people in his years, and had come out on top. Melrose's past was squeaky clean as far as Decker knew. Amazing – a lawyer and a politician with nothing to hide. He shook hands all the way around and requested that he speak to his client, the young Ernesto, in private.

His request was granted.

The twenty minutes that followed were protracted and tense.

When they came back into Headmaster Williams's CEO office, Ernesto looked upset, but Melrose was unreadable. He said, 'Can you tell me the basis for this detainment?'

Decker said, 'Your client has a stolen cup in his possession.'

'Have we determined that the cup was stolen?' Melrose asked innocently. 'My client claims that the cup was an heirloom.'

Decker said, 'Counselor, the cup belonged to the synagogue, Bet Yosef, that was vandalized this morning—'

'That's impossible!' Jill broke in.

'Impossible that the synagogue was vandalized, or impossible that your son could have some involvement in the crime—'

'Don't answer that!' Melrose interrupted.

'Ernesto, what is going on?' Carter asked.

'I wish I knew, Dad.' Ernesto tapped his toe and made eye contact with the floor.

A good bluff, but not a great one. Decker said, 'The cup was taken from Ernesto's backpack. That's a fact. Dr Dahl was there as a witness.'

'Did he give you permission to search his backpack?'

'Absolutely not,' Ernesto stated.

'It's irrelevant whether or not you gave him permission!' Carter Golding spoke out. 'I'd like to know what it's doing in your possession?'

'So you're saying it's *not* a family heirloom?' Decker remarked.

'Carter, please!' Melrose said. 'He's not saying anything. He's not the subject of this inquiry. What I'm hearing is that no one was granted permission to check Ernesto's backpack!'

Dr Williams came alive. 'The school's bylaws state that faculty can search lockers and personal property of any student at any given time to hunt out contraband or unlawful substances. Mr Golding is aware of the bylaws. He has signed an honor code, acknowledging such laws with a promise to abide by them. So have Mr and Mrs Golding. It is a requirement of attending the school.'

'Lieutenant Decker is not faculty.'

'Dr Dahl is faculty,' Decker countered. 'She was the one who ordered Ernesto to open his knapsack.'

A few seconds of silence before Melrose turned his curious eyes on Jaime Dahl. 'If you do routine searches for contraband, I'm assuming you have a list as to what constitutes contraband?'

'Of course.'

'And does it say specifically what items are contraband?'

'Stolen items are contraband,' Williams interjected.

'So a cup is not illegal.'

'The stolen cup is illegal,' Decker said.

'According to you, Lieutenant, a silver cup was reported stolen from a synagogue,' Melrose pointed out. 'How do you know for certain that *this* is the cup in question? There may be hundreds like it.'

'Do you want proof that the cup belongs to the synagogue? That can be arranged. I can even probably dig up the original sales receipt. But I'll tell you one thing for your own benefit, in case your client wants to change his story. That cup isn't an heirloom. We bought it a year ago when the synagogue began having regular *kiddushes* after services.'

'What's a *kiddushes*?' Jaime Dahl asked.

'Hors d'oeuvres after the Sabbath prayers. Before you eat, you need to make a benediction using wine. Hence, the silver cup.' Decker just realized that suddenly he was the resident Jewish expert, a position usually reserved for Rina. He felt strange occupying it now.

Melrose said, 'You know a lot about this particular synagogue. May I ask if you're a member?'

'You may ask, and I'll even answer it, Counselor. Yes, I am a member.'

'So you're hardly an unbiased party in this investigation.'

'That may be. But that doesn't negate the fact that I can identify this cup as stolen.'

Melrose bluffed out, 'None of this will hold up in court. It's an illegal search and seizure done under false pretenses. You told the students that this was a routine contraband check.'

Carter stood up. 'Aren't we missing the main issue? What were you doing with a cup from a vandalized synagogue, Ernesto?'

'It isn't the right time to talk about this,' Melrose said.

Jill said, 'This is all a mistake. Our son would never have anything to do—'

'Are you going to arrest the boy?' Melrose asked. 'Yes or no?'

Decker sat back. He addressed his comments to Ernesto. 'Mr Golding, this isn't going to go away. I am going to find out what happened, and if you're involved, it's going to come out. You can be in the catbird seat, or one of your cohorts can bring you down. Take your pick!'

'Ernie, what's going on?' his mother asked.

'Nothing, Mom,' Ernesto answered. His breathing

suddenly became audible. 'He's trying to psych you out. He's a part of an organization of brutality. Police lie all the time. They're never to be trusted. How many times have you told me that?'

Decker saw Jill Golding's cheeks turn pink. 'Ernesto,' he said, 'you talk to me, I can ask a judge for leniency. Most you'll do is some community service. More important, if you cooperate, I can try to get your records sealed even though you're almost eighteen. The Ivies would never have to hear about it.'

'I don't believe a word you're saying,' Ernesto answered. 'Cops are pathological liars.'

Decker raised his eyebrows. 'Fine, son. Have it your way. I'll recommend that you're tried as an adult.'

Ernesto stood up. 'You can't bully me into submission! I've had way worse nightmares!' He stomped out, slamming the door as he left. Mom was the next one out the door. Dad waited a beat, swore under his breath, and then took off as well. The quiet ticked away for a few moments.

Decker said, 'You want to bring him down, Mr Melrose, or do I take out the handcuffs?'

'I'll get him.' Melrose left.

Again, the room fell silent. Jaime Dahl broke it. 'I can't believe it! Almost anyone but him!' She regarded Decker. 'You still have a few boys left to search. Would you like me to do that?'

'I'll do it when I'm done with Ernesto. I'll need a list of his friends—'

'I don't think I can do that, Lieutenant,' Jaime answered. 'Finking is not part of the contract.'

'Finking?'

'It's one thing to catch a student with stolen goods, it's quite another to have a boy rat another out.'

'The synagogue was a horrible mess,' Decker said. 'Pictures of dead Jews were thrown all over the place. He didn't do it alone. I want names!'

Williams was about to offer some words, but discussion was cut short. The door opened, and Ernesto tromped in. Still short of breath, he gasped out, 'I want to talk to you.'

Decker pointed to his chest. 'Are you talking to me, Mr Golding?'

'Yeah, I'm talking to you . . . sir.'

'I like the "sir" part,' Decker said. 'It shows civility.'

The parents and Melrose materialized. Carter Golding was red-faced and furious. 'I am the boy's father. I demand to know what's going on!'

'I'm trying to get that done, Dad,' Ernesto said with anger. 'Can you just . . . like lay off for a few moments—'

'You've been accused of vandalizing a house of worship, and you want me to *lay off*?'

'Carter, I know you're upset, but please, let's deal with one issue at a time,' Melrose said.

Ernesto said, 'I'll tell this cop what's going on, but first you've got to guarantee me what you just said . . . about it being sealed.'

Melrose said, 'Ernesto, the man is a police lieutenant. If you want someone to do you favors, start acting appropriately humble.' He looked at Decker. 'What can you do?'

'I could probably get his part pled down to malicious mischief, which will require some explaining since it's a hate crime. But if it turns out he's jiving me, all bets are off.'

'What is malicious mischief?' Jill asked. 'What does it mean?'

'It means it's a misdemeanor,' Melrose stated flatly. 'I'm still not sure this is the best way.'

'Why the change of heart?' Decker asked Ernesto.

'I have my reasons,' the teen answered. 'If you want to know about them, give me a guarantee.'

'I'll do the best I can,' Decker said.

'Not good enough,' Ernesto stated.

Decker stood and took out the cuffs. 'Fair enough. You're under arrest—'

'Wait a damn minute!' Carter broke in. 'Ernesto, once this man *arrests* you, you can't be unarrested! Are you aware of that?'

Ernesto was quiet.

'It won't hold up, Carter,' Melrose assured him. 'He doesn't have any rights here.'

'Can you guarantee that?'

No one spoke.

'This is the situation, Ernesto,' Decker said. 'You talk, I listen. If I like what I hear, I go to bat for you. If I don't, you're no worse off. I'll still arrest you. But what you told me will be inadmissible because you spoke without a lawyer.'

'No, no, no!' Melrose broke in. 'Who said anything about his talking without representation?'

'Counselor, if you're there, then it's official. I have to

read him his rights. Then, as we all know, I can use his statements in a trial. If you're not there, I can't use anything.'

'So what happens if you like what you hear?' Carter wanted to know.

'He writes it all down in a witnessed confession statement. We seal it. Then I take it to the D.A. and probably he'll plead him down to a simple wrist slap—'

'Probably?'

'Yes, probably. I can't say for sure. This is the best I can do.'

'I'll take it,' Ernesto said.

'Ernesto, you're seventeen. You don't have the final word. Do you understand that?'

'And you're fired, Mr Melrose. Do you understand that?'

'Ernie, what in the world is wrong with you?' Jill screamed. 'Apologize!'

'This is precisely why I can't trust him without representation,' Melrose said.

Ernesto tightened his fists. 'This is my life here, Mr Melrose. Not yours, not my mom's, not Dad's . . . *my life*.' He looked at Decker. 'I can speak for myself.'

Melrose said, 'Carter, you can't let him do this!'

'Yes, he can,' Ernesto said. 'My parents raised me with independence. Now they're going to put their money where their mouths are and trust me to do the right thing!'

And what could the Goldings say to that? Decker couldn't have scripted it better. He broke in. 'Where do you want to talk, Mr Golding?' A pause. 'Is there a vacant classroom somewhere?'

'You can have the faculty lounge annex,' Williams stated.

Ernesto said, 'I have a calculus test last period. That's in an hour. Can we wrap it up by then?'

'That depends on what you have to tell me,' Decker said.

'I'm not gonna miss my test,' Ernesto insisted. 'I studied two hours for that sucker.'

'Ernesto, calculus should not be foremost on your mind!' Jill barged in.

'Calculus isn't foremost on my mind, Ma, only getting an A in calculus. If I don't get an A in calculus I can kiss off the Ivies.' To Decker, he said, 'You said the records would be sealed?'

'If I like what I hear, I'll make that recommendation.'

'So I wouldn't have to put anything on my college applications?'

'Not if they're sealed.'

'So the universities wouldn't know—'

'Forget about college right now!' Carter snapped.

'How can I forget about college, Dad!' Ernesto exploded. 'Other than sex, college is all I ever think about. Because it's all *you and Mom* ever think about!'

7

The prep school supplied lots of perks, among them the faculty lounge. It was set up like a café in a bookstore with tables, chairs, a few comfy sofas, and several computer stations, allowing teachers to go on-line and check their E-mail. Plenty of reading material – novels, nonfiction, magazines and papers – sat on the built-in shelves that lined the walls. A few excellent pieces of student artwork were displayed. The biggest benefit, in Decker's mind, was the in-house laundry service. When Dr Dahl saw him gaping at the counter, she explained that the faculty worked long hours. It was the least they could do.

Decker had to strain to hear her because as they walked, Ernesto was sandwiched between them. He followed the administrator through the area, ignoring the steely looks of those who occupied the space. He said, 'A place that does the wash. What's your starting salary?'

The woman actually cracked a smile. 'It's on the high side because all of our teachers have postcollege education.'

An obvious slap in the face meant to put him in his place. Decker just shrugged. 'I'm an attorney. Does that count?'

She slowed, giving him a quick glance. 'You're an attorney?'

'Once upon a time.'

'You actually passed the bar?'

'Now you're getting insulting.'

She blushed. 'I didn't mean——'

'Yes, I passed the bar,' Decker said.

Gently, Jaime guided Ernesto. 'This way.'

The annex was a blip of a room off the lounge. It was paneled, cozy, and held two tables, each with a computer, and several couches. It also had its own private rest rooms, which Decker found very impressive. They had interrupted a couple involved in a deep conversation. The young blonde woman stood up, red-faced and red-eyed, smiling nervously at Dr Dahl. The man – a bit older, in his thirties – remained on the couch, trying to adopt a casual demeanor, raking his hair with his fingers.

Jaime said, 'We need the room, Brent.'

Slowly, the man got up. 'Sure. Of course.' He walked out with the blonde woman, a healthy distance between them.

Dahl tried to stifle a sigh. To Decker, she said, 'Can I get you some coffee?'

'How about some water for the both of us?'

Ernesto said, 'I'm fine.'

'I'll bring some in, just in case.' Jaime left.

'Where do I sit?'

'Anywhere you want,' Decker answered.

The teen looked around, deciding on the couch. 'Are you really an attorney?'

'Yes.'

'Why are you a cop then?' Ernesto looked down. 'Not that it's any of my business.'

'I like the job.' Decker took out his notebook.

Ernesto said, 'I saw this documentary once . . . about cops. Once they retire, they have a hard time readjusting to the civilian world. That's what they call it, right?' He looked to Decker for confirmation, but Decker didn't react. 'Anyway, the moderator or narrator said something about cops being adrenaline junkies . . . that the regular world was a boring place compared to what they were used to. A high percentage of them commit suicide. Because they've been hooked on the adrenaline like others get hooked on drugs.'

Decker said, 'Are you hooked on drugs?'

Ernesto shrugged. 'Nah. Drugs are just for recreation. Something to do because the parties are so damn boring.'

'Is that why you vandalized the synagogue? Because you were bored?'

Jaime Dahl came back in the room with a bottle of Evian and two glasses. 'Anything else?'

'No, thank you.' Decker couldn't keep the edge off his voice. He had wanted to say, *Leave us the hell alone.*

Dahl picked up on it. 'I'll be waiting in the lounge.'

'Where are my parents?' Ernesto asked.

'With Dr Williams.'

'Is Mr Melrose there, too?'

'Yes.'

Decker said, 'Any time you want to stop and consult your parents or your lawyer, just let me know.'

Ernesto took a deep breath and let it out. 'I'm all right. I can handle myself.'

No one spoke. Jaime said, 'I'll be going, then.'

Decker smiled. He even kept the smile after she closed the door, as he waited for the kid to speak. He tried to make eye contact. It lasted for a few seconds, then Ernesto's gaze fell on other things. The computers' screen savers, the candy machine, the landscape on the wall. His posture was casual, but the vein in the kid's temple was pulsating, his jaw taut and bulging. He didn't appear the least bit cocky. On the contrary, Ernesto was worried . . . troubled.

'Actually, this is a good thing.'

'What is?' Decker asked.

'You and me here. I don't want my parents or their lawyer to hear the full details of what happened.'

'Their lawyer is your lawyer. You're going to have to tell him.'

'I will, but he doesn't have to hear the details, either. I mean he needs details, but he doesn't need . . .' Ernesto groped for the words.

'Explicit details?' Decker tried.

'Yeah. Exactly. I'll tell you and maybe you can soften it around the edges.'

'You can present it to your lawyer however you'd like.'

'No one was hurt, you know.'

'Yes, that's true.'

'You think we can work something out?'

'I'll know better once I hear what you have to say.'

'And if you can't work something out?'

'Then you're no worse off than you were a few minutes ago.'

He folded his hands into his lap, a sheen of sweat draped across the big forehead. 'I am not out of control. I know you think I am, but I'm not. Despite what I did, I am not angry with anyone or anything. My life's okay. I don't hate my parents. I got friends. I'm not hooked on drugs even if I do drop dope occasionally. I'm a top student, a lettered athlete. I got lots of spending cash. My own set of wheels . . .'

Silence.

'But you're bored,' Decker said.

'Not really.' The teen licked his lips. 'I got this problem. I need help.'

No one spoke. Then Decker said, 'Are you asking me to suggest that the judge recommend counseling in lieu of punishment?'

'No, I'm willing to do community service. I fucked up. I know that. It wasn't anything personal, Lieutenant Decker. I want you to know that. I just have this . . . obsession. I . . . had to do it.'

'You felt obliged to trash a synagogue?' Decker's voice was neutral. 'How so?'

'Just kept thinking about it. Over and over and over and over. I need help. But I've got to make sure I have the right therapist.'

'I'm not sure what you're asking for, Ernesto. I have no recommendations.'

'My parents would love to see me in therapy.' Head down. 'They've been in therapy like forever. They think everyone needs therapy. So I guess by going to a shrink, I'll make them happy.'

Decker waited.

'I don't want their therapist or his recommendation,' Ernesto said. 'He's not what I need . . . a *good friend* to talk things over with. I need some guidance here. That's why I'm talking to you.'

'I'm not a therapist, Ernesto.'

'I know, I know. You're only interested in a confession and putting this baby to bed. But maybe if you know the background, you can go to the D.A. and get some suggestions.'

If the kid was acting, he was doing a great job. He seemed genuinely perturbed, down to the fidgets and the squirms. Decker, ever the optimist, was willing to hear him out. Perhaps this boy, who had desecrated a synagogue with obscene slogans and left horrific pictures, had a story to tell.

'Ernesto, I'll do what I can. But first I have to hear something. So if you want to tell me certain things, I'll listen.'

'Okay, I'll do that. It's hard, though. Despite my family's liberal bordering on radical attitudes, we're not a family with open communication. I know what my parents want, and if I deliver, I get the goodies. I don't rock the boat, I sail on smooth waters. So here it goes.'

Decker nodded encouragement.

'When you asked me if my family is Jewish, and I said way back when, I wasn't being snide. But I wasn't being entirely truthful and that's the problem. My last name is Golding. My father's father . . . my paternal grandfather . . . was Jewish. My paternal grandmother was Catholic. My mother's mother was Dutch Lutheran, her dad was Irish Catholic. I'm a real mutt as far as any faith goes. So my parents – like the good liberals they are – raised me with no organized religion and just a concept of justice for all. Not that I'm putting my parents down . . . do you know what they do?'

'Golding Recycling.'

'Yeah. Did you know that they are among L.A.'s top one hundred industrialists?'

'Your parents are an entity.'

'I've got to give them credit. They're sincere. Everything they do has the environment or civil rights or the homeless or AIDS or some other cause behind it. They are the consummate fund-raisers. Sometimes it got in the way at home – it's just my brother and me – but at least fifty percent of the time, one parent was there for me or for Karl. That's Karl with a K.'

'As in Marx. And you're named after Che.'

'You got it. My parents weren't masters of subtlety. They've become more sophisticated since the naming days, but even in their most radical days, they talked the talk, but they never crossed the line. That's why they're living in a seven-thousand-square-foot house in Canoga Estates instead of creating false identities and running from the law.'

'You like your parents.'

'Yeah . . . yeah, I do. I . . . admire them although I'm aware of their faults. That's why this is all so screwed up.'

'What's screwed up?'

'Me. I'll tell you my part in the mess, but that's as far as I'll take it. I'm not a rat, I don't name names.'

'So there are others?'

'I didn't say that. For your purposes, I was the sole perpetrator.'

'That's ridiculous.'

'That's my story. Should I go on?'

'I'm still here,' Decker said. The boy didn't seem to know how to start. Decker helped him out. 'Why did you vandalize the synagogue?'

'That's a good question. I have nothing against Jews.' He looked away. 'It has more to do with my personal problems. I've always been obsessive-compulsive, and I'm not just throwing out psych terms. I've always had weird rituals. Some of them, I've outgrown. But some . . . I can't help it. We don't have to go into specifics, but my obsessions are relevant because once I get a thought into my head, I can't let go. And that's the problem. I have these dreams . . . more like fantasies because I'm awake when I think about them. It has to do with my Jewish grandfather – Isaac Golding. Well, it turns out that he wasn't Jewish. Matter of fact, I think he was a Nazi.'

Decker kept his face flat. 'Isaac's a strange name for a Nazi.'

'That's because it wasn't a real name. I found this all

out about six months ago. Remember I told you about the honors civics assignment?'

'The family tree. Dr Ramparts.'

'Yeah. Exactly. It's a semester project. Dr Ramparts wants it done in detail and correctly. So I've been working on this for a while, mostly getting oral history down from my parents because all my grandparents are dead. But then I figure I should do paper research for the sake of completion. So I started going through trunks of old documents that my dad has buried in the attic.'

'An attic?' Decker asked.

'Yeah. I know that's weird for L.A. homes. But like I said, we have a big home.'

'I didn't mean to interrupt you. Go on. You're digging through old documents.'

'Yeah, right. I think my dad didn't even know about the shit. It was given to him after his mother died.' Ernesto hesitated, then drank some water. 'Anyway, my grandfather supposedly escaped the Nazis and moved to Argentina in 1937. Except old papers showed me that Grandpa's account was off by ten years. From what I could tell, Grandpa actually came to South America in 1946 or 1947 under the name of Yitzchak Golding. Yitzchak is Isaac in Hebrew. I guess I don't have to tell you that.'

Decker nodded. Yitzchak was the name of Rina's late husband – the father of his stepsons.

Ernesto took a breather and went on. 'So I figure okay . . . so Grandpa came after the war. He made a mistake. When I knew him, he was old and a little senile, so his absentmindedness is completely within context. So, I point out this little discrepancy to my dad, expecting a logical explanation. Instead, Dad freezes up, then accuses me of trying to stir up trouble . . . which was totally ridiculous. Usually, if Dad doesn't want to talk about it, he just kind of gets this condescending smile and says something like, "Another time, Che." Dad calls me Che when he's trying to prove a point. But this time, he gets mad. He gets red in the face. He stomps off. I'm shocked. This means, you know, I hit a nerve.'

Silence.

Decker said, 'So what happened?'

'Nothing. I never brought it up, and certainly Dad never brought it up again.'

'So now you're curious and you have no logical explanation and no one to talk to.'

'*Exactly!* I technically dropped it, but it's been plaguing me. It's on my mind all the time. Because I get to thinking that if Grandpa did come over in '47, that must have meant that he was in Europe at the time of the war. And being a Jew during the war, he must have suffered somehow. Because I have a couple of friends whose grandparents were European and Jewish, and they have war stories. But I never remember hearing any war stories. Nothing about the . . . the Holocaust . . . the death camps. No survival tales, either.'

'I understand.'

'And furthermore, my grandfather's family was intact – his parents and a sister . . . which would make sense if they all had come to South America in 1937. The camps weren't in full operation until later on. But it wouldn't make any sense for all of them to be alive if Grandpa came over in 1947. You get my drift?'

'Your grandfather was an imposter.'

'That was my conclusion. My dad told me that I got the dates mixed up. But I don't think so.'

'Do you have your grandfather's birth certificate?'

'No, and that's a problem. Just some old papers. I did some further probing . . . a little of this and that. Called up some resources. I did find a Yitzchak Golding who was sent to Treblinka, a camp in Poland, in 1940. He never came back. His brothers and sisters were also sent to the death camps. So were his parents. None of them came back. No aunts, uncles, cousins . . . all of them gone. Dead. The family is as extinct as dinosaurs. I'm carrying the name for a bunch of Jewish ghosts. They're haunting me, Lieutenant Decker. Day in and day out, they're haunting me. Their faces and their corpses.' Golding looked up, his stormy eyes wild and wet. 'I had to get rid of them. So I did what I had to do.'

'You vandalized the synagogue.'

He nodded.

'Are the ghosts gone now?'

He shook his head. 'Of course not. They'll never be gone unless I make peace with them. I don't know if that's possible. It's hard to talk to ghosts. They only talk in dreams, you know.' Ernesto swiped his eyes. 'I had this girlfriend for over a year. Lisa. She was wonderful – terrific, beautiful, smart. I broke up with her when I found out about Grandpa. I just couldn't be with her anymore.'

'She's Jewish?'

'Yeah.'

'And that's why you broke up with her?'

'Of course. I was afraid of hurting her. Because of these dreams . . . these fantasies I have. I would never want to hurt her. I loved her. I still love her. But even after breaking up with her, the fantasies won't go away.

'The fantasies . . . they're sexual. They repel me, but they also – in some sick, primal way – they excite me. We were having sex, but it was the normal kind. Now all I can think about is the sick kind. Demeaning her . . . hurting her. It makes me sick to think I'm like that. But I can't help myself. Certain things you can't hide, you know.'

His pants were bulging.

'All this shit going through my brain while I'm trying to take my SATs and SAT IIs . . . *I . . . need . . . help!*'

It was a compelling case, and a sympathetic teenager. Decker was no shrink, but the kid seemed sincere. Not overly done, but clearly troubled. And what would Rina think if she found out that Decker was feeling sorry for the kid?

'Tell me the details about the vandalism,' he said. 'Where did you get the pictures? They looked original. Were they from a neo-Nazi group or part of the stuff you found in your attic?'

'What difference does it make? I just got them.'

Decker was blunt. 'Who else from your school was involved?'

'Look, I admit that I did it. That's as far as I'm going. I'm not taking anyone else with me. That's your job, not mine.'

Decker could have pushed it. And maybe on down the road, he would push it. But his motto was to deal with issues one at a time. And now that Decker knew about Ernesto's involvement, other things would fall into place. 'I'm sure that whoever adjudicates the case will demand that you get some kind of rudimentary counseling.'

'I need more than that.'

'I agree.'

Ernesto jerked his head up, surprised by Decker's honesty.

Decker said, 'You'll have to talk to your parents—'

'Oh, no, no, no, no, no! That's not possible! As a matter of fact, I am forbidding you to say anything to them about this. I'll admit to the vandalism. I think Dad understands where it came from because deep down, I think he knows about Grandpa's past, too. But he hasn't faced the truth yet. Maybe he never will. In any event, they don't need to know the details. My fantasies . . .'

'You'll tell your therapist?'

'I'd like to. If I can find one I can trust.'

Yet he told Decker all his thoughts without much hesitation.

Ernesto seemed to have picked up on the thoughts. 'My parents have this elevated image of me. Why spoil it for them *totally*? So what if you think I'm an asshole – a spoiled rich kid flirting with neo-Nazism because I'm bored and a jerk. What do I have to lose? I'm telling you what you already think. I'm not that way, really. I mean, I've got my problems but I'm certainly not a Nazi freak. Just ask Jake.'

At the mention of his stepson's name, Decker felt his heart skip a beat. He didn't answer.

Ernesto said, 'We used to go to the same parties. Everyone knew that Jake's stepdad was a big shot cop. We weren't close, but we knew each other.'

Meaning they probably toked together. Decker remained quiet.

'Not that Jake talked about you.' Ernesto looked somewhere over Decker's shoulder. 'Actually, he didn't talk about anything personal. He had this way of talking to you without ever talking about himself. Like he was really interested in what was going on in your life. It made him a girl magnet – that and the fact that he looks like he does. Me? I always felt he was hiding something. Kind of like being a cop, I guess. I haven't seen him around in a long time. How's he doing?'

'Let's keep the conversation on you, Ernesto. What do you want me to present to the D.A.?'

'How about if . . . I like give you a statement? And we'll play around with it until we're both satisfied.'

'How about if you give me what you want me to present to the D.A.?'

'You can't help me?'

'No. That's called putting words into your mouth.'

'All right. I figure it out on my own. What do I do?'

Decker reached into his briefcase and took out a piece of paper and pencil. 'You can start by writing.'

8

His orders were to pick up Hannah after school at three-thirty on the dot! This was not subject to debate, this was something he had to do because Rina was still busy cleaning up the *shul*. She refused to leave the sanctuary until it had been restored to pristine condition. No matter that Decker was in the middle of a pressing investigation of the crime that had caused it all, he'd just have to stop and do this parental duty.

He understood his wife's agitation. The thought of the synagogue in a state of obscene disarray was something she – the daughter of camp survivors – couldn't handle. Cleaning was a way not only of negating what had taken place, but of doing something. *Action* as opposed to sitting around and being victimized. The techs had taken the better part of the afternoon to do their thing, so not only was the synagogue messy from vandals, but it was covered with print dust. The hate-filled leaflets and horrible pictures had been bagged and carted away for evidence. And though it might take a while to pull all the pieces together, Decker was sure that it would work out. Now it was just a matter of retracing the kid's steps, finding out whom he had associated with. This was a good case for Wanda Bontemps to sink her teeth into. As a newly arrived detective, she'd get a chance to show her mettle. And if she needed mentors, she couldn't ask for better ones than Webster and Martinez.

Decker pulled the unmarked next to the schoolyard. Which is what it was: a school*yard*, because it certainly wasn't a playground. Not much more than a six-car parking lot sided by two basketball hoops. Twenty minutes, twice a day, the little kids were let out to ride tricycles, hit a tetherball around a pole, and run around. He got out of the car and stared at the asphalt.

'*Where are the swings and slides?*' Decker had asked his wife.

'*Where's the money? You find money, you'll find swings and slides.*'

Waiting among the group of gabbing mothers, he once again felt like a wart on a beauty queen. One of them attempted a smile. Decker tried to smile back, but from the look on the woman's face, he had probably retorted with a sneer. She gave him the back of her head and went back to talking with the other moms.

Rina wouldn't have approved of his reserve, but she'd never tell him. She knew his heart was in the right place – as were his hands. He had revamped the bathroom of the *shul* practically single-handed. Although they had thanked him heartily, he had known what they'd been thinking. *The Goyim . . . they're good with their hands* – as if he couldn't be smart and coordinated at the same time.

Everything in their small Jewish Orthodox community was operated on spit and prayer. The primary school had originally been a thirty-year-old medical building. A step away from being demolished, then someone had stepped in at the last moment with a down payment. The architect – the brother of a member of the *shul* – had managed to join all the suites under a common ceiling. The classrooms weren't much bigger than closets, but it was home. At least one of the docs had had the courtesy to leave a skeleton behind for the science lab – their most up-to-date prop. There had been a to-do about keeping the bones. Although the body was plastic, the head had once belonged to a genuine human being. In the end, the more modern outvoted the less modern, and Mr Skeleton stayed.

Hannah came running out of the gate. 'Dad-dddeeeeee!'

'Hannah Roseeeeee!' Decker answered back, picking the seven-year-old up in his arms. 'How was school?'

'Great! How many bad guys did you catch today?'

'A zillion billion.'

'Yes!' Hannah's feet kicked the air. She squirmed her way down until she was standing on her own power. 'Where's Eema?'

'She's busy.'

'Is she at the *shul*?'

Decker looked at her. 'Uh, yeah, she is.' He bent

down and looked his daughter in the eye. 'What do you know about the *shul*?'

'The teachers told us that a bad man made it messy.' Her brow was knitted in sorrow and fear. 'Someone who doesn't like the Jewish people. Is he going to hurt us, Daddy? Like that bad man who shot the kids at the Center?'

'No, honey. No one is going to get hurt. It's all under control.'

'Did you catch the bad man, Daddy?'

'Sort of.'

'I'm scared. Why is Eema there?'

'To clean up the mess, that's all.'

'But no one got shot?'

'No, honey, no one got shot.' What a world! 'Let's go, Hannah. Cartoons are waiting.'

Hannah was quiet on the ride home. Decker tried conversation, but the little girl didn't respond. Four blocks before home, she started talking, although it had nothing to do with the *shul*. It was a diatribe about how Moshe always took her pencils . . . just grabbed them from her hand without even asking!

'That's very rude,' Decker concurred.

'He never even once asked,' she said in outrage. 'And . . . he never said thank you.'

'*Very* rude.' Decker parked the car in the driveway, helping his daughter out of the car. Then he took out Hannah's backpack which must have weighed twenty pounds. 'How do you carry this?'

'On my back.'

'No. I mean it's so heavy!'

'Yes, it is,' Hannah agreed. 'Sometimes I use the wheels. Can I have Mike and Ike for snack?'

'No candy before dinner. How about milk and cookies?'

'I don't like cookies. How about milk and Mike and Ike?'

Decker was too tired to argue. 'Sure.'

'Oh, Daddy!' Hannah crooned, hugging his waist with thin little arms. 'You're the best!'

Translation: Between you and Eema, you're the sucker. He parked her in front of the TV and used the quiet time to call his wife. 'Just wanted to let you know that I got her.'

'Thank you, Peter. Is everything okay?'

'As long as you don't mind her snacking on Mike and Ike.'

'And if I did?'

'I'd say, next time you pick her up.'

Rina laughed over the phone. 'I do appreciate you picking her up. I can't stand the *shul* in this state.'

'Are you almost done?'

'Not even close. I don't know who made the bigger mess – the vandals or the techs. Judith Marmelson and Renée Boxstein are here. Renée's husband, Paul, is bringing over cans of paint. If you want to leave Hannah with her friend, Ariella Hackerman, you can join the party.'

'This time I'm going to have to pass. I'm waiting for Yonkie to get home. I'd like him to baby-sit while I go back to work. I cut short what I was doing to pick Hannah up. But that's okay. Actually, it was good to get out.'

'How's the investigation going?'

'Promising. I can't tell you any more.'

'Promising is good. Promising is encouraging.'

'It is indeed.'

'A suspect—'

'I can't tell you any more.'

'You're no fun.'

'Yeah, but you knew that when you married me.'

Yonkie was home on time. Decker waited until he settled into his room before intruding on his life. A moment later, he heard ear-blasting punk rock coming from Yonkie's stereo. Decker had to bang on the wood to be heard over the din. The music volume took a nosedive, and then his stepson opened the door, looking at him with grave eyes. 'Hey.'

'Hey.' Decker tried out a smile. 'Can I come in?'

'Sure.' He stepped aside. 'What's up?'

'Are you still mad at me?'

'No, not at all. Sorry about today. I spoke without thinking.'

'Did you get a lot of flak from your friends?'

'It's okay. I can handle myself.'

Same words as Ernesto. It was the adolescent creed.

Yonkie licked his lips. 'What I don't want is help, okay?'

Neatly stated. Decker nodded.

Yonkie was restless, clearly anxious for him to leave. 'Anything else?'

'I left work early to pick up Hannah,' Decker said. 'I've left some things unfinished. Can you watch her for a couple of hours until Eema gets home?'

'No problem.'

Being agreeable, but there was anger behind it. 'Are you all right, Jacob?'

'Fine. Don't worry about it.' A pause. 'How's Eema?'

His voice took on concern. The kid loved his mother. That made two of them. 'She's scrubbing out the synagogue. It was pretty bad.'

'Does she need help?'

'You're helping her by watching Hannah. You sure it's okay?'

'Positive. If she gets bored, I'll take her out somewhere.'

'Thanks.' Decker patted the boy's shoulder, but there was no response. Like Jacob was made of stone. Or maybe he was just plain stoned.

Jacob knew he was being sized up. He didn't flinch from Decker's scrutiny. 'Uh . . . are you going out now?'

'Yeah, give me a few minutes.'

'Take your time. Call me when you need me.'

He closed the door in Decker's face. Jake's life was a giant tumor of repressed anger. Decker tried not to take it personally, but the tension left him queasy. He went over to Hannah who was steadily working her way through the box of candy.

'How about a grilled cheese sandwich?'

The girl's eyes were glued on the TV – Scooby-Doo. Man, that had longevity. The talking Great Dane had been around when Cindy was a little girl.

'Hannah, did you hear me?'

'Grilled cheese is okay.'

She had heard him. Decker made up a grilled cheese sandwich, courtesy of an electronic sandwich maker that not only grilled, but also molded the bread into an attractive shell shape. The aesthetics were lost on Hannah. She asked him to wrap it in a napkin so grease wouldn't get all over her fingers. Meticulous at times, downright messy other times. Kids never failed to mystify him.

He said, 'Hannah, I'm going back to work now. Yonkie's here if you need anything.'

'Where's Eema?' she asked again.

As if repeating the question would make her mother appear.

'She's at the *shul*.'

'Okay.'

'I'm going now.'

'Okay.'

'I love you.' He bent down and gave her a kiss. 'Bye.'

The little girl chewed off a piece of dripping cheese. 'Bye.'

The child was in TV narcolepsy. He patted her head, then heard Jacob summoning him. Actually, Jacob had called out 'Dad' and that was good. When Jacob was angry, he called him Peter.

'Are you still here?' Jacob yelled from his room.

'I'm still here. What's wrong?'

'Can you c'mere for a sec?'

Decker patted Hannah's head again, then entered the inner sanctum of Jacob's private space. Jacob always made his bed and kept his floor cleared of junk, but his desktop was covered with books, papers, candy wrappers, doodads, and other odd-shaped items that Decker couldn't identify. Sammy's bed and desk had been left in pristine condition, completely cleared of anything extraneous. Jacob refused to let his mess carry over to his absent brother's side of the room. It was as if Jacob kept it clean in hopes that Sammy would materialize.

'I think you'd better hear this.' Jacob turned on his answering machine.

Hi, Jake. This is Ernesto Golding. Long time, huh? I don't know if your stepdad told you what was flying. Probably not. At least, he shouldn't be talking about me, but you never know. Anyway, don't go postal, but you'll probably hear it from someone. So I figured you might as well hear it from me . . . that I B-and-E'd your temple . . . messed up some stuff, spray-painted some swastikas, and threw around some Nazi shit on the floor. I was just fooling around a couple of days ago, getting stoned, and one dare led to another and things kinda got outta hand. I dunno . . . it was nothing personal against Jews or anything. It was just something to do. I feel bad about it, but like I said, it was nothing personal. And I don't know how much you and your stepdad talk, but you can tell him that if you talk about it. I'm sorta rambling, I know. Anyway, I haven't seen you around in a while. I suspect I won't see you around anymore. I'm going to hang up now.

There was a click, then the droning buzz of the phone line.

Jacob looked at his stepfather with curious eyes. 'Did

you arrest Ernesto Golding for vandalizing the *shul*?'

'What he tells you is his business. But as far as I'm concerned, he's a juvenile, and I don't talk about juveniles.'

'I'll take that as a yes.' Jacob shook his head. 'What an absolute . . . prick!'

'Why do you think he called you?' Decker asked.

'I don't know. I barely knew him.'

'Do you have any opinions about him?'

Jacob gave out a breathy laugh. 'I have four grandparents who are camp survivors – two of them with numbers. This guy vandalizes the *shul* and leaves Nazi crap and hate graffiti all over the place. But I'm not supposed to take it personally?' He bit his lip. 'Yeah, I have opinions about him. I think he's a butt wipe.'

Decker restrained a smile.

'He's a rich kid,' Jacob said. 'But he makes a big point of not flaunting it. He's so concerned about not flaunting it that he flaunts it. Money meant nothing to him because he was always flush.'

'Is he a smart guy?'

'No dummy. He took the SAT twice. Did over 1400 the second time.'

'Better than I could have done,' Decker said. 'Of course, that's not in your league—'

'Stop it!' Jacob snapped.

'Good Lord, take it easy, will you!' Decker barked back. 'I'm trying to be nice.'

Jacob looked away. 'I'm sorry.' He touched his forehead. 'I think I've inherited your tendencies toward headaches. Pretty good trick, considering we're not genetically related.'

Decker wanted to smile but couldn't get it out. 'I'm going now. If you need anything, call me, not Eema. She's got her hands full.'

'Yeah, sure.' Jacob kneaded his hands. 'Look, if you want to ask me stuff, it's okay. I don't *know* much about Golding. I knew him from the parties. I haven't seen him or any of them in six months. I hope you know that.'

'Yonkie, I'm not looking over your shoulder.'

The teen considered the words, but gave no indication that he agreed with them.

'You miss Sammy?' Decker asked.

'Yeah.' He licked his lips. 'Yeah, I do. We E-mail each other almost every day, so in a way, I talk to him as much as ever. But then things come up . . . things you don't want to write about. It's not the same.' He caught Decker's eye. 'Golding had a really nice girlfriend . . . Lisa Halloway. They were real tight, and then he broke up with her. She was upset about it. Totally baffled. At least, that's what she told me. I felt bad for her. I almost asked her out. Not because I felt bad for her, but because I liked her. She was smart enough and really good-looking.'

'So why didn't you ask her out?'

'What's the point?'

'I'm sure she would have gone out with you, Jacob,' Decker said. 'Besides the brains, you got your mother's baby blues.'

'No, I didn't mean that. I *know* she would have gone out with me. But it wouldn't have lasted, so why make

Eema upset? Eventually, I would have been too Jewish for her, and she would have been too goyish for me.'

He shrugged with resignation.

'You know, it's not the rabbis and all the mantras they feed us at school that keeps me Orthodox. It's idiots like Ernesto Golding. It makes me realize how alienated I am from the vast majority of this country. I can't be a typical American teenager, starting with the fact that I've never eaten a cheeseburger. So maybe the rabbis did their job on some level.'

'Do you like being Jewish?'

Jacob turned hostile. 'What kind of question is that? Do *you* like being Jewish?'

'Most of the time, yes. Can you stop biting my head off?'

'Sorry.' Jacob tapped his toe. 'I'm okay with being Jewish. Better with it than I was six months ago. Now that the pressure's off, and I can choose a secular college without feeling guilty, I feel a *lot* better about it.'

'That's good.' Decker leaned down and kissed Jacob's head. Not that he had to lean down much. The kid was inching his way to six feet. 'I've got a mound of paperwork that's weighing down my desk.'

'Go jam,' Jacob said. 'Don't worry about anything. Hannah will be fine.'

'And you?'

'I'm fine.' A pause. 'A bunch of us are thinking of going to Magic Mountain Saturday night. I'm driving, but the guys are chipping in for the gas. I have enough for admission, but that'll bust me. Do you have any odd jobs I can do for a couple of bucks?'

'I suppose baby-sitting counts for something.' Decker handed him a twenty. 'That should tide you over for a while.'

'This is very generous.' A big smile . . . a genuine smile. 'Thanks a lot. I'd better go study. I'm pulling high B's in Gemora and would like to keep it that way.'

'Absolutely.' Decker left the boy in peace. Money. It certainly wasn't love, but sometimes it acted as a damn good imposter.

9

Microwaving the pizza had left it tasteless with soggy crust to boot, but it was hot and filling and that was the best that Decker had hoped for at this point in time and space. He made it back to the station house by five with a belly full of grease and a head spinning with ideas. He knew that Ernesto Golding had not worked alone, but other culprits continued to be elusive. Decker would have liked to question Ernesto's friends extensively – find out if they had information – but he knew that their parents wouldn't allow contact. Without proof of involvement, Decker couldn't muscle his way into their living rooms, and no other evidence was forthcoming because Ernesto insisted he was the sole perpetrator. Furthermore, since Ernesto had cooperated with the D.A., Melrose had high hopes of getting the charges knocked down to a malicious mischief misdemeanor – probation combined with community service, *and* a sealed record.

Now that Ernesto had entered into the legal system, Decker's part in the play had been relegated to the role of supporting cast. He didn't have a lot of working time. If he didn't come up with something new very soon, the entire case would slip from his grasp – officially closed, naming Ernesto Golding as the one and only vandal.

Entering the detectives' squad room, Decker was heartened to find Martinez and Webster at their desks. Wanda Bontemps was also finishing up her paperwork. She was hunched over her desk, her fingers playing with a cap of tightly knit curls. She wore black pants and a blue turtleneck. A black blazer was draped across the back of her chair. He flagged her down, along with Martinez and Webster, and the quartet convened in Decker's office.

Webster said, 'Was Golding arraigned yet?'

'An hour ago,' Decker answered. 'No Contest. He's back home – own recognizance. Court date will be in about six weeks.'

'Was he expelled from school?' Wanda asked.

'That I don't know,' Decker said. 'I have this gut feeling that there've been some quiet negotiations behind the scene. You know how it is with institutions and money.'

'The way of the world,' Webster said. 'Nothing you can't buy with money. Even money.'

Decker said, 'I don't know what the headmaster is planning to do. In a perfect world, Golding should be expelled.'

'In a perfect world, he should be in jail,' Wanda said.

'This is very true. But given the fact that Melrose pushed through a rush job, it's unlikely.' Decker felt glum, as if he somehow had failed Rina. 'What'd you find out about the Preservers of Ethnic Whatever?'

'It's run by a guy named Darrell Holt, who is a mixture of lots of races,' Martinez said. 'So I can't figure out how he reconciles his own genetic variety with his ethnic purity crap. Anyway, he's wangled endorsements for his cause from some token minorities – one Filipino, one Hispanic, one African-American, one Asian, one Jew, and for the sake of completion, one Anglo.'

'What kind of endorsements?' Decker asked.

'You can see for yourself, sir.' Webster handed him the flyers. 'It's all the same crud. Y'all can't pin them down just by reading the articles. They play the separate but equal over and over and over.'

Decker thumbed through the pages, scanning the paragraphs. 'Here's one that recommends an English-only policy.'

'Yeah, that's the one by the Marine.'

'Hank Tarpin.' Decker scanned the printed material. 'Superficially, there's lots here that my wife would agree with. She would kill her sons if they married outside the religion.'

'She isn't the only one,' Wanda said. 'I'd like my daughter to marry a good African-American man. Life is hard enough. At least in your own community, you can go around without getting stares and snickers. I talk from experience. About three months ago, she had a Hispanic boyfriend.' She looked at Martinez. 'People gave them looks.'

'What happened?' Martinez said.

'They broke up, but not because of the race . . . although I'm sure that didn't help. He was a cop and she's a cop and that wasn't good.'

'One of my kids married an Anglo,' Martinez said. 'The other married a nice kid whose family was originally from Cuba. I'm from Mexico, and that's another ball of wax. I can't say I feel more comfortable with one son-in-law over the other. But that's not the case with my parents, who don't speak English all that well. There's a language barrier. Which is why, personally, I'm big on an English-only policy in school. If you don't speak and write the language of the country, you're second class. No way my kids and grandkids are going to be second-class citizens.'

'I agree with you, Bert,' Webster said, 'but I reckon that you and the Marine are coming at it from different angles.'

'That's true but irrelevant.' Decker put down the papers. 'The only pertinent question now is, do we have anything to link Holt to the vandalized synagogue?'

'Nope,' Martinez said. 'But we talked to Holt before you arrested Golding. Maybe if we went back and mentioned Golding—'

'And then maybe Golding's lawyer would be all over our asses for giving out the name of a minor,' Decker interrupted. 'Pulling the Ernesto card is out. If the Preservers of Ethnic "Racists" is involved, we've got to get them without asking about Golding.'

'How about harboring a fugitive?' Bontemps said. 'Tell the Loo what you told me about Ricky Moke.'

'Who's Ricky Moke?' Decker asked.

Webster explained. 'Supposedly Moke has been implicated in blowing up university animal laboratories. Supposedly Holt knows Moke. Supposedly Moke has dropped by their office. Supposedly Moke is an ardent racist.'

'That's an awful lot of supposedly,' Decker said. 'Does this bad guy have a sheet?'

'Nothing I could find,' Martinez said. 'But I've only checked locally.'

'If he's implicated with bombs, FBI would have information on him. Make a couple of calls tomorrow.' Decker sat back. 'What about Darrell Holt? Does he have a sheet?'

Webster shook his head no.

'Any information on him?' Decker asked.

'The Preservers have a Web site,' Webster said. 'But that's all fluff.'

'Find out what you can about him.' Decker scanned through the leaflets. 'Are these the only papers you found? I'm wondering if Golding ever wrote anything for them.'

'I'll check it out tomorrow.'

Decker thought about what Golding had told him, about his German grandfather and his dubious past. 'While you're looking up people in the computer, find out what you can about Jill and Carter Golding. I want to know everything I can about Ernesto, and it doesn't hurt to start with the parents. Since they're well known, it should be easy to find information about them. Also do a search with Golding and Holt and/or Golding and

Ricky Moke as a common subject and see if the computer throws out any association.'

Webster said, 'The Preservers also have a girl working there. She looks about twelve.'

'Name?'

'Erin Kershan.'

'Look her up.'

Wanda said, 'Should we put a watch on them, Lieutenant?'

Decker considered the idea. 'Are they local?'

'Yes, they are,' Martinez told him. 'Matter of fact, they live in the same building although different apartments. I'll do it.'

'I'll do it, Bert,' Webster volunteered. 'I got the two A.M. feeding anyway.' He looked at Decker. 'Could I leave at about one?'

'Sounds fine, Tom. You can put in for overtime.'

'I can use the money, sir. Thank you.'

Decker started writing down a schedule. 'While you're doing stakeout, I'll drop by the Goldings' and run Holt, Moke, and the Preservers of Ethnic Integrity by Ernesto. The boy isn't going to admit to anything, but a good nuance is worth a thousand words.'

The Goldings weren't home, leaving Decker to wonder if they were hiding out somewhere. Just as likely, they were out to dinner. It was only a little past six. Decker called Jacob and was apprehensive when no one picked up the phone. He tried Jacob's car phone. The boy answered after two rings. 'Yo.'

'Are you two all right?'

'Oh, hi, Dad. We went out for ice cream.'

In the background, he heard Hannah scream, 'Hi, Daddy!'

'Hi, Hannah Rosie.' To Jacob, Decker said, 'Is she in the backseat?'

'Backseat with her seat belt on,' Jacob replied. 'We're on our way home.'

'I was thinking about stopping by the *shul* to see Eema.'

'That's fine. Don't worry about us. I can put Hannah to bed.'

'Could you do me another favor?'

'What?'

'Before you put her to bed, can you two come down and bring me down some junk clothes and my sneakers from home in case I want to help paint later tonight.'

'No problem.'

'Or maybe I should just go home, so Hannah won't be subjected to—'

But the line had already gone dead. He thought about calling Jacob back. He didn't want Hannah reading all that hate-filled graffiti or seeing those dreadful pictures. Then again, Rina had been there for a while: the *shul* was probably somewhat sanitized by now.

He arrived at the *shul* by seven and parked on the street because the tiny lot was full. A few broken windows had been boarded up, but light shone through the translucent curtains covering the intact glass doors. When he went in, he entered a construction site. Tarps and drop cloths had been laid down everywhere. More than a dozen people were working, brushes and rollers in hand. The walls had been primed, and open paint cans were everywhere. Rina was wearing overalls and a big red bandanna over her head. Her face was dotted with Navaho white. She gave him an air kiss.

'How's it going?' Decker asked.

'*Baruch Hashem!*' She was smiling and it was genuine. 'Let me introduce you to some of our volunteers that you don't know.' She walked over to two African-American women. One was tall and skinny, the other was short and fat. Mutt and Jeff. 'This is Letitia and this is Bernadette. They're friends of Wanda Bontemps from her church. As soon as she called them, they came right down to help.' She patted Decker's shoulder with a paint-splattered hand. 'This is my husband, Peter.'

'Your husband.' It was the one named Bernadette. She had a smooth, round face and a stern expression. She rocked from side to side. She was as tall as she was wide. 'The police lieutenant.'

It sounded as if she was holding his title against him; in light of the past allegations of his department, that could very well be the case. He held out his hand to her and she took it.

Decker said, 'Nice of you to help out.'

'It was nice of Wanda to call them down,' Rina said.

'Our church has an outreach program to help,' Bernadette said. 'No one should be able to get away with defaming a house of God.'

'I agree,' Decker said.

'We need to start something like that in our community.' Rina turned to her new friends. 'It's not that we're so provincial, although that's part of it. It's just that we've been so busy trying to make this congregation work. We barely have enough time and money to get our own services in order. But that's going to change. We have to get more involved.'

'This was an eye-opener to me,' Letitia said. Her face was long and she had a wide, horsey smile. 'I always thought the Jews had the big synagogues.'

'Some do,' Rina said. 'We sure don't. We're lucky to pay the rent.'

'Yeah, I guess that's my own prejudice talking,' Letitia said. 'I'd better stop yakking and get back to painting.' She smiled again. 'Go with my strengths.'

'How about some more coffee?' Rina asked. 'I need more coffee.'

Decker was happy to see Rina so charged up and filled with action. It helped mitigate the pain of why she was there in the first place. He said, 'The way you're flitting around, do you think you really need more caffeine?'

'I don't flit, I move in a purposeful manner,' Rina explained.

Bernadette said, 'She just appears to be flitting because she's so graceful.'

'Uh-huh,' Decker said. 'Whatever you say, ma'am.'

Rina yelled out, 'Moishe, we could use some fresh coffee.'

Moishe Miller – a big bear of a man – was standing in front of several folding tables, piled high with shredded paper and abused books. At the moment, the bearded dentist was painstakingly piecing together torn bits from prayer books. 'Reg or decaf?'

The women looked about the room, then at each other. 'Full strength,' Rina ordered. To Decker, she said, 'Are you going to help out? We took down all the bookshelves. We need someone to paint them and put them back up.'

'Yes, I'm going to help out. Jacob's bringing over some junk clothes. I have a little more work to do, and then I'm all yours.'

'Good to have someone who knows what he's doing. House painting is a lot harder than it looks. It's not just slopping paint over the walls.'

'So you've discovered.'

'It actually takes some practice.'

'Does this mean you appreciate me more?'

'I've always admired your manual skills. You just don't work fast enough.'

'But I do a good job. And the cost is cheap. You get what you pay for.'

Rina nodded, then smiled at the women. But the expression was a taut one.

Bernadette caught the tension. 'Well, nice meeting you . . . Lieutenant.'

'Peter is fine,' Decker said.

'Peter then.' Again, Bernadette shook his hand, then nodded to Letitia. The two of them went back to their artwork. Rina used the moment to take Peter aside. She said, 'Yonkie called me—'

'I can't talk about it,' Decker said. 'The party is a minor.'

'The party is a kid named Ernesto Golding,' Rina

whispered. 'You didn't tell me, Yonkie did.'

'Do you know this kid?' Decker asked Rina.

'Never heard of him until Yonkie told me. There must be someone else involved. This isn't the work of just one person.'

Decker shrugged.

'C'mon. Yes or no? Is there someone else?'

'No comment.'

'Now you're sounding like a politician.'

'If you're trying to get me angry, I've had worse insults.'

Rina grew impatient. 'Peter, this is *your shul*, too.'

'I'm painfully aware of that, Rina.' Then he said, 'Please tell me that you haven't mentioned Golding's name to anyone else.'

'Do I look like an idiot?'

Now she was glaring at him. He said, 'Don't we have enough on our minds without fighting?'

'This isn't a fight,' Rina announced.

'It isn't?'

'No. It isn't. This is . . . both of us glaring at each other because we're both under a lot of stress.'

'I'm *glaring* at you?' Decker asked.

'Yes, you're glaring at me.'

'You're glaring at *me*!'

'I know,' Rina said. 'That's why I said we were glaring at *each other*!'

Decker paused, then started laughing. It broke the strain, allowing Rina to laugh with him. She reached out and took his hand and squeezed it. 'I'd hug you except I'd get paint all over your suit.'

'Hug me anyway.' Decker took her into his arms.

They hugged – a long and romantic one. And she did get paint onto his suit. He didn't care. That's why God invented dry cleaning.

10

It was past eight and the Goldings still hadn't made it home. Decker would try them in the morning. Still, he wasn't ready to call it a working day. Six months ago, Ernesto Golding had a girlfriend named Lisa Halloway. Golding had mentioned her, and so had Yonkie. His stepson had stated that she had been devastated by the breakup. Decker wondered if she had picked up any telltale signs of Ernesto's antisocial behavior before the actual vandalism.

The problem was getting past the parents. But that turned out to be the easy part: the parents weren't home.

At least she didn't slam the door in his face.

Under the illumination of a porch lamp, he noticed the winking of metal – multiple studs in her ears and a small stone in the side of her nose. Who knew what was in her belly button? Decker realized he shouldn't judge by externals – if Yonkie had liked her, she must be a girl of some substance – but he was a middle-aged guy with old-guy prejudices. Trying to be objective, if he looked beyond the holes, he saw a pretty, dark-eyed girl with a clear complexion, an oval face, and dimples in her cheeks. Lots of long curls framed her face. She had her shoulders hunched over as if she were cold, and her arms were strapped across her chest. She was unhappy and not afraid to express it.

'I don't know anything about the vandalism.' Her voice was raspy and low. 'But even if I did know anything about the vandalism, I wouldn't rat on Ernesto.'

'All I want to do is talk for a few minutes,' Decker said.

'Why should I let you in? You could be a rapist!'

Decker smoothed his ginger mustache, aware of Lisa as an angry, young girl wearing a clingy, white tank top and jeans and no underclothes. He could see her nipples even in the poor light. Being alone with her – in private – was not a good idea. He said, 'So we'll talk out here.'

'For all the neighbours to see?'

'Yeah.' Decker smiled. 'That's the point. You'll feel more comfortable that way.'

'You can come in,' Lisa sneered. 'I don't seriously believe you're a rapist.'

'Thank you, but I'm fine out here.' Decker kept his face flat. 'Can I talk to you on a conceptual level for a moment, Lisa? Let's say we are given competing attributes – loyalty and justice. Both are admirable traits, agreed?'

'I don't see the point of all this!' She rubbed her arms. 'Also, I'm cold.'

'I'll wait while you get a sweater.'

'Never mind!'

She was thoroughly sullen, but Decker continued anyway. 'If the party in question is accused of doing something criminal, but there is no definitive guilt or innocence, maybe the party deserves the benefit of the doubt, ergo loyalty. But if you know for sure that he did it – because he himself has admitted it – doesn't his criminal act abnegate his right to expect loyalty, *and* isn't loyalty moot because he already admitted the act?'

She swished her curls. 'I don't know *what* you're talking about.'

'Why be loyal when you know he did it?'

'Lieutenant Lazarus, it's all moot. I don't know anything about the vandalism. Can I go now?'

Lieutenant Lazarus – using Yonkie's surname. 'It's Lieutenant Decker,' he corrected. 'And it's a free country. You can leave anytime you want.'

But she didn't leave.

Decker said, 'You went with Ernesto for a while, didn't you?'

'You know I did. Otherwise, why would you talk to me? What's the point?'

'Any of his friends twang your antenna?'

'You mean did he hang out with Brown Shirts?' She rolled her eyes. 'And if he did, do you think he would have told me about it? I'm Jewish.' She gave a snort. 'Not the *right* kind of Jewish, for you.'

Decker's eyes bored into hers. '*What* did you say?'

The intensity in his voice threw her off-balance. She blushed, and pressed her lips together and turned away, the implicit message being she blew it with her mouth. The other implicit message was that it probably hadn't been the first time.

'Who have you been talking to, Lisa?' Decker pressed.

He knew damn well to whom she'd been talking. Now Decker had the advantage. She knew she had gotten Jacob in trouble. She'd have to call him and explain. But first she'd have to deal with Decker. If she remained snotty, she would add to Jacob's woes.

Now she was scared, didn't make eye contact. 'Can I go now?'

Decker was relentless. 'Have you been talking to my son?'

'Stepson—'

'I stand corrected. *Where* do you know him from?'

'Just around—'

'*Where?*'

'I met him at a party. What's the big deal? Je*sus*! Now I know why—'

Again, she stopped herself.

'Go on!'

Lisa rubbed her hands together. 'Look! I met Jake at a party. Ernesto was there. Maybe Jake mentioned Ernesto or me to you in passing.'

'Maybe he didn't.'

'Well, then, okay. Maybe he didn't. I'm just saying that parents don't need an excuse to rag on their children. Even my parents . . . who are pretty cool . . . they still snoop. All parents snoop. Jake told me you snooped. Maybe it was true, maybe it wasn't. But let me tell you something about your son—'

'*Step*son.'

'He feels brainwashed by your stifling way of life. He struggles with it. But in the end, you must have succeeded because he hasn't answered my phone calls for the last four months. Congratulations.'

So she had made a play for Jake, and it had failed. So not only was it his fault that Jake was conflicted, but it was also his fault that she didn't succeed in getting him. 'You know what, Lisa? I'm going to do you a big favor. I'm going to forget what you just said, and how you just insulted four thousand years of my *step*son's heritage. Let's go back to talking about Ernesto—'

'It's my heritage, too, you know,' she defended herself.

'Then if it is, you should be even more offended by what your ex-boyfriend did. I'm going to ask you straight out. Did Ernesto have any friends that made you nervous?'

She paused for a long time. So many emotions walked past her face – defiance, shame, insecurity, embarrassment, anger, hate – the whole gamut. Finally, she settled on resignation. 'I hope I'm not sounding spiteful. I don't want to appear like the scorned woman.'

'Go on.'

She sighed. 'There's a kid in our class – Doug Ranger. He has an older sister – Ruby. She's around twenty-two or -three . . . graduated from Berkeley with a degree in computer science. She's smart . . . sexy . . . not to me, but to the boys. She's full of ideas . . . more like full of shit!' Wet eyes. 'I've seen her car at Ernesto's house a couple of times.'

'Maybe it's Doug's car and he's visiting Ernesto.'

'It's not him, it's her.'

'I guess parents aren't the only people who snoop?'

She wilted, her voice soft and plaintive. 'Please, Lieutenant.'

'So you've seen Ruby Ranger go into Ernesto's house? Yes or no?'

'Yes.' Totally defeated now. 'Several times.'

'What's she like?'

A long sigh. 'Politicized.'

'What kind of ideas does she have?'

'Libertarian stuff. Government should stop being everyone's baby-sitter. And it certainly doesn't have any right to be a censor when it's so corrupt itself. She's really big on a free Internet. That's her raison d'être at the moment . . . to maintain an uncensored Internet. You're twelve years old and wanna talk about porn in the chat room with convicted sex offenders, that's fine with her. You wanna talk about incest or NAMBLA, fine. You wanna talk about scoring drugs, fine. You wanna talk about neo-Nazis and Hitler as heroes or buy Nazi stuff over the Internet, that's fine, too. She said that . . . those exact words.'

Decker nodded.

'She also said – right to my face while people were listening in – she also said that I would have been perfect concentration camp fodder because I have typical Jewish looks.'

Decker winced. 'That's awful. Not that you look Jewish, but the Nazi fodder part. That's absolutely disgusting.'

'It creeped me out.'

'I can certainly understand that.' Immediately, Decker was thinking about how this woman might be stoking Ernesto's sadistic sexual fantasies. Her prodding would be especially potent if Golding felt that he was from Nazi heritage. 'What'd you say to her?'

'Nothing. I was too shocked to respond. And, of course, that's exactly what she wanted. To get attention by being outrageous.' Her eyes were focused somewhere on her bare toes. 'Jake wasn't there. I told him about it afterward. He told me his grandparents were in concentration camps.'

Decker nodded.

'But they're not your parents?'

'My parents are American,' Decker said.

'So are mine. And my father isn't even Jewish. I was very offended by her statement. Then, there's this side of me . . . I was embarrassed by looking so Jewish, because Jewish girls don't have a reputation for being hotties. That's why I got the nose pierce. You probably think that's awful, right?'

He did think it was awful. Awful and an awful shame. But he tried to keep his face neutral. 'Feelings aren't awful.'

She wasn't buying. 'Not true. Self-destructive feelings are very awful.'

Decker softened his tone. 'Do you know where Ruby Ranger lives?'

Lisa nodded. 'With her parents. Are you going to go talk to her?'

'Definitely,' Decker said. 'But it didn't come from you, all right?'

'She'll think it came from Jake. He *hated* her. Every time she walked in the room, he'd leave. She once confronted him . . . something about him living an outdated life. That was a mistake! Wow, he got real scar—'

She suddenly shut down.

Jake got real scary, she had wanted to say. Decker would bring it up with him, a task he dreaded. A father part of him just didn't have the energy to deal with another crisis. But the cop part kept pushing him on. He folded his notebook. 'Thank you. You've been helpful.'

'Maybe I've been helpful to you,' she said. 'But I certainly have not been helpful to Jake or Ruby.'

He was minutes away from the *shul*. But his head was still spinning from what Lisa Halloway had just told him. He decided to make a quick pit stop at home. Be a concerned father and check up on his children. Besides, the longer car ride to his house would give him a few more minutes of thinking time.

How to approach Ruby Ranger. At twenty-two, she was not a minor, but he imagined that her parents still exercised monetary control over her. If he could get them on his side, maybe that would give him an in to

Ruby. Still, if the young woman were so strongly opinionated with such outrageous ideas, it indicated that she wasn't dominated by her parents. The age, early to mid-twenties, was unpredictable.

It was getting late. The best thing was to wait until tomorrow. Maybe he'd have some other clever idea as to how to approach her. Maybe if she enjoyed baiting people, baiting a cop would be a big kick for her. He'd play dumb. If she hated Jacob, it would be even more of a kick to mess up his cop father.

Which brought him back to his stepson. After fifteen years of having a no-fuss, no-hassle kid, he was getting paid back in spades. Jacob was moody, sullen, and sarcastic. But scary? The kid never failed to surprise him.

He opened his front door, then went into the kitchen. Jacob looked up from the kitchen table. He was in his pajama bottoms, eating a sandwich, and reading *Beowulf*, yellow highlight marker in his hand. 'Hi. What are you doing home? I thought you were going to the *shul* to help out?'

'I decided to come home first . . . see if you need anything.'

'I'm fine. Hannah's asleep.'

'Any problems?'

'Nah, she's a great kid.'

'Yes, she is.'

'You look tired,' Jacob said. 'Like you just had a very bad conversation with a hysterical seventeen-year-old girl.'

Decker sat down at the table. 'I'm loath to get you

involved. But I need help. As a cop, the more information the better.' He stared at Jacob's food. 'What are you eating?'

'Tuna. There's more in the fridge. I'll make you dinner.'

'I'll do it.'

'Sit.' Jacob got up. '*Kibud Av.* Honoring your dad gives you brownie points upstairs. I could use extra.' He fixed Decker a tuna on rye, complete with lettuce and tomato. Decker ritually washed his hands, then said the blessing over the breaking of bread. Within two bites, half the sandwich was gone.

'You are hungry.'

'I'm always hungry.' Decker patted his stomach. Still firm but a bit wider. 'Can we talk about Lisa?'

'If you want.'

'Actually, I'm more interested in a woman named Ruby Ranger. Lisa told me you knew her, also that you disliked her.'

'That is a *gross* understatement. Ruby Ranger is psycho!'

'Lisa said that Ruby tried to bait you once. You took offense and got pretty aggressive.'

'What really happened was I told her if she ever got in my face again, I'd blast *her* face to smithereens.'

Decker didn't answer, too stunned to talk.

Jacob said, 'I not only threatened to kill her, I told her how I'd do it. Then I told her how I'd cover it up. Then I told her I knew all about homicide investigations and how to trip them up because I was your son, and I'd seen you conduct enough of them to know the pitfalls.' He looked at his lap. 'Actually, I think she believed me.'

Decker bit his lip, trying to figure out how to respond. He couldn't get any words out.

'She never talked to me again,' Jacob said. 'Course, I never saw her again. I stopped going to the parties. So I guess I'll never know what she really thought.'

'Did people hear you threaten her?'

'Yeah, we attracted quite a crowd. For a while, I was worried that someone was going to report me to the authorities – the real authorities, not you. Which would have been the correct thing to do. But no one did. All of them . . . the convictions of a turnip.'

Silence.

Jacob said, 'Being arrested would have been consistent with my self-image. I was in the nadir period of my life. I was smoking weed and taking pills and screwing around and screwing up. I was out of control. Thank God, you got to me first.' He looked up. 'That's a compliment.'

'Thank you.' Decker stared at him, as if looking at a stranger. 'You didn't tell me you were taking pills.'

He waved Decker off.

'What else didn't you tell me?'

Jacob threw his head back. 'You're a good guy, Dad. You try to be understanding. But even good guys have their limits.' He faced his stepfather. 'I'm scaring the hell out of you, aren't I?'

'Yes, you are.'

'I hate everything and everyone,' Jacob said. 'I'm furious all the time. But I'm the problem, not the world. I'm trying to channel it all into constructive endeavors. Probably sounds like a crock of crud to you, but it's true.'

Decker was quiet.

Jacob looked away. 'I really am trying. For Eema, especially, because she deserves better. I haven't touched anything chemical beyond an aspirin in six months. I'm doing well in school. I'm still working the suicide hot line once a week. I feed the homeless once a month. I am *trying*! But it's *hard*!'

Decker put his hand on his son's shoulder. He leaned over and kissed his forehead. 'What can I do for you, Jacob?'

He shook his head. 'I guess you can just keep doing what you're doing. Like not freaking when I tell you these things.'

'It's hard,' Decker said. 'Inside, I'm freaking pretty badly.'

The teen pushed his plate away and closed the book. 'You've seen a lot of psychos in your day, right?'

'Right.'

'Do I fit the profile?'

Decker didn't dare to contemplate the thought. 'No.'

Jacob smiled with watery eyes. 'You're just being nice.'

'You have a conscience,' Decker said. 'Psychos don't. But that doesn't mean that you couldn't do damage if you blew.'

'I know that.'

'Were you just spouting off at Ruby Ranger or did you really mean it?'

'At the time, I think I really meant it. She's a bad person. She defends people like Hitler and Stalin and Pol Pot. When I threatened her, she played it real cool. In truth, I think she liked it. I *know* she liked it. She got excited – aroused. Her nipples got hard.'

'That could have been fear.'

'It was a sexual thing, Dad. Believe me, I know. These people . . . they are so rich, so privileged. Nothing is novel to them, so they're always looking for kicks. When drugs don't do it anymore, they move on to other things. Ruby Ranger thinks mass murderers and serial killers are misunderstood geniuses. Do I think she's behind the vandalism after what Lisa told me – that she and Ernesto are playing the mating game? Absolutely! I wouldn't be surprised if Ruby did it just to get to me, that she was waiting for me to come after her with a gun. She's probably all wet and horny about it—'

'Jacob please!'

'I'm sorry, I'm sorry.' He covered his face. 'I'm such a pain in the butt.'

'You're not a pain . . . yeah, you are a pain. You're very worrisome. I'm stymied. I don't know what to do.'

'Don't worry. I'm not going to do anything stupid, I promise you.'

'Are you being open with Dr Gruen, Jake?'

'Bit by bit. Like I am with you. I tell him partial truths until I get the nerve to tell him the whole truth. He can tell what I'm doing, but lets me go at my own pace. He's much better than the first one. I didn't like her at all.'

'Did you tell him about your threatening remarks to Ruby Ranger?'

'Yeah. We've been working on that.'

'Okay.' Decker chose his words carefully. 'Would you mind if I called him? I could use some guidance on what to do for you.'

'You're doing fine, Dad. I probably talk to you as much as I talk to him.'

No, I am not doing fine! Mildly, Decker said, 'So you'd prefer that I don't call him?'

'Let me talk to him first, okay?'

'Fair enough. Is there anything else you'd like to tell me?'

'About Ruby Ranger or about me?'

'At the moment, I'm more interested in you than in Ruby Ranger.'

'What specifically? Drugs? Yeah, I took pills, too. Mostly downers when pot wasn't enough. I liked being zonked out. It took the edge off the anger.'

'What else, Yonkie?'

'That's it.'

Silence.

'No, really. That's it.' He showed Decker his forearms. 'See? I'm clean. I'm very angry, but I'm not chemically altered. You're seeing the unadulterated Yonkel.'

Decker tried out a smile. He thought he was partially successful. 'What about sex?'

'What about it?'

'Are you sexually active? I'd like to be sure that you're protecting yourself.'

'Very much so.' Jacob smiled. 'I'm not *doing* anything.'

Decker's laugh was real. 'Okay.'

'I made this deal with myself, that I'd wait with girls until I go away next year to Johns Hopkins. I have to work to keep the grades up, and girls are a distraction. Mostly, I'll be older, the girls will be older. It ain't easy, but I can wait.'

'That's very smart.' Decker stalled. Somehow, he got the words out. 'Actually, when I asked you if you'd like to tell me something, I was thinking about criminal activity, Jacob.'

Jacob turned red and looked away.

'Am I way off base?' Decker asked.

Jacob continued to stare off. 'I shoplifted.'

'B-and-E's?'

'No.' He looked at Decker. '*No.*'

Decker was about to say, 'Okay, I believe you,' but he couldn't find his voice.

Jacob said, 'I shoplifted. Mostly booze, but I also stole about a dozen CDs over about a three-month period.' A pause. 'Sixteen CDs. Don't ask me how I did it with all those metal detectors. There are ways. I'm doing *kapparah* for it.'

'What kind of atonement?' Decker asked, using the English word.

'I never opened the CDs. They were still in their wrappers.' A beat. 'Two months ago, Dr Gruen called the store manager. He explained the situation without mentioning names. Then he returned the CDs for me, no questions asked. As far as the stolen booze goes, I screwed up my nerve and did that myself. I used to hit this mom-and-pop liquor store. The owner – Mr Kim – he's being decent about the whole thing. We reached an agreement – a price. I'm working it off – manual labor stuff. Stocking shelves, sweeping, cleaning . . . watching kids for theft. Now, that *is* ironic, Alanis Morissette. I do it on Shabbos because it's the only day I have off. Eema thinks I'm with friends, but I'm not. You can check it out if you want.'

'Where is this place?'

'About four miles from the house. I walk there after lunch. Yossie picks me up after dark. I used to see some of the old crowd there. Now they stay clear of me and of Mr Kim. I may not have scared Ruby Ranger, but I think I scared lots of them.'

Decker rubbed his head.

'I've given you a headache.'

'I'm just glad you told me all this after the fact.'

Jacob said, 'I'm doing better, Dad. It's hard, but I'll be all right.'

'Yonkie . . .' Decker cleared his throat. 'Am I wrong in assuming that the bastard who molested you did more than you've admitted?'

Again, the teen turned red. 'I told you everything that I remembered. But there may be stuff that . . . that I blocked out. I was only seven, so . . . you know.'

Decker felt sick to his stomach. *What did that motherfucker do?* Calmly, he said, 'Are you talking about it with Dr Gruen?'

'Bit by bit. When it comes back to me.' Jacob flashed him a quick smile. 'You want to talk about Ruby Ranger?'

Decker was happy to change the subject. Did that indicate a weakness on his part as a parent not to probe deeper? Or was he rationalizing it by telling himself that it was best left to the professional? Decker was only human. There was only so much he could absorb at one time. 'What can you tell me about her?'

'Objectively, she's smart – a computer person. I bet she's an amateur hacker. She's sexy enough to get plenty of guys if you're into that severe Goth look. I could see her talking Ernesto into vandalizing the *shul.* She'd get off on that. But she'd never get her own hands dirty. That wouldn't be fun for her. Her thing is manipulation, getting you to act out her pathology.' He grinned. 'I sound pretty shrinky, don't I?'

'You've learned the lingo.'

'When in Rome . . .' He looked at Decker. 'If you talk to her, tell her to go to hell for me.'

'She'll be interviewed but not by me.'

'Ah!' Jacob smiled. 'Conflict of interest.'

'Exactly.'

'I'm sorry to be such a burden to you. Don't worry. I'm out of your hair in a few months. Surely, you can hang with that.'

'Jacob, you're not in my hair.'

'Sure, Dad.' He gave him a sour smile. 'Actually, I'm looking forward to Johns Hopkins and getting out on my own. And I'm not going to shoot anyone. Although if I did pop Ruby Ranger, I'd be doing the world a service.'

'That's not funny, Jacob.'

'I didn't mean it to be.'

11

Installing and painting bookshelves gave Decker much needed downtime, using his body instead of his mind. By two in the morning, the chemical cleaning fumes had become overwhelming, so the *shul* gang broke for the night. Rina was out as soon as she hit the pillow, but Decker remained fitful, dreaming in dribs and drabs about rebellious boys, his own stepson included. He awoke with a start at five-thirty – it was still dark – and drowned his lethargy with three cups of espresso coffee. At six, he took his prayer shawl and his phylacteries and rushed over to the synagogue to join the men in morning services – an anomaly because usually their small house of worship couldn't round up a quorum. But the events of yesterday motivated the community to try a little harder.

Right before the services started, half of Yonkie's school – including Yonkie – came in to join them. Some smart kid even had the grace to bring in

Danishes and juice as a reward for participation. It was downright homespun and everyone seemed friendlier, more social and a lot more grateful – praying with sincerity . . . making it count. By eight – after demolishing the snacks – the men started leaving to begin their working day. Rina, along with several other women, came in just as the men were filing out. They were holding pails, scrub brushes, scouring pad and lots of Scotch tape to piece together torn bits of the holy books. Decker helped them unload the cleaning material.

'I've never seen the place so spotless,' he remarked to his wife.

'Almost like it never happened,' Rina answered. 'What's with *that* kid? Why on earth would he do such a terrible thing? I know you can't answer me. I'm just wondering out loud.'

'Darling, I'm just as confused as you.'

Rina regarded her husband. 'Poor Peter. You look tired.'

'I'm fine.' Decker smiled to prove the point. 'How come you look so good? It's not fair.'

'It's called foundation to hide the dark circles.'

'Ah.'

'Also, you're not wearing your glasses.'

'I don't need glasses!' Decker insisted. 'Only with medicine bottles. Let's not rush things.'

Rina grinned. 'Did I tell you I love you this morning?'

'No, you didn't.'

She did. Then she stood on tiptoe and kissed him.

Then she handed him a paper bag. 'I packed you lunch. Please remember to eat it.'

'That's never been my problem . . . not eating.'

She pinched his ribs. 'Yeah, you're right.'

'Below the belt, kid.'

'Stop talking that way.' Rina smiled. 'We're in a *shul.*'

Decker laughed and hugged her. She felt tense and tight. He said, 'Don't overdo it with all the cleaning, Rina. You're punishing muscles that you're not used to using.'

She broke away and rubbed her shoulder. 'I'm aware of that.'

'I'm going to remember that "below the belt" comment,' Decker said. 'Especially tonight.'

'I sure hope so.'

Decker laughed again, then gave her a final wave and returned to his car. Before he started the engine, he tried the Goldings' home phone number. When no one picked up, he again left another message. He had almost made it to the precinct's parking lot when impulse overtook reason. He did a safe but illegal U-turn in the middle of the street, backtracking until he hit the Goldings' neighborhood – a ritzy area containing blocks of spacious homes on acre lots. The development had its own tennis courts, swimming pools, saunas, Jacuzzis, workout gymnasiums and recreation rooms as well as its own private patrol. As Decker groped around for the specific address, a white-and-blue rent-a-cop slowed his cruiser to check him out. Decker flashed his badge. The private nodded, then parked in the middle of the street and got out. He showed Decker the route to the Golding abode.

Ernesto lived in a house that was an amorphous blob, resembling a mound of melting chocolate ice cream. It was constructed out of adobe and probably would have looked great in Santa Fe, but since it sat in a lane of traditional Tudor, colonial, and Mediterranean houses, the place looked unfinished. More than unfinished, it looked like a project that someone forgot to start. The front landscaping was an assemblage of rocks and stones, sitting in beds of sand, and drought-resistant plants, mostly varieties of cacti, but there were also ice plants for ground cover and other flowering mint-colored foliage. A couple of stunted pines framed an old, carved door – the front entrance.

Decker knocked, but didn't expect anything. To his surprise, Carter Golding answered with Jill peeking over his shoulder. Even more surprising, they acted as if they wanted to see him.

As a matter of fact, we were just about to call you.

He was invited inside.

The area was sumptuous and airy, utilizing an open floor plan. Furniture and screens were arranged to define rooms with different purposes. The staircase to the upper levels was also free-form and made of brown adobe. The mud-colored walls were textured and lumpy, holding tiny windows that let in large amounts of light. Lots of muted colors, probably because the sofas and chairs were covered with faded and worn upholstery. Nothing was formal or structured, as if every piece of furniture, every knickknack, every painting and wall hanging had been someone's castoffs. Not that the interior looked junky, more like designer funky.

Jill caught him staring. 'Everything here has been recycled. All the upholstery is either the original coverings, or we recovered it with discarded material. The glass windows for instance, all recycled.'

'All the architectural features came from demolition projects,' Carter explained. 'It's a point of pride with us. Even the wood used for framing up the house was recycled from other estates.'

'You've certainly held a consistent stance,' Decker said.

'We do our share,' Jill stated.

'Probably at a fraction of the cost, too,' Decker stated. 'I'm about to redo my kitchen. This is giving me ideas.'

Jill lit up. 'If you want, I'd be happy to show you around our plant. We get old cabinets all the time. Beautiful cabinets, Detective, made of solid wood. Not the current processed plywood.'

It sounded very tempting. But not only was it unethical, Decker could just picture how Rina would react, knowing that the cabinets came from the family of a boy who had tattooed the synagogue walls with *Hitler should have killed more of you.* It had taken Decker a while to convince her to ride in his revamped Porsche.

Carter was offering his business card. 'The number on the back is my private work number. Feel free to use it.'

Decker took the card to (a) have the number and (b) be polite.

'Please sit down,' Jill said. 'Anywhere is fine.'

Decker decided on a rose-on-the-vine patterned sofa. It was very comfortable. Carter took up an overstuffed chair and looked around the house as if observing it for the first time.

'My wife has a designer's eye.' Carter's smile was open – a slash of solid white among his gray and brown facial hair. 'She knows how to put stuff together. It's an art.'

The man was acting all too jocular. Thin and short, he was nearly swallowed up by the chair's ballooned pillows. 'Can I get you anything to drink?'

'No, I'm fine, Mr Golding.'

'Call us Jill and Carter,' Jill said. Her elfin face had been freshly scrubbed, leaving her skin clear and shiny. Her long hair was pulled back into a ponytail. She looked less stressed and years younger. Both of them wore denim work shirts and jeans. Decker felt stiff in a suit.

Jill said, 'It is so fortuitous that you dropped by. It's so much easier to talk face-to-face.'

'I'd be happy to talk.' But Decker's mind was on Ricky Moke and Darrell Holt: if they had anything to do with Ernesto and the vandalism. 'But if it's okay with you, I'd first like to have a few words with Ernesto.'

'He's not here,' Carter said. 'He's with some relatives. All the hullabaloo has left him zapped. More than that, he needs time and solitude to think about the magnitude of his actions.'

'Maybe I can stop by . . . where he is right now.' Decker smiled. 'It would help me out a lot to ask him a few questions.'

Jill sighed. 'I'm so sorry, Detective, but his lawyer will not permit you to see him without his counsel. But if you'd like to leave a message, we'll relay the words.'

'I really wanted to see him in person.' Decker sensed he was working with someone cooperative. 'Is there a way you can arrange a quick visit? Maybe you can take me over? I sure don't mind if you stay while I ask him a couple—'

'No, that won't work,' Carter broke in. 'Not without the lawyer. I hope you understand.'

Decker nodded. 'I have no objections if Mr Melrose is there.'

'Everett is on a tight schedule,' Jill stated. 'I'm afraid yesterday took up most of his time. I'll run it by him, though. Maybe he'll have a spare moment.'

'Would you?' Decker asked.

'It would be my pleasure,' Jill said.

But Decker knew she wouldn't do it. 'What about Karl?'

'What about him?' Jill responded.

'Perhaps I can talk to him?'

'Whatever for?' Carter broke in. 'No use dragging him into the mess. We don't believe in guilt by association, sir.'

'Of course.' Decker was getting nowhere. He stood up. 'Thanks for your time—'

'Please stay for a moment.' Carter waited a beat,

stroking his neatly trimmed beard. 'We have a couple of favors to ask of you.'

'Me?'

'Please sit,' Jill requested. 'Are you sure I can't get you something to drink?'

'No, I'm fine.'

Jill was still waiting for him to park his butt, so Decker sat back down. Jill followed suit, then beamed at him. 'We have some very good news. We've found a terrific therapist for Ernesto. It took us all night, but we found the perfect people to deal with him.'

Carter said, 'The vandalism was inexcusable – outrageous and disgusting. Even so, we feel we need to get to the root of the problem, don't you agree?'

Decker agreed.

'His behavior definitely shows lack of parental understanding on our part.' Carter looked down and shook his head. 'You try your best, but sometimes it isn't enough. You need a professional.'

'Do you have children?' Jill asked.

Decker nodded.

'Teenage children?'

Carter said, 'Jill, that's a bit personal.'

Obviously Ernesto hadn't told his parents about Jacob. Decker said, 'I have teenage children. I know they can be full of surprises.'

'Exactly!' Jill exclaimed. 'I'm glad you're on our team!'

'Your team?'

'Yes, in a way.' Carter was excited now. 'Because you can be of enormous help. Ernesto has asked that *you* talk to the therapist.' He smiled. 'I don't know what you said to our son, but obviously you have developed some kind of trust . . . a rapport if you will. I, for one, think that's marvelous. I must tell you that this kind of . . . bonding is very unexpected . . . coming from a policeman.'

He almost spit out the last word.

'Not that we don't support the local law, but given the past history of the LAPD, the department leaves much to be desired—'

'Cart, we don't have to go into that right now,' Jill said tightly. 'Detective, we'd like you to talk to Dr Baldwin. We would really appreciate that.'

Decker was stunned. 'Mrs Golding—'

'Jill—'

'I'm glad Ernesto is going to get some professional help. But I'm not the one who should act as a go-between.'

'Quite the contrary,' Carter protested. 'I'm interested in your opinion. More important, Ernesto is interested in your opinion.'

'Sir, to align myself with a suspect – even for societal good – is a conflict of interest. Furthermore, even if I approved of this man—'

'Dr Baldwin,' Jill interrupted.

'If I liked him, ma'am, it would mean nothing. If I didn't like him, it wouldn't mean anything either. I couldn't tell a good therapist from a bad one.'

'All we want is your opinion,' Jill said.

'I can't do that.'

'This is very disappointing.' Carter was pensive and grave. 'Ernesto insisted to us that you had his interest at heart.'

The manipulating little bastard. 'I'd like if things worked out for everyone. But my job puts me in direct conflict with what you're requesting.'

Carter stroked his beard. 'How about this? You agree to talk to Dr Baldwin, and we'll let you talk to Ernesto and ask him your . . . couple of questions.'

They're all manipulating bastards.

Jill broke in. 'Ernesto seems to trust you. He wants your opinion.'

'I can't give him an opinion. I don't know anything about therapists and psychology.'

'Surely you've seen therapists in your line of business,' Carter added. 'You can't work with oppressed and desperate people day in and day out without some kind of stress management.'

Decker said, 'The last therapist I talked to specialized in child psychology.'

Jill said, 'Really? What's his name? I'm sure I know him.'

'Jill, that is also a bit personal.'

Decker said, 'Why would you know him?'

'Because I have an MFCC – Marriage and Family Counseling Certificate,' Jill explained. 'I thought you knew that.'

'No, I didn't know that.'

'I thought the police knew personal things about their suspects,' Carter said.

'Pardon?' Decker said. 'Last time I checked, you two weren't suspects.'

'Well, the family of a suspect. You can't mean to say that we're not under a cloud of suspicion.'

'Cart, we can go into that later,' Jill interrupted. 'What's the doctor's name? The child psychologist, I mean.'

'Jill, wouldn't that come under confidential information?' Carter asked.

'Oh, yes, I suppose you're right about that.' She nodded solemnly. 'Sorry. You seemed so open with us that I seem to have forgotten my boundaries. Anyway, it is important to Ernesto that you speak with the therapist. Also, I'd be curious about your opinion. We all want to help Ernesto. I mean, you do want to help him, don't you?'

'If you help us out, Lieutenant, I'm sure we could work something out with Everett,' Carter said. 'If he sees that you have Ernesto's interest at heart, I don't see how he could object to your speaking with our son.'

Jill added, 'In the end, it is our decision . . . whether or not we permit you to talk to Ernesto.'

'So we're swapping favors, is that it?'

She blushed. 'I'm just saying it is our decision. Surely, you can see that Ernesto's not a criminal.'

Decker couldn't see anything of the sort. But he had a half hour for lunch to spare. Rina had packed him a pastrami sandwich topped with mustard, mayo, sauerkraut, and spicy pickles. He figured he might as well get indigestion from something other than food.

12

Crimes more pressing than vandalism still plagued the city, leaving Decker to contemplate the wisdom of using valuable time to interview a couple of shrinks even if it meant a second chance with Ernesto. Still, he might as well try to understand someone else's kid, because his own stepson left him abashed.

Wanda had found quite a bit of material about Mervin Baldwin and his psychologist wife, Dee, on the Internet. They had been interviewed by the top news-lite magazines, and had had a cover article about them as a power couple in *Psychology Now*. There were also several 'in-depth' profiles on them in in-house papers for local psychology organizations, both city and state. They had written about a dozen pieces for journals, most of them having to do with 'Oppositional Behavior in Teenagers'. From reading the abstracts, Decker gleaned that Merv Baldwin's speciality was working with troubled teens.

There were essays devoted to his own unique treatment entitled Nature Therapy. It espoused being at one with the earth and land, using a combination of intense group programs out in the wild as well as individual therapy. The articles contained lots of psychological jargon that Decker didn't understand, so he took notes. He wasn't sure what it meant to be 'at one with the land', but to him it sounded a lot like camping.

The Baldwins had several satellite offices, but the main digs were in Beverly Hills; the exact address was given to Decker by the Goldings before he left. Wanda had downloaded several pictures of the psychologists, but they hadn't reproduced that well. From the photos, Merv was bald but dressed expensively. Dee was meticulously groomed, as stiff as her coifed hairdo. He looked to be in his fifties, about ten years older than his wife.

Traffic was thick over the hill because of freeway construction. Decker pulled off at Sunset and took it east, passing through Westwood, then the opulent residential area of Beverly Hills. The sinuous boulevard had been narrowed to two lanes because of roadwork, and was treacherous because of a sudden May downpour. The asphalt had a thin coating of slick mud, and that had brought the flow down to a crawl. Los Angeles was always unprepared for rain, and when it came, the locals drove like beginners, going either too fast or too slow.

Turning left onto Roxbury Drive, he kept going until the street turned one-way, and of course, it was the wrong way. He maneuvered the unmarked through the maze of crazed shoppers and tourists until he was finally going the correct way on the street – except that the curb parking was taken up. To make matters worse, the public lots were full to capacity. By the time he had successfully landed a place to leave his vehicle, he was ten minutes late.

It didn't seem to matter, because the Baldwins kept him waiting. Decker didn't expect that they'd do a kiss-up number, but he didn't think they'd leave him cooling his heels. He was about to leave when the door opened, and a young African-American woman who introduced herself as Maryam Estes apologized for the delay. Lovely and curvy, she swayed as she ushered him into the 'intake suite', an interview room with very low ceilings. Decker didn't have to duck to make it through, but he could touch the wood beams with a simple arm stretch. The space was large and done up à la Frank Lloyd Wright with lots of rich, wood built-ins, a conference table, and a gleaming ebony desk. The couches were constructed from slats of wood and covered with dozens of colored pillows. There were lush floral still lifes on the walls, and a stone fireplace was going full blast.

Even though the surroundings had improved, Decker wasn't about to wait anymore. He was about to vocalize his displeasure to the next person he saw, but then a woman came in, took his one hand in her two-handed grip, and introduced herself as Dee Baldwin. She looked even younger than she had in the photographs, in her late thirties. But she did have the same coifed honey-dipped hair that wouldn't survive too long in the wild. She had a round face with round brass-colored eyes and white teeth, her visage reminiscent of a lioness. She was quite petite except for shoulders that were very broad, made even bigger by the shoulder pads of her black pant suit jacket. Her earlobes dripped gold, her neck as well. Her perfume was light and airy.

'I am so sorry for the delay.' An apologetic smile. 'A crisis came up . . . one even bigger than Ernesto Golding. This boy is in *real* trouble. Merv is still dealing with the parents, but he'll be here soon. I know you're a busy man, so perhaps we can start without him.'

Dee sat down opposite him.

'You were so kind to see us in the first place. Especially because I'm sure your personal feelings about Ernesto are less than laudatory.'

Decker said, 'Since we're both on a tight schedule, maybe you can tell me why everyone was so anxious for us to meet.'

'We deal with the police all the time, you know.'

'I didn't know.'

'Perhaps I should tell you a bit about Merv and me. Our therapy is rather unorthodox in the conservative field of psychotherapy.'

'I never thought of psychology as conservative.'

'Oh, but it is!' Dee crossed her legs. Fabric rubbed against fabric, producing a swishing sound. 'The field has utilized the same disciplines and methods over and over. It's Freud and psychoanalysis, or Skinner or some variation of behavior therapy, or Rogers and client-centered therapy or some kind of humanism – gestalt therapy. Then there are the various therapies that deal with anxiety and fear – hypnosis or meditation or relaxation. But nothing in psych has yet addressed the fact that we – human beings – have had our core essence stripped by domestication and urbanization. We have moved from the primitive to the advanced. That's good – don't get me wrong – but there is still this residual part of us that longs to be harmonious with nature.'

'That's why there are national parks, I suppose.'

'Camping, hunting, fishing . . .' She waved them away. 'They have become hobbies instead of livelihoods. We have become such Urban Irvings that we have forgotten how we were fashioned. Not that we can turn back the clock – time steadily marches forward – but we must deal with this issue of our animalistic side. If we don't harness it into constructive means, the destructive takes over. Hence boys like Ernesto Golding. This is a young man who needs his *primitus* guided to *constructo* rather than *destrudo*.'

Decker smiled. 'What does that translate into?'

From the doorway, a voice boomed out, 'He needs to be challenged physically, is what it translates into!'

Decker turned around. Now, Merv Baldwin looked *older* than the computerized image – in his mid-fifties, which meant there was about a fifteen-year difference between Dee and him. Not that Decker was judging – he was twelve years older than Rina – but it was something he just noticed. Dee was as pretty as Merv was plain. The man was bald and paunchy with a round face vanquished by sag. He had short limbs and short fingers, and no doubt had short toes, since his shoes – croc loafers with a tassel – looked to be a tiny size. He wondered how the man balanced on such wee soles. He was dressed in an expensive suit – hand-fashioned because of his size and with working button-holes. Good color sense – blue pin-striped suit, white shirt, and a gold tie.

'Merv Baldwin.' A hearty handshake. 'I apologize for being late. Crisis! Not unexpected, not to me anyway, but it caught certain parties by surprise.' He began pacing. 'So you're the detective who extracted the confession from Ernesto. A physical confession as well as a confession of the soul. I must tell you that I did not approve of this meeting.'

'Neither did I,' Decker said.

He stopped pacing, regarded Decker, then continued to walk back and forth. Decker looked at the distaff Baldwin, trying to gauge her facial reaction to Merv's perpetual motion. But her face was relaxed, as if this was totally natural.

Merv called out, 'Perhaps we both didn't approve because we're on opposite sides of the fence, eh?'

'I don't know about that,' Decker said. 'We both want to know the truth.'

'Yes, but you want to know a tangio/sensory truth. A truth you can see or hear or feel. I, on the other hand, want to know the truth up here.' He pointed to his temple. 'To me, what happened at that synagogue, although terrible, is not as significant as what was happening in the boy's mind. The *why.* With you, the why isn't of chief importance. Oh sure, you'd like to have a motivation. It helps clinch a case. But the mere fact that it was done – that is your primary concern.'

'That's not entirely accurate,' Decker said.

'Oh, no?' Merv shouted as he trod the carpet. 'The law takes into account some extenuating circumstances, but not all of them. In the mind, there are *always* extenuating circumstances.'

The man was irritating. Decker was irked. 'Why am I here, Doctor?'

Merv hopped about. 'Ernesto requested that I present my therapy for your approval. Not that I care if you approve or not. I'm just trying to do an old friend a favor.'

'You're friends with the Goldings?' Decker asked.

'We marched together.' He stopped to regard Decker's face. 'You must be of that same generation vintage.'

'As a vet, I was on the opposite side, Doctor.' Decker smiled. 'Seems to be a pattern.'

Merv smiled. 'Not as much as you think. I did my tour – not in action, so I suppose you think less of me. But I was not anti-army, only anti-Vietnam. I was a staff psychologist in Germany – the one called in to help the mental basket cases that the confrontation created. It was a very ugly war.'

'Yes, it was.' Decker checked his watch. 'It's been nice talking politics, but I have other obligations awaiting.'

'We know you must be very busy,' Dee stated. No sarcasm in her voice. 'Thank you for taking time out for us and for Ernesto. Over the years, we have seen many cases of boys-will-be-boys. We deal in the extremes, helping young men bleed energy in constructive means. And they can't contact the constructo within until they feel a sense of harmony with nature. That's why we call our therapy Nature Therapy. We take our clients out of the city and back into the untamed. During the day, our clients are challenged with the physical: the construction of a shelter, the search for food, protection from animals, insects, and the forces of nature. We have Nature Masters who preside over these exercises. Our guides are professional survivalists. They are instructed to teach the client about the physical, but offer no therapy. Even if a client wants to confide in them, they are instructed to tell the client to hold the question or statement until group or individual therapy times. Each of our boys gets individual as well as group therapy. Integrating the mind with the body is what puts our clients back into harmony.'

Merv continued the speech. 'We have had a tremendous success rate. It's not perfect, but no therapy is a panacea, especially if the clients aren't willing to change. In Ernesto's case, we feel he is ripe for our self-awareness therapy. He is bright, physical, and troubled by what he did. Surely, you must believe that the boy, given the right intervention, would prove to be a productive citizen and an asset to the community.'

Decker said, 'If you think you can turn him around, great.'

'That would please you,' Merv stated.

'You bet.'

'It wouldn't be cognitively dissonant with your preconceived notion of the boy?' Merv stated. 'I'm sure you have assessed him as problematic.'

'More like criminal,' Decker said. 'But, hey, prove me wrong.'

Dee smiled. 'Oh, we will do that, Lieutenant. Have no doubt. We will do that.'

'It sounds to me like a summer camp for troubled kids.' Decker sat back in his desk chair, regarding Martinez, Webster, and Bontemps. They looked like an updated and older version of the Mod Squad. 'Ever look in the back of *Sunset* magazine or any other similar periodical? It's filled with nature camps for troubled teens. I really don't know what makes this one so different.'

Martinez rubbed his tired face. It was close to five and his stomach was rumbling. 'Maybe it's different because the Baldwins appeal to a rich clientele.'

'All those places appeal to a rich clientele, Bert. Ever call up and ask the prices?'

Wanda said, 'Maybe they have a higher staff-kid ratio. Or maybe the docs are just real good with the therapy.'

'Or maybe they've got a good racket going,' Decker said. 'However, if it straightens the kid out, I'm all for it.'

'But you have doubts,' Martinez said. 'Me too. Let me hear your reasons.'

Decker made his hands into a teepee. 'If the kids were redeemable, it might work. Frankly, it's garbage in, garbage out. I think the survival camps just turn the psychos into better psychos. Because now they've learned the survival skills to be great fugitives.'

'Ditto,' Martinez stated.

'You really think Ernesto is all that hopeless?' Webster said. 'I'm not excusing the sucker – I think he deserves more than just CS – but his acting out is probably rebellion against radical parents. Y'all know how it is. Kids experiment and if they don't succeed in really buggin' their parents, they didn't do it right.'

'This is beyond the ordinary rebellion,' Decker said. 'The kid left pictures that showed piles of dead Jews. It was totally repulsive!'

'I know you were offended, but consider this, Loo.' Webster wasn't ready to concede the point. 'How do teens act out. Drugs? Sex? Weird dress and loud music? Given the Goldings' background, I couldn't see them being too worked up about any of those things. But racism or violence – swastikas and horrific photos – that would get them where it hurts.' He paused. 'They *were* upset, correct?'

'I think so.'

'You *think* so?' Martinez said.

'Put it this way. They were very glad to see their son get therapy. That was the important issue, not the degradation of a synagogue. Jill Carter is a therapist, and in the Baldwins, they think they've found a cure for Ernesto's problems. Total bullshit. That boy knew what he was doing. In answer to your question, Tom, he could be redeemable, but it's out of my hands now. The deal's been cut, and I was part of it. The therapy and community service will satisfy a judge, and that's that. If I want more, I'm going to have to do it on my own.'

Decker smoothed his mustache.

'Ernesto may have gotten the Nazi crap out of his system, but he didn't vandalize the synagogue by himself. I'd sure like to find out who else was behind the vandalism. Ernesto won't name names, but maybe we can uncover someone who will.' He turned to Webster. 'I take it the stakeout was worthless?'

'Not entirely. I heard some cool books on tape.' Tom shrugged. 'I didn't see either Holt or the girl go in or out of the place. I left at one-fifteen.'

'We don't have any suspects at the local level except the Preservers of Ethnic Integrity,' Wanda said. 'But there are lots of fringe groups on the outer areas . . . in the mountains and canyons.'

Martinez said, 'Speaking of mountains and fugitives, remember Ricky Moke?'

'The friend of Darrell Holt's?' Decker asked.

'Yeah, him. The FBI has a file on Ricky Moke. But not for bombing.'

'What?'

'Computer hacking. He's a mystery. The Feds have almost nothing on him.'

'What do they have?'

'There was a guy who used the screen name Ricky Moke whom the Feds caught hacking into Lunar Systems Inc. from a location near Frisco. When the Feds went to check it out, the port belonged to a grocery store that had no awareness of the crime. Someone had wired the port to a condemned building. No one knows who this Moke guy really is.'

'No picture?'

'Nothing.'

'So we don't even know if Moke is a real person or not.'

'Darrell Holt claims to know him,' Webster commented. 'I could ask him for a description.'

'We could do that for the sake of completion. But it's irrelevant if Moke isn't tied to any hate crimes.'

Martinez said, 'Personally, I think Moke's a dead end as far as the vandalism is concerned.'

Decker said, 'So forget about Moke. Concentrate on the hate groups we have. Lord knows there's enough of them.'

'If y'all want to take this hate thing to the next level, we need to go regional,' Webster said. 'That could take a while. Is this a good use of our time, especially since Ernesto has admitted to doing the vandalism?'

'Ordinarily, I'd say it would play very well with local politics. Showing that the police have zero tolerance for racism, especially after what happened with Buford Furrow at the Jewish Center. On a personal level, I want to take these bastards out. But . . .' Decker sighed. 'But we can't do much with Ernesto because he's a minor and the deal's gone down.'

Martinez said, 'Where does an upper-class kid like Ernesto get such graphic pictures? Off the Internet?'

'Maybe,' Decker said.

'So maybe someone should check out what's available out there . . . on the Web sites.'

'That's a good idea,' Decker said.

'I can do that in my spare time,' Webster said. 'As long as we make sure that the powers know what's going on. I don't want the Feds at my doorstep, demanding that I download my computer.'

'I'll clear it for you,' Decker said.

'I'll do it, too, if you want,' Wanda said.

'I'll clear you both,' Decker said. 'Or better yet, you two should just go over the hill to the Tolerance Center. I'm sure they have everything you need.' He thought for a moment. 'Rina knows some people who work there. I'll have her make a few phone calls.'

'Good,' Webster said. 'So where are we now?'

Decker said, 'I've got one more lead – a possible girlfriend of Ernesto Golding. From what I've been told, she's into some very scary stuff. But we've got a problem with her. She's over twenty-one, so we can't scare her parents into allowing us to interview her.'

'Maybe we can scare her,' Wanda suggested.

'This one doesn't sound like she scares easily.' Decker shrugged. 'But since we don't have much else, we'll give it the old college try.' He checked his notes, then wrote the vitals on a piece of paper. 'Here you go.'

Martinez took the paper. 'Ruby Ranger?'

'She sounds like a porn star,' Webster said.

'Maybe she is,' Decker said.

Webster brightened. 'Want me to check out the adult tapes at the local Blockbuster?'

'There are better ways to use your time, Tom,' Decker answered.

'My wife has been preoccupied with our daughter for the last six weeks. If you can think of a better use for my time, I'm all ears.'

'It's just that his hand is getting tired,' Martinez said.

'Do I have to hear this?' Wanda held her ears.

Decker smiled. 'Do me a favor, Wanda. You drive. At the moment, you're the least likely to get distracted by fantasies.'

13

The brass plate on the gate named it Hacienda del Ranger. The villa was several levels of pink plaster, green shutters, and red-tiled roofs, with a round two-story turret that contained the front entrance. To get in, Webster rang a bell that connected to an intercom. Once buzzed in, he, Martinez, and Bontemps stepped through a shaded courtyard lushly filled with potted plants, the floor tiled with Mexican pavers. The centerpiece was a three-tiered, scallop-shell fountain that dribbled rather than spouted.

The woman who answered the intercom was of average height and terminally thin, with a weathered face made even older by her big bleached-blonde hair. Her hands were snaked with veins and knobs, and sprouted long red nails. She was dressed in black knits, which gave her a spectral look. The three detectives gave her proper ID, but she didn't bother to read any of the information. 'What do you want?'

'Mrs Ranger?' Martinez asked.

'Yes, what do you want?'

Wanda said, 'If you don't mind, we'd like a word with your daughter, Ruby—'

'She's not in.'

'Alice, stow the bullshit!' a female voice broke in. A moment later the thin woman was unceremoniously shoved out of the way. She teetered on black spiked heels.

'What are you doing, Ma?' The voice came from a young woman who stood with her hands on her hips. She was tall and bony except for ample breasts. Her hair was black and poker-straight, clipped just below the earlobes, with bangs grazing the tops of her eyebrows. Her complexion was chalk white, red lipstick outlined her mouth, and green eyes peered from black-lined sockets. Her hands were long, but unlike Mom's, her nails were short and ragged. She wore black leather pants and a midriff denim vest that barely contained her cleavage. Her navel was pierced, as were one eyelid and her nose.

'I've been expecting this, Alice. They know I've been with Ernesto. It's guilt by association. Wrong, but what the fuck?'

Alice said, 'Do you have to use such crude language?'

'Yes, I do—'

'Why do you have to do it in front of me?'

'Because it's so much fun to see you squirm. But don't sweat it, old cow. I'm leaving.'

Mom marched off, tears in her eyes. Ruby flashed the cops some white teeth and a tongue pierce. 'Ah, the unholy trinity. I must rate to send over three little coppers.'

'Ruby Ranger?' Martinez asked.

'Duh, yeah!' She knocked her temple. 'Anyone home?'

'May we come in?' Wanda asked.

'Yes, you may come in.' Ruby swung the door open. 'You can talk to me while I pack. Because when I'm done, I'm gone.' Abruptly, she turned and headed up the stairs.

Wanda raised her eyebrows. 'Oh, my, my!'

'Whatever she is, porn star ain't that bad of a guess,' Webster said.

They started in after her, but then Alice suddenly reappeared. 'Can I get any of you some coffee or tea?'

'No thank you, Mrs Ranger, we're fine,' Webster said.

Alice was filled with short, spasmodic movements, as if tension was delivered through her nervous system in discrete bundles. 'You shouldn't think badly of Ruby. She's a free spirit because we've raised her that way. Maybe too much a free spirit, but I know she'll settle down.' The woman smiled, but her eyes were still moist. 'We were all free spirits and look at us now.'

In Wanda's mind, that wasn't an endorsement. 'We'd like to talk to your daughter before she leaves. So if you'll excuse us.'

'Of course. I'm just trying to explain . . .' She stopped. 'To understand and explain . . .'

They left her groping for words, still trying to explain. The door to Ruby's room was open. She was literally throwing her things into an oversize black duffel. Most of the clothes were black, waving like funeral banners as they leapt from the drawer to the bag. Her room was prison cell spare – a full-size bed with a blanket on top, and a dresser topped with a boom box. Nothing hung from the walls, and there was nothing on the floor other than the hardwood. No mirrors, no TV. Yet the woman was immaculately groomed. Wanda walked a few steps and peeked into the bathroom. It was filled with bottles and jars sitting on the rim of the bathtub. And it did have a mirror over the sink.

'Where are you going?' Wanda asked in a disinterested tone.

'None of your business.' Ruby didn't bother to look at them when she talked. 'Now that I said that, I'll tell you. Probably back up to Northern Cal. But maybe not.'

'Silicon Valley?' Webster said.

'Depends what's in it for me.' She stuffed a pair of Levi's into a side pocket. Then she took out a very skimpy leather bustier and placed it over her midriff top. 'What do you think?'

No one answered.

'Yeah, yeah, I know what you're thinking . . . no support for my boobs.' She cupped her breasts. 'Thirty-six D. All flesh, no implants. Weep your heart out.' She tossed the bra over to Martinez. 'Give it to your wife or your girlfriend.' She tossed him a pair of panties. 'Think of me the next time you fuck.'

Martinez tossed both articles back at her. 'I'll pass.

Where were you yesterday morning?'

'Masturbating in my bed.'

'What time?' Martinez said, evenly.

'I dunno. Nine, ten . . . I didn't bother looking at the clock.'

'The act doesn't take that long,' Wanda said. 'What did you do afterward?'

'I dunno. Showered, shaved my legs, took a dump . . . the usual. I wasn't anywhere near the synagogue. Yes, I admire Hitler, but painting juvenile slogans on walls and leaving pictures of dead bodies is infantile.' She smoothed her polished hair with bitten fingernails. 'I'm not a Nazi . . . fascism holds no interest for me. It's the evil leaders that I find utterly fascinating. Those who start out in the extremities of society and somehow wangle their way to the top. It's more of an indictment of the public than it is of them. Nothing can exist without public support.' She grinned at them. 'Even cops . . . especially cops.' She tossed the leather bra to Wanda. 'How about it, sister? Goes well with your complexion.'

Wanda tossed it back. 'I'm not your sister, and I prefer colors. I outgrew Goth a long time ago.'

'Judging from the crow's feet, I'd say it was a long, long time ago,' Ruby answered. 'Do you get what I'm saying here, folks? That totalitarianism can't exist in a vacuum. I mean, look how fast the Berlin Wall fell. Seventy years of entrenched, hardened Communism brought down like *that*.' She snapped her fingers.

'Did you and Ernesto ever talk about Hitler?' Webster asked.

'About Hitler, Stalin, Ivan the Terrible, Louis XVI, Marie Antoinette, Bluebeard, Jeffrey Dahmer, Gacy, Ed Gein, Lizzie Borden, Richard III . . . what else? So I have a fixation about the dark side. The country hasn't retracted the First Amendment so far as I know.'

Webster said, 'You look like you're in a hurry to leave.'

'You're a clever one for a hick.' She sat on the edge of her bed. 'If you're assuming that my rapid exit implies some kind of guilt, you are out of the ballpark, my cutie pie. Ernesto admitted that he vandalized the synagogue. If he had help, I don't know about it. We didn't talk much. We had a sex-shu-al relationship. He's large and that was why I put up with him. I'm twenty-three and a genius on many levels, he's seventeen – bright but no Einstein. Not that he doesn't have promise, but he needs a few more years for his brain to gel. We fucked more than we talked.'

'You just opened yourself up to statutory rape,' Webster said.

'I fucking quake. But sure, if you want to arrest me for rape or putting ideas into his head, give it your best shot.' She stood and hefted the duffel. 'Not too bad.' She disappeared, then came out of the bathroom holding an armful of hair and bath products, dumping them into the nylon bag. 'You talk to your superior's kid about me? Jacob Lazarus. Now that kid had some genuine gray matter. A certified cutie, but very disturbed. Man, he really hates me!' She grinned. 'I'd keep an eye on him. Because isn't it always the hotshot's kid who's the most fucked up?'

She paused.

'Although I can identify with his anger. Life is so stupid when you're that smart. I think that's why I'm so obsessed with those who make an impact, albeit an evil one.' She zipped up the duffel and lifted it again. 'Man, this fucker is heavy! You want to help me?'

'No, not at all,' Wanda said.

She smiled. 'Suit yourself. I'm outta here. Tell my mother that Dad's still fucking his secretary, so she may as well have that piece of chocolate cake.' She winked and lifted the bag about two inches off the ground. 'Bye now.'

They followed her down the staircase. Alice was waiting at the bottom. 'When will you be back?'

'I dunno.' Ruby kissed her mother on the cheek. 'Buck up, Ma. There's always the pool man.'

She dragged her bag across the hardwood floor and onto the porch outside. It left a scratch atop the planks. She towed the duffel through the courtyard and onto the sidewalk, then she heaved it into an open trunk on a four-wheel-drive Jeep. She slammed the lid shut, hopped into the driver's seat, and gunned the engine. Minutes later, she was gone.

Wanda took down the license plate, then said, 'I wouldn't fret too much, Mrs Ranger. Kids always return when the money runs out.'

Alice regarded Wanda, her eyes red and still brimming with water. 'You-all don't know the hell I've been through. You try to give up and let them go, but something inside of you keeps trying. One more conversation, one more *attempt*!' She wiped tears from her cheeks. 'She was once a baby . . . goo-goo-ing and ga-ga-ing in her crib, just like any other baby. Her brother isn't like that. I just don't understand what happened!'

Martinez rubbed his neck. 'Kids are tough. But she isn't a kid anymore. She's an adult. You can take the yoke off your neck. She isn't your responsibility anymore.'

The woman shook her head. 'No, sir, the yoke is there . . . always. Like that African tribe whose women have iron rings around their necks permanently. The rings stretch the neck. They stretch it and stretch it and stretch it. It is said that if the rings were removed, the stretched neck could no longer support the head, and the woman would die. That's me, Detectives. The yoke is the only support I have left.'

Before Jacob had left the synagogue in the morning, Decker managed to secure the boy's permission to talk to Dr Gruen. He knew he had caught his stepson in a weak moment, and felt bad about exploiting him, but Decker needed some guidance. He left a message with the doctor's answering service, figuring that the psychologist would call him back later in the evening. To his surprise, Gruen was on the phone five minutes later.

'You caught me right before my six o'clock patient.'

'You caught me right before I left,' Decker said. 'Thanks so much for calling me back.'

'You're welcome. What can I do for you, Lieutenant?'

'Jake gave me permission to talk to you.'

'I know. He called me.'

'Oh, good.' Decker stalled. 'I was wondering if you could help me out with some of his issues . . . without breaking confidentiality, of course.'

'What in specific?'

Again, Decker paused. 'He's very angry . . . self-admitted.'

'This is true. He is one pissed-off kid.' The psychologist's voice was not only calm, but conversational. He could have been talking about a plumbing bill.

'What's he pissed off about?' Decker asked.

'Pick a topic,' Gruen answered.

'I think he's worried that he's a sociopath,' Decker told him. 'He asked me if he fit the description of those I have arrested.'

'What did you tell him?'

'No, of course.'

'And that's how you feel?'

'Of course.' But Decker hesitated a little too long.

Gruen said, 'His life would be much easier if he were sociopathic. Then he'd just do his thing, and with his intelligence and good looks, he'd probably be a top corporate raider. Instead, the kid is saddled with an overly developed conscience and a pathological sense of guilt. He's ashamed by his recent behavior – the drug use that he has admitted to you – and is terrified that his mother is going to find out. I've suggested family therapy so he can admit certain things to her in a controlled environment and rid himself of some of the guilt. But he's not ready for it yet. He has a big stake in protecting her. Does your wife have a clue as to what's going on?'

'Much more than he thinks she does.' A pause. 'I don't think she knows anything about the molestation. Jacob's intimated to me that more went on than he had admitted.'

'Uh-huh,' Gruen said.

'Is it bad?'

'That's what we're working on.'

'You can't say anything more?'

'At this point, we're trying to sort out fact from fantasy. Even he's not sure. For instance, one of his recollections is his molester threatening that his mother would die if he told her what went on. That's the one he admitted to you, correct?'

'Yes.'

'I think the threat might have been more like, "If you don't let me do what I want to do, I'm going to kill your mother." '

'He said that?'

'No. This is my interpretation. But put yourself in Jacob's seven-year-old mind. This animal tries to rape and kill his mother. The kid's got to be thinking that it was somehow his fault. If he had let this pederast do what he wanted to do to him, his mother would have been safe. Which is totally false. Now I can tell him, and you can tell him, and the whole world can tell him, that it isn't his fault. That a monster is a monster is a monster. And intellectually, he'll believe you. He'll say, "Of course, it wasn't my fault." But getting rid of the entrenched guilt is a whole nother animal.'

'How does he get rid of it?'

'I'm not sure he can. So I'm telling him not to even bother to assess blame. Instead, he should look at the outcome. Mom is fine. More than fine. She's happily remarried, and has kids she adores. Now maybe she isn't fine. Maybe she's miserable. But that's not the point. If he perceives her as fine, that's good enough.'

'She is doing fine,' Decker said. 'At least, she never hinted that she wasn't fine. Maybe she isn't fine. I'd think she'd be a lot finer if Jacob was happy.'

'Ain't that the mantra of all parents. Anyway, you want my opinion. Behaviorally, Jacob should excel in college. And hopefully, he'll find socially acceptable outlets for all his energy. Emotionally, it would be good if he continued seeing someone when in Baltimore. His problems aren't going to be solved in TV time, before the last commercial break. He's aware of that, too.'

'What should I be doing?'

'He's talking to you. Whatever you're doing, it's working. I've got a patient in two minutes. I've got to go pull her chart.'

'Can I call you again?'

'How about if I call you if Jake and I think I should call you? That way you don't have to keep asking Jacob's permission, and he won't feel you're horning in too much.'

Decker resigned himself to being kept in the dark.

'That sounds acceptable. Thank you.'

'You're welcome. Bye.'

In other words, no news would be good news. Decker's take on it was no news meant less excess stomach acid.

14

The vandalism case stalled, but crime did not. With new homicides, rapes, assaults, burglaries, robberies, domestic disturbances, and car thefts, even Decker couldn't think too much about a once defaced synagogue now freshly painted and restored to its former mediocre glory. The vandal or vandals did succeed in mobilizing community support for inter-faith dialogues on hate crimes. Rina had thrown herself into the thick of it, organizing this panel and that panel. It was her way of dealing with the insult. Once in a while, she asked him about the progress of finding more culprits. When he made excuses, Rina didn't push it.

For months, things proceeded apace, Decker's family mercifully going through a quiescent period. His daughter Cindy had completed her second year as a cop, and had done so without major incident. This year, all the bad guys against her were actually felons.

Jacob had been officially accepted to a joint program with Johns Hopkins and a local yeshiva in Baltimore. He worked hard without complaint and kept most of his opinions to himself. Decker resisted the parental urge to pry. Instead, he concentrated his energies onto Hannah, who truly wanted his attention.

By school's end, in June, Ernesto Golding had completed all of his ninety days of community service. From time to time, he had dropped in on Decker just to shoot the breeze, speaking at length about therapy, and how he was finally getting it together. And how good community service had been for him: to get out and not be so spoiled and see what was happening in the real world. Because he sure as hell knew he didn't live in the real world. And he was glad that Ruby was out of his life because although she was a good lay, she was very bad for him. She had filled his head with all sorts of weird ideas. And now he wasn't even so sure about his grandfather being a Nazi, and maybe he made it all up in his head because Ruby had messed with his brain.

In three weeks, Ernesto was off to the Baldwins' nature camp.

'I'm glad you're doing well,' Decker had found himself saying.

'I guess.'

'You're satisfied with Dr Baldwin?'

'Actually, I think I talk more to you than to either one of the Baldwins. I think you should start billing my parents for your services.'

Tempting, considering the Baldwins were making

around three hundred an hour. He was making around three hundred a day: good money when he didn't compare it to anything else.

'I'd like to talk more, Ernesto, but unfortunately, I have a meeting in about ten minutes.'

'I know you've got to go. Look, I'm graduating in two days. If you aren't doing anything, maybe you could come to the ceremony. I wouldn't mind.'

'What day of the week is it on?'

'Friday at six.'

Saved by the bell. Decker said, 'It's the Sabbath—'

'Oh, yeah. Right. Anyway, I'm off to Brown. Pretty good for a felon, huh? Thanks for saving my butt, by cutting me a deal and keeping it all quiet. Thanks for giving me another chance. I'm going to do better. You'll see.'

'Are you looking forward to the nature camp?' Decker asked the teen.

'I don't think I need it anymore, but it was part of the deal. What the hell? It'll teach me good survival skills. The main instructor is a former Marine. Sounds like fun, huh?'

'A riot,' Decker said.

Ernesto rolled his eyes. 'It'll be okay. I'll be okay. How's Jacob?'

'Fine.'

'He's got one more year to go, right?'

'Yes, but he's going back east actually.'

'Really? Where?'

'He's in a joint program with Johns Hopkins University and a local Jewish high school.'

'That's cool,' Ernesto said. 'That's real cool. Say hello to him for me. I know he doesn't hang with my buds from Prep, but you know, that's okay. Tell him I said hi.'

'I will.'

The young man's smile turned into a grin. 'I'll write you from the wilderness. Send you a postcard by carrier pigeon.'

Decker laughed. 'Good luck!'

After he had left, Decker realized that he almost liked the boy. And he did wish him well. Which was why he felt sickened to the core when he caught the call.

15

It was a short hop from residential real estate to woodlands, from homes and civilization to what once was the dominant terrain of Southern California mountains. Hills abloom with early summer wildflowers – a palette of deep lilacs, sun-kissed yellows, and a spectrum of greens. Mervin Baldwin ran his back-to-nature camp a few miles into the region where the knolls segued into rocky peaks and the unruly vegetation was lush and thick through endless wilderness. The solidly built, teenage boys whom Baldwin claimed as his clients could walk back to the strip malls in just a few hours, and often they did. Eventually, they were found, reclaimed, and given even more duties to make up for their truancies. Mervin Baldwin found it exhilarating as well as redeemable that these boys could negotiate and navigate their ways from foreign territory back to home base.

He would exhilarate no more. Mervin Baldwin, along

with Ernesto Golding, was dead.

The sun had just jumped over the horizon, but was still low enough to cause that blinding postdawn glare. It was a little past six in the morning, and Decker had already finished a Thermos of coffee. Usually, he depended on a brisk workout on the treadmill to get the heart started, but today it was a chemical rush that kicked the system into action.

He drove a Jeep Cherokee, once black, but now turned charcoal thanks to a layer of fine-grained dust. Driving up a gravel road until it dead-ended, he then switched into four-wheel drive and took the Jeep off-road up the stony incline. The SUV bounced and bumped, the motor straining as it neared the Baldwin campsite. Within moments, official vehicles and uniformed people came into view, their vehicles taking up the precious level ground. Decker maneuvered the Jeep about fifty yards to the left where he found a relatively clear patch to park, but it left the wheels at a slant. He got out with great caution. Below him was a hundred feet of rock, not a sheer drop, but if he were to fall, he'd get pretty banged up from rolling downward.

The actual stomping ground was a mesa, fronted by a panoramic view and surrounded by a moat of deep drops and gorges. Not a whole lot of room to square-dance, but it did allow the camp officials to do roll call with a sweep of the eye. Off to the left, two large canvas huts had been erected. The rest of the flattened ground was covered with sleeping bags. Eleven dazed teenagers – Decker had counted them – were seated on the ground, resting, staring or playing cards using sunflower seeds as money. They were in various states of dress – from pajamas to jeans and an undershirt. None of the kids made eye contact as he walked by, but Decker could feel them watching his back with suspicious, hardened eyes. It took an act of will not to look over his shoulder.

The wilderness was an unincorporated area, co-manned by Decker's substation, the conservatory park rangers, and the Sheriff's Department. Usually, homicides up in the hills were taken over by the Sheriff's, but since Mervin Baldwin and Ernesto Golding were locals, someone had been smart enough to phone him up. Decker hoped that the call indicated interdepartmental cooperation instead of a macho-uniform pissing contest. He wanted the case and the other agencies would give it to him if he treated all involved with respect. He smiled first and then flashed his badge, approaching one of the park rangers. Her name was Landeau, and she was a big woman with thick wrists. Her hair was tied back in a ponytail, and sweat dotted a protruding forehead. It wasn't that hot, so Decker surmised that the perspiration came from physical exertion.

She said, 'The crime scene's the bigger of the two shelters.' Her voice trembled as she spoke. 'There're about a dozen officers combing the area.'

Decker stared at the view. 'What are they looking for?'

'Pardon?'

He turned to face her. 'What are the officers in the mountains looking for?'

'Oh. The perpetrator, of course.'

Which meant the area was already trampled upon.

Decker said, 'Do they know who the perpetrator is?'

Landeau stuttered, 'N-no . . . I mean I don't know . . . maybe someone else does.'

Decker didn't say anything. He looked around, his gaze taking in the boys, then skipping over to a man dressed in battle fatigues, being questioned by two uniforms. In the background, he heard the strain of more vehicles making their way up the mountain.

Decker pointed to the combat guy. 'Who's that?'

'Corporal Hank Tarpin.' She consulted her notes. 'Formerly from the USMC. He calls himself the Chief Nature Master – the camp coordinator in charge of the day-to-day activities. He found the bodies and identified them.'

'As Golding and Merv Baldwin.'

'Yes.'

Decker nodded. 'I'll go talk to him.'

'Yes, sir,' Landeau answered. She was clearly glad to get rid of him.

Tarpin was over six feet and built with a broad chest and very big arms suggestive of an iron pumper. He had a remarkably small head for the thick frame. Or maybe it just looked smaller because his scalp was shaven clean. Deep, brown eyes, prominent nose, thick lips, and a big chin. He reminded Decker of the T-shirted genie on the household liquid cleaner, only without the earring.

The officers looked up and Decker flashed his badge, making sure Tarpin took it in. The man's face was emotionless. Not hostile or defiant, just a total blank. It could be shock; it could be a controlled effort not to give himself away. Decker introduced himself.

'Lieutenant Decker.' Tarpin's voice was muted. 'Good you made it down so quickly. I know you had some prior dealings with Ernesto, because the kid told me.' A pause. 'He liked you. I thought you should know that.'

'Thanks for telling me.' Decker regarded the khaki-clad sheriffs. They were clearly below him in rank, but didn't like being usurped. From the stripes, Decker could tell that the smaller man was a sergeant. 'I had prior experience with the deceased minor. That's why I'm here.' Decker's eyes fell upon the two domed huts, waterproof and colored neon orange. 'That's the crime scene?'

'Yes, sir,' the sergeant answered.

Tarpin said, 'It's unspeakable in there. Not that I haven't seen bodies in Serbia and Rwanda, but . . . it's been a while. And I knew them . . . shook the hell out of me.'

That's what his words said. But Tarpin's face was still empty.

'You identified them as Ernesto Golding and Mervin Baldwin?' Decker asked.

'Yes, sir, it's them.' Tarpin looked away, his nose wrinkling for a split second – as if he smelled something rotten.

'When did you discover them?'

'When I got up . . . around five in the morning.'

'And you immediately went into the tents?'

'The closest hut is where the provisions are kept. The

farther shelter belongs to the Baldwins. I went to get breakfast going, and . . . something didn't smell right. If you've ever been in combat and had a whiff of the stench, you just don't forget it.'

Decker took out his notepad. 'What did you do?'

'Lifted the flap to Dr Baldwin's tent.' He averted his gaze. 'God help them now . . . He's the only one who can.'

'And you knew right away that they were both dead.'

'Yes, sir. No doubt about that.'

'Look for a pulse?'

'Of course . . . nothing.'

'Were the bodies warm?'

He waited a moment. 'I don't recall.'

Decker thought a moment. 'So Ernesto Golding was in Merv Baldwin's hut.'

'Yes, sir.'

'Doing what?'

Once again Tarpin wore an enigmatic expression. 'Therapy. That's where Dr Baldwin does therapy with the boys.'

'At five A.M.?'

'I beg your pardon?'

'You said you found them at five in the morning. They were already dead. Does Dr Baldwin do therapy in the wee hours of the morning?'

'He does therapy twenty-four hours a day, Lieutenant. That's what makes him remarkable. I hope you're not implying something.'

'No, I'm just asking questions.'

'Then you should start asking questions about the

other Dr Baldwin – Dee Baldwin. I can't seem to reach her. She's not answering her pager or the phone. I'm concerned.'

'Can you give me the numbers? I'll send over some officers to her residence.'

'You bet.' Tarpin fished through his pockets. 'Have a pencil?'

Decker handed him his notepad and pen.

'I hope this isn't any kind of vendetta. They've worked with all kinds of unbalanced teenagers.' Tarpin scribbled down numbers. 'This is her pager, this one's the cell phone, this is the office, and the residence.'

Decker reclaimed his pad and pen, then dialed from his cell phone – dead in the wilds. 'I'll have to use the mike in the SUV. This isn't working in this range.'

Two murdered, one missing.

Decker said, 'All the rest of the camp's boys are accounted for, Corporal Tarpin?'

'Yes.' Tarpin turned his head and spit on the ground. 'Are you going to question them?'

'I'd like to.'

'It wasn't one of them. None of them could pull this off and be so quiet about it. I didn't hear a damn thing. Besides, these boys here are rank amateurs. The Baldwins don't take the hardened juvenile cases in their camp. Too much risk.'

'What did these boys do to bring them here?'

'Petty stuff . . . or just acting out with Mama and Papa. They're on the wrong track, but when push comes to shove, they're basically spoiled, rich-kid pussies. They think they're tough, but wouldn't last a week on the mean streets.' Tarpin's bald head was sweating. 'He deals with other kids, more disturbed kids. You might want to start looking there.'

'I'll start with these boys.' Decker walked toward the Jeep to make his calls. 'Mainly because they're here and so am I.'

Tarpin dogged him. 'They didn't do it. They're all like Ernesto. You think a kid like Ernesto could have done that?' He answered his own question. 'Not a chance. None of them could do it. You'll see when you talk to them.'

Decker opened the door to the four-wheel drive. 'I have every intention of doing that just as soon as I put in the call to find Dee Baldwin – the living before the dead, Corporal.'

He didn't need to go inside to know what had happened. The ground was veined with streaks of blood, oozing out from under the bottom of the waterproof dome. Several bloody partials of shoeprints formed a trail from the door flap to the edge of the drop. Decker chalked them and looked over the escarpment. No continuing trail down the mountainside as far as he could see, but that meant nothing. Someone would have to climb down there and check it out, because from the way it looked, it appeared that the shoeprint went over the edge. Weird, but not impossible.

Gingerly, he trod on the dusty ground below, watching where he stepped. He opened the door flap and lowered his head. Then, trying not to breathe too deeply, he peeked inside.

The wind of death registered first. It stank of blood and guts, reeking like the back of a butcher shop. The stretched fabric walls had been bombarded with splatter marks; on the ground were puddles of crimson and brown plasma. There once was a double bedroll, but now it was a blotter of blood-soaked sheets. The two bodies lay on the ground, side by side, both doubled over. No arms hiding their faces: they didn't even have enough time to assume protective positions. Ernesto had been bare-chested; Baldwin had on an undershirt. The rest of their clothes lay in a heap near the entrance to the tent.

Decker closed his eyes in order to think. A tinge of nausea made pinpricks in his stomach, but he swallowed it down. If the victims' state of dress implied that this meeting had been more than just therapy, it put a different cast on Dee Baldwin's disappearance. Was she running from the bad guys or hiding from the cops? Or maybe she had just gone grocery shopping at seven in the morning.

He opened his eyes. The scene did not improve. The faces were bluish white and streaked with blood. They had been shot repeatedly and, from the bullet holes that dotted the bodies, they'd been shot impulsively. No execution-style shooting, this was rage, giving full meaning to the word *overkill.* Exit holes from the shells had made Swiss cheese out of the tent walls. Judging by the sizes of the apertures, the weapon was probably a .32-caliber. The assailant must have had a silencer, because otherwise there would have been lots of noise. If the couple had been awake and had been seized with such firearm force, there would be no way for them to fight back. If they had been asleep, they wouldn't have known what had hit them.

The coroner would determine a range for the time of death. In this case, Decker's knowledge as a detective would be just as accurate. The bodies were still warm. At this elevation, things cooled off at night. The murders appeared more recent than not.

If Tarpin was innocent and to be believed, he didn't hear anything. Which meant it happened in the deepest part of the sleep cycle – usually two hours before wake-up. If Tarpin said he woke around five, the murders probably took place sometime around or after three.

From three to five . . .

Where was Dee Baldwin?

He closed the flap and gave himself a moment to catch his breath while scanning for details. In the last few minutes, Webster, Martinez, and Bontemps had surfaced. Martinez was writing in his notepad, but stopped when he saw Decker. The trio walked over, Webster saying, 'How bad is it?'

'It's awful.' Decker turned to Bontemps.

Before he could talk, Webster broke in. 'I called Wanda down because she was involved with Golding in the vandalism case. I thought if this was another hate crime, a bigger hate crime, she should be here.'

'It's a hate crime, but not a "hate" crime,' Decker said. 'But it's good that Wanda's here. We could use someone in Juvenile since the majority of our suspects are under eighteen.'

They all regarded the stunned teenagers.

Decker said, 'Let's divide the kids into two groups according to their ages. The ones over eighteen can be questioned. As far as the minors, we can't do much without parental consent. Get their names and phone numbers, and start contacting the parents. You can also ask them very casually if they heard or saw anything, and judge their reaction.

'But remember that we're working with a different population here. They're all going to look like they're trying to hide something, because that's their normal behavior. They're fuckups. They've got years of experience masking guilt or shifting the blame. We're looking for something out of the ordinary.'

Webster said, 'Y'all really think one of them did it and stuck around to be questioned?'

Martinez said, 'Maybe we have a real psycho in our midst.'

Bontemps looked at the motley crew. 'That very well could be.'

'I'm going to see if I can get Tarpin's permission to open up the kids' knapsacks,' Decker said. 'When the parents placed their kids in the program, they explicitly gave Tarpin and Baldwin permission to do random checks of their personal possessions for drugs and contraband.'

'This is sounding familiar,' Webster said.

'I realize that,' Decker answered.

'Who's Tarpin?' Martinez asked.

'The dude in the camouflage,' Decker said.

'He looks like he could do some damage. What's his

role in the camp?' Martinez asked. 'Boot kicker?'

'Chief Nature Master,' Decker said. 'The activity coordinator. I think he does everything except the actual talking therapy.'

'Why does the name Tarpin ring a bell?' Webster said.

'You're right,' Martinez stated. 'But I can't place it. What's his gimmick? Is he a survivalist expert or something?'

'Probably.'

'*That's it!*' Wanda looked up with triumphant glee on her face. 'Remember the Preservers of Ethnic Integrity? Darrell Holt and Erin Kershan?'

'Yeah, yeah!' Webster said. 'The flyers they were printin' up!'

'Tarpin's name was on it!' Martinez said. 'He was the English Only guy.'

'This is sounding *very* familiar,' Wanda remarked.

Decker raised his eyebrows. 'The flyer should be in the original case file. I'll look at them later.'

Wanda said, 'At the time we didn't have anything to connect the Preservers of Ethnic Integrity to Golding and the temple vandalism. I don't know if Tarpin and Golding knew each other before this tragedy, but it would be interesting to find out.'

'Whatever happened to that other racist kid? The hacker.' Decker snapped his fingers. 'Ricky Moke. Or whatever his name really is. Wasn't he also a supposed survivalist?'

'I think that's how Darrell and Erin saw him,' Wanda said.

'Graduate of Mervin Baldwin's program?' Martinez asked.

'Let's check it out.' Decker paused. 'In the immediate, I'd sure like to locate Baldwin's wife. She's not at her house or at the clinic, and that's making me nervous. I gave the go-ahead for immediate entrance on the grounds of imminent danger to her welfare, but then we had to retreat from the premises. I'm trying to get a court-ordered search warrant, especially for Baldwin's clinic. Tarpin suggested some kind of vendetta. Maybe something'll pop up in his case files.'

Martinez said, 'Aren't his case files confidential?'

'Not if someone's in imminent danger.' Decker paused. 'A crazy patient coming back to get you. What's the likelihood of that? Probably as likely as old criminals coming back to hunt us down.'

'It happens,' Martinez said.

'Not very often. Know what the most dangerous occupation for that kind of thing is? Law. People get real pissed at lawyers. Anyway, I don't know for certain if Dee Baldwin is in imminent danger. As a matter of fact, she just might be the perp.' Decker described the scene inside the hut. 'A wife finding her husband and a kid in that kind of pose, I could see her going into a rage.'

'I dunno, Loo,' Martinez said. 'You think the camp shrink would have a homosexual affair with a minor with all these kids *and* Tarpin *and* his wife hanging around?'

Wanda said, 'Maybe Dee paid him a surprise visit.'

'At three in the morning?'

'At three in the morning, it would really be a *surprise* visit,' Wanda said. 'And that's why she waited. She had suspicions. Wives know that kind of thing. She wanted to catch him when he least expected it.'

Decker said, 'That could explain the premeditation aspect of this crime. The murderer had to have used a silencer. Otherwise, he or she or they would have woken up the entire camp. She comes up here with a gun and a purpose . . .' Decker thought a moment. 'She would have had to use a vehicle to get up here. So somewhere among these umpteen tire tracks would be an impression that matches her vehicle. So let's get a casting on every single tire print here and let's say a . . . half-mile radius, assuming she might have parked a ways down so as not to create too much noise. Wanda, you chalk off every single tire track you see, and have the techs do the plaster work.'

She frowned. 'That's gonna take up a lot of time.'

'Yes, it will,' Decker said. 'You have a problem with that?'

'Uh, no, sir, not at all.'

'Good. Tom and Bert will help you after they're done. Tom, you take the older kids – which'll take time because the questioning will be more involved. Bert, you take the information on the minor kids and also, you handle Tarpin because you've been in the service. He claims to be a Marine . . . mentioned something about Serbia and Rwanda. To me, Tarpin looks like a mercenary. I'll call Oliver to do a background check on him. I've got to call on Jill and Carter Golding before they hear the news from somewhere else. Of course, if anyone wants to switch places . . . ?'

Silence.

'Thought not.' Decker squinted into the hot sun, felt its fire spitting in his face. It was shaping up to be one hell of a day.

16

They had to have known something was really wrong, because if it had just been another minor run-in with the law, Decker wouldn't have come in person. But there was no way for them to expect news as bad as this. And there was no palatable way for Decker to deliver it.

Standing like a robot, witnessing all the horror, shock, and pain known only to other grieving parents – the screams, the sobs, the sudden clutching of the breast. The father trying to comfort the mother, the mother refusing all of it. Then came the immediate denial.

You must be mistaken.

Are you sure?

You could have made a mistake.

How can you be certain?

You're wrong!

But Decker was not wrong. This part never got easier. He only got older.

At first, they would hate him because he had told them the unspeakable. Then, a week would pass . . . two weeks . . . a month. They would come to view him as the link, the one who would impart some logic into the madness, their conduit to the investigation, the one they could call, yell at, scream at, cry with. Eventually a relationship would grow – maybe a symbiotic one, maybe an antagonistic one – but some kind of relationship.

Still standing at the doorway – because no one had invited him in yet – Decker spoke in short sentences. Even so, his words weren't registering.

Jill's eyes had turned feral. She hissed when she spoke. 'You didn't know him all that well. You could have made a mistake.'

Decker said, 'Maybe we should all go inside.'

They stared back at him: Jill with her red, pinched nose dripping clear snot all over her green sweats, and Carter, pale green in complexion and stymied by shock. He was dressed in a work shirt and jeans. Decker lowered his head, attempting to cross the threshold. Passively, they split ranks and let him enter. Carter immediately fell into a chair, battling a bad case of nausea, dropping his head between his knees. But it was Jill who made the sudden run for the bathroom. They could both hear her retching.

Carter whispered, 'How do you know? How are you certain?'

'The camp's coordinator – Corporal Tarpin – positively identified him.'

'Oh, God!' Tears flowed down the man's cheeks.

'But just maybe he made a mistake?'

Pleading, begging. It was pure pathos, heart wrenching.

'I'm afraid not, Mr Golding. I saw him as well.'

More awful silence. The questions would come. Slowly at first, then they'd barrage him, getting angrier at each query. It was a pattern that Decker was all too familiar with.

Carter said, 'I'm grateful I was home.'

Talking from a male perspective. He had been there to take care of his wife. Carter didn't know what Decker knew, that she wouldn't want his care and she wouldn't want his protection. What she wanted was her son back, and since she couldn't have that, he was of no use to her at this time.

Carter looked up. 'At least she didn't hear it alone.' A pause. 'You're sure?'

'I'm sure.'

Carter pointed to a chair.

Decker sat.

'What . . .' That was all he could get out.

'Perhaps we should wait for your wife. She'll want to know, sir. She'll have to know.'

Carter didn't argue. And eventually Jill did return, with mottled white skin and shaking hands.

Carter said, 'He was going to tell . . .'

Silence.

She bit her lip as tears rushed from her eyes. Then she nodded quickly.

Short and simple. Decker said, 'Right now, this is confidential. Dr Baldwin was also murdered. They were found together in a double bedroll.'

Jill looked up and covered her mouth as her eyes widened. 'Oh, my God!' Breathing hard. 'Oh, my dear God! Together?'

Decker nodded.

'So where was Mervin?' Carter said. 'Are you implying that *he* did it?'

Decker nearly kicked himself, realizing his error. 'Mr Carter, it was Mervin who was murdered. It's Dee Baldwin who's missing.'

Carter stood up, full of venom. 'Just what are you saying?'

'I'm just telling you what we saw—'

'You didn't *see* anything!' Carter yelled. 'Furthermore, I don't care what the hell you saw, I'm telling you it's impossible! I know Ernesto enough to know that what you're saying is pure bullshit! Someone is trying to discredit my son and I want to know why!'

More than discredit. Someone had murdered his son. Dad appeared more outraged by the inference of his son's homosexuality than the actual murder. But that was only because the diversion was easier to digest.

'Why would someone do such a thing!' Carter was still screaming. He shook a finger at Decker. 'This is . . . this is . . .' And then he melted, sinking into a chair. He laid his head in his hands and wept openly. His wife watched with wet eyes, still shaking and still ashen. She observed him without comforting him. It was horrible to watch. Decker knew if he spoke, the man would stop crying. But that wasn't to anyone's advantage. He let him go on for a few more moments, then said, 'I don't know what happened, sir. But I *will* find out.'

Carter looked up. 'Why would . . . what do you think?'

'I don't know yet.'

'You must have some ideas,' Jill whispered.

'I'm sure I will have some ideas,' Decker said. 'And when I do, you'll be the first to know.'

'When can we see him?' Jill's voice was barely audible.

'As soon as I hear it's okay, I'll come down and get you personally.'

'We can't see him now?' Carter asked. 'I want to see him now! I demand it!'

'Please, please, Mr Golding.' Decker had his eyes closed, seeing the horror and knowing it was too much. 'You must trust me with this one. I'll tell you when it's okay.'

Silence. Then came the muted sobs and the hand-wringing.

'How did . . .' Carter couldn't say it.

'He died instantly,' Decker said. 'I'm positive he didn't feel a thing.'

'That's not what I meant.'

'But that's what you want to know,' Decker said. 'He didn't suffer.' He paused. 'I know you have another son, Karl. I'd like to talk to him as soon as you'll allow it.'

'Why?' Carter asked.

'Because sometimes brothers confide in each other. I know this from personal experience. I have two sons who are very close to each other and protective of one another. I'm sometimes regarded as the common enemy. Or just too overprotective—'

'Oh, my God!' Jill blurted out. 'Do you think that Karl's in danger?'

'No, that's not what I'm saying,' Decker answered. 'I just want to find out what he knows about his brother.'

'Our children are very open with us,' Carter said. 'If you have something to ask, I demand that you ask it of me.'

'Nothing specific to ask at the moment.' A lie. 'Just walking down all avenues. Mr Golding, do you have any information that might help me?'

'No! Of course not! Why did you ask that?'

'Please don't take offense at anything I ask, sir. And I beg the same of you, Mrs Golding. I am so sorry. The last thing I want to do is contribute to your pain.'

Jill stared at him through deep pools of sorrow. 'So you don't know who did it?'

'No,' Decker replied.

'And Dee Baldwin is missing?'

'Right now, we can't locate her, that is correct.'

Jill clasped her shaking hands. 'So what do you think?'

'I don't know.'

'Is Dee involved?'

'I don't know.'

'And it was brutal?' Jill asked.

'It was instantaneous,' Decker replied.

Jill's lower lip trembled. 'He didn't suffer?'

'No.'

'How do you know?'

'I know. He didn't suffer.'

Jill started crying again. 'I want to see my son,' she sobbed. 'I *need* to see him!'

'As soon as it's okay, I'll take you down personally—'

'You already said that!' Carter snapped.

'I know. I'm repeating myself.'

'Can't you speed things up?' Carter barked.

'The case is my top priority,' Decker said. 'I'm moving as fast as I can, because that's what we both want. That's why it's so important for me to get information early on. I hate to belabor this, but when do you think I could meet with Karl?'

Jill dried her eyes on a crumpled tissue. 'What do you think Ernesto was hiding from us?'

'I don't know. Maybe nothing. But kids hide things. Even kids who love their parents. And Ernesto loved you both very much—'

Carter made a snorting sound. 'Don't patronize me—'

'I'm not, sir. He told me that he loved and admired you both very much. Actually, he told me that the first time we talked alone . . . the day he confessed to the vandalism of the synagogue.'

Another protracted silence. Then once again Jill started to weep. 'Thank you for saying that.'

Decker waited a moment before speaking. 'This is just a gut feeling, so I could be completely wrong. I'm just wondering if this wasn't connected to the vandalism. That maybe Ernesto had dealings with some dangerous thugs. That maybe he had gotten himself into a bad way and was too embarrassed to tell anyone.' A long pause. 'I don't know. I'm just pecking around.'

'Do you have some specific thugs in mind?' Jill demanded to know.

'When the temple was first vandalized, we checked out some neo-Nazi groups—'

'Ernesto wouldn't know anything about that!' Carter insisted. His voice rose in pitch. 'Why would he know anything about that?'

Decker said, 'For a boy like Ernesto to vandalize . . . I was thinking that he somehow had been influenced by some pretty rotten people. People he wouldn't mention to you, but perhaps Karl might know—'

'If you suspected that Karl knew something about the vandalism, why didn't you talk to him when it happened?' Carter growled out.

'I believe I had asked to talk to him,' Decker said. 'I think you had said no.'

Carter looked away. 'I don't remember that!'

'Well, maybe I'm wrong,' Decker said.

But they both knew he wasn't wrong.

Jill bit her lip. 'Karl doesn't even know yet . . . does he?'

'You're the first ones I've told.'

'But he'll find out soon. It's bound to make the news.' She jumped up and started pacing. 'Carter, you have to call—'

Carter bounded out of the chair. 'I'm on it.'

Jill said, 'Can you please go now? We need some . . . I have to . . .' Her eyes watered. 'I have to make some phone calls.' She sank back into the couch. 'I don't know if I can do it!'

Decker said, 'Is there someone I can call for you?'

'My sister.' Jill gave him the number. 'I really don't feel well.'

'I'll call her right now.'

'I'll be in the bedroom upstairs.'

'Can I help you up?'

'No, I can . . .' She trudged over to the staircase, an old woman bound in shackles that would never come off. Climbing one step, two steps, then three and four. She stopped, turned and faced him. Her voice was filled with tears. 'When did you want to meet with Karl?'

'As soon as possible.'

'Come back in an hour.' She continued her climb to hell.

Decker looked around the chock-a-block furnishings and eventually found the phone. Three lines; one was lit up in red. Decker punched in the second line and called Jill's sister. Her name was Brook. He told her to please come by her sister's home now. When Brook asked for an explanation, Decker said he'd talk to her once she arrived on the premises. As a rule, he didn't deliver this news over the phone.

Carter came back. 'Where's my wife?'

'Upstairs in the bedroom,' Decker said. 'I'm waiting for her sister.'

'Which one? Brook?'

'Yes. There are others?'

'Philippa,' Carter said. 'She lives in San Diego. Jill's

not that close to her. But I suppose she'll have to be . . . told.' He looked about at nothing in particular. 'I have to go pick up . . . my son . . . Karl. They've pulled him out of class. I didn't tell anyone why . . . just that it was an emergency.'

'Would you like me to pick him up?' Decker offered. 'Not to question him, just as a taxi service so you can stay with your wife.'

Carter looked somewhere past Decker's shoulder. 'No questions?'

'No, not in the car. Your wife said I can come back in a hour to talk to your son.'

Carter was silent.

'Or . . .' Decker tried, 'I can wait here until Brook arrives. And you can go pick up your boy.'

Carter shook his head in confusion, tears in his eyes. 'I don't know. What do you think I should do?'

'Honestly? There's nothing you can say or do for your wife at this moment. She's in a state of shock. Your son will need you. And he'll remember who came to pick him up. If you're too unsteady to drive, I'll send a car out for you.'

'I can drive.' Carter checked his pockets, then pulled out his car keys. 'The school is ten minutes from here. I can make it.'

Decker nodded.

'You'll wait here for Brook?'

'Yes, sir.'

'You'll tell her?'

'Yes, if you want me to.'

'Yes, I think . . .' He brushed back tears. 'I suppose

I'll have to call my siblings as well. I have two younger brothers.' His wet eyes were frozen in grief. 'Thank God, my parents are dead.'

Karl was also broad across the chest and had iron-pumper arms, indicating to Decker that somewhere in the ectomorphic Golding lineage was a rampant meso-morphic gene. His face was fairer, but his complexion was rumpled like tapioca pudding. No beard growth yet, so lumps and bumps were visible in all their glory. His eyes were bluer than his brother's, swimming in a sea of red. His nose was also red. He peered at Decker, but nothing registered in his eyes. It was as if Decker were inanimate.

Decker said, 'Just a few questions, Karl. Tell me when you've had enough.'

'Okay.' It was a whisper. 'It's important that we talk now?'

'Yes.'

The boy averted his gaze. 'All right.'

They were sitting on a leather couch in the boy's bedroom, as spacious as Decker's living room. It held the same plaster adobe-colored walls as the rest of the house and was furnished very sparsely – a bed, a desk and computer, a TV on a stand, bookshelves containing more videos than the printed word. With the air-conditioning on full-tilt, the place was crypt cold.

Decker said, 'First off, let me tell you how sorry I am.'

Tears leaked from the fifteen year old's eyes. He rubbed them away.

'Your brother said a lot of things to me in confidence,' Decker continued. 'Things that bothered him, and things that bothered me. I'm wondering if he expressed the same concerns to you.'

Karl looked up from his lap. 'Like what?'

'Ernesto spoke to me about some of the fantasies he was having. Did he ever speak to you about them?'

The moments ticked on. One . . . two . . . three . . . four . . .

The boy whispered, 'What fantasies?'

Decker kept his face emotionless. 'I'm telling you this, not to be lurid, but to help me understand Ernesto. The more I know about him, the more it'll help me with the investigation. Ernesto was interested . . . no, that's the wrong word. He was plagued by awful images of Nazi brutality. Plagued by them, but fascinated by them. The images bothered him very much, but he couldn't get rid of them. Furthermore, he felt that . . . that your father's father – Isaac Golding – hadn't been up front about his origins.'

Silence.

And then more silence.

'Did he ever express any concerns like these to you?'

Karl sighed. 'May I ask what the point of . . . the point of this is . . . sir?'

He was trying to be polite, and that counted for a lot, especially under these circumstances. 'I'm wondering if Ernesto had had a secret life and had slipped into the wrong crowd. I'm wondering also if he had tried to get out of it, by confessing it to Dr Baldwin. Perhaps someone wanted the information transfer permanently silenced.'

'Do you think that's what happened?'

'I don't know, Karl. That's why I'm asking you such sensitive questions.'

'Did you talk to my parents about this?'

'Not yet.'

'Can I ask that you don't?' The big kid swallowed. 'I don't think my mom . . .' Tears. 'She's in enough pain.'

'Tell me what you know. And then we'll see if we can work out a plan.'

'First, you tell me what you know . . . sir.'

'Okay, I will. According to Ernesto, your grandfather's name was Yitzchak Golding.' Decker pronounced the name with the correct gutturalization, something he couldn't have done five years ago. 'Ernesto had done some research and had found out that a Yitzchak Golding had died in a Polish concentration camp. Now it's entirely possible that there's more than one Yitzchak Golding. But Ernesto was under the impression that your grandfather had stolen the dead Yitzchak Golding's identity. Did he ever mention anything like that to you?'

'Something.'

'So this sounds familiar?' Decker asked him. 'That your grandfather was a Nazi in hiding?'

'A little.'

'Like how.'

'Just that Ernesto had some . . . questions. He went to Dad about them. Dad freaked and that was the end of it. Ernie dropped it.'

Decker took in the kid's eyes. 'So if I mentioned this to your dad, it would strike a nerve?'

'I don't think you should do that right now.'

'I'll keep that in mind. What about your mother?'

'He never said anything to her as far as I know.'

'Okay. So we'll keep her out of this.' Decker smoothed his mustache. 'How about you, Karl? Did he stop talking about it to you?'

The boy's eyes overflowed. He threw his hands over his face and cried out, 'It's all my fault.'

'No, it isn't—'

'Yes, it is! I should have *said* something! I should have *done* something! I didn't *know*!'

Decker watched him gulp in big, breathless, heart-wrenching sobs. Seconds passed, then minutes. Finally, Karl was controlled enough to speak. 'It started out as a school project – the family tree.' A big sniff. 'When this came up . . . and Dad wigged . . . Ernie knew that he'd hit something awful. I told him to drop it with a capital *D*! What's done is done, you know. Grandpa was dead, the Holocaust is more than a half-century old, and stirring stuff up wasn't going to bring back any lives. He wouldn't *listen*.'

'You must have been frustrated—'

'More like angry. Ernie was acting like this . . . like . . . a *possessed* person!'

Decker nodded encouragement. 'What did he do?'

'He wanted to find out who Grandpa really was. He wrote to Argentina, he wrote to Berlin, he wrote everywhere. He went nuts with the idea of who Grandpa was . . . and his Nazi origins. He started talking to some real strange people. I should have told Dad. I should have told Dr Dahl. She would have done something smart. But then the temple vandalism went down. And Ernie went into therapy. So I kept my mouth shut and decided to let the experts handle it.'

'You did the right thing—'

'No, I didn't,' the boy broke in. 'Ernie's dead! I *didn't* do the right thing!'

'Yes, you did,' Decker said. 'You have to believe me on this, Karl.'

The boy didn't believe him. But he didn't refute him, either.

'Are you scared, Karl?' Decker asked. 'Do you think you need protection?'

'I *don't know*!' The boy's lower lip trembled. 'I don't know!'

'Do you have any names?'

'No, goddamn it! I wish to God I did, but I don't, sir. I swear I don't.'

'I believe you.'

Karl said, 'The whole synagogue thing was . . . I had no idea that Ernesto had gotten involved so deeply! *I* thought he was making the whole thing up just to look like a badass to his girlfriend.'

'Ruby Ranger.'

'Queen Goth. If anyone was behind this, it would be her! She's crazy and mean!' He looked up at Decker. 'I'm not the only one who feels that way. Your stepson hates her, too, you know.'

Decker knew.

Karl looked away. 'I probably shouldn't have mentioned him.'

'No, it's fine. Several people, including Jacob, had told me that Ruby and Ernesto were an item.'

'You should arrest her!' Karl looked at Decker. 'You are gonna talk to her, right?'

'Last we heard, she had left town right after the vandalism. When was the last time Ernesto saw her?'

'I don't know.'

'So you don't know if she and Ernesto had maintained contact after the vandalism?'

A long, suffering sigh. 'There were a few letters. I think I know where he hid them . . .' Karl got up. 'But it could be that Ernesto took them to camp.'

'Why did Ernesto hide the letters?'

'Because my mother snoops. Ernie did drugs. It nearly did him in.'

'Literally?'

Karl nodded. 'About a year ago, we found him unconscious one Sunday morning. It was a miracle that he survived. Up until that time, my parents were really on his case – study, study, study, study. Do this because it'll look good on your college application, do that because it'll look good. Ernie's a bright guy. But these days being plain bright isn't good enough. When Ernie OD'd, all hell broke loose. My parents were one step from sending him away to boarding school. Then suddenly, they eased up.' The boy snapped his fingers. 'Their therapist probably told them to do it. They wouldn't do anything without talking to the therapist. Even so, Ernie felt that they didn't trust him. So he hid stuff. Mostly weed, but personal stuff, too.'

'Like the letters?'

Karl nodded. 'I just can't understand *why* Ernie was taken in by that *bitch*! I know sex was part of it. But Ernie had lots of girls. Why her?'

Because she was forbidden, dangerous, and Ernesto had been a rebellious boy. But Decker maintained silence. It seemed like the smartest option.

'I'll be right back.' Karl walked off to his dead brother's room. Ten minutes later, he came back empty-handed. 'Nothing. Sorry. I would have liked to help you nail her.'

'You think the letters might be at the camp?' Decker asked.

'Possibly.'

'Did he ever read you any of the letters?'

'Once or twice, Ernie read me parts – sexual stuff. Explicit stuff about how she loved it, but in graphic terms. Ruby thought she was this hip anarchist. She was loco!'

'Do you think she was behind the temple vandalism?'

'Probably.'

'Ernesto never mentioned any names to you after he vandalized the synagogue?'

'No.'

'How about names of Nazi or white supremacist groups?'

'No.'

'Does the group the Preservers of Ethnic Integrity sound familiar?'

A shake of the head.

'Erin Kershan?'

'No.'

'Darrell Holt?'

'Nope.'

'Ricky Moke?'

'No. Sorry.'

Decker said, 'Do you know if Ernesto got involved in any supremacist groups maybe over the Internet?'

'I don't know what he found or where he found it,' Karl said. 'Ernie was my brother, but we're very different.'

'Did he ever mention to you any of his motivation behind vandalizing the temple?'

'Motivation?'

'I'm thinking that maybe it was some kind of ritual needed to prove his dangerous side to his girlfriend?'

'Beats me.' Karl looked down. 'After it happened, Ernie said, "Don't ask!" He was upset about it, though. I could tell that.'

'Did he say anything about being in danger?'

'No, not worried upset. Upset upset. He felt bad.'

'He told you he felt bad?' Decker asked.

'Not in words. But I know he felt bad.'

'Do you think that he kept you in the dark to protect you?'

'Possibly.'

'And Ruby Ranger's name never came up?'

'Nah. I think he would have rather died than to rat on the bitch.'

Neither one said the obvious: Maybe that was exactly what had happened.

17

As he drove back to the crime scene, Decker spoke over the tactical lines. The reception was much poorer from the squawk box than it was through the digital cell phones, but supposedly, the conversations were restricted. Not that there was any real privacy nowadays: the Luddites had a point. 'Are the bodies still there?'

'The wagon left about twenty minutes ago,' Martinez answered. 'Police photographer is still here. Do you want me to tell her to wait for you?'

'No, I'll work from the photographs. Did you search the bodies for personal effects?'

'We didn't find anything *on* them. We're rooting through their belongings now. Anything specific you're looking for?'

'Letters to Ernesto from Ruby R.'

'How many?'

'Maybe three or four.'

'I'll ask Tom about it. So far, Ernesto's possessions are pretty minimal – a bedroll, a canteen, a metal dish, and the basic cutlery. Standard issue according to Tarpin.'

'We'll get back to him later. How many boys have we interviewed?'

'There are only two boys here who have reached their majority. Tom talked to both of them. You can ask him about it.'

'Anything promising?'

'Not so far.'

'And how about the others? The minors?'

'I know that Wanda and Tarpin have been busy notifying the parents. It hasn't been a cakewalk. I'd say about seventy percent of them are out of town. They took advantage of the time without junior to hightail it off to the Caribbean. Seven of the nine kids volunteered to have their belongings searched. Predictably, they were all clean. Wanda has been questioning them with a light touch. I think they're disappointed. I think they keep expecting us to read them their rights.'

Decker smiled. 'You said seven out of nine boys.'

'Yeah, I did. The two remaining lads are more hard-liners. Could be they're hiding something. Or, they just don't want to cooperate because they're wary of the cops.'

'Priors?'

'I wouldn't know. They're juveniles. Wanda knows the ins and outs of Juvy. If they're hot, she'll know about it.'

'I'll deal with them when I come up. Who are they?'

'Brandon Chesapeake and Riley Barns. Not that they're dancing on anyone's grave. All of a sudden, the lure of crime isn't so glamorous. And it doesn't smell very good, either.'

'Did you talk to Tarpin at length?'

'I was about to do that . . . unless you want him. We've got parents to deal with. I'm certainly not lacking for something to do.'

'All right, wait for me,' Decker said. 'I'll take Tarpin because I have a job for you – Dee Baldwin. I know she's not at her residence or at the office. I want you to talk to some of their friends and find out if they – she and Mervin – had a special vacation spot or cabin retreat up in the mountains – a place where she could be hiding out.'

'You think she did it?'

'Ernesto and Mervin looked pretty cozy, so who knows? Or maybe she's hiding out because she's scared. Another avenue is Ernesto as the target. He didn't do the vandalism alone. Which means that he may have fallen in with some very bad dudes. Specifically, I'm interested in Ruby Ranger. You need to find out where she is, as well.'

'I can certainly go back to Alice Ranger, but I don't think she'll be too cooperative.'

'Lean on her. It's important.' Decker paused. 'Also, did we ever get an actual photograph of Ricky Moke?'

'No. It never seemed important because Ernesto confessed. Do you want me to go back to Darrell Holt with a police artist and a kit?'

'After we find out about Dee Baldwin, then go back to Holt.'

'Not a problem if you trust his eye . . . if you trust him period. He could be lying.' A pause. 'He probably is lying. Those types lie outta force of habit.'

He sat with Tarpin overlooking the precipice of the mountain, side by side, because Decker knew that men talked more freely without eye contact. The corporal's face glistened with sweat, beads forming on his sizeable nose. He wore a camouflage cap over his bald head and had his shirtsleeves rolled up to his elbows. He wore the same stony expression, making him hard to read, and Decker supposed that that was the objective.

Taking out his notebook with pen poised in hand, Decker took a few moments to breathe in the scenery. The mountains were wide and vast, their tips iced with a brown translucent layer of summer smog. Oven hot, he could feel himself drip underneath his clothing even though they were shaded by the canopy of a sycamore. Staring outward, Tarpin asked about Dee Baldwin.

'She's not at her residence or at the office.'

'That's not good.'

'No, it's not. Do you know of anywhere else that she might be? Did she and Dr Baldwin have a second home anywhere? We checked locally, but maybe they had something out of state?'

'Sometimes they went to the beach for weekends.'

Decker started writing. 'Good. Where?'

'Malibu.'

Decker waited for more. 'Do you know where?

Malibu's a long stretch of sand.'

'Nah, not my territory. I think they rented.'

That narrowed it down to fifty zillion people. 'A house? A condo?'

'A condo.' Tarpin paused. 'It could be she's there. They're renovating their home in Beverly Hills. From what Dr Merv was saying, their house was a mess.'

'So they moved out during the construction?'

Tarpin shrugged. 'I don't know. The only thing that Dr Merv said was the house was a mess and the renovation was costing him a fortune. Probably Dee's idea. She's the decorator . . . redid their office about two years ago.'

'Okay. That helps.' Immediately, Decker phoned Martinez and gave him the news, telling him to coordinate with the Malibu Sheriff's Department. After Decker got off the cell, Tarpin took off the cap, wiped his bald pate with a handkerchief, and then re-covered his head.

He said, 'You trust people outside your division to do your job?'

'Pardon?'

'The Sheriff's Department. Do you trust them?'

'Why do you ask?'

Tarpin said, 'Delegating responsibility. Frankly, I believe that if you want something done right, do it yourself.'

'Does that extend to murder?'

Tarpin's eyes focused in on Decker's face. The first hint of emotion from the man and it was anger. 'I won't dignify that with an answer.'

'I'm not implicating you, Corporal. Just that this looks professional . . . delegating out. What do you think?'

Tarpin didn't answer.

Decker said, 'You know I have to ask you certain questions, sir, because you were in charge of the camp. Also, you were the first one to find the bodies. We always ask pointed questions to those who find the bodies. Plus, these mountains are pretty secluded. I'm just wondering why no one heard anything.'

'You can wonder. It's a free country.'

'Sounds like an inside job.'

'Sounds like the job of some insane man.'

'Or a very evil man,' Decker corrected.

'Well, Lieutenant, I'm not crazy and I'm not evil.' He turned and took in Decker's expression. 'I'm just about as straight arrow as they come.'

Uh-huh, Decker thought. 'Let me ask you this. If you did do the murder, what motivation did you have?'

'You're asking me?' Tarpin said.

'I'm asking you.'

'I don't have any motivation, because I didn't do anything.'

'But if I wanted to pin something on you, where would I go? For instance, to find a hidden motivation, maybe I should check out your association with the Preservers of Ethnic Integrity. See what they have to say about you?'

Tarpin stared straight into the mountains. 'Sure, you could do that.'

'Did the Baldwins know about your membership in PEI?'

'What the hell does this have to do with Merv's murder?'

The words were strong, but Tarpin's voice was deep and mild.

'Maybe nothing—'

'Definitely nothing.'

'I've heard that the Baldwins are very liberal. I'm just wondering how they felt about your association—'

'They wanted the best person for the job,' Tarpin interrupted. 'I'm the best.' Laughter erupted from his broad chest. 'So you're thinking I murdered Merv because I didn't like his politics? The Baldwins knew about my associating with PEI. Merv even proofread a couple of articles I wrote for their official newsletter. We were at political ends of the spectrum – them and me. I respected his right to believe what he wanted to believe; he respected mine.' Finally some emotion had entered the Marine's eyes. 'If you'd like to get on with solving the case, that would be nice.'

'I just don't picture you having much in common with those PEI clowns.'

'National PEI is composed of over two thousand members. Suddenly you've met them all?'

'Two *thousand* members?'

A slow smile came to Tarpin's lips. 'Surprised?'

'Actually, yes, I am.' Decker shook his head. 'I hope they're less marginal than the mouthpieces in the local front office.'

Tarpin was quiet.

'What's his name?' Decker scanned his notes in mock confusion. 'Darrell Holt. What do you think of him?'

'You met Darrell?'

'Yep,' Decker lied.

Tarpin looked across the valleys. Picked up a stone and threw it down the mountainside. 'Darrell ain't no dummy. He went to Berkeley. They don't let stupid people into college.'

Having gone to college, Decker knew that *that* was definitely debatable. 'What about his girlfriend? Don't tell me she went to Berkeley. She doesn't even look eighteen.'

'I don't know Darrell's girlfriend.'

'Erin Kershan?'

'Nope. Don't know her.'

No one spoke for a moment. Decker remarked, 'I'm just thinking why Darrell Holt would pick the most radical of all UCs to go to. It hardly fits his politics.'

'That's because you didn't know Darrell in his younger days.'

'And you did?'

'Yes, sir. Kinky hair down to his shoulders, unwashed, unkempt, spouting that radical, racial gibberish. His dad put him in Dr Merv's camp about seven years ago. But the boy quit therapy, then went off to college. You can't change a light bulb if it don't want to be changed. But like I said, Darrell had some smarts. He came to reason on his own.'

Decker was astounded. 'So Darrell went to Baldwin's nature camp.' He tapped his pencil against his notebook. 'Is that how you two met?'

'Yes, sir.'

'And you were active in PEI at that time, Mr Tarpin?'

'Correct.'

'Did you introduce Darrell to PEI?'

'No, sir, I don't use the nature camp to recruit membership for my beliefs.'

Uh-huh, Decker thought. 'So Darrell just fell into the group again happenstance?'

'Happenstance? That means by accident, don't it? I think Darrell went into the group because he was interested in what we had to say.'

'But you never mentioned the PEI to him?'

'I might have,' Tarpin admitted. 'Frankly, I don't remember. It was a long time ago.'

'How long has Darrell been with the group?'

'Three, four years, I think. Go ask him.'

'I will,' Decker said. 'Do you know if Darrell and Ernesto knew each other?'

'No, sir, I would not know.'

'Have you ever heard of a guy named Ricky Moke?'

'No, Lieutenant, I don't know the name.'

'Darrell told my men that Ricky was also a member of the Preservers of Ethnic Integrity.'

'That very well could be. Like I said, PEI has over two thousand members.'

The stone face was back, so Decker couldn't tell if he was lying. 'What can you tell me about Darrell Holt . . . when he was at the camp?'

'Bright boy, but very troubled.'

'How was he troubled?'

'Acting out all the time. Lord knows Merv and Dee

tried. Darrell wasn't going to have it. Like I said, he settled down on his own.'

'Did he talk to you much?'

'Not too much.'

'What about Ernesto?'

'What about him?'

'Did he talk to you?'

'All the boys talk to me, Ernesto included. I don't encourage it . . . the Baldwins don't like it. It interferes with their therapy.' He faced Decker. 'I'll tell you one thing, Lieutenant. Ernesto felt bad about what he'd done to the temple – genuine remorse. What do Ernesto's problems have to do with the murder anyway?'

'Right now, we don't know who the intended victim was. Could be Baldwin. But maybe it was Ernesto.'

'Why would it be Ernesto?' Tarpin asked. 'He's just a kid.'

'Let me turn it around on you, Mr Tarpin. Why would it be Baldwin?'

'Because the Baldwins dealt with some really bad kids – psychos with the flat, lizard eyes that you see on snipers. The doctors tried, but some kids are beyond redemption.'

'But why murder someone up here . . . in the mountains? Bad access, hard to escape, plus you have all these witnesses and potential enemies.'

'Not if the man was a survivalist.'

'Are you saying the killer was a graduate of the camp?'

'Maybe.' Tarpin faced him. 'Why do you think the intended hit was Ernesto?'

Decker hesitated. How to talk without revealing too much. 'To this day, I don't believe he acted alone in the vandalism. I think Ernesto might have fallen into bad company, had remorse about it, and maybe some of those neo-Nazis were coming after him.' Decker tapped his pencil against his pad. 'Did he ever mention a young woman named Ruby Ranger?'

Again, Tarpin broke into a disaffected stare. 'Ernesto talked about her from time to time. She sounded like a bad egg.'

'Was *she* ever a patient of the Baldwins? Or don't the Baldwins take girls?'

'They take anyone who needs them. I don't know about Ruby Ranger. Why don't you look her up in the office files?'

'That requires a subpoena.'

'So go get one.'

'You see her as a suspect, Corporal?'

'Yes, I do.' He spat on the ground. 'Used to be that the worst things that girls did was smoking dope or kiting checks. Now they're just as bad as the boys. There's progress for you.'

18

Getting a search warrant on criminals with probable cause was one thing. Getting a warrant on patient files when one of the doctors was still alive was proving to be more difficult. As the hours dragged, Decker decided to send a team over to the Baldwins' Beverly Hills office to see if they could talk their way into information. Since Martinez was hunting down Malibu condos for Dee, and Tom and Wanda were still tied up at the scene, Decker gave the daunting task of being charming to Scott Oliver and Marge Dunn.

Neither sounded overjoyed at the assignment.

Riding on the freeway over the hump, Oliver sat in the passenger's seat of the unmarked and tried not to dump on Marge. He was cranky because he hated officious people, and those that practiced in Beverly Hills tended to be full of themselves – or maybe the correct word was *successful*. Scott figured that Deck had given him the detail on purpose, that the Loo was still upset over Oliver's all-too-brief relationship with Deck's daughter Cindy. Never mind that the girl had dumped him and was on *her* way to being a rising star in LAPD. Never mind that he was on the dark side of forty and had reached the pinnacle of his career ten years ago. No, forget all that crap. Oliver decided that Decker's animosity came from the fact that he was better looking, and could get tons of women anytime he wanted just because—

Marge interrupted his fantasies with business. 'I talked to one of their psychology associates. Her name is Maryam Estes.' She picked a speck of dirt off navy linen/polyester blend slacks. They were supposed to wrinkle a little, but still look presentable. The garment definitely had the wrinkle part down pat; presentable was another matter. Still, the deep tone looked good with her pale complexion, her brown eyes, and her dishwater, thin hair. Along with the pants, she wore an oxford weave shirt and a matching blue jacket. Sensible navy shoes with rubber soles, but stylish – a Tods knockoff. She always felt lucky when she found decent shoes in size ten wide. Her feet were proportional to her height and weight, but the fact didn't make it easier to find things in the stores. 'She didn't sound very cooperative over the phone.'

'Did she sound pretty?'

'By pretty do you mean young?'

'Yeah, young is definitely okay.'

'She sounded young.' Marge got off at Sunset and turned left, heading toward Beverly Hills. 'Young and very nervous.'

'She doesn't have the best job security right now.'

'For the moment, Dee's still alive.' Marge slowed the car as she hooked around the twists and turns of the boulevard.

'Think so?' Oliver adjusted the air-conditioning up a notch. The wool of his charcoal suit was supposedly lightweight, but in today's sticky, smoggy heat, the fabric was oppressive.

Marge thought a moment. 'Either Dee whacked them or she's running from the people who whacked them.'

'Either option ain't good for the young-sounding Ms Estes.' Oliver checked his hair in the vanity mirror. Still relatively thick and still in place. 'Or is it Dr Estes?'

'She didn't say.'

'What exactly does Decker want?'

'To sniff out the Baldwins' patients and see if any of them are violent psychos. We're also supposed to find out all we can about Ernesto Golding and his problems, plus ask about a twenty three year old named Ruby Ranger who was Ernesto's girlfriend. But we have to be careful because we don't have a subpoena and there's a confidentiality problem.'

'Okay,' Oliver said, 'so what's the plan?'

'Just get her talking.' Marge stopped at a red light, and turned to face him and smiled. '*Enthrall* the words out of her, Scott.'

He straightened his tie and slicked back the salt-and-pepper hair that lined his temple. 'Piece of cake.'

Marge turned the cruiser right, onto Camden Drive, a street of eclectic large houses that sat on lots too puny for their size. The sidewalks were lined with magnolias that bathed the lawns and homes in muted light. When she hit Santa Monica, she realized that the street had turned one-way and she was going the wrong way. 'I hate this city.'

'So do I.'

'Or maybe I'm just jealous because I can't afford to live here.'

'I don't mind not living here. I mind not being able to shop here.'

'You could always hit the sales.'

'Fifty percent off a fortune is still too high.' Oliver looked around. 'We're not too far away from Cindy's, you know.'

'Now that would be a very bad idea.'

'I wasn't thinking about anything, just stating a fact—'

'A very, very bad idea—'

'Yeah, yeah. Just concentrate on your driving.'

'Do you still see her?'

'We don't stick pins in each other's voodoo dolls if that's what you mean.'

'I'm not asking if you're enemies, I'm asking if you still *see* her?'

'What do you care?'

Sore point. Marge smiled. 'You're right. It is none of my business.'

'No, I don't *see* her. Cindy's idea, not mine.'

No one spoke.

Oliver said, 'You passed up the address.'

'I should concentrate on my driving,' Marge said.

'Now I'm going to have to go around the block again.'

'God is punishing you for asking about Cindy.'

'That's very medieval thinking. Besides, you brought her up!'

'I'm entitled. But you can't say anything about it. Isn't that the way it works?'

'You're right.'

'Damn right, I'm right.'

'Can we be friends now?'

'That's implying we were friends to begin with.' When Marge didn't respond, Oliver frowned. 'Okay. We're friends. Happy?'

Marge patted his knee. The car crawled around the block until she finally parked in an underground lot. Silently, they rode the elevator to the eleventh floor – Oliver looking very sour – then got off and turned right, walking down a plush, quiet hallway to the Baldwins' office. A young woman with mocha-colored skin and a nest of tumbling black curls met them at the door. She wore a white, short-sleeve, silk blouse tucked into a maroon skirt that brushed the top of her knees. Maroon pumps completed the look. They pulled out their badges, and the woman stepped aside so they could come in. She was breathless.

'I'm Maryam Estes.' Once inside, she closed and locked the door. 'This way.'

They followed her down the thick carpeted hallway, her chunky heels leaving depression marks in the nap. Her walk was stiff and quick.

'Are you a doctor as well?' Oliver asked.

She spoke over her shoulder. 'Ph.D.'

Silence.

Oliver whispered to Marge, 'I think she likes me—'

'Shut up.'

Panting, she led them into the Baldwins' resplendent office. Paneled walls hosted verdant landscape oil paintings set into gilt frames; the polished parquet floors were adorned with several Persian rugs. The space was filled with handsome furniture that was old-fashioned in style but looked brand new – tables, chairs, sofas, and bookcases – the centerpiece being a walnut partners desk, its sides intricately carved with flowers, vines, and leaves. Strategically placed mullion windows showed off a city view.

Marge looked about. On the desktop sat two computers, blotters, pens, pencils, file folders, and piles of papers. She ran a finger over an empty spot on the smooth walnut surface – no dust. Someone had recently cleaned up.

Maryam said, 'Sit anywhere you'd like.'

Marge settled into a rose upholstered sofa, but Oliver elected to walk around the room, dissecting the young woman in his head. She wasn't pretty – her face was too round, and her eyes were too close set – but she still was attractive. Hot bod, good skin, and thick, biteable lips.

'Huge place.' He took in her dark eyes and smiled. 'You could waltz in here!'

'They hold lots of group therapy sessions.' She averted her gaze. 'They need the room.'

'What's the rent on something like this?'

The woman stiffened. 'I don't know.' Another bristle.

'I hardly think that's important right now.'

'Probably not.'

Good job of enthralling her, Scott. But Oliver often had some method behind the incompetence. Marge looked at the partners desk. 'Did the Baldwins share the same office?'

'They both have private space. There's also an "intake" suite for interviews.'

'So in addition to the waiting room, an intake suite, and this ballroom, they have individual offices?'

'If you're doing individual therapy, you can't be interrupted because your partner needs to look at the files.'

'So these . . .' Marge pointed to the back wall lined with oak veneered cabinets. 'That's where the case files are kept?'

'The recent ones, yes.'

'You don't lock them up?'

'Of course they're locked!' Maryam was offended. 'Pardon my impudence, but why exactly are you here? Shouldn't Dee Baldwin be your concern? Shouldn't you be out *looking* for her?'

'We're doing that, Dr Estes – well, not us personally – but the police have made Dee Baldwin a top priority. We are here because we need some help.'

'Help?' Maryam licked her lips. 'How?'

'Information kind of help,' Oliver said. 'We're looking into culprits. Since Dr Baldwin treated some disturbed people, we were wondering if one of his patients might have done this.'

'Like a revenge thing,' Marge added. 'Do you know

of any patient that swore a vendetta against either one of the Baldwins?'

A shake of the head. 'Nothing comes to mind. And even if someone came to mind, I couldn't help you. Patients have confidentiality.'

'Not when it conflicts with the immediate well-being of someone who's alive,' Marge said. 'You know the Tarasoff case.'

'It doesn't apply when the person's already dead.'

'Now, that's a good point,' Oliver said. 'So you shouldn't mind answering a couple of questions about Ernesto Golding.'

'I can't help you because I don't know anything about Ernesto Golding.'

'Maybe we can take a peek at his file?' Oliver said.

'Certainly not!' Maryam protested. 'I can't give you that kind of permission. You'll have to wait for Dee.'

'That may take a long time,' Oliver said. 'Like in forever.'

'That's a horrible thing to say!' Suddenly, Maryam burst out crying. 'This is just awful! Who could have done something so dreadful? Dr Merv didn't have an enemy in the world.'

The two detectives let her cry for a few moments. Then Oliver asked, 'How well did you know the Baldwins?'

'Except for the occasional holiday party, I only knew them professionally. I've worked here for eighteen months, and not a cross word has been exchanged. They've been wonderful to me and wonderful to their patients. Dedicated psychologists and fabulous mentors.'

Again, the tears overflowed. 'My God, this is so . . . so upsetting!'

Sobbing once again. Marge got up and placed a soft hand on her back. 'I know that you feel as if you're violating them . . . by talking about their cases.' A meaningful sigh. 'Let's do this. Tell me what you can about them and their patients. What *you* would feel comfortable with.'

'That's a very tall order.' She blew her nose into a tissue. 'Very tall. As psychologists, our bread and butter is confidentiality. If our patients can't trust us, they find someone else. And with both of the Baldwins out of commission, it's going to fall on me. The patients, I mean. I have to ensure that they know I'm trustworthy.'

'Then how about if you just start with the basics,' Marge suggested. 'You know . . . how long you've known them . . . what kind of therapy they did . . . did they see adults or teens or kids . . . things like that.'

Maryam looked up and dried her eyes. 'His specialty was oppositional teens.' She noticed they were waiting for more. 'Kids with behavioral problems.'

Marge nodded. 'Any of them seem particularly prone to violence?'

'I'm sure some were, but I didn't see them personally. Mostly, I handled Dee's overload. She focuses on anxiety disorders that lead to antisocial behavior. You know, things like acting up in high school.'

'That's a problem?' Oliver said. 'For me, acting up in high school was a pastime.'

'*Serious* acting up.' Maryam gave him a cold look.

'Teens with suicidal thoughts, alienation, and lots of anxiety in test taking. I'm talking about entrance exams in the main – mostly college, but some high school and elementary school as well. It was Merv who handled the obstructionist boys, and handled them through his group therapy and nature camp. The off-site retreats were the main focus of Merv's therapy, although Dee does participate by giving seminars—'

'Wait a minute, wait a minute,' Marge interrupted. 'Can you back it up a moment? What do you mean by entrance exams for *high school*?'

'For the private preparatory schools,' Oliver said. 'They give entrance exams. You gotta apply to those kinds of schools. You knew that, right?'

Marge was silent.

Oliver refrained from sighing. It wasn't Dunn's fault. With altruism as her banner, Marge had adopted a teenager a year ago, and there was a brickyard of knowledge that she just didn't know.

'So I have to worry about Vega?' Marge asked. 'I mean she's brilliant. Isn't a brilliant mind enough?'

'They're all brilliant!' Maryam commented. 'It's how to bring your brilliant teenager to the attention of the admissions committee. Did you know that there are applicants with straight A's, and 4.3 averages, *and* 1600 on the SAT who don't make it into Harvard?'

'No, I didn't know.' Marge looked pale. 'How do you get past a 4.0 average?'

'Honors classes. They're worth five points instead of the usual four. And then it always helps if the student has had college courses.'

Marge pondered this. 'So the kid has to *be* in college before the kid can get into college?'

'There are honors programs at the local universities,' the psychologist informed Marge.

'So what's the point in sending them to college, if they've already had college?' Marge grabbed her temples. 'Talk about anxious kids. What about anxiety for the adults?'

'We deal with lots of anxious parents,' Maryam stated. 'A lot of the time, they're the problems. They want perfection from the kids, while they were anything but perfect in their own youth. Things are much more rushed these days. You have to get a jump start if you want the results. It's the digital generation, Detective. Gen-D. The computer waits for no man.'

'In the old days, we called this kind of behavior being a pushy parent.' Oliver smiled. 'It was considered a big no-no among the shrinks.'

'Pushy is one thing. Motivation is quite another,' she preached. 'Most of the Baldwin clientele are highly motivated. They want to do the right thing.'

'The right thing?'

'What will help out the odds.'

'Like what?'

Maryam gave them a half-smile, and it was condescending. 'That's what the therapy is all about. Even if I told you trade secrets, you couldn't do anything with them anyway. You have to be in the hands of the right therapist. Anyway, I do believe we have digressed. In answer to your original question, I don't know of any disappointed child who would have come back to wreak havoc because he or she hasn't gotten into their first-choice university.'

'You never know,' Oliver said. 'Look at that mother in Texas – the one who tried to murder her daughter's classmate because she was competition for the cheer-leading squad. People have been murdered for very trivial reasons.'

Her face turned ashen. 'You don't have to be so brutal.'

'Dr Baldwin's murder was brutal.'

'It has nothing to do with his patients—' Maryam's pager went off. 'Oh boy! Another one on the emergency line. They've been calling almost nonstop since the dreadful news came over the media. They must be in a state of shock. I must take the call.'

'That's fine,' Oliver said.

'But I can't talk while you're here.'

'I thought you said there are other offices.'

Maryam frowned. 'It may take a while.'

'We can wait.' Oliver tried to look earnest.

Slowly, she got up. 'I'll be back. And I trust you won't touch anything.'

'Of course not,' Marge said.

'That would bode very badly for you . . . if I found you rifling through things.'

'It's a felony,' Oliver stated. 'You know what they say about cops who go to jail.'

She still was dubious. A final look over her shoulder, then she left without closing the door. Oliver waited for a few moments, until one of the phone lines had been illuminated. Then he jumped up and shut the door softly. 'Keep your eyes glued to the line.' He headed for the file cabinets that lined the back of the room. 'Tell me when the light goes off.'

'Oliver, what are you doing?'

He yanked on a drawer. 'Locked. Well, I've done harder things.' He took out a lock pick.

'Are you out of your mind?'

'Instead of scolding me, why don't you help me out?' Oliver inserted the pick into the cabinet's weak standard lock. Moments later, it popped. 'I'm not bothering with all the files, just one file – Ernesto Golding. C'mon, Margie! We're under the gun here!'

'You do your B-and-E's by yourself. Besides, I gotta watch the phone for you.'

'Yeah, yeah,' he dismissed her. Frantically, he rifled through the files. 'God, this man generated paperwork. Gold, Gold, Golden, Goldenberg, Goldenstein, Goldin, Golding. Yes, Ernesto Golding! Voilà! Jeez, it's not all that big for someone so screwed up.'

'You're crossing the line.'

'Actually, I've crossed it. The kid is dead, Dunn. What difference does it make?'

'Don't expect me to lie for you.' Absently, Marge yanked on the top desk drawer. To her surprise it opened. The line on the phone machine still glowed red. 'However, maybe I'll take a quick look at his schedule planner since it's not in a locked drawer—'

'That's the spirit!'

'Shut up before my senses get hold of me.' Marge scanned the book. 'Isn't it going to look suspicious, Scott? That Golding's file is missing?'

'You're right!' Oliver stuffed a few papers back into the file folder. 'I'll come back for the rest.'

'There are lots of two-hour bookings.' Marge read the pages. 'Isn't the standard therapy time one hour?'

'So the guy had a racket going.'

'I don't know about that . . . but there are lots of funny notations after lots of the names.'

'Funny notations? What do you mean?'

'Letters: S, S, S, PS, PS, S, I, S, S, E, I, E, S2, E, G, L, S, S, S2, L, M . . . What do you think it all means?'

'How should I know?'

'There are more S's than anything else.'

'So maybe S stands for "psycho".'

' "Psycho" is spelled with a P.'

'Yeah, you're right. So maybe "psycho" is PS,' Oliver stated.

'Somehow, I don't think so.' Marge's eyes searched the room. 'I wish there was a copier somewhere.'

Oliver said, 'It's a binder notebook, Marge. Just take out a few pages and put it through the fax machine.'

'I can't believe I'm doing this.' She took out a page and ran it through the fax machine. 'What happens when the machine prints a report?'

'That's only a phone report. Keep going.'

She ran another sheet through the machine. It was coming out when the red phone light went off. 'Uh-oh. The doctor hung up the phone.' She quickly placed the original pages back in the binder.

'Shit.' He slammed the file cabinet shut, sat down, and plastered casual across his face. 'I wonder if we could stall her for a few more minutes.'

'Just shut up and act like you were cooling your heels.'

'I'm sorry,' Maryam announced as she came back into the office. 'I was on so long because of call waiting – one phone call after the other. Everyone is panicked about Dr Baldwin's death. Such a terrible, senseless tragedy!' Her eyes became moist. 'And the worst part is Dee. We still don't know about her.'

'No, we don't,' Marge said.

'Truly frightening.' Maryam shuddered. 'It gives me goose bumps to be here . . . alone. But someone has to hold down the fort.'

'Are you the only psychologist associate?'

'There are four assistants in addition to me. But I'm the only one that's licensed in clinical psychology. I'm the only one qualified enough to take over if something happened to Dee . . . I don't even want to think about that. But I guess I have to. Their patients are going to need support and help. I have to be there for them!'

An instant practice of rich people! Not a bad rise in income. Then Marge wondered why she was thinking so cynically.

'I have work to do,' Maryam said. 'I'm sorry but you'll have to leave.'

'Thank you anyway,' Oliver stated. 'Can we come back if we have a few more questions?'

'Maybe when things aren't so hectic.' She started to choke up. 'When things aren't so *emotional*.'

'Thank you,' Marge said. 'I know you tried.'

'I just wish I had something to tell you.'

Oliver smiled patiently. 'We all do the best we can.'

She escorted them out the door, even walked them to the elevator. When they were safely underground, Marge said, 'So what do you think?'

'Nice ass and she's probably clean. What do you think?'

'Narcissistic as hell, but I didn't detect any duplicity.' She unlocked the car door and went inside. Once Oliver had settled himself in the passenger's seat, she started the motor. 'You ever want to hang up the shield, you could have a dazzling career as a felon.'

'Cops and felons.' Oliver grinned. 'The line is very thin, Detective Dunn.'

19

They literally had lined Decker's office because there wasn't enough initial seating, prompting Oliver to bring in four brown folding chairs. Though the act of altruism got them off their feet, it did little to improve the mood. It was almost three in the afternoon, and the air conditioner wasn't doing much in the way of circulation. Every once in a while, Decker felt a waft of tepid air across his sweaty neck, but that was as good as it got. At least his chair was his own and had a nice padded seat. Both Webster and Oliver had taken off their jackets, shirtsleeves rolled up to the elbows. Dunn and Bontemps had on short-sleeved blouses. Decker's coat hung over the back of his chair, but he still wore a tie and had his cuffs buttoned at the wrists. It set a neat example for his detectives, and besides, he never knew when the captain might appear. Not that Strapp would say anything, but Decker knew how things worked. One of the reasons he was where he was.

Webster said, 'Where's Bert? Still checking out beach property? Must be twenty degrees cooler out there. Why don't I get those assignments?'

Ordinarily, Decker would have let it go. But today he wasn't feeling charitable. 'Are you done bitchin' or is there more?'

'I don't know, Loo,' Webster drawled. 'It's awfully hot and it's only the end of June. I'd say you have a summer of bitchin' ahead of you.'

'Thanks for the warning. Let's move on.'

Wanda was geared up. Her cheeks had taken on a deeper hue, and her brown eyes glinted with excitement. 'Okay, remember we told you about two minor kids that wouldn't talk or have their backpacks gone through?'

'Brandon Chesapeake and Riley Barns,' Decker said. 'What do you have?'

'First a little background.' Webster dabbed sweat off his forehead. 'It seems that Brandon's big problem was repeatedly violating his parents' curfew, sneaking out at all hours of the night.'

'Typical kid stuff,' Oliver said.

'Not my kid,' Marge said.

'Your kid's from Mars,' Oliver answered.

Marge sneered at him, but deep down she agreed.

'You're just jealous 'cause Vega's so darn smart!' Wanda snapped.

'Who let this woman in here?' Oliver grumped. 'Last I heard this was a murder investigation, not a truancy case.'

'Can we all cut the snide remarks?' Everyone was hot and tired, and nerves were frayed. Decker turned to Wanda. 'That's your cue to keep going.'

Wanda had hit a sore spot in Oliver. Being as he *was* a D2 in Homicide, and she *was* a D1 in Juvenile, she needed to make amends, and fast. 'Oliver's right. That kind of thing is typical teenager garbage, no big deal except that Brandon was caught for city curfew violation in Westwood. The kid was issued a citation and his parents found out and hit the ceiling. They forced him into therapy with the Baldwins. Mervin suggested the camp, and that's how Brandon came to be where he was.'

Webster said, 'The second kid, Riley Barns, was also caught for truancy along with Brandon. Except his parents didn't care much about how late Riley stayed out because they were never home themselves. The deal was this: Riley and Brandon are best friends. Where one went, the other went. So that's how they both ended up with the Baldwin camp. Now you're up to date.'

'We're not talking hard cases,' Oliver said.

'Exactly,' Webster answered. 'So Wanda and I are thinking, why would those two do the tough bit at a time when their psychiatrist and fellow camper were reduced to hamburger? So we both do the old bore-into-the-eye trick, and see more fear than anything else. Y'all combine it with the fact that their sleeping bags were closest to Merv Baldwin's tent. I think we got a clear deduction.'

'They saw something.' Decker wasn't surprised.

Someone should have witnessed *something*. 'What?'

Wanda said, 'We managed to pull out of Riley Barns the fact that he *was* awakened by a popping sound. He didn't get up, he didn't even move – just opened his eyes from his sleeping bag, not too sure about what he heard. Then he thought he saw a tiny beam of light, like a penlight. He said he might have seen a couple of shadows come out of the tent area and disappear into the brush.'

'A couple of shadows?' Decker said. 'As in two people?'

'Maybe.'

'Go on.'

'That's it,' Wanda concluded. 'No details beyond that.'

Webster stated, 'He was half-asleep. And since everything was quiet after that, he went back to sleep.'

'Any idea what time it was?' Decker asked.

'No . . . nothing.'

Marge said, 'You think the boy was scared into losing his memory?'

Wanda said, 'Nights are pitch black out there. Plus, the kid was awakened from a deep sleep. *I* don't think he's holding back.'

'So why didn't he say anything when he was first questioned?' Marge asked.

'I think he was freaked when he found out what had happened,' Webster said. 'He told Brandon Chesapeake about his experience right after Tarpin made the announcement.'

'What announcement?' Decker asked.

'He told the boys what had happened,' Webster said. 'Not the details, just that there had been a crime in Dr Baldwin's tent and everyone should stay where they were and not do anything until the police got up to the mountain. It was at that point that the boys decided the best plan of action was to keep their mouths shut. I can certainly understand their reticence.'

'It's generic shit,' Oliver said. 'We know that someone came in the tent and out of the tent. I say either the kid's lying to get attention and he didn't see or hear a damn thing. *Or* he saw more than he's letting on. He should be interviewed again.'

'Agreed,' Webster said. 'The problem is he's a minor and his parents are scared and aren't going to let us talk to him anymore. But maybe if the Loo came down . . .'

'No problem.' Decker looked at the framed picture of his family on his desk. 'I've got to figure out how to approach the parents. How many shadows did Riley see?'

'He said a couple,' Wanda said.

'And he has no time recollection.'

'He claims no,' Webster said. 'Just opened his eyes and saw these shadows coming out from the tent area and crawling back out into the woods. His first thought was that they were doing some kind of nighttime survival maneuvers.'

'Have they done that before?' Marge asked. 'Nighttime maneuvers?'

Webster shrugged. 'Beats me. I'll ask Tarpin.'

Wanda said, 'The main thing is that after a full day of

being pushed through Marine-type survival drills, Riley was very tired and it didn't take much for him to fall back asleep.'

'Did you tape the interview?' Decker asked.

'No, sir, we did not.' Wanda wiped her face with a tissue. 'We caught the kid and the parents at a weak moment – when they were too shocked to protest – took whatever we could get. We knew they were going to bolt any second, so once we got Riley to admit that he heard something, we just started flinging questions until Mr Barns put up the legal fence. We tried to keep it friendly because we figured you'd want to come back.'

Decker nodded. 'And you're sure the other kid – Brandon – he didn't see or hear anything?'

'He says he didn't,' Webster answered. 'We interviewed them all as best we could. Most of them were minors.'

'A stunned population of teenage boys who were scared witless, but still trying to keep up the macho front. Then you add hysterical parents into the mix . . .' Wanda shook her head. 'It wasn't a beach party. We didn't see or find anything suspicious.'

'Where are Ernesto's belongings?'

'They've been bagged,' Webster said. 'We didn't find any letters from Ruby Ranger if that's what you're asking. They do exist, right?'

'His brother claims they do. No reason to doubt it.' Decker took out his notepad and wrote down, *Riley Barns*. 'So none of the other kids look hot on the perp list?'

'Not from what we could see,' Webster said. 'It's the same story, Loo. The boys in the camps are what I might call overly rambunctious, but not carved-in-stone psychos.'

'So why were they there?' Marge asked.

'Different reasons.' Webster took out his notepad. 'Most were brought in to the Baldwins for drug problems. The parents found a stash or some pills and freaked out.'

Decker knew that feeling. 'A normal reaction.'

'Yeah, I suppose.'

Wanda was flipping through her notes. 'One got in trouble for getting drunk, taking the family car and totaling it. Another got arrested for malicious mischief at a shopping center.'

'That's pretty serious,' Marge said.

'Yeah, but it ain't shooting your teacher because she wore the wrong type of athletic shoes,' Wanda stated. 'The boys had been brought to the Baldwins by the parents without the kids getting in official trouble with the law. Some were school recommendations. Ernesto Golding was an exception, because he was charged and convicted of something.'

'I'll tell you one thing that they all had in common,' Webster broke in. 'The parents could afford the Baldwins' hefty fee – twenty grand a kid for three weeks.'

Oliver and Decker broke into whistles. Marge's eyes widened in diameter. She said, 'The Baldwins have carved out a nice niche in rich, bad boys.'

'Psychiatry is the province of the rich,' Webster said. 'That's nothing new.'

'Not always,' Decker said. 'I'll tell you this much. Twenty grand buys a lot of shrink time – like a hundred hours. Which would be seeing a shrink an hour a day, two times a week for almost a *year*. How many camps a summer does he run?'

Webster said, 'Three.'

'How many kids per session?'

'Twelve,' Webster said. 'We did the math: seven hundred and twenty thousand a summer. And that doesn't include the sessions they run during winter and spring break – that's only ten grand a pop.'

'A bargain,' Marge said.

'Nor does it include the follow-up sessions—'

'And they say a diploma is just a scrap of paper!' Decker shook his head. 'I definitely went into the wrong field.'

'What do they do with all the money?' Oliver asked. 'Surely that kind of income brings about some kind of vice.'

'Tarpin told me they might be renting a Malibu condo while they were remodeling their Beverly Hills home,' Decker said. 'That'll chew up a hell of a lot of income.' Decker added *money and debts* to the list. 'Here's another tidbit for your consideration. Darrell Holt – the kid from the Preservers of Ethnic Whatshis-face – he attended one of Baldwin's camp sessions about seven years ago. He must come from money. We should find out about him.'

'What?' Oliver said. 'Why didn't you tell me this two hours ago? I would have stolen his file—'

'I didn't hear that,' Decker said.

Oliver smiled. 'I'm talking theoretically.'

Before Decker could delve, Marge broke in. 'What did Holt do to get shunted into the Baldwins' camp?'

'I don't know,' Decker said. 'Tarpin wasn't forthcoming with details. He did say that Darrell was radical in his younger days and that he went to Berkeley. It would be interesting to know what brought about Darrell's shift to the right.'

'The day's still young even if we aren't,' Webster said. 'I'll go back to the PEI and see if I can't catch up with Holt.'

Decker looked at his notes. He had to investigate Holt, Ranger, Riley Barns, and money and debt with regard to the Baldwins' finances. And of course, there was Bert out looking for Dee Baldwin's supposed beach getaway.

Webster said, 'You want me to interview Holt or surf through racist Web sites?'

Decker said, 'Let's do this, Tom. Before you go to Holt, let's do some homework. Go to the Tolerance Center in the city. I'm sure it has details on all the hate groups. I didn't bother with it after the vandalism because Ernesto confessed. But a double murder justifies the man hours. I want to know everything there is to know about Holt and Tarpin – and that Moke character while you're at it.'

'I can make an appointment to go down there tomorrow,' Webster said.

'I'll go you one better. I'm going to hook you up with Rina. She knows the lingo because she's done research on white supremacist groups, as part of her outreach program in the community. You set it up, and when you have an appointment time, I'll make sure that Rina meets you down there. She'll love it and it'll be beneficial to you.'

'Sounds good.' Webster certainly didn't mind working with Decker's wife. She was smart and competent, and a comely lass at that. 'I'll let you know when I got something set up.'

Oliver consulted his notes. 'How long has Darrell Holt been with PEI?'

'Tarpin claims four years.'

'And what's Tarpin's role in the camp?' Marge asked. 'Besides being a fascist Marine.'

Decker gave her a smile and a wistful one at that. There were times – when Marge asked a certain question in a certain way – that made him sorely miss working with his former partner. 'He's a Baldwin henchman. Discipline guy for the day-to-day activities. I didn't grill him on his activities with PEI.'

'Regarding this Holt guy,' Oliver said. 'It's totally possible for me to . . . theoretically get into Baldwin's files. I know where they're kept . . . theoretically.'

Decker said, 'It's totally possible that if you were to do that, you would find yourself in jail with a bunch of eager felons waiting to ram a hard rod up your butt.'

'Loo, you have a vivid way of describing things. So I won't bother telling you the details that theoretically might be in Ernesto Golding's file – a file that we could have gotten into anyway because Ernesto is dead and there's no confidentiality with dead people.'

'Anything we can use?' Decker asked.

'Lots of jargon and abbreviations. Still, what came out was that he had a kinky sexual thing going on with this girl, Ruby Ranger.'

'Nazi shit?' Decker asked.

'Exactly. Except I think some of it might be fantasy because it was pretty wild. I think that was Baldwin's conclusion, too.'

'We need to fix on this Ranger girl. Last we heard, she went up north. Earlier this morning, I called six police stations in the greater Bay Area. They're looking for her and her car, but they're going to forget unless we follow up. Wanda, I'll leave the job of pestering to you.'

'Yes, sir.'

'You wanna see Ernesto's file, Loo?' Oliver asked. 'You went to college. Maybe you'll understand it.'

'No, I don't want to see it. I don't want to even know about it until the warrants come through.'

'While we're on the subject of theoretical incidents . . .' Marge cleared her throat. 'Just suppose I found some things lying around on Baldwin's desk, copied them down, and had a question about the shorthand Baldwin used by his patients' names?'

Decker stared at her. 'I don't believe this.'

Oliver said, 'Blame it on me. Show and tell, Margie.'

'I don't want to see it,' Decker said.

'So don't look,' Oliver retorted.

But Decker did look. Marge had brought out several copies of what looked to be a desk calendar. She felt guilty – but not that guilty. 'At first, we were thinking that the shorthand could be describing his patients' psychiatric conditions. But the abbreviations don't seem to correspond to psychiatric ailments.'

'Like C for "crazy" or N for "nutcase"—' Oliver said.

'How about N for "neurotic"?' Webster said. 'Not the kids, the parents. Doesn't anyone ever just work things out anymore?'

Decker bristled. 'Maybe these kids have real problems, Tom.'

'Yeah, the problem is they're spoiled rotten. Y'all wouldn't find any of us desecrating a temple and getting away with a slap on the wrist.'

'In the end, Ernesto got more than a slap,' Decker said.

Webster paused. 'Yeah, that's too bad. I'm not saying he deserved to die or anything. And I'm not saying that kids don't have troubles. I'm just wondering if some of the parents aren't using the Baldwins as high-priced baby-sitters?'

'I'm sure there's some of that,' Decker said. 'But I'm also sure that most of the parents are very sincere in wanting the best for their kids.'

'Whether the kids want it or not,' Wanda said.

Oliver said, 'Getting back to the shorthand, I was thinking that PS could stand for "psycho".'

'Shrinks don't use the term "psycho", Scott,' Marge answered. 'You know, Maryam mentioned Dee Baldwin acting as kind of a guidance counselor . . . getting kids into the right colleges. I'm thinking that maybe the shorthand stands for names of colleges. Since S is the most frequent, and we're talking about smart, rich kids, it could be Stanford.'

'What's PS?' Oliver said. 'Pseudo-Stanford. And notice I knew "Pseudo" started with a P.'

'Very good, Oliver,' Marge said.

'Maybe University of Pennsylvania,' Webster said. 'That's an Ivy. PS equals Pennsylvania.'

'What's E then?' Wanda asked. 'What's M?'

'E could be Emory in Atlanta,' Webster said. 'That's also top ranked. Maybe M is for U of Michigan in Ann Arbor. That's considered a public Ivy.'

'How do you know that?' Oliver sneered.

'I got into Michigan.'

'Bully for you.'

'No need to get nasty.'

'If the abbreviations are top universities, where is the H for Harvard, or the P for Princeton, or the Y for Yale?' Decker asked. 'And what is I? Or L? Or S2?'

'Stanford waiting list?'

'No, I don't think so.' Decker rubbed his forehead. 'Any other ideas?'

His question was met with silence broken by the ring of his telephone. The tension in Rina's tone was audible. So was her voice. Everyone could hear it.

'The murders are all over the news,' she said. 'Yonkie's beside himself. In case you forgot, he knew Ernesto Golding—'

'Hold on, Rina.' Decker covered the receiver and looked at his staff. They were on their feet before he even spoke. 'Give me five minutes.'

They all nodded and were out the door. Rina said,

'Are you in the middle of a meeting?'

'I was.'

'About Ernesto Golding's murder?'

'Yes.'

'Did Jacob tell you where he knew Ernesto from? He's being vague with me.'

Decker didn't answer right away.

Rina broke in. 'You've got to tell me, Peter.'

'Rina, he spoke to me in confidence—'

'Peter, *I'm his mother!*' Rina shouted. 'Oh, just forget it! I know anyway. From the drug parties, right?'

Decker was momentarily stunned. He couldn't speak.

'I'm religious, Peter, but I'm not blind,' Rina stated. 'More important, I have a nose. His clothes used to reek of pot. Combine that with his formerly poor grades, and the fact that he was a gross underachiever, it doesn't take Sam Spade to figure it out.'

'So why didn't you ever say anything about it to me?'

'Stop throwing the blame back in my corner—'

'This isn't about blame, Rina; I'm just trying to understand you, for heaven's sake!'

Silence over the phone. Then Rina said, 'I didn't want to upset you. You were nervous enough about Sammy being in Israel.'

Decker said, 'Did you ever talk to Jacob about his drug . . . his former drug use?'

'It is former?'

'Best of my knowledge, it's former.'

'No, I didn't. Because frankly I didn't know how to handle it without getting hysterical. And the last thing that Yonkie needed was an hysterical mother. I figured he just had to mature. That was probably pretty stupid of me, but sometimes, Peter, I just get tired of parenting.'

'I hear you loud and clear, darlin'.'

'I did talk to Shmueli about it. I knew if Jacob confided in anyone, it would be his brother. He told me to let it ride, that Yonkie was feeling bad enough for the both of us.'

'So I'm not the only one who was keeping secrets.'

'I suppose that's true,' Rina said. 'We can talk about that later. Right now, Yonkie's the issue here. Peter, he's very scared.'

'About what?' Decker sat up. 'Does he know something?'

'I don't know.'

Decker's duty was clear. 'Is Jacob home now?'

'Yes. He was going to come with me to the airport to pick up Shmueli. But if you're coming home, I'll tell him to stay and wait for you.'

'I'll be there in twenty minutes.'

'Was he good friends with this Golding boy? He claims he wasn't, but I think he might be lying to protect me.'

'I think he's being honest. Yonkie had told me that he hadn't seen the boy in months. It's probably the murder itself. You know kids. They think they're immortal. Then reality smacks them in the face . . . Don't worry.'

'Just when he was doing so well with the therapy and his grades. I don't want him to start Johns Hopkins an emotional wreck!'

'It's the start of the summer, Rina. He'll be okay by the fall.'

'Except he's taking his Calculus and Physics SAT II next week. I know he's a good test taker but—'

Again, Decker sat up straight. 'What did you say?'

'I don't know,' Rina said. 'What did I say?'

'You said that Yonkie is taking the SAT II in Calculus and Physics,' Decker answered.

'Right. He's trying to exempt out of freshman Calc—'

'S2 is SAT II, S is SAT, PS is PSAT . . .' Decker replied. 'Of course. That's it. That's what their specialty was . . . getting kids into top universities.'

'What's it?'

'A code we were trying to crack. Now it's obvious. None of the others could know because none of them have college-bound teenagers. Scott's sons didn't go to college. Neither did Bontemps's daughter. Webster has school-age kids, and Vega hasn't reached that point yet. Only me. I'm a very dull boy sometimes.'

'What are you *talking* about?' Rina exclaimed.

'Rina, what's a standardized test starting with M?'

'How would I know? I haven't been in school in eighteen years. Are you coming home?'

'Yes. So you don't know of any test that starts with M?'

'Oh for goodness' sakes, can you ever stop thinking about work?'

'I'm on my way home—'

'How about the test to get into Medical school?' Rina threw out. 'I think it's the MedCat or the

M-CAT. Something like that.'

'You're a genius.'

'Great!' Rina was irritated. 'Will you come home to your son now?'

'Absolutely. I bet L is for the LSAT. Jesus, *I* took the LSAT.'

'Way back in the Stone Age.'

'Now you're being nasty.'

'You deserve it.'

'How about E?'

'E?'

'Yes, E. What about E? What tests begin with the letter E? A test for Economics or something?'

She thought a moment. 'Are we dealing only with college tests?'

'I don't know. What do you have in mind?'

'How about the ERBs? Hannah's school gives them every year. Some schools give the Iowa instead—'

'So that's the I,' Decker said. What was Baldwin doing? Helping kids prepare for their standardized tests? And what, if anything, did it have to do with Ernesto's murder? His second phone line lit up. He asked Rina to hold a moment.

It was Martinez.

The news didn't surprise him. But it did sadden him.

To his wife, he said, 'I'm sorry, Rina. I'm not going to make it home. You may as well take Jacob with you.'

'That sounds bad.'

'They found Dee Baldwin's body. An apparent suicide, but it could be homicide. I've got to go.'

'Oh, my goodness! I'm so sorry, Peter.'

'Tell Jacob not to worry. It's under control.'

'Is it?'

'Not yet. But it will be.'

He spoke bravado. He spoke lies.

20

Over the hill, it was fifteen degrees cooler, and being as the condo sat atop the sand, Decker felt a pleasant ocean breeze riffle through his suit jacket as soon as he got out of the car. He had squeezed the unmarked into the last spot on the gravel lot, which was already filled with two Mercedes, two Beemers, one Porsche, one Range Rover, one Ford Explorer, one Jeep, one Honda (Bert's), three squad cars, and a half-dozen scantily dressed people – dazed and confused – milling in the open spaces. At five in the afternoon, daylight was still strong, but the sun had begun its westerly descent. Decker hadn't taken more than a couple of steps before Martinez pulled him between the Beemer and the Explorer, a place for temporary privacy.

'I put in the call to Malibu Sheriff's.'

Decker nodded. 'It's their jurisdiction, even if it is our case.'

'The guys they sent over seem nice, but not too familiar with the rigors of homicide investigation. They probably don't get a lot of opportunity out here.'

'I don't know, Bert. Murder of the rich and famous isn't an alien concept. When did you call it in?'

'About an hour ago.'

Decker wagged his finger. 'But you called me almost two hours ago.'

'Well, you know . . .' Martinez's smile was sheepish. 'I wanted to look around and make my own notes first.' He flipped the cover off his notepad. 'First a little background. I checked with the assessor's office: no record of the Baldwins' owning anything around here. So I started going from realtor to realtor, figuring like you said that they rented. I struck oil. The Baldwins seem to be creatures of habit, renting the same beach condo every summer. Except that this summer they rented for the entire year.'

'They're remodeling their house in Beverly Hills. I suppose they need somewhere to live.' Decker raised his eyebrows. 'I'm surprised the rental agents were cooperative. Aren't they supposed to be protective of their clients?'

'Not the ones I interviewed,' Martinez answered. 'They love to name-drop. Besides, they had a personal interest in making things easy for me. It doesn't look good to have bodies moldering in your rental units. From the initial glance, it points to suicide.'

'Because . . .'

'Single shot to the head. No defense marks – cuts or scratches on the arms or the palms of her hands. No ligature marks around her wrists. Superficially, nothing to indicate force or a struggle.'

'Any note?'

'I didn't find anything. But if she did whack hubby and the kid, it's easy to find a motive. Ernesto was barechested. She might have interrupted something.'

'It was a hot night,' Decker said.

'Now you're making excuses.'

'You're saying that she went up to the mountains at three in the morning . . . with guns and silencers . . . and happened to discover her husband and a young boy in a compromising position . . . and went crazy?' Decker frowned. 'C'mon, Bert. That kind of damage done quickly and quietly points to a pro.'

'Then maybe Dee knew about the affair and hired out. Afterward, she felt extreme guilt and whacked herself.'

Decker wasn't happy with that picture, either. 'Webster questioned one of the kids . . . Riley Barns. He saw a couple of shadows lurking around the tent in the early hours.'

'That's news to me.' Martinez shrugged. 'Anyway, the rental agent's name is Athena Eaton, and she informed me that this little ditty here – a two-bedroom, two-and-a-half-bath number – rents for ten grand a month. The last time she saw Dee Baldwin was when Dee and Mervin signed the contract three weeks ago. A full year at ten grand a month, including a first, last and a one-month cleaning deposit. That's one hundred and twenty G's out the window. Their practice must be cleaning up.'

'It was cleaning up,' Decker said.

'Speaking of cleaning up, the owner is going to need every bit of the damage deposit. The bedroom carpet is white.'

'Lots of splatter?'

'Enough that it can't be cleaned. Dee's lying in a good-sized pond of blood. Single shot through the mouth with a .32.'

'Through the *mouth*,' Decker said. 'You said "to the head".'

Martinez reddened. 'I meant it came out in the back of the head.'

'You examined the body?'

The blush deepened. 'Sort of.'

'Gunpowder residue?'

'Appears that way.'

Decker smoothed his mustache and said nothing.

Martinez said, 'We'll know more after Shot Squad and Forensics examine the angles, and the position of the body after she fell . . . Uh-oh. Heads up, Loo. The Sheriff's main man is on his way. We gotta look friendly.'

Martinez introduced Decker to a man around forty years in age, with a deep tan, a good suit, and blow-dried hair. His face held lines, some of them deeper than others, and he had cop's eyes despite the trappings of being Mr Beachcomber.

'Detective Don Baum.' He shook Decker's hand. 'I want to thank Detective Martinez for calling in the local authorities right away. It shows cooperation, not to mention good manners. And that's what we're going to give you in return. Cooperation. It gets things done. And that's what it's all about – getting the job done.'

'You bet!' Decker answered. 'Is the coroner here?'

'Yes, sir, Lieutenant. The coroner just came. Let's have a look.'

They started walking toward the building – a series of white stucco townhouses covered with blue Spanish tiles.

Decker said, 'Who found her?'

'I went in first,' Martinez said. 'Unfortunately, Ms Eaton – the real estate agent – followed me. From the look on her face, I think she sincerely wishes she hadn't.'

'Where is she?' Decker asked.

'In one of the squad cars, catching her breath,' Baum said.

'The smell might have been the *coup de grâce*,' Martinez said.

'Did she touch anything?' Decker asked.

Martinez had to think a moment. 'Maybe the bed frame for support. Then I propped her up and escorted her out. I was gloved.'

'We're dusting for prints,' Baum said. 'It's going to take some time.'

'What about the photographer?' Decker asked.

'She's in the unit as we speak,' Baum said. 'I'll get you copies of everything. I've got six of my people canvasing the area for witnesses. I'll forward you their reports.'

'Thank you,' Decker said. 'And what about Dee Baldwin's car?'

'It's the Range Rover in the lot,' Baum said. 'We'll impound it and dust it for prints.'

A four-wheel drive, Decker thought. *Maybe she did go up. Or someone went up using her car.* He said, 'I'd like the tires gone over, see what Forensics can pull from the treads. Then, I'll need an imprint. I want to find out if she was up at the camp recently.'

'Consider it done.'

And if she had been up, what would that prove? A fat zero, but that didn't matter. Now was the time to gather information. Behind them, a news van pulled into the parking complex, its tires bumping along the gravel road.

Decker said, 'We'd better speed it up.'

Baum led them to the unit. 'It's this one.'

Planted against the front wall of the building was a compact flower garden abloom with showy multi-colored impatiens and leafy, purple-flowered statice. A cop was stationed at the front door of the Baldwins' unit, yellow crime scene tape stretched across the jambs. Baum peeled it back, and they walked into a petite entry hall with a powder room off to the left. Ten paces forward and two steps down put Decker into an open space: a living room/dining room combination, and a well-equipped kitchenette punched out of the side wall. The décor was mild and warm like sand, done up in ecru and white with slipcover muslin furniture resting upon soft, muted oatmeal carpeting. The coffee and end tables were free-form shapes of high-lacquered elm burl resting on stands of driftwood. The dining table was a slab of country oak. The walls were adorned with prints of terns, ducks, pelicans, game fish, blue whales, and dolphins. Large pieces of black coral as well as cowry and conch shells sat in bric-a-brac shelving units that sided a large fireplace. A wall of sliding glass doors led out to decks and provided an unobstructed full-range view of the Pacific – blue and infinite, a testament to the insignificance of man.

Another cop held guard at the foot of the stairway. He nodded to Baum as they ascended the steps.

The second story held two bedrooms, each with its own bath. The master bedroom had its own deck and its own cerulean view. The bed was a king and dressed with white lace pillows piled high over a white down-filled comforter. Very serene except for the black powder all over the walls and bed frame, not to mention the dead body smashed up against the wall. It spoiled the Zen effect.

Decker stared at the corpse. Dee was semi-upright, the angle of her limbs obscured by a flowing, pink peignoir. She resembled strawberry sauce falling over a sea of vanilla ice cream. Her head was tilted to the left, blood dripping from her nose and mouth. Beside him, a gray-haired, four-foot-ten, seventy-pound grandma was snapping pictures.

Grandma aimed and fired, Dee sitting perfectly still for the camera. 'A perfect waste of good lingerie.' She looked up and saw Decker's stoic face. 'Haven't you ever heard of black humor?'

'How'd you get into this business?' Decker asked.

'I'm seventy-seven,' she replied. 'How many bar mitzvah pictures can I take in a single lifetime?' She removed the lens from her Nikon. 'I'm done here. That should give you a little more breathing room.'

'Thank you,' Decker said.

'You're welcome,' Grandma answered. 'I know I'm cute. You don't have to hold back the smile, sir.'

Decker smiled. She was cute, but murder wasn't. Dee's death had been the cop's road to the void – suicide through the mouth, severing the brain stem – an instantaneous death. Unusual for an amateur who usually chose the temple, but maybe Dee had seen enough detective movies to go that route. What was unusual was *where* they found her – on the floor beside the bed instead of *on* the bed. True, she could have fallen off the bed to the floor, but the splatter marks didn't bear that out.

The coroner was several feet from the body, holding up a vial of blood to the light. He was young and moved with a jerky rhythm. Vanilla skin was stretched over broad cheekbones. He had a wide smile and big teeth and a dab of the Occident, rounding his Asian eyes. He had broad shoulders and a lean frame. His name was Chuck Liu.

'A little neat to be suicide.' With gloved hands, Liu wrote something down on a label, stuck it on the tube of plasma, then bagged it in plastic. 'But I heard it through the grapevine that her husband was found in a compromising position with a teenager – a male teenager.'

Decker made a noncommittal gesture.

Liu said, 'Was she the jealous type?'

'I don't know anything about her except that she and

her husband were in the same profession and worked out of the same office.'

'That's always a recipe for disaster. What do you think?'

'I'll reserve judgement until I know what's going on. Should I ask for a time of death?'

'Eight to twelve hours. Rigor is moderate. The inferior portions of her thighs and calves are swollen and red – lividity combined with the upward percolation of the blood that she's sitting in. That takes time.'

Decker nodded. Dee had died somewhere between five and nine in the morning. Certainly enough time for someone to come down from the mountain and take her out as well.

The coroner proceeded to bag Dee's hands. 'There's gunpowder residue here.'

'She fired the gun,' Baum said.

'Not *the* gun,' Liu corrected. '*A* gun. If she had been deep asleep or drugged up, someone could have done it for her. Just popped it in her mouth and fired the trigger. We'll know more once we've done the blood work-up.'

'Does it look like suicide to you?' Baum asked.

'Sure.'

'But it could be homicide,' Martinez said.

'Sure.'

Decker said, 'Anything left of her mouth?'

'Some of the front portion of the maxilla is still intact.' Liu took out a dental mirror from his bag and slipped it between blue lips. A small beam of light that had been attached to the handle gave him some visibility inside the dark cavity. 'Yeah, the incisors and canines are still there. It looks like the bullet caught the back edge of the bony palate, deflected upward and backward through the brain stem.'

'Any soft palate left?' Decker asked.

'Nothing.'

'Hard palate?' Decker asked.

'Yeah, a few tissue shreds behind the incisors . . . more, actually. It goes to the premolars. I can even see the start of her palatal torus, but everything's pretty roasted back there.'

'Any cuts or lacerations on it?'

'Can't tell.' Liu pulled the mirror out. 'What are you thinking?'

'If she had been coerced, she might have struggled and the nose of the gun might have cut her palate and cheeks.'

'Her buccal mucosa is charred from the heat of the bullet.' He considered Decker's thoughts. 'I'll look when I have her on the table and opened up.'

'Also, if you can say something about the amount of powder on her hands,' Decker said. 'If someone did this to her – had his hand over Dee's hand when the trigger was pulled – some of the powder must have wound up on the shooter's hand as well.'

Liu said, 'So maybe you should go out and look for someone with gunpowder residue.'

'So you're saying it wasn't suicide,' Baum said.

'I'm not saying anything,' Liu said. 'I'm just saying if you have a suspect, test him for gunpowder residue.'

A great idea, except at the moment, there was no suspect. 'Where's the gun?'

'It's been bagged,' Martinez said.

'The bullet?'

'Embedded into the wall,' Baum said. 'Techs'll get it.'

'I'm just about done, so you can get the meat wagon ready.' Liu looked at his bloodied gloves and shirt. 'I'm not exactly dressed for prime time.' He snapped his gloves off and threw them in a 'contaminated materials' bag. 'I'd appreciate it if someone could distract the cameras so I can get out of here with minimum effort.'

Baum said, 'We'll handle the press.'

'I can tell you more once I've got her laid out on the slab. When do you want the autopsy done? Yesterday?'

'That would be nice,' Decker said.

'Typical,' Liu said. 'I'll do my best. It's too late to hit the waves anyway.'

'You're a surfer?' Martinez asked.

Liu's look was wistful. 'Nothing like drowning out the ugliness of the world in one magnificent seven-foot curl.'

Athena Eaton was fifty and anorexic, with jet-black hair and a face slathered with makeup. By the time Decker was ready to interview her, she had popped three pills, and her behavior alternated between woozy incoherent and hysterical incoherent. In the end, Decker had the cops take her home with a promise to come back and check in on her tomorrow. Since Baum had his people canvasing the area, there were no pressing reasons for Decker to stay on the scene.

Crammed with information overload, he needed a good hour of solitude to sort everything out. The amount of paperwork was staggering, and he wouldn't finish it up until sunrise. But before he went any further, he had to put in an appearance at home. His stepson Sammy was coming back after a full year away in Israel, and if he didn't show up, he'd live to regret it. Not to mention the fact that he actually missed his stepson terribly and wanted to see him.

And they talk about women balancing work and personal obligations.

When he pulled up into his driveway, he felt a stab of apprehension. Rina's car was still gone. Even allowing for bad traffic, by Decker's calculations, Sammy should have been home a couple of hours ago. Maybe she took the family out for dinner at one of the kosher restaurants in town. He certainly hoped that was the case.

When he opened the front door, he immediately heard noises – the distorted, high-pitched squeals that could only belong to toons getting smashed, squashed, electrocuted, or fried. He went into his daughter's bedroom.

'Hi there.'

Hannah looked up. 'Dadddeeee!'

'Hannah Roseeeee!'

She jumped up, and he spun her in his arms. Then he kissed her cheek and set her down.

'I'm hungry,' she complained.

'Where's Eema?'

'At the airport.' She sat back down in front of the TV. 'Can you get me a snack?'

'Who's taking care of you?'

'Yonkie.'

'Where's Yonkie?'

The little girl shrugged. 'Chocolate milk and chips?'

'Have you had dinner yet?'

'Not an Eema dinner. But Yonkie made me cheese and applesauce and a glass of milk. Does that count as a dinner?'

Decker wasn't sure if the food qualified or not. 'I suppose it's okay.'

'So can I have chocolate milk and chips. Oh, and a plum, too?'

'I suppose.'

'Great! You want to watch TV with me?'

'Maybe a little later.'

'Okay. I'll wait for my snack.'

'Uh . . . shouldn't you be doing something else?'

The seven year old looked at him. 'What?'

'Like shouldn't you be reading or playing outside . . . something other than watching TV?'

She sighed with exasperation. 'Eema already took me ice-skating, then I went to the liberry and took out two new books that I'm 'posed to read before I go to bed. Then I drew six pictures with my new berry-scented markers. Then Yonkie and I played Street Fighter II for an hour. Now I'm tired. But if you want me to be bored and turn off the TV, I'll do it.'

Putting it that way, TV watching seemed perfectly reasonable. 'No, no,' Decker said. 'It seems like you've had a busy day.'

'I've had a very busy day, Daddy. I'm tired and

hungry. Cheese is not enough for a growing girl.'

Decker smiled. 'I'll get you your snack.' He retreated into the kitchen, where he found Jacob engrossed in some kind of test study guide. The teen had finished off his junior year with straight A's for the first time. He looked up. 'Hey.'

'Hey,' Decker answered back.

'You look wiped.'

'A bit,' Decker admitted. 'Where's Eema?'

'The plane was delayed . . . and delayed . . . and delayed.'

'Poor Sammy. You didn't go to the airport?'

'Eema felt the wait might be too long for Hannah.' He shrugged. 'I volunteered to baby-sit. I might as well enjoy her and the comforts of home before I'm confined to a ten-by-twelve cell with nothing but a hard cot to sleep on and bread and water to eat.'

'I don't think the accommodations at the yeshiva are that bad.'

'That's what you think.' He closed his book and sat back in his chair. The boy's face was flushed and pained. 'I've heard a couple of the newscasts, you know.'

'Saying?'

'That the other Dr Baldwin – the lady . . . you know. They're saying it was suicide. What'd she do? Kill her husband and Ernesto in a fit of jealous rage, then kill herself?'

Decker shrugged.

'That's how TV's telling it.'

'Let's hear it for little screen journalism.' Decker sat down. 'Are you freaked?'

'Yeah, I'm pretty freaked. It's horrible!'

'Are you talking to your friends about it?'

'What friends?'

'Are you talking to anyone about it?'

'I'm talking to you.'

Decker was quiet.

Jacob sat up. 'A few people have called me up.'

'Lisa Halloway?'

Jacob nodded. 'Yeah, she's devastated!' He sighed. 'It's terrible. I got my own feelings about this, and people are calling *me* up, asking *me* questions. Like I'm a hotline to your investigation.'

'Can I do anything for you?'

'I don't suppose you want to take the calls.'

'I'm a little busy right now.'

'Then how about if you read all this junk for me.' He held up a SAT II chemistry study guide. 'You can take the test for me.'

'Sure, I can fail it for you,' Decker answered.

The boy cracked a smile. 'Actually, I know the material pretty well. I'll be fine.'

'That's good.'

A long pause. Then Jacob said, 'Ernesto never struck me as gay, by the way.'

Decker sat down. 'Why?'

'I'm a pretty boy,' Jacob said. 'The kind of looks that girls and gays love. He never came on to me.'

'Maybe you're not his type,' Decker said.

The teenager smiled. 'I'm everyone's type.'

Decker smiled back. 'So you're basing Ernesto's sexual inclination on your universal sex appeal?'

'In all seriousness, it's just that he . . . he was comfortable with girls. Also, he never made any antigay jokes, which is a tip-off with someone trying to hide it.'

'People have secret lives, Yonkie.'

'Uh, yeah, I think I know something about that.' The boy looked down. 'Just giving you my perception, for what it's worth.'

'It's worth a lot. You knew him a lot better than I did.'

Silence.

Decker broke it. 'What should we do for dinner? Hannah's hungry and I'd like to give her more than snacks.'

'There's always takeout,' Jacob said. 'Hannah will always eat pizza.'

'We should actually cook something. I'm sure Eema and Sammy will be hungry when they come home.'

'What can you cook?' Jacob asked.

'Hot dogs and scrambled eggs,' Decker answered.

Jacob got up and went to the refrigerator. 'Hey, guess what? There're a half-dozen veal chops in the freezer.'

Decker said, 'I can broil veal chops.'

'There are also a couple of salad bags. That would really impress Eema. A fresh salad.'

'Yes, it would.'

'Well, there you go.' Jacob pulled out the package. 'A gourmet delight.'

'Jacob, are you okay?'

The boy sat back down. 'Not really. It's too surreal. Eema and I were talking about it before she left for the airport. She's convinced that I'm holding back. I'm not. I told her all I knew about Ernesto – which wasn't much. I didn't like him. But knowing someone who was murdered so brutally is awful. How do you face this, day after day?'

'I swallow back personal feelings so I can do the job.'

'You never take it to heart?'

'It affects you.' Mental pictures of today's victims played in Decker's mind. 'But if you want to get the job done, you push things aside.'

'Is that what you're telling me to do?'

'Of course not, Yonkie. This must be absolutely shocking to you even if you didn't know him all that well.'

Jacob made a face. 'I'm also upset about Eema finding out about the parties. Apparently, she knew about it all along.'

'Apparently.'

'Did you know that she knew?'

'Not until a few hours ago. She's also good at hiding things.'

'She said all the right things,' Jacob said. 'But deep down, I know she doesn't trust me.'

'Jacob, she loves you so much. She's much more concerned about your future than your past.'

'I know. She wants me to be happy.'

'Yes.'

'You want me to be happy.'

'Yes.'

'I'm sure Ernesto Golding's parents wanted him to be happy.'

Decker's eyes clouded with sadness. 'Yes.'

'Did you talk to them?'

'Yes.'

The boy looked down. 'Was it awful?'

'Yes.' Decker drummed his fingers on the table. 'Before this happened . . . had you ever heard about either of the Baldwins from any of your old party friends, Jacob?'

The boy looked up. 'Of course. Everyone knows the Baldwins. It wasn't only that group, Dad. Several kids from the yeshiva had seen them. They've got a real racket going.'

Decker's interest was piqued. 'What kind of racket?'

'I don't mean racket.' The teen searched for the right words. 'Just that he was very successful in getting kids into prestigious universities.'

'Did he tutor kids for their entrance exams?'

Jacob thought a moment. 'His wife – the other Dr Baldwin – did a lot of college counseling. You know, schools are supposed to have guidance counselors. But a lot of them are not very good, so parents hire out private college counselors.'

'*Private* counselors . . .' Decker thought a moment. 'At big fees, no doubt.'

'I guess.'

'Whatever happened to kids just reading the catalogues?'

'It's a tough world out there, Dad. Lots of universities and lots of competition. The key is to match the right kid to the right counselor, because certain counselors have more pull with certain colleges.'

'What do you mean by pull?'

'Just what it sounds like.'

'To me, it smacks of nepotism . . . or something illegal.'

'Not any more illegal than the old boys' networks that excluded blacks, Jews, Hispanics, Asians—'

'Discrimination is illegal, Yonkie.'

'That doesn't mean it doesn't exist. The top universities are private and can basically do whatever they want to do. You know about legacies, right? If you're a legacy and pay full tuition, that's better than a 4.0 for lots of private universities. It's different in the public universities like UCLA. It's totally based on points on the first round.'

'Points?'

'Points for grades, points for the SAT, points for the SAT II. Which isn't really fair either. A black kid from South Central, who's been dodging bullets to make it to English class, has more baggage than a white kid from Encino. Now *if* you don't get in to the UC the first round, you can appeal the decision and bring in all the extraneous stuff. So when you get right down to it, nothing's completely objective.'

'I didn't realize the process was so complicated.'

'Yeah, it is. Not so hard for me because you and Eema never really cared about the Ivies. I know if it were up to her, I'd go to Yeshiva University. So I was spared all this major league anxiety. But even in the Orthodox circuit, there's intense pressure to go to good schools. Believe me, I've seen the most arrogant guys reduced to tears because of poor SAT performance.'

'So that explains services like Dr Baldwin's tutoring,' Decker said.

'A kid explained it to me like this: Suppose a certain guidance counselor always sends the university top students. If you sat on the admissions committee, wouldn't you trust his or her opinions?'

'Did the Baldwins write recommendations for the kids?'

'I suppose. I mean you can have lots of letters of recommendation in your applications. Supposedly, the ones that mean something are the ones from the teachers – the people who know your academic skills. But I'm sure that the right character references can tip the scales. There was a kid who graduated from Torah V'Dass about two years ago who got a recommendation from some honcho politico who, in turn, had gone to school with a man on the acceptance committee of the university that he was applying to. Now the guy was smart, but c'mon. A letter like that? It clinched it.'

'Did the Baldwins have that kind of muscle?'

'The Baldwins had a tag for working magic. I never thought about it, because I thought I was going to YU and that was that. But then this thing from Hopkins and Ner Yisroel came up: to do my last year of high school and my first year of college together. My whole perspective changed, people telling me how lucky I was. It wasn't luck. It was Eema who pushed and pushed and pushed for them to consider me. That's what you need, someone pushing for you. I was *lucky*, even if it means I got to wear a black hat.'

'It'll match your hair.'

'Great!' he said stiffly. 'I'll be color coordinated.'

'So having the Baldwins behind you meant something.'

'Definitely.'

'What about Ernesto Golding? What was he aiming for?'

'Ernesto got into Brown – no easy feat. I don't know if he got into Berkeley. Probably not. I'm sure he would have gone there if he could have. It's Ruby Ranger's old alma mater.'

Decker paused. 'That's right. You told me that Ruby Ranger went to Berkeley.'

'Did I?'

'Someone did.'

'No one ever said she was dumb. Just evil.'

'Is she up there now?'

'Beats me.'

'How old is Ruby Ranger?'

'Around twenty-two or -three.'

A little younger than Darrell Holt – who had also gone to Berkeley. 'Did she ever see Dr Baldwin?'

'How would I know that?'

'You seem to know lots of things, Yonkie,' Decker said. 'Did Ruby ever bring older guys to the parties?'

'She may have, but I don't know. I tried to stay clear of her.'

'Have you ever heard of or met a guy named Darrell Holt?'

Jacob thought a moment, and then he shook his head. 'No. Who is he?'

'What about Ricky Moke?'

'Nope. Can I ask who he is?'

'A cipher.'

Hannah came into the kitchen, wiping her eyes. 'I'm hungry.'

'How would you like some veal chops and fresh salad?' Decker asked.

'*Eeeeuuuuuwwww!*'

Decker was resigned to the inevitable. 'How about a hot dog?'

'Yum!' The little girl started running in circles. 'Yum, yum, yum!'

Just then, they all heard a car pull into the driveway. Hannah shouted, 'Shmueli's home!'

Jacob swept the little girl in his arms. 'Let's go see your big brother!'

'Yeah, yeah, yeah!' Hannah shouted.

'Yeah, yeah, yeah!' Jacob answered.

Decker couldn't tell which one was the more excited.

21

Rina regarded her husband as he wiped the last dish, his face a study in concentration. He was thinking about the case. Still, she tried to make small talk.

'It's good to have Shmueli home, no?'

Decker grinned. 'Never thought I'd say it, but I missed his mouth. I missed his pithy observations. I missed his quick wit that bordered on sarcasm, and his strong opinions on everything. It's great to have him home.'

'Even if it's for a very short time.' Rina sighed. 'At least they'll be close to each other. We'll do a weekend in New York, then a weekend in Baltimore. You know . . . alternate so no one feels left out.'

Decker looked at her. 'How often do you plan to visit?'

'What does it matter?' Rina blurted out. 'You're never home anyway.'

Decker was shocked, not by the observation, but by her frankness.

Rina stammered, 'That was terrible—'

'No, it's true, Rina.' He nodded. 'You visit whenever you want. It's fine.'

But the look on his face told her it wasn't fine. 'Peter, don't shut me out. I'm very sorry. It just . . . slipped out.'

'I know.' He put down the dishtowel and hugged her. 'Maybe I should take a sabbatical.' A pause. 'Or . . . being as I'm only three years away from twenty-five, maybe I should call it quits.'

'You'd be miserable.'

'Not as miserable as you think,' Decker said. 'I know we have a mortgage. There are other things I could do. You know, I could hire myself out as an expert witness – a cop and lawyer. I'm very articulate, and extremely calm under scrutiny. You know what the top guys get? Five hundred an hour portal to portal.'

'You've always called them whores.'

'I wouldn't say anything that I didn't believe.'

Rina shook her head. 'They have ways of making you say things you don't mean.'

'Yes, I know that.'

She kissed his lips, then pulled away, busying herself with straightening up the kitchen. 'I don't think you should do anything rash just because I made a rude remark.'

'Okay.' Decker thought a moment. 'How about this? After I get some resolution with this case, I take a week off. We'll fly down to Florida, leave Hannah and the boys with my parents for two days. They can go to Disney World or Epcot while we bask in the sands of St Croix.'

'Now that sounds like a fabulous plan!'

'A lot less impulsive than quitting?'

'Yes, indeed.' She smiled. 'You know I have lots to do, Peter. I don't sit around and wait for you to entertain me. For instance, I'm in charge of the scholar-in-residence lunch at the *shul*. Someone from the Tolerance Center is going to speak about hate groups. We're going to have a tremendous turnout because I sent out flyers to everyone in the community. I have over a hundred positives. We're getting twenty people alone from the First Baptist Church.'

'That's a lot of *chulent* under one roof.'

'Don't hold me responsible for the gas levels,' Rina said. 'Then the next weekend after that, I promised that I'd be on a panel on Sunday.'

'Maybe you should hire yourself a full-time policy wonk on hate crime. Have your people call my people. Think you have time to work your husband into your busy schedule?'

She looked at him with mischief in her eyes. 'I have time now.'

'I didn't mean sex, but hold that thought. I mean literally work for me. I need your help.'

Rina visibly brightened. 'You do?'

'Yes, I do,' Decker said. 'Since the vandalism, you've been buried in hate crimes.'

'Just H.R. 1082. We're about this close to getting the

law passed.' She pinched off an inch of air between her thumb and forefinger. 'It's not only a moral law, but a just law. And a broader definition of hate crimes will also make your life easier.'

'I'm sold. While you've been lobbying for it, I know you've been researching hate groups on the Net. If you could talk to Tom Webster about hate groups, it would be helpful to me.'

'My pleasure!' Rina said. 'If he wants the total picture, I'll introduce him to some people at the Tolerance Center.' A pause. 'You're not just doing this to make me feel good, are you?'

'No, honestly. I spoke with Tom about it today. Why should he struggle when you've done all the background work? It would help me tremendously.'

'Great!' Rina felt her spirits lighten. 'In the meantime, now that our family's together, maybe we should do something.'

'Like what?'

'How about a movie . . .' She hit her head. 'You've got to get back to work, don't you?'

'Yes. But don't let that stop you all from having a good time.'

'Sure.' Rina's smile lost some of its brilliance.

Decker said, 'While you were at the airport, I talked to Jacob.'

'About Ernesto's death?'

'Yes.'

'And?'

'Naturally, he's very upset. It's horrible. I hope I helped him, but I don't know if I did.'

'You must have said something right. Yonkie actually looked *happy* over dinner.'

'It's probably Sammy's presence. He really loves his older brother. I didn't realize how much until I saw the two together.'

'They're very close.'

Decker felt his throat clog. 'Thank you for providing me with such amazing children.'

Rina threw her arms around her husband's neck. 'Let's see if you still say that after you get the tuition bills.'

Oliver raked fingers through black, and by now, greasy hair. He felt hot and sticky and really needed a shower. 'If what Jacob says is true, that the Baldwins were using pull to get kids into college, I can suddenly see some new reasons for someone wanting them dead.'

It was nine in the evening, and Decker had decided that they should meet in an interview room because there was more space. He sat at the head of the table. The left side held Webster, Martinez, and Wanda Bontemps. The right side had Oliver and Dunn. Arranging themselves by partnership rather than by sexes. They were spent, but Decker gave them a great big A for effort. Files, folders and papers were spread over the table, intermixed with empty paper plates of pizza and lukewarm Styrofoam cups of coffee.

They were waiting for all the initial reports to come in. Ballistics was especially important. All were anxious to see if the bullet that killed Dee Baldwin matched any of the bullets responsible for the deaths of Ernesto Golding and Mervin Baldwin. Decker had put a rush on it, but a rush only meant something if someone in the lab was willing to speed it up.

'What are you saying, Scott?' Webster put down his coffee cup. 'Disgruntled parents whacked the Baldwins because their kid couldn't get into Harvard?'

Oliver said, 'Remember that mother who tried to murder a sixteen-year-old classmate of her daughter's because the other kid made cheerleading squad and her daughter didn't?'

'That was extreme.'

'Well, so is this,' Oliver said. 'Someone paid lots of money to Mervin to get little Jimmy into the big H, and the Baldwins failed to work their magic?'

'So why not return the money?' Wanda asked.

'What if there was no more money to return?' Oliver said.

'Maybe the guy was broke,' Martinez said. 'He sure spent a lot. One hundred and twenty grand to live in a beach condo while his house was being remodeled.'

Decker said, 'Did the Baldwins owe money?' No one spoke. 'So let's look into it.'

Webster said, 'Could be he owed money. Or could be he owed favors. Sometimes money and favors have a definite connection. You do favors in order to avoid paying money.'

Wanda said, 'So what did poor Ernesto have to do with any of this?'

'Wrong place at the wrong time?' Oliver suggested.

'I'm not so sure about that,' Decker said. 'Ernesto

had fallen in with some edgy folk before all this happened. He could have been the target.'

'I agree,' Martinez said, 'You should see these PEI weirdos. Besides, Oliver, you don't kill just because your kid doesn't get into Harvard—'

'Maybe it was Stanford.'

Martinez turned to Decker. 'You agree with me, right?'

Decker shrugged. 'You should have heard Jake talk about what kids are doing nowadays to get into the right colleges.'

'You should have heard what Maryam Estes said about it,' Oliver said. 'You wouldn't believe it.'

Marge said, 'Prep courses for the entrance exams, prep courses for the prep courses. And this is after they take prep courses to get into the right high schools and middle school. And of course you have to go to the right elementary school to even be considered by the right high schools. Which leaves us with pre-school. You know that kids have to apply for these hoity-toity *nursery* schools.'

Wanda made a face. 'How do you test kids for nursery school? They can't read.'

'Shapes,' Marge answered. 'Counting to ten. Colors.'

'Well, what if your child is two and still sucks her thumb?'

Marge said, 'According to Maryam, if your child gets rejected, it'll be an uphill battle.'

Wanda said, 'Maryam sounds idiotic.'

'I don't disagree, Wanda, but thems are the facts,' Oliver stated. 'Twenty grand a year so you can brag that your kid can tell the difference between a triangle and a square.'

Decker spoke to Martinez. 'Apparently the parents are very cutthroat about this kind of thing.'

Martinez said, 'So who'd you bribe to get Jacob into Johns Hopkins?'

'Jacob did it on his own. And even he claims that he got help . . . that his mother got him in by pushing the right buttons.'

Martinez said, 'But the fact remains that you didn't need Baldwin.'

'I might have hired him if I cared about the Ivies,' Decker said. 'The fact is I'm basically a blue-collar-type guy, and my wife is Orthodox. She cares more about how many nice religious Jewish girls there are on campus rather than the IQ of the student body.'

'Where's Sammy going?' Marge asked.

'Yeshiva University,' Decker said. 'No shortage of gray matter floating around there. Still my kids have friends who are pushed by their parents. Which to me is funny because my generation was supposedly the do-your-own-thing generation.'

Martinez laughed. 'Yeah, aren't we a bunch of old hypocrites.'

'I take exception to the word "old",' Oliver replied.

Decker said, 'Supposedly, even if you go to the right high school, you need people like the Baldwins to assure you get into the right college.'

'Exactly,' Oliver said. 'Now you're a parent, you invest all this money and time and effort into little Timmy getting into Harvard—'

'I thought it was little Jimmy,' Wanda said.

Oliver glared at her.

Wanda smiled back. 'Go on.'

'And then, little Timmy or little Jimmy doesn't get in,' Oliver said. 'I can see some unbalanced person taking his frustrations out on Dee and Mervin Baldwin.'

'What can people like Dee and Mervin Baldwin actually do for a kid who just isn't all that with it upstairs?' Webster said. 'No matter how much you drill the kid, if he doesn't have the raw matter, it isn't going to help.'

Decker said, 'They can practice test-taking with the kid. I'm sure there's some holdover from one test to another. If you practice enough, maybe you can raise your score a few points.'

'A *few* points, yes,' Webster said. 'But not several hundred points. I know enough about these entrance exams to know that much. As a matter of fact, if you take the SAT, then take it again and improve too much, it looks suspicious.'

Decker said, 'But maybe being psychologists, the Baldwins knew *how* to take the tests to maximize results. Also, since psychologists usually design the IQ tests, I'm betting the Baldwins had a pretty good idea about the contents.'

Webster said, 'How could they know better than anyone else? The tests are guarded secrets until they're posted.'

'I'm not saying that the Baldwins did know. Just that if test-taking was their specialty, they might make it a point to know.'

Oliver blurted out, 'Or maybe he actually did know.' He grinned. 'Inside info, ladies and gentlemen? It's happened before.'

Webster said, 'It would kill the Education Testing Service's reputation if an errant test was leaked prior to release date.'

'So Baldwin paid someone off,' Oliver said. 'The man was minting money, doing course preparation. I can see that college is big business. And that's what it always boils down to anyway. Business.'

'It would have to be more than just a payoff,' Webster said. 'It's not like the tests are posted on the Internet. The center's computers have their own nerve center not connected to any service provider. And I'm sure very few people have access to the pass code.'

'C'mon, Tommy!' Oliver barked. 'Computers aren't fail-safe. Look at this "I love you" virus back in 2000. Apparently, it was pretty damn amateurish and it shut down . . . what was it? Three major net providers?'

'He's got a point,' Marge said.

Martinez said, 'FYI, wasn't Ricky Moke under FBI investigation for hacking?'

'Interesting,' Decker said. 'But what does Moke have to do with the Baldwins?'

'A connection through Hank Tarpin?' Martinez suggested.

Decker sat back in his chair and looked at the ceiling. 'We've gone from the Baldwins as hapless victims to the Baldwins as white-collar, high-tech criminals with Moke as a fugitive neo-Nazi cohort. I think we need to back it up.'

'I think we need to get a warrant to search the Baldwins' office,' Oliver said. 'So what's up with that?'

Decker said, 'I'm hoping to get one first thing in the morning. It took a while to find someone who was even willing to listen. Rifling through the files of current, ongoing patients violates confidentiality agreements. You can shout Tarasoff as precedence, but since there's no immediate danger, I had to fudge a bit. I found a judge willing to go out on a limb, but he wants to sleep on it.'

'What should we do now?' Marge asked. 'The banks are closed, so we can't examine finances.'

Oliver said, 'We don't have a warrant, so we can't investigate the Baldwins' files.'

Webster said, 'By the time I got over to the PEI, Holt was gone.'

'How about Liu and the autopsy?' Decker asked.

Martinez said, 'I just checked. He hasn't even begun. Logjam. He hopes to know something by tomorrow.'

Decker said, 'So how about . . . we finish up the paperwork and call it a night.'

Everyone seconded the motion. Oliver even thirded it.

22

A mother's sleep was eternally light, a quick dash into Neverland where the conscious lay dormant, rousing to action at the wail of a hungry infant or the moans of a sick toddler. So ingrained was the reflex that even after the children had grown to independence, Rina's slumber remained permanently altered; the reason she awoke as soon as the bedroom door opened. It was not much more than a mere crack, but she sensed it even if she didn't hear it. It wasn't light yet, although the sky had turned from black to gray in anticipation of dawn. According to the nightstand clock, it was five-twenty-eight. Sammy stood at the door. She put her finger to her lips and waved him away, not wanting to wake up Peter. She didn't know what time Peter had come home, but she had gone to bed at midnight.

Quickly, she slipped on her robe and quietly closed the door behind her. She squinted as harsh lamplight seized her eyes, blinking several times as she tried to clear her thoughts. Sammy was dressed in street clothes, the leather straps from his small black prayer box – the *tefillin shel yad* – coiled around his right arm. On the widow's peak of his sand-colored hair sat the other prayer box – the *tefillin shel rosh*. Tall and handsome, her elder son cut an imposing figure.

'Are you all right?' she whispered.

'Yeah, yeah, yeah,' he replied. 'I'm just jet-lagged. I've been up learning since four in the morning. Then I saw daylight and decided to daven. I'm not the problem. There's some guy at the front door who wants to see Dad—'

'What? *Now?*'

'Yeah, he says it's important. He seems very agitated. I didn't know if I should wake Peter or what.'

'Did he give you a name?'

'Yeah, but I didn't get it totally. Something Gold—'

'Oh my goodness!' Rina slapped her hand to her breast. 'Carter Golding?'

'Yeah, yeah. Who is he?'

'His son was murdered—'

'Oh no! *He's* the one?'

Rina nodded. 'I'd better go see what he wants.'

Sammy stopped her. 'Don't you think you should wake up Dad?'

'First let me see what he wants.' She hesitated before she opened the door, then made the commitment. The man facing her was small and thin, his features blurred by lack of light and by facial hair. He was in constant motion, rocking on his feet, kneading his hands together, his eyes jumping about.

'I'm so sorry,' he coughed out. 'I thought that maybe . . . that your husband . . . that maybe he wasn't sleeping . . . I'll come back—'

'No, no, please come in, Mr Golding,' Rina pleaded. 'Please.'

He crossed the threshold of the door, stepping in just far enough to let Rina close the door. Wrinkled and disheveled, it was clear that he'd been wearing his clothes for a very long time. His movements were jerky, spasmodic – like a pinball confined to a very small machine. 'I shouldn't have come here.' Breathless. 'Waking you like some madman. I'm not a madman!'

'Of course you're not.'

'Your husband is still asleep? Don't wake him. I'll come back.' He stared at Sammy, then pointed at him with a shaking finger. 'What's on his arm . . . his head?'

Rina looked over his shoulder. '*Tefillin* . . . phylacteries.'

'My father had them. I don't know what he did with them. But I know he had them.' A pause. 'I wonder what became of them?' Golding began to pace, throwing his arms behind his back. Groucho Marx on methamphetamines. 'You're the one who sent out the flyer for the hate crimes council at the synagogue. We sent you some money, you know.'

'Yes, I know. Thank you.'

'You sent us a thank-you card – a nice one considering it was Ernesto who trashed the place.' Tears welled up in the man's eyes. 'He wasn't a bad kid, you know.'

'Of course.'

'He used . . .' Golding coughed to hide a sob. 'He used to talk about your husband. Did your husband tell you about that?'

'No, sir, he keeps his business confidential.'

'They used to talk . . . your husband and Ernesto. Ask him. Ernesto wasn't a bad kid.'

'I know—'

'No, you don't know!' Golding grabbed her arm until he and Rina were almost nose to nose. 'You *don't* know. But I'm telling you the truth. He had his problems, but he was a good kid!'

In the background, Rina could see Sammy walking toward the bedroom. Rina shook her head ever so slightly. Instead of pulling away, she placed her hand atop his. 'A parent knows his child better than anyone; I believe you, Mr Golding.'

The man's face crumpled, his chin quivering as a tear fell down a cheek. He let go of her arm, leaving behind fresh finger marks. 'Thank you!'

'Please sit down.'

'I shouldn't be here,' he whimpered. 'Bothering you—'

'Please sit down, Mr Golding. Let me get my husband for you.'

'You're being very hospitable . . . especially after what Ernesto did to your synagogue.' Then, Golding broke down, crying out dry, heavy sobs.

A few tears escaped from Rina's eyes. 'I'm so sorry. Let me get Lieutenant Decker. I know he'd like to see you.'

'No, he wouldn't!' The man continued to sob. 'I *yelled* at him yesterday! I *insulted* him!'

'I'm sure you did nothing of the sort,' Rina said softly. 'Besides, I yell at him all the time and he still talks to me. I'll get him for you.'

She started toward the bedroom, but Golding jumped up and grabbed her arm again. 'Please, I don't want to put you out.'

But Sammy had already gone into the bedroom. In a flash, Decker appeared, still bare-chested underneath a terry-cloth robe. His eyes were bloodshot, his hair was a red nest of tangles, and his skin felt as if it was on fire. Part of that was the adrenaline rush, his heart beating as fast as a jackhammer.

'Oh, God!' Golding exclaimed. 'I woke you up!'

'I'm fine, Mr Golding.' Decker noticed Sammy staring, his big brown eyes agape.

The boy said, 'Uh, I'll be in the kitchen.'

'I'll come with you.' Rina started to leave, but Golding grabbed her arm again. Decker moved in, but Rina held him off with the palm of her hand. Golding was too distraught to even notice Decker's defensive stance.

'Please stay,' Golding sobbed. 'You were so nice to write such a thank-you card.'

She looked at her husband, then said, 'Of course I'll stay.'

'Thank you!'

Again, Rina patted his hand. No one spoke for a few minutes, the only sounds being Golding's choked tears. Wordlessly, Rina extricated herself from his grasp and fetched a box of Kleenex. She handed it to him. 'How about a glass of water?'

'No, I'm all right.' He blew his nose into a tissue. 'I'm . . .' Another blow. 'Thank you.'

'You're welcome,' Rina said. 'Why don't we all sit down?'

When he didn't respond, Decker said, 'Please, Mr Golding. Have a seat right here.'

Decker sat him down in his special place – an oversized leather chair-and-a-half stuffed with down, complete with ottoman, his reading sanctuary whenever he was home. The rest of the furniture was feminine and frilly, upholstered with lots of blue gingham checks, and blue and white paisley prints. Lacy pillows and doilies abounded. A sweet little hand-loomed rug sat under an old-fashioned white rocker. Decker's chair looked like the fat sheik in the middle of his harem. He perched himself next to Rina on the couch.

Golding said, 'I'm sorry to have woken you up like this.'

'No, no,' Decker said. 'It's no problem, sir. Can we make you a cup of tea?'

'Don't bother.'

'It's no bother.' Rina was up. 'Herbal maybe? I have cinnamon, orange, chamomile, lemon—'

'Chamomile.'

'Sugar, lemon?'

'Plain.'

'I'll be right back.'

Golding whispered out a 'thank you', then turned his

attention to Decker. 'You must think I'm crazy.'

And how could the man be anything less than crazy after what had happened? Golding had on a light gray, coffee-stained sweatshirt and jeans.

Decker said, 'Is there something specific on your mind, Mr Golding, or did you just need to talk . . . or ask some questions maybe?'

He played with his beard. 'There is something I want to talk about. I just don't know how . . .' He swallowed back pain. 'Do you think you're going to find this monster?'

'Yes.'

'Then you have some ideas?'

'You'll be the first one to know when I have something definite.'

'When do you think that will be?'

'I don't know.'

'Soon? A week, a month, a year?'

'Every case is different. Right now, this case is top priority.'

He nodded. Rina brought in two giant-sized steaming mugs. 'Here we go!'

Golding took the tea, but didn't drink it. He used it to warm his hands. Tremors seized his body. He was shaking from internal cold. 'Sit down, Mrs Decker . . . please.'

Rina sat back down, giving Decker the other mug. He thanked her with a nod.

Golding said, 'There is something on my mind.'

Silence.

'I wanted to talk to you about this family thing.' He

pointed to his chest. 'About my father. Ernesto thought things about him. Things he told you . . . about my father being . . . you know . . .'

'I know,' Decker said.

'It isn't true,' Golding said. 'None of it. I swear to you, it isn't true. My father was a good man: a very righteous man and devout man. He wasn't a Nazi! He couldn't have been a Nazi.'

'Okay—'

'No! Not okay!' Golding's hands were shaking, and he splashed hot tea over them. He hardly seemed to notice, but he did put the cup down. 'You've got to believe me!'

'I believe you, sir.' Decker spoke calmly. 'Kids dream up the wildest things. Sometimes, I think they like to create problems for themselves. My own children are no exception.'

Golding sighed. 'They do, don't they?'

'Seems like it.'

'So why do you think Ernesto would make up something like that?'

Decker was thoughtful. 'He told me something about the dates not matching—'

'Dates?'

'When your father immigrated to Argentina, was it?'

Golding nodded.

'According to Ernesto, your father told you he had gone to South America in 1937. Ernesto told me that he had really immigrated later, in 1946 or 1947 – after the war. But kids oftentimes make mistakes.'

'Even if it wasn't a mistake, that doesn't make my

father a Nazi!' He bit his bottom lip. Blood trickled out. 'I just don't know much about my father. That's why I'm here.'

More silence.

'My father didn't talk about his past. No one did. I learned very quickly not to ask questions. But that doesn't make him a monster. He was kind and gentle and wouldn't even kill . . . b-b-bugs! Honestly. He used to wrap them up in a tissue and let them go outside.'

'My wife does that,' Decker said.

Golding's hands were rubbed raw. 'He wasn't a Nazi. But . . . Ernesto had some reason to be curious about him. He said he found an Isaac Golding who had died in the camps.'

'There could be more than one,' Decker said.

'True,' Golding answered. 'Either way, I want to find out who Isaac Golding really was. So I've come to you.'

It was Rina – the daughter of concentration camp survivors – who offered him absolution. 'It's past history. Does it really matter, Mr Golding?'

He looked up. 'Please call me Carter . . . and yes, it does matter. In a few days, I will bury my . . . my boy . . .'

He threw his palms over his face and wept, heart-wrenching sobs that were painful to witness. Rina and Decker had no choice but to wait him out.

Finally, Golding said, 'Nothing . . . no pain can compare to that. There is nothing you can do or say or tell me that will hurt worse than that. You cannot even hope to understand my pain, but as parents, you can . . . maybe imagine it.'

Decker noticed that Rina was silently crying. What was she thinking about? The unimaginable horror of losing a child? Her own set of baggage that included the death of a husband to cancer, the murder of a dear friend, and an untimely hysterectomy?

'So nothing you could tell me could be worse,' Golding said. 'My father's past is a mystery to me, and was a mystery to my son. I'd like to find out about it . . . to honor Ernesto. It was of interest to him, and I shut him down. Now I owe it to him to find out the truth.'

Decker was impassive.

Golding said, 'You don't think I should do it?'

'You're whipping yourself,' Decker said. 'You don't have to do that. You were a wonderful, caring father. I know that because Ernesto told me so.'

Water streamed down his cheeks. 'I was a good father.' He nodded vigorously. 'I was. I spent time with my children. I did my best. I wasn't perfect, but I tried.' Again, Golding blew his nose. 'But I owe this to my son's memory. And . . . I'd be lying if I didn't say . . . it would . . . complete something inside of me.' His eyes met Decker's. 'I don't know how to do it, though. You're a detective. I thought that maybe you could help. Maybe you know someone who specializes in that kind of thing.'

Decker ran fingers through his mussed hair. 'I know a few private detectives, but they're not genealogists. Plus, they're expensive—'

'Money isn't an issue.'

'There are no guarantees,' Decker said.

'There never are. I know that better than anyone.'

Rina said, 'Where was your father born?'

Golding regarded her. 'Somewhere in Eastern Europe. He never mentioned a specific place. You cannot believe how close-mouthed he was.'

Decker took a moment to digest that. 'Does he have any living relatives?'

'All gone,' Golding said. 'My grandparents died when I was quite young. There was also a sister . . . my aunt. She never married. She died when I was about ten.'

'I suppose you could try a genealogist,' Decker suggested.

Rina said, 'Mr Golding, what languages did your father speak?'

'Please call me Carter.' Golding thought a moment. 'English and Spanish, of course. He spoke a foreign language to his sister. I was under the impression that it was German.'

'German?' Rina asked. 'Are you sure it wasn't Yiddish?'

'I wouldn't know,' Golding said. 'The two languages are similar, correct?'

'Yes,' Rina said. 'Assuming your father was Jewish, there is a world of difference between the German-speaking Jews and the Yiddish-speaking Jews. Yiddish-speaking Jews were usually poorer – manual laborers, farmers, or merchants. German Jews were a different ball of wax. Lots of them were much more integrated into German society. In general, German-speaking Jews came from Germany. Hungarian-speaking Jews – like my parents – came from Hungary. Rumanian Jews came from Rumania. Lots of Czech Jews spoke Czech. But Jews from Poland usually spoke Yiddish if they came from what we call the pale area – a border area between Poland and Russia.'

Decker asked, 'Polish Jews didn't speak Polish?'

'The rare educated ones did; those that lived in the city did. But most Polish Jews were very poor and lived in these small border villages. They were ghettoized even before the Warsaw Ghetto became official . . . do you know about the Warsaw Ghetto?'

Both of them shook their heads.

Rina ran her hand over her face. 'When the Nazis were stepping up their eradication of the Jews, they herded them all in an area in Warsaw to keep track of them. It made the extermination easier. It's not important right now. Maybe it'll be important later on.'

Golding tapped his nose. 'And what does it mean if my father spoke Polish?'

'Did he?' Rina asked.

Golding waited before answering. 'Ernesto showed me some papers . . . in my father's handwriting. The language wasn't German. And it wasn't a romance language either. Maybe it was Polish.'

'All right,' Rina said. 'That tells me that your father was either an educated Jew or city Jew or . . . he wasn't Jewish, but a Pole.'

Decker said, 'Where did Ernesto get his information from?'

'I haven't the faintest idea. I . . .' His eyes misted

up. 'I haven't gone through his school papers. I suppose there might be information there.' He sighed. 'He told me that an Isaac Golding had died in a Polish camp. I don't remember the name. At that point, it didn't seem consequential. Maybe the written language was Russian.'

'You'd know if it were Russian,' Rina said. 'They have a different alphabet.'

'Yes, of course.'

Rina said, 'The big cities in Poland have some records, you know.'

'I know, but I don't know how to . . .' He sighed. 'Everything in that part of Europe is so foreign to me. My father . . . he gave me nothing about his past. He used to say that now we were in America, and that was all that mattered. He considered himself an American. He was very angry with me when the Vietnam War came and I protested against it. Though he never raised his voice, I'm sure he thought I was ungrateful. The subtleties of First Amendment rights were as foreign to him as the sixties' hippie, drug-laden culture.'

Rina cleared her throat. 'I was planning on going to the Tolerance Center in the next day or two. They have archivists there whose specialties are filling in blanks. If you give me Ernesto's school papers, maybe I can look through them—'

'Not until we do,' Decker interrupted. He regarded Golding. 'I'd like to go over your son's room first thing this morning.'

Golding nodded permission. 'If you think it will help

bring the monster to justice. I have my own opinions, of course.'

'Which are?'

'That the horror had nothing to do with my son,' Golding stated. 'Dr Dee Baldwin was murdered miles away from my boy. He was just in the wrong place . . .' The man looked away. 'You can go through his room if you have to. But I have my doubts.'

'Thank you,' Decker said.

'And if you find anything relevant to my father, you will give the papers to your wife . . . so she can check it out with the Center's archivist?'

And what could Decker say to that? 'Mr Golding—'

'Carter, please.'

'Carter, what if the information is . . . painful to you?'

'I already said that nothing could compare. I owe this to Ernesto. And I will do this for him! And if you can help me, you'd be doing something for Ernesto as well. But if there's a conflict, I'll hire someone privately.'

'It may come to that,' Decker said.

'In the meantime, maybe your wife can find out something.' Golding reached into his pocket and pulled out a colored Polaroid of an elderly man, Carter, and two burgeoning adolescents. 'The most recent picture I have of my father. Dad was notoriously camera shy.' He looked down. 'If he were a wanted man, that would make sense.'

Rina took the photograph and examined it – a study of three generations. Grandfather Yitzchak was flanked by Carter on the left and the boys on the right. Carter and his sons wore T-shirts, jeans, and big smiles. Grandfather Yitzchak had on an old narrow-lapel black suit, white shirt, and a thin tie to match. His expression was not exactly stern . . . more like shy. 'How old is this?'

'Four years ago. Dad was seventy-eight. He was the last of my family to go. Mom died ten years earlier.'

Rina nodded. 'And the boys?'

'Ernesto was thirteen, Karl was eleven.'

'All I can do is try.' Rina stood, snapshot still in hand. 'I'd better go check on Sammy.'

'The boy with the phylacteries?'

'Yes, he just got back from Israel.'

'Go check on him.' Golding stood and held out his hand. 'Thank you, Mrs Decker.'

She took his hand, securing the agreement to help him. As soon as Rina left, Golding began to pace, making tracks with mindless, nervous motion. 'I need to get back to Jill . . . and Karl.'

'When may I look at your son's room?'

Golding checked his watch. 'My goodness, it's early. How about in two hours? At eight or eight-thirty?'

'I'll be there.'

'Lieutenant, when can we bury our son? I know you're conducting an investigation, but my wife and I need some . . . some . . .'

'Closure.'

'Something tangible to weep over.' Again Golding looked away.

Decker said, 'I'll try to have him released as soon as possible. Can I help you with anything else?'

Golding shook his head. 'Not unless you can raise the dead.'

Rina's late husband's name was Lazarus. Decker kept his face neutral, not knowing if the name was an omen for positive outcome or irony.

23

Sipping coffee, Decker sat at the kitchen table, the paper opened in front of him, and pretended to be casual. 'I have problems with your searching for the identity of Golding's father, Rina. For all I know, it might be the reason behind the murder.'

Rina adjusted the kerchief on her head, then sliced strawberries into a bowl of cereal. 'All the more reason for you to find out what's going on.'

'I agree.' Decker looked up. 'It's exactly how you said it. All the more reason for *me* to find out. Me, not you.'

'And *which* of your detectives knows the area of post-holocaust Jews?'

'Rina—'

'Excuse me. I have to go feed your daughter.' She marched out of the kitchen, marching back in a minute later. 'You had no idea what questions to ask Golding. And even if you had stumbled upon the right questions, you'd have no idea what the answers would have meant.

And *you're* the best of the lot.'

'Now you're being chauvinistic.'

'Peter, I am doing the man a favor – parent to parent.'

'And I am trying to run a murder investigation.'

'Even better. I'll tell you everything I find out.'

Decker rolled his eyes.

'Don't give me that!' Rina scolded him. 'Didn't you ask me to take Tom Webster to the Tolerance Center?'

'To give him information on hate groups. Not for genealogy.'

'So while he's looking at hate groups, I'll talk to the archivist.' She looked at him with defiant eyes. 'Don't you have to be somewhere?'

'You're trying to get rid of me?'

Rina regarded her husband's hurt face. Sighing, she pulled up a chair and sat next to him. He put down the paper, took a final drink of coffee, and shrugged her off. 'I'll go now.'

'Stop.' A pause. 'I'm sorry.'

'Why do we have these stupid conflicts?' Decker growled. 'You shouldn't be involved in my business.'

'You had no qualms about asking me to take Tom Webster—'

'So now I changed my mind. Tom can figure it out himself.'

It was Rina's turn to be offended. 'Fine. Solve your own cases.'

'Thank you very much, I will.'

No one spoke.

'What is it, Peter?' Rina blurted out. 'An ego thing?'

'C'mon!'

Silence.

Rina checked her watch. 'Are you taking Hannah to school?'

'I will if you want me to.'

'She likes it. She enjoys time with her father.'

She got up. Decker held her arm. She looked at him with downcast eyes.

'I hate this!' he said. 'You're giving me heart palpitations.'

'That's caffeine. Or old age. Don't blame your palpitations on me!'

'Old age? That's mean, Rina! True . . . but mean.'

It was mean. Rina sat down. 'Sorry.'

'I'm worried,' Decker said.

'Peter, no one is going to come after me for trying to find Isaac Golding's true identity.'

'I'm sure you're right.'

Rina was touched by his admission. His fear came from caring. She leaned over and kissed his cheek. 'Peter, this is *your* case. I have enough obligations without adding conflict with you. Okay?'

'Yeah, yeah.'

'You're brushing me off.'

'I'm in a terrible bind. I want information that you can help me with, but I feel like I'm betraying some protective husband code by getting you involved.'

'Why don't you let me be the judge?' Rina hesitated. 'What do you *really* need from me?'

A good question. He said, 'Tom is perfectly capable of getting information from the Tolerance Center. But since you've been setting up this hate prevention council, I figured you've done lots of research work on local hate groups . . . You could give him some background, so he'll know how to ask the right questions.'

'That's certainly true.'

'And by your being there, you can help him ask the right questions if he gets stuck.'

'Fine.'

'Also, by being with someone he knows . . . even tangentially . . . he'll feel less like a fish out of water.'

'I have no problem going to the Center with him, Peter.'

Decker gave her a weak smile. 'I really do appreciate your help.'

She smiled back. 'I know.' A pause. 'Anything else?'

'No, that's it.'

'All right,' Rina said. 'But now I have a problem. You have to figure out a way to help Carter Golding so I don't appear to be going back on my word.'

A quandary. Decker said, 'Exactly how does one go about finding an anonymous concentration camp victim?'

'First of all, Isaac Golding isn't anonymous. He has a name. There are lists, Peter. The Center has archives.'

'So all that you'll be doing is looking at lists?'

'I don't really know.' Rina got up and poured a cup of coffee for herself. 'What exactly did Ernesto tell you?'

'That there was a discrepancy between the supposed date of his grandfather's arrival in Argentina and the actual date he did arrive. Then he told me that he had found an actual Yitzchak Golding, but he had died in the camps. I was thinking that maybe his grandfather just made up the name.'

'Could be, although it doesn't sound random to me. If Grandpa had been a Nazi who had wanted to pass himself off as a Jew after the war, what better way to present yourself than as a dead man? No one showing up to prove you wrong. Where was Ernesto's Yitzchak Golding from?'

'I don't know, but he supposedly died in a Polish camp.' Decker mulled over his thoughts. 'I believe he told me a name. I have his entire confession on tape. I'll replay and tell you the name he told me if you promise not to fink on me.'

'Scout's honor.'

'The camp wasn't Auschwitz, that much I remember. If you name some others for me, I may recognize it.'

She furrowed her brow. 'Auschwitz was the main camp in Poland. I don't know all the others by heart. Hold on. Let me get a Jewish encyclopedia.'

Rina was gone for several minutes. She came back holding a big blue tome. 'Let's see . . . Auschwitz, Betzec, Sobibor, Treblinka—'

'That's it.'

'Treblinka?'

'Yes, I'm positive.'

'Hold on.' Rina left and came back moments later, holding another blue volume. 'In operation from 1941 to 1943. It was designed as a liquidation camp – about 870,000 people exterminated—'

'Good Lord!' Decker couldn't fathom that many

people dying on one geographical spot.

'Auschwitz killed more,' Rina said. 'That's because Auschwitz was around longer. Almost three years longer.'

'What do you mean "designed" as a liquidation camp? Weren't they all . . . that?'

'Some of them – like Auschwitz – were officially labeled "forced labor" camps, others were "holding centers". Both are misnomers because the end results were the same. People were either murdered or died due to starvation, exposure or disease. According to this article, there are very, very, *very*, few survivors from Treblinka because its specific purpose was to exterminate the Jewish population of Poland.'

'Who was in control of it? The Germans or the Poles?'

'Germans, with the Poles being willing accomplices.' Her eyes skimmed across the pages, taking in the horrors with little emotion. 'Escapees who were caught were shot on the spot or hanged as examples . . . those that did make it into the surrounding area were turned in by the villagers. There were some efforts of resistance . . . Dr Julian Chorazycki . . . SS men's physician. He was an inmate—'

'Jewish?'

'Yes . . . he and some others gathered contraband weapons with the help of the Ukrainians, but he was caught and put to death. Zelo Bloch led an uprising of fifty to seventy men. He was also put to death. Then the Germans burned the camp down . . . about seven hundred and fifty escaped, but only seventy survived to see liberation.' Rina looked at her husband. 'If that was

Carter Golding's father, he was certainly one of the rarefied few – seventy out of eight hundred and seventy thousand. It defies logic.'

Decker said, 'Even if he had been one of the lucky ones, what are the odds that his mother, father, and sister also survived?'

'Nil,' Rina said. 'Ernesto was onto something. Where did he say he got his information from?'

'He claims he got it off the Internet,' Decker said. 'I think that's bogus. Does the Center have lists of survivors from Treblinka?'

'I'm sure they do.' Rina thought long and hard. 'Peter, what did you do with those awful pictures Ernesto left behind after he vandalized the synagogue?'

'We bagged them. They're somewhere in the bowels of the evidence room. What are you thinking? That they could be a link to Isaac's identity?'

'Maybe the dress or faces or area would point to a specific camp.'

Decker said, 'As I recall, most of them looked like anonymous dead bodies.'

'Anonymous dead Jews.' She was dispirited.

'I'll pull them from the evidence room, Rina. You never know.'

From the hallway, they both heard Hannah asking if it was time to go yet. Rina looked at the clock. 'Oh my goodness, it's a half hour past the start of school!'

Decker stood. 'That means I'm a half hour late.'

'I'll take her—'

'No, I'll take her. I want to take her.' Decker grabbed Rina to his chest before she could run off, and kissed her hard on the lips. 'I love you.'

'I love you, too. And you're not old, by the way!'

'I am old. But I don't care because I have a young wife . . . well, not so young anymore—'

'Now who's being mean?' Rina slugged him on the shoulder. 'Are you feeling okay about this, Akivelah?'

'I love when you call me Akivelah. It means you're not mad at me.'

'I'm never mad at you.'

'Nonsense, you're mad at me all the time.' He grinned. 'I'm just not home enough to see it. Watch yourself. Lots of kooks out there.'

'I could say the same for you.'

'You could. But it wouldn't help.'

The room was depressing because it was so static, as if expecting its occupant to walk in at any moment, like a puppy waiting for its tardy master. Decker could tell that once the space had been alive: a changing diorama reflecting Ernesto's whims and wishes, from the choice of CDs to the posters on the wall. The boy's workstation was almost 360 degrees of desktop, hugging the room. Ernesto had an elaborate stereo system, an elaborate computer system, a VHS player, a DVD player, a fax machine, and a phone – state-of-the-art wherever Decker looked.

The boy with everything: now he was a statistic.

On the shelving above the counters were rows of videos, stacks of CDs, dozens of athletic trophies, wrinkled candy wrappers, old letters, overdue library books, piles of papers, notebooks, textbooks, and about thirty paperbacks, most of them fiction. The room held three doors – one to the bathroom, another leading to a walk-in closet, and a third that connected to a common hallway. A queen-size bed sat in the middle of the floor and was covered by a comforter emblazoned with a leopardskin print. It made a perfect spot for sorting and stacking the piles of paper that Ernesto had left behind.

Decker pulled out the first stack and dug in.

Two and half hours later, he had gone through six years of Ernesto's life via his schoolwork. The boy was a decent student – better than Jacob had been in his old days – but not a superior student. He had organizational problems with his homework, with his math problems, with his essays. No surprise, judging by the entropy of the room, although the two aspects – neat room and organized schoolwork – weren't always correlated. Sammy was a slob, but systematic when it came to his papers. Jacob was compulsively neat, but disorganized. Paying arduous attention to detail, Decker checked every drawer and every shelf and went through the bedding. He looked behind the machines, knocked on walls, and checked the floorboards. He found lots of loose paper, but nothing regarding a family tree project. Furthermore, Decker couldn't even find notes or drafts or a hint of his research.

Maybe Ernesto had come to terms with his origins and had thrown out all the ancient history. There were no newsletters or computer printouts from any white supremacy or neo-Nazi groups, no flyers from PEI, and no photographs of SS officers or dead Jews. Decker didn't find any obscene letters from Ruby Ranger.

The bathroom was just as devoid of clues. On the countertops were acne creams, pills for seasonal allergies, a prescription dandruff shampoo. He searched through the towel cabinet, the sundry cabinet, the medicine cabinet. He opened old bottles and smelled them. Shook out a bottle of talcum powder, sniffed it, put it to the tip of his tongue and grimaced. It was talcum powder. Ernesto had no telltale colored pills, no hidden hypodermics, no contraband that Decker could detect. The most controversial item on the shelves was a box of condoms.

He moved on to the walk-in closet.

It had been stuffed with shirts – polo shirts, casual shirts, Hawaiian shirts, T-shirts (lots and lots of T-shirts), muscle shirts and tank tops. He had slacks in every color, he had jeans in every style, he had khakis, he had twills, he had corduroys, he had woolens, he had cottons, he had suits and a half-dozen sports jackets, including two preppy blue blazers. Ernesto owned racks of shoes.

Decker sighed and refrained from rubbing his forehead because his hands were gloved.

He began to open the built-in drawers.

More T-shirts. Dress shirts, too, laundered and folded. Shorts and bathing trunks. Underwear consisted of both jockeys and boxers – all of it very ordinary, except for the quantity, and very depressing.

Two separate sock drawers – one for athletic white crew socks, the other for colored dress socks that smelled slightly herbal.

Decker began unraveling balls of socks. He found a

stash, not more than a few ounces of marijuana. That was it for drugs. But he did notice something unusual about the athletic sock drawer. When it was pulled out to its maximum, it was shorter than the other drawer by at least six inches.

Decker tried to remove the drawer from the gliders so he could look behind it, but it remained firmly affixed. Resisting the urge to yank it off by brute force, he applied reason instead of frustration. There had to be some kind of release button. He removed all the socks and pored over the empty drawer. Seeing nothing, he felt with his fingertips, and discovered a small depression not much bigger than a pen nub in the back left-hand corner. He took out a pen and punched the depression. Immediately, the drawer loosened from the brackets. Decker took it out and peeked inside the dead space.

Behind it was a tiny lock box, shut tight by a combination lock. He took out the box and hefted it. It was surprisingly light. The dilemma now was whether to bother the parents for the sequence of numbers or just to pick it.

He opted to bother the parents, specifically Carter, who wasn't aware of the combination because he hadn't even been aware of the box. He was defensive, but it was born out of protectiveness of his son's memory.

'What do you expect to find?' Golding said.

'I don't know. Maybe drugs.'

'And if it's drugs, it hardly matters, does it?'

'Unless he was dealing, sir. That could be a reason for his murder.'

'He wasn't dealing.'

'He was using. I already found a small stash in his socks. It could be he has a brick in there, that he broke off a little for personal use.'

Golding said nothing, a tormented and torn man.

Decker said, 'What was Ernesto's birthday?'

An easy question that even Golding could answer. He gave it to him, albeit reluctantly. After fiddling with the right/left of the dial, the lock finally popped. No drugs, no firearms, no letters, no family report, but lots of incriminating pictures that filled the entire space. Not pornography, but obscene. Men in striped prison garb, all of them dead. About twenty black and white snapshots and all of them in perfect focus, with each man holding a different death mask. Some had open mouths, others had open eyes, but they all wore the skeletal face of starvation.

Golding stared in horror. 'These are repulsive . . . disgusting. Get them out of my sight!'

'I want to take them—'

'Take them! Get them *out* of here!'

Decker hid them from Golding's view. 'These are original photographs. Any idea where Ernesto might have picked these up?'

'No!' Golding whispered in abject dread. 'No! How would I *know*?' His eyes began to leak tears. 'Please just take them and get out of here!'

'I'm sorry to intrude—'.

'Please, just *go*!'

'Mr Golding, are you sure that you still want us to delve into your father's past?'

'Yes.' Slowly, Golding focused his eyes on Decker's face. 'Yes, I want your wife to look into my father's past. I want to know about it. I *need* to know about it. But that doesn't mean it has to be shoved in my face.'

24

Usually, she took a combination of freeways and canyons to go 'over the hill'. But today, since she wasn't stopping at her parents' house, it was pure speed until she hit the Robertson Boulevard exit on the 10 East, heading north though the haunts of her childhood.

It had been almost two decades since she had lived in her old neighborhood. The area had become so Jewish that, except for the palm trees, it felt as regional as Brooklyn. Not that she didn't have occasion to go back to the city, but she rarely went beyond her parents' house in North Beverly Hills. The valley's *Frum* community was self-contained – from cheap pizza joints for the kids, to family restaurants with booths and wine. Kosher butchers and bakeries weren't problematic, so why should she bother to travel? Still, the area felt nostalgic, passing all the kosher establishments, the fruit and vegetable storefronts, as well as the Jewish bookstores that sold *sepharim* as well as religious articles. Even the independent food market, Morry's – which was actually owned by Irv – catered to the neighborhood inhabitants, carrying hard to get items such as kosher cheeses and kosher flour tortillas.

So many religious schools and yeshivas in the area, they overflowed with children, spitting in the face of Hitler. So it was only natural that a holocaust memorial would find its permanent home among those who had lived through the inferno firsthand.

Rina's own parents – both of them camp survivors – were getting on in years. Her father now walked with a cane, and her mother was slower in gait as well as in speech. They were still sharp mentally, but sometimes the pain of old crimped their smiles. They loved Hannah, but oftentimes Rina could sense that the little girl was just too much for them. She didn't bring her as often as she had brought the boys, and that saddened her.

She glanced at Tom Webster, seated beside her, hands in his lap, eyes staring out the windshield. She had gotten the Volvo washed before she picked him up, but it still smelled a little stale. But perhaps that was due to L.A. smog rather than the condition of her station wagon. The detective hadn't said much since she picked him up from the stationhouse. No doubt he was a little nervous being around the boss's wife, a strange Jewish lady who wore kerchiefs on her head, and long sleeves rolled up to her elbows even in the summer. Tom was about as gentile as it got with his blond hair, blue eyes, and sharp features, as well as that thick southern accent. Perhaps he was antsy about visiting the Tolerance Center as well. Webster was as out of his element as she was in. She knew she should make an effort to talk to him. He sat stiffly in a blue suit, white shirt, and blue tie. Since both of them were dressed in hot clothing, she blasted the air-conditioning in the car.

'Anything you want to ask me?'

Tom turned and looked at her, his hands remaining in his lap. 'No, ma'am, not at the moment.' His voice was tight. 'Although I reckon later on I'll have lots of questions.'

'We're not going to the museum. The research offices are across the street. That's where the library and the archives are located until they finish remodeling.'

'All right.'

'Have you ever been in this neighborhood before?'

'I can't say that I have, though I've been in Beverly Hills a couple times when they had the classic car shows on Rodeo Drive. Ever been down there? They close off the roads and make a big street fair out of it. It was fun, especially for my boy. He likes cars.'

'I imagine they have some impressive automobiles.'

'To me, they were very impressive. But I guess they're run-of-the-mill for the city's well-heeled residents.'

Rina said, 'My parents live in the area and drive a Pontiac.'

Webster blushed and stammered out something by way of an apology.

'Oh please!' Rina smiled. 'My parents are well-heeled, but not interested in cars. Peter likes cars. He loves his Porsche. My younger son, Jacob, likes cars, too. He likes hot rods.'

'A kid after my own heart.'

'He likes the Viper and the Sheldon . . . is that right?'

'Shelby?'

'Yes, that's it.' Rina laughed. 'My elder boy couldn't care less. He lives in his head. Funny how that works.'

'Yeah.' Webster stretched uncomfortably. 'So . . . you grew up around here?'

'Yes, I did.'

'But not the lieutenant.'

'Oh no . . .' Rina smiled. 'He grew up in Gainesville, Florida.'

'Really?' Webster seemed surprised. 'He's more of a good ole boy than I thought.'

'Very much so.'

Webster started to talk, but stopped himself. Rina, however, knew what his question would be if he dared to ask it. How in the world did she and Peter meet? They met on a case. He was the principal investigator; she was a principal witness. They didn't have anything in common. He was worldly, she was provincial. She was religious, he was secular. He was divorced, she had been widowed. They had come from different worlds, and it shouldn't have ever come to pass.

Except that there was this incredibly strong physical thing.

She smiled to herself.

That was what Webster wanted to know. But she didn't tell him any of it, instead returning her attention to the road, maintaining a professional distance that made them both feel comfortable.

The actual museum was a towering edifice of pink and black granite; the offices across the street much more utilitarian. They walked into a tiny lobby secured by a guard, Webster showing his badge, Rina writing down their names on the sign-in sheet. The sentry radioed their arrival through a walkie-talkie, and a minute later a fifties-plus, pencil-thin woman came through the parted doors of one of the four elevators. Dressed in a sheath of black, she had startling blue eyes and her head was a nest of inky, short curls. She could have been Rina's much older sister. She kissed Rina's cheek.

'How are you doing, darling? Your husband must be going crazy with those awful murders.'

'Yes, it is awful. That's one of the reasons why we're here. This is Detective Tom Webster. He needs information.'

The woman gave him her hand. 'Did we ever meet before?'

Her Long Island accent was as broad as a put-on.

Webster said, 'I don't b'lieve—'

'Yes we did, yes, we did.' She hit her head with a hand topped by long, red, manicured nails. 'But it wasn't in a professional capacity. It was at . . .' Again, she hit her head. 'Wait, wait . . . Baja Mexico, the fast-food joint, not the country. Your son ordered a chicken fajita grande and shared it with my grandson, who ordered that vegetarian burrito. Your wife was very pregnant. That must have been like . . . seven, eight months ago at one of those car rallies in B.H.' She jabbed the elevator button. 'What'd she have – boy or girl?'

Webster stared at her. 'Uh, a girl—'

'Oh, how wonderful! She got her girl. She really wanted a daughter, but didn't say anything to you because she didn't want to upset you in case she had another boy. Tell her congratulations.'

Webster was struck silent. The elevator doors opened and they all stepped inside. As soon as they closed, the woman smiled, showing white teeth. 'Did I say my name? Kate Mandelbaum. What was your wife's name? Karen?'

'Carrie.'

'That's right. And don't look so concerned about not remembering me. I make it a practice to memorize people. It comes in handy in my line of work.'

They got out on the third floor. Kate took them down a long corridor, her buttocks swaying because she was marching in ultra-high heels. As soon as she got into her office, she pressed the blinking message-machine button and listened while sorting through a stack of written phone numbers.

'Hi, Kate—'

She disposed of that message.

'Hey, Katie—'

Fast-forwarded through that one.

'Kate, it's Neil. I was wondering if you could take on the Farkas file—'

'No, I cannot!' She erased that one.

'Hi, Grandma. It's me . . . Reuven. I was wondering if you could come to my school for Grandparents' Day.

I'm gonna be in the choir, too. But I don't have a solo. Call me back at—'

She fast-forwarded the message. 'Like I don't know the number.' She punched it in via speed dial. 'Hello, darling. I got your message and of course I'll come to the school. Tell me when and where. I love you, darling. Bye.' She fell down on the chair and fanned herself with a flyer. She spoke to Rina. 'You want me to tell him about hate groups? By now, you must know as much as I do.'

'That's quite a compliment,' Rina answered.

Webster took out a notebook. 'I b'lieve you've talked to one of my colleagues in the past . . . Wanda Bontemps.'

'Sure, I know Wanda,' Kate answered. 'So, you work with her?'

'Same geographical area, different detail. I'm in Homicide.'

'Then you must think white supremacists had something to do with the murder of those two psychologists. Wouldn't surprise me. Racists hate shrinks almost as much as they hate Jews.'

'Most of the shrinks are Jewish,' Rina said.

'Yeah, that just adds to their sense of paranoia that the Jews are out to get them. Turn their brain into mush . . . like there was something there to begin with.' Kate turned to Webster. 'Actually, I heard it was a gay thing. The wife caught her husband and the boy in a compromising position.'

'It's an ongoing investigation,' Webster said.

'That means he can't talk about it,' Rina said.

Kate said, 'Ernesto Golding – the boy who was murdered along with Mervin Baldwin – he vandalized your synagogue, right?'

Rina nodded.

'So you think there's some kind of connection?'

'Beats me,' Rina said. 'I'm just here to help Detective Webster.'

'C'mon, your husband must tell you things.'

'No, he really doesn't.'

'I don't believe you.'

'America's the land of free thought,' Rina answered.

'Very funny. Anyway, Detective, what do you want to know that Wanda couldn't tell you?'

Webster said, 'Wanda's great at investigating hate crimes like Ernesto Golding – vandalism by bored, white, rich kids. Triple murders are another ballgame. Right now, we're looking into everything including local white supremacy organizations.'

'How local?'

'Southern Calif—'

'So-Cal is teeming with the critters. Starting in San Diego environs is Tom Metzger territory. You know about Tom Metzger?'

'Yes, ma'am. American Nazi Party—'

'No, the ANP was started by George Lincoln Rockwell, and that's based in Chicago. Not to be confused with the home of the NSDAP which is based in *Lincoln*, Nebraska. Metzger's party is the White Aryan Resistance – WAR.'

'What's the difference?' Webster asked.

'Nomenclature. They're all hatemongers.'

'How many groups are there in Southern California?'

'Twenty . . . twenty-five. That doesn't mean So-Cal is being overrun with these clowns, only that it's hard to tell you specific numbers because the groups are constantly shifting.'

'How about some names?'

'I know there's a chapter of the World Church of the Creator—'

'Who are they?' Webster asked.

'An offshoot of the American White Party . . . Matthew Hale,' Rina answered.

Kate said, 'Hale took over in 1995, maybe '96. They're white supremacists based on social Darwinism – survival of the fittest. They don't care who you are as long as you're white. They're atheists as opposed to the Christian racist sects who obviously use Christianity to rationalize their racism. Each ethnic group more or less has its own racist counterpart – the Latinos have Aztlan, African-Americans have the Nation of Islam. Whites have lots to choose from – branches of the Klan, the neo-Nazis, the Straight Edges, the Skinheads, the Peckerwoods—'

'Peckerwoods?' Webster laughed. 'Why would anyone in their right mind call themselves a Peckerwood?'

'It was a derogatory term for blacks,' Kate said. 'Peckerwoods use drug money to finance their neo-Nazi activities, as opposed to groups like the Hammerskins, who supposedly disavow the drug trade. Now, that's the overt party line. The differences are teeny-tiny and becoming more teeny-tiny everyday.'

Rina said, 'I think Detective Webster is specifically

interested in the Preservers of Ethnic Integrity, because its home base is in the North Valley.'

'The Preservers of Ethnic Integrity.' Kate nodded. 'They were originally a splinter from the World Church of the Creator. Over the last four years, they've worked really hard to sanitize their act. For instance, they don't talk about white supremacy or even the white race. Instead, they use terms like the integrity of the *European-American*, to put it in the same category as African-American or Hispanic-American.' She sat down at her desk, moving the computer mouse until her flying-object screen saver disappeared. 'I'm sure that PEI has a Web site.'

'They do.' Webster gave her the URL page number. 'I was just hoping that you could tell me more than the stuff I picked off the Internet.'

'Well, first let's look at what they're preaching. Often the buzzwords will tell me something about who they associate with.' As soon as Kate brought up the Web site, she flinched. The screen was alit in vivid color and was three-dimensional. It showed a detailed, three-dimensional Uncle Sam standing guard over a topographical map of the United States. 'Well, the graphics are new . . . very high quality. A pro job. They must have gotten an infusion of money somewhere.'

'Where would the money come from?' Webster asked.

'I don't know, and that's a problem. Recently, two white supremacists up in Silicon Valley sold their business to a major computer company for over a hundred million dollars. They financed this massive mail-out of hate literature up in the tri-state area – Washington, Oregon, Idaho. Right now, their dot-com money is paying for Garvey McKenna's defense.'

'I don't know him,' Webster said.

'He's a violent racist,' Rina said. 'Sacramento area. He was involved in the arson of two synagogues and one black Baptist church. He's currently being tried on robbery and assault charges of a Jewish jeweler in that area.' Rina frowned. 'Wasn't he convicted?'

'It's on appeal,' Kate answered. 'It's really depressing. One of the ways we hit these bastards is with lawsuits – sue 'em until they're broke. With an influx of techno-money, it makes it harder for us to do our job.'

'What about the Preservers of Ethnic Integrity?' Webster asked.

'I don't know who's funding them.'

Rina asked, 'How many people log on to this kind of Web site?'

'This one in particular . . .' Kate punched up some keys. 'It's got about seventy hits a day. Some of the users have cookies – identifiable pixels – that act as a computer trail. We can find out where they go from here, what other sites they have visited. A lot of them have traceable pixels, so we can tell the point of origin for their messages.'

'The exact residence?' Webster asked.

'No, but the city oftentimes. The Internet is a sneaky thing. It professes privacy, but in reality it leaves a large electronic trail. You just have to know where to look for it.'

'So you keep tabs on the people who've hit these Web sites?'

'We can't possibly keep tabs on all of them, but if a name pops up a certain amount of times on different sites, we'll start a file on him or on her. I can't get over the sophistication of these graphics.'

'Ever hear of a guy named Ricky Moke?' Webster asked.

'Ricky Moke,' Kate said. 'No. Who is he?'

'That's what we're trying to figure out,' Webster said. 'His name showed up on the FBI list for computer hacking. When the synagogue was vandalized six months ago, I interviewed Darrell Holt at PEI. His assistant, a child named Erin Kershan, mentioned him to us. But no one seems to know who he is.'

'I'll look him up.'

'What about Darrell Holt?'

'He's been around for a while,' Kate said.

'Somebody told me he's been with PEI for about four years. Does that sound right?'

'Yes, it does.'

'So Darrell came right when PEI started to clean its image,' Rina commented. 'Maybe he was behind the sanitation effort.'

'That sounds logical,' Kate said. 'Darrell comes down with a college education – UC Santa Cruz—'

'I thought it was Berkeley,' Webster said.

'Maybe it was Berkeley. He was a radical turned conservative – which isn't at all unusual for these guys. Tom Metzger was a communist before he became a Nazi. I'll plug Holt into the computer later. Right now, let's see what PEI is up to. Okay, okay, here's their pitch. They're now railing against the New World Order—'

'Which is?' Webster asked.

'Anything that espouses cooperation and peace between countries,' Kate said. 'When Bush senior was president, he often made mention of a New World Order. That fed these crackpots' paranoia of government conspiracies. They began to profess anarchy like blowing up government buildings. Willis Carto, who lives in So-Cal, out in Escondido, publishes a newspaper called *The Spotlight* – one of the oldest anti-Semitic machines. Now it's almost exclusively anti-NWO. Maybe PEI is some sort of outcropping from Escondido. Maybe that's where they're getting their funding for the fancy graphics.'

'If Ricky Moke exists,' Rina said, 'and if he's a computer person who's also aligned with PEI – maybe he's doing the graphics gratis.'

Webster liked that idea and told her so. He looked over Kate's shoulder as she scrolled down the site. She said, 'No, PEI can't be aligned with TWCOC. They're anti-Third Position.'

Rina said, 'The Third Position states that nationality is irrelevant as long as you're white.'

'You're white,' Webster told Rina. 'Could you join?'

Kate broke in. 'Actually, she could because The Third Position doesn't believe that white Jews are really Jewish. So if she dropped her identity as a Jew and preached white supremacy, they'd probably take her in.'

Webster said, 'You know that Darrell Holt is kinda black.'

Kate raised her head from the screen and thought a moment. 'How can you be kinda black? That's like being kinda pregnant.'

'He looks biracial or multi-racial,' Webster said. 'You've never seen him?'

'Just pictures. He claims he's Cajun. To me, he looks typical Na'leans.'

'Actually, he claims he's Acadian from Canada – Nova Scotia. Which I'm thinking might be true, because Nova Scotia Acadians have black descendants.'

'Then it would make sense that he'd be anti-Third Position,' Rina said.

'So now we got a guy who's a segregationist and a racist, but not a white supremacist because he's got black blood in him,' Webster said. 'So why didn't he align himself with a group like Nation of Islam?'

'Maybe he tried to do that up at Berkeley, and he wasn't black enough,' Rina said.

Webster smiled. 'Wouldn't that be a hoot? Someone wanting to be a racist, but too much of a mix to fit in with any of the groups.'

'So he starts his own group,' Rina said.

'No, PEI was started longer than four years ago,' Kate said.

'But it changed images four years ago,' Webster reminded her.

'You said it yourself, Kate,' Rina said. 'Holt made several transformations.'

'Why don't you look Holt up?' Webster suggested.

'First let me shut this down . . .' She exited the official PEI site and plugged in Darrell Holt as a keyword. 'He has his own Web site . . . linked to PEI.'

Webster said, 'Who started PEI?'

'I believe that it was originally a splinter group from the Methods of Mad White Boys – one of Garvey McKenna's survivalist militia groups up in the Idaho area.'

'Survivalist militia group,' Webster repeated. 'Is the man from military stock?'

'I believe so. Marines if I'm recalling correctly.'

'Why doesn't that surprise me?' Webster said. 'Does the name Hank Tarpin ring a bell?'

'Not until thirty seconds ago,' Kate answered. 'Holt's Web site is linked to Tarpin.'

25

Decker said, 'If Tarpin murdered the Baldwins because of his racist beliefs, why did he wait so long?'

'He needed help,' Oliver answered. 'The Baldwins had a variety of psychos going through their nature camp. Tarpin had to find the right one.'

'So you're saying it took him, what . . . eight years to find the right psycho?' Wanda Bontemps was skeptical.

'Tarpin is a patient man,' Oliver answered.

Wanda didn't dispute this. Scott had seniority, and she didn't want to piss him off by arguing with his conjectures that nobody else was buying, either. It was almost two in the afternoon, and Decker's office was as stuffy as a gym sock. The desk fan had been turned up to the max, but it wasn't cooling much. It *was* blowing papers all over the place. Decker had run out of coffee mugs to use as weights for his paper piles. The group was fanning itself with flyers of the police Fourth of

July picnic at Rodgers Park. Have a safe and sane fourth and enjoy the city fireworks. The Loo was waiting for the pathology reports, waiting for the ballistic reports. Maybe Forensics would point to a killer.

Marge said, 'Pardon my ignorance, but aren't the Baldwins, being therapists, supposed to be savvy when it comes to reading people? You're saying that they didn't have an inkling that Tarpin was out to get them?'

'They were arrogant,' Oliver persisted. 'You know, kind of like that Greek thing . . . pride before the fall.'

'*Hubris*,' Marge answered.

'How'd *you* know that?'

Marge stiffened. 'First of all, Scott, I'm not a moron. Secondly, Vega's studying *Oedipus Rex* in school.'

'Tarpin was the first one to find the bodies,' Oliver said. 'He was the only one capable enough to pull it off. The kid that Webster talked about . . . Riley Barns. He thought he saw a couple of shadows.'

Decker said, 'Barns was vague. He might have seen shadows; he might have been dreaming.'

'He wasn't dreaming,' Oliver insisted. 'He saw two shadows – Holt and Tarpin. They're both survivalists; they're both militia based. They wait until everyone's asleep, they slip into camouflages, do Baldwin and Ernesto, then slip back into the woods. Tarpin goes back to the boys, Holt does Dee—'

Martinez said, 'Scott, it's just as likely that Dee Baldwin whacked herself in remorse for whacking her husband in a fit of rage after she found him with Ernesto.'

Marge made a face. 'I don't believe that for a minute.'

'Well, you didn't see her positioning. Consistent with suicide.'

Webster said, 'Tarpin associated with bad news, Bert. Y'all should've seen the literature on Garvey McKenna and his militia – the Methods of Mad White Boys.'

'They're crackpots,' Martinez said.

'That don't mean they aren't evil,' Webster retorted.

'So maybe that's why Tarpin broke away from them,' Martinez suggested.

'Why are you defending a jerk like Tarpin?' Oliver asked Bert.

'I'm not *defending* him,' Martinez said, bristling. 'I think it's odd that Tarpin and Holt – even with their racist views – would twiddle their thumbs for years before murdering the Baldwins. Especially since he and Holt may have known each other for years.'

'Maybe a money motive was introduced,' Wanda said.

'There's a thought,' Oliver said. 'Someone in PEI paid Tarpin to murder the Baldwins because the Baldwins were liberals, asshole shrinks, and PEI knew that Tarpin could get them easier than anyone else.'

Decker made a face. 'I don't remember hearing that the Baldwins were crusading against PEI or any hate group. They seem like an odd target.'

'Isn't Ernesto's father very liberal in his politics?' Wanda asked.

'Aha!' Oliver said triumphantly. 'Tarpin got three in one day.'

'Ernesto was murdered, not his dad,' Marge said.

'You want to cripple someone, you attack their children,' Oliver said.

'That's true.' Decker formulated his thoughts. 'But if Tarpin did it, he certainly cast himself in the limelight. There are safer ways to murder someone.'

Martinez said, 'Exactly. Why would Tarpin set himself up?'

' 'Cause he's a dumb-shit racist,' Oliver said.

'Give me a motive, Scott,' Martinez said, 'other than "he's a dumb-shit racist".'

'That isn't enough?'

'No, being a dumb racist doesn't mean you're a triple murderer,' Martinez said.

'Doesn't mean you're not.'

'This is beginning to sound infantile,' Marge said.

Wanda interjected, 'Is it possible that one of the camp boys glommed on to Tarpin and took one of his racist ideas to the extreme?'

'Anything's possible,' Decker said. 'I suggest we start with what we know. Plot A – a triple murder. Plot B – double murder, suicide.'

'The killer used a silencer,' Marge said. 'If it were an impulsive thing for Dee, she wouldn't have brought a gun and a silencer.'

Martinez said, 'Maybe she suspected her husband years ago and was just building up the courage. The thing is, we don't know.'

'Bert's right,' Decker said. 'What we do know is that Hank Tarpin is still alive and was up there at the time of the shooting. We know that Hank Tarpin found the bodies. We know that Tarpin – along with Holt – is a member of PEI. We know that Tarpin is a Marine, like Garvey McKenna. We need to talk to Tarpin again.'

Martinez said, 'Even though we've already interviewed him for four hours without an attorney and couldn't come up with anything?'

'Try him again,' Decker said. 'See if you can invent a plausible story that won't send him running for legal cover.'

Marge said, 'How about . . . we suspect that the Baldwins were using pull to get kids into universities, and we want Tarpin's opinion about it.'

'That isn't a story, that's the truth,' Oliver said. 'The Baldwins *were* using muscle to get their kids into the top schools.'

Decker said, 'Even better. It'll make us more believable.'

'Loo, Tarpin isn't going to know anything about that,' Martinez said. 'He's basically a drill instructor.'

'I'm not so sure,' Decker said. 'Maybe some of the kids have talked to him about how they were depending on the Baldwins to get them into universities, and that's why they agreed to attend the Baldwins' nature camp. If you have a better ploy, Bert, I'm here to listen.'

Silence.

'Good, so I'm putting Bert and Tom on Tarpin.' Decker wrote down the assignment in his logbook. 'Next, we need to get hold of Maryam Estes at the Baldwins' office.'

'Did the warrant come through?' Marge asked.

'Not yet.' Decker looked up from his notepad, his

eyes jockeying between Marge and Oliver. 'But even if you could technically look through every single file, you'd need to narrow it down. So try to get Estes to help you. I want you two to find out if there were any kids or parents who held a grudge against the Baldwins. Any questions?'

There were none.

'We're on a roll.' Decker regarded Bontemps. 'You can call up the Board of Psychological Examiners and find out if there have been any complaints against the Baldwins in the past . . . oh . . . how about ten years? Also, check out the Baldwins' bank account, real estate holdings, assets, anything you can get your hands on. See if you can't get an idea of what they're worth or if there was big money going in and out. When you're done with that, check out insurance. What kind did they have, who was the beneficiary, who had something to gain by the Baldwins' deaths.'

Martinez said, 'Someone should find out if the Baldwins had marital problems. It would support a murder/suicide theory.'

Decker said, 'Wanda, nose around into their marriage as well. Anything on Ruby Ranger's whereabouts?'

Wanda said, 'I do a round of calls each day. No one up north has spotted the car.'

'So maybe she's not up there. But keep checking.' He wrote her assignment in the book. 'I think we're all set for the time being. I'm going down to the morgue to see what Pathology has come up with. The body was released an hour ago. The funeral is set at six o'clock and everyone should be there. Whatever happened, even if Ernesto was involved in his own demise, it still was a terrible tragedy for the parents. Anyone have something important to add, talk now.'

Silence ensued.

Decker stood up. 'Adios, amigos, and good luck.'

Most of the library's free floor space had been taken up with boxes and folding chairs from last night's lecture – a very successful event with over two hundred in attendance according to Georgia Rackman, the Center's primary archivist. She was a big woman with thick wrists and ankles and big hair – bleached blonde and sprayed stiff. Her face was round, open, and smooth, her brown eyes emphasized by a heavy coat of eyeliner. She spoke with a heavy Texas drawl, and made no excuses when her voice elevated above acceptable volume levels.

'In Dallas,' she exclaimed, 'we do everything on a grand scale!'

The library was filled with standard bracket shelving that held thousands of tomes, all of them dedicated to the ashes of war. So many titles . . . too many memoirs: *The Archives of the Holocaust*, *The Holocaust and the History of the Rise of Israel*, *The Jews of Warsaw*, *The Death Camp Diaries*, *The Warsaw Uprising*, *Walking with Ghosts* . . . But Jews weren't the only ethnic group represented. There were also sections on the massacres of the Armenians, the bomb drops and subsequent carnage wreaked upon the cities of Hiroshima and Nagasaki, the annihilations of the Cambodians under Pol Pot, the civil war between the Hutus and Tutzis in

Africa, the bloodbath in the Belgian Congo. It was clear to Rina that no one group could claim its persecution as unique – a very sad commentary on the human condition.

The small library supported one full-time librarian, one full-time archivist, one part-time archivist, and two male exchange students from Austria who satisfied their country's military obligations by working for the Center for a year.

Georgia sat at her desk in front of her computer and sifted through the black and white photographs that Rina had given her. 'They don't tell me much. I don't even know if they're authentic. The paper looks too new.'

Rina mulled over the options. 'You can do a lot with computers nowadays. Or maybe they're recently printed but taken from old negatives.'

'Now, there's a thought.' Georgia looked. 'Unfortunately, they don't tell *me* anything specific. But I'll show them around. Almost no one survived Treblinka. You know that.'

Rina sat next to her. 'I know that.'

'It would help a great deal if you had that piece of paper with the Polish writing. It could be a work permit, it could be a visa, it could be transport papers . . . it would tell us a lot.'

Rina sighed. 'I'm sure if Mr Golding had it at the tip of his fingers, he would have given it to us.'

'And he's not sure if the language is Polish?'

'That's correct.'

'It makes a difference. Because there were lots of

Jews who came through the Warsaw Ghetto, especially at the end – before the city was bombed out of existence. There were Czechs, Estonians, Latvians, Lithuanians, Danes, Swedes . . .' She held up her hands. 'The Nazis were liquidating them as quickly as they could find them. It would really help to have more information.'

'I bet Mr Golding wishes he had more as well. When I spoke with him this morning, he was in a terrible state. I'm sure he doesn't remember hardly any of the conversation.' Rina sighed. 'Poor, poor man.'

'Why is he bothering with this now? Doesn't he have more important things to think about?'

'Maybe he doesn't want to think, Georgia. Besides, men deal with pain by being proactive. Females talk.'

'I see you've been reading those pop psychology books, eh?'

'No, not at all. I just observe my husband. Whenever he's nervous, he starts fiddling around the house. Which is really good because Peter is very talented with his hands. All the drippy faucets get fixed when he's anxious.'

Georgia smiled. 'And you're not even sure if this Yitzchak Golding is alive or dead?'

'No, I'm not,' Rina said. 'Ernesto Golding, the murdered boy, had claimed that he had found some information about a Yitzchak Golding who died in Treblinka. All his relatives died there as well. But there could be another Yitzchak Golding and that could have been Mr Golding's father. I don't know,

Georgia. That's why I'm here.'

'From what source did he find that piece of data about Golding dying in Treblinka?'

'I don't know.'

'Could he have been making it up?'

'Sure.'

'Do you know the year Yitzchak Golding died?'

'No.'

'I'll start with the Records of American Gathering. If that doesn't pan out, we'll go to the Red Cross, the registry at Yad V'shem, the Central Archives, the HIAS . . . the list is long. Except most of them deal with those who survived to '45 or beyond. As you well know, Treblinka was liquidated way before that.' Georgia hesitated, then looked down. 'Hmmmm.'

'What does that "Hmmmm" mean?'

'If Golding's father *was* a Nazi, and if he took on Yitzchak's name, first off, he would have to have known that Yitzchak Golding was dead. Secondly, to take on his name . . . Yitzchak Golding would have to have made an impression in his mind. Because remember the camp was leveled by '43 and the war wasn't over until '45. Millions of Jews died after Treblinka was long gone. Golding had to have been on the impersonator's mind for at least two years. So you know what that says to me?'

'What?'

'That the dead Yitzchak Golding was a force to be reckoned with. I'm thinking that maybe he was involved in some kind of revolt and had made a name as a local hero. Like in the Warsaw Ghetto Uprising.'

'But the Jews in the uprising died defending the Ghetto, not in Treblinka.'

'So maybe he was involved in one of the camp's uprisings. There were several of them, you know.'

'I'm aware of that. I didn't see the name Golding in any of the accounts.'

'Thousands were involved and died anonymously. He could have been one of the forgotten masses.'

'Not so forgotten,' Rina said. 'Someone has his name even if he isn't a relative.'

'Curiouser and curiouser.' Georgia glanced at her watch, not because she was in a hurry but because she was tense. 'What I tell you stays between us, all right?'

'I hear you.'

'I know this man – Oscar Adler. He's around ninety . . . from Czechoslovakia. But he was transported to Warsaw, then to Treblinka at the very end of the camp's existence. When the Nazis tried to burn the camp down – this was right before the Russian invasion – a rarefied few souls escaped and hid out in the woods of Poland. Even of those who escaped, most of them were returned to the Nazis by the Polish police. This man is a real survivor in every sense of the word. He's very coherent and very alert. But there's a problem.'

She let the words hang in the air – either for dramatic effect or it was hard for her to vocalize them.

'He won't talk about his experiences, Rina. I've begged and begged him to record his story for posterity. I've used every tactic known to mankind – he remains mute.'

Not unlike Golding's father. 'Where do you know him from?'

'He's in the same rest home as my uncle. You know me: I've got a big mouth, and old folk are the talkiest people in the world when you give them a chance. He let it slip one day that he survived Treblinka – kind of accidentally on purpose. You could have picked me off the floor. I was shocked beyond belief. I started thinking about how much good he could do for the Center. But when I mentioned it, he froze like an icicle. He turned red with fury and hypertension and told me under no circumstances was I allowed to mention his experience to anyone. I thought that was terribly unfair, but I was not about to give the man a coronary. So I've kept my promise, and as much as I'd like to bombard him with questions, I've kept my mouth shut. So far.'

It was unfair, but who was Rina to judge someone who had gone through that monstrous ordeal? She said, 'It's a shame. I'm sure there are people out there who don't know what happened to their loved ones.'

'Not in this case. Treblinka wiped out entire families – all generations. Now, once in a blue moon, I'll mention a name to Oscar. If he knows the name, he'll tell me yes or no. But so far, he hasn't known any names. That's because by the time he got to Warsaw, the Nazis were killing the Jews at such a fast rate, he never got a chance to know anyone for more than a week at a time. He only survived because he hid out until the bitter end.'

'I guess at ninety, he feels that he has earned the right

not to talk.' Rina thought for a moment. 'Is there anything he especially likes to eat?'

Georgina rocked her hand back and forth. 'Soup may be good.'

'How about if I made him some homemade chicken soup? Or better yet if I made him some old-fashioned cabbage soup with boiled flanken?'

'How about both?'

'Easy enough. I'll make two pots. And I'll even include matzoh balls and kreplach with the chicken soup. Noncontingent upon his talking about his awful experience. He gets the soup no matter what.'

'You may have something there.' Georgia shrugged. 'But don't be disappointed if he refuses to talk to you.'

'Once he tastes my soup, he won't say no.'

Georgia stared at Rina. 'I'll tell him you're pretty. In addition to soup, Oscar's a sucker for a pretty face.'

26

When Emma Lazarus wrote her famous words underneath the Statue of Liberty, she must have had places like the Foothills Division of the LAPD in mind, the area being a multicultural mix of displaced and struggling whites, blacks, Hispanics, Asians, and other ethnicities thrown into the immigrant salad. It was arid terrain, making it Saharan hot in the summer-time, swimming in the smoggy haze of vehicular combustion. It had been the division that Decker had called home for fifteen years, working there even as it sat under microscopic scrutiny after the Rodney King beating. In this lonesome geographical glitch called the Northeast Valley, the title of 'Hero of the Century' still belonged to Ritchie Valens. To Bert Martinez, the deceased singer was still tops.

At the helm of the unmarked Dodge, he sped along the 5 North, driving by groups of peeling stucco houses and apartment units, disassembled car parts spangling weed-choked lots. In the harsh sunlight, the chrome and steel reflected heat but no warmth.

'I went to school not far from here,' Martinez said.

Webster glanced at him. 'Really?'

'Yeah. Pacoima High. My prom date lived off the freeway . . . before this was a freeway. In the old days, the only thing out here were houses and a White Front discount department store.' He changed lanes. 'My old man was a housepainter, you know.'

'No, I didn't know.'

'Yeah, him and his brother. Between the two families, we were seven boys. My father wore a big, black belt and felt free to use it on our butts.' A smile. 'Those were the days when Children's Services meant a hot lunch at the cafeteria.' He shook his head at the passage of time. 'I'm not saying corporal punishment is a good thing, but neither me nor my three brothers resented him for it. Just the way it was.'

'Or maybe your old man knew when to stop.'

'Maybe.' Martinez exhaled. 'When I lived here, it was home. Now it just seems like another blighted area – depressing as hell. And it hasn't even changed all that much. Amazing what perspective does.'

'Do you still have relatives out here?'

'Nah. The minute any of them got a little money, they moved away.'

'Where does Luis live?'

'Montebello.'

'Where he works.'

'Yeah. Did I tell you he made sergeant?'

'No. Tell him congratulations from me.'

'I will. The other two live in the Union Station area.'

'That I know. I think my wife has taken half our neighborhood down to the store. They all like the part when your brother takes out the screwdriver and starts pounding the shit out of the wardrobe to prove how strong that fabric is.'

Martinez chuckled. 'He's got the routine down pat.'

The Dodge whined as it ascended the smooth grade up to the mountains. The temperature gauge started to rise. Not precipitously, but enough to cause some concern.

'Open the windows?' Martinez suggested.

'It's better than overheating.'

Immediately, a scorched wind filled the Dodge. Webster sighed and unbuttoned his shirt. 'When you think about it, we work in a division that has all ends of the spectrum. Some very wealthy live in the area, some not so wealthy . . .'

'Go on,' Martinez said.

'Sometimes, I go to a house . . . like Alice Ranger. She's living in this spanking-new mansion with every kind of amenity, drinking herself comatose. Here I am, a college graduate working my ass off, sweating like vegetables in a frying pan for fifty-two grand a year.'

'Plus benefits.'

'I'm not complaining,' Webster said. 'I reckon there were lots of ways I could have gone, but I chose this, and I'm not complaining—'

'You already said that.'

'So it sounds like complaining?' Webster smiled.

'I'm all right. But I do wonder what the hell people like Alice have to bitch about. And we don't only see women like Alice Ranger. We deal with lots of working stiffs. So what must it be like for a macho, hyper-American Marine like Hank Tarpin to work with the rich day in and day out? It's got to eat at you.'

'Not if you never aspire to it.'

'C'mon, Bert. No one ever aspires to grow up average.'

'Tommy, if your life was below average growing up, average can look pretty damn good.'

Webster didn't say anything.

Martinez hesitated. 'Being poor isn't the reason that these buttholes wind up racists.'

'It's one of the reasons.'

'It's one of the excuses,' Martinez answered. 'One among many.'

'Our exit is coming up. It's right past the Honor Farm.'

Martinez moved over into the right-hand lane, then got off into a land of hay-colored, parched hillside undulating in the distance. Heat radiated off the asphalt. Scrub oak – gnarled and bent – thrived in the baked earth. Tall eucalyptus trees shimmered silver while exhaling fiery, menthol breath. Chaparral had managed to sprout and grow from the cracked ground below. The Dodge pitched through the lonely terrain, through air that was hot and still. But the visibility was better. Out here, even the smog had retreated, burning away in the unforgiving sunlight. Sweat was pouring off skin surfaces that Webster shouldn't have been aware of.

Martinez said, 'How far is this place?'

'Canyon country.'

'Which canyon?'

'Sierra Canyon. Next to Placerita Canyon – the nature reserve. Y'ever been there?'

'No.'

'I was there about five years ago. Not in this heat, but in the springtime. My hay fever went haywire.'

'You really are a city slicker.'

'So far as I know, no one's allergic to cement.'

'How do I get there?'

'Wait a minute.' Webster regarded the map. No grid lines – the roads in the Thomas Guide weren't much more than a series of random squiggles. He gave Bert directions to the best of his ability – a mile here, two miles there. Martinez negotiated the series of twists and turns, and within minutes the car descended into the protective covering of the glens, mercifully shaded by towering sycamore trees that dropped the temperature a few degrees. The Dodge's temperature gauge dropped as well.

'Try the air-conditioning again?' Webster suggested.

'Sure, live dangerously.'

They closed the windows and blasted the fan. But all it did was throw tepid gusts throughout the car's interior. Small wooden homes – some no more than shacks – blended into the landscape. Deeper into the winding canyon, they passed a biker bar, replete with blinding chrome-studded Harleys. Shirtless, bearded, fat men were hanging out of the place, bellies protruding like tongues from panting dogs. Martinez smoothed his mustache and reduced the speed, just long enough to cast a couple of glances.

'Think PEI has any sympathizers out there?'

'I reckon it may have one or two.'

'Want to catch a beer, Tom?'

'There're 'bout sixty of them and two of us. I'll pass.'

The men laughed, but it was a jittery one. Delving into the wilderness, farther from the telephone poles, farther from civilization.

Webster said, 'From the looks of it, I'd say that Tarpin felt right at home at Baldwin's nature camp.' He stared at his map, looking at the small dirt roads that he had outlined in red. ''Bout a mile up you got to look for an unpaved pathway – Homestead Place. But there aren't any street signs.'

'I'll use the odometer.'

'It'll be on our left.' They rode in silence, looking for the turnoff. Webster squinted. 'How 'bout there?'

Martinez slowed. 'It's as good a guess as any.'

The car rattled as it plowed against the rock-hard dirt lane, both of them praying the tires wouldn't give out. As the car hugged the tortuous paths, makeshift shacks and lean-tos could be spotted nestled in the copses. The structures held addresses, but the street numbers seem to defy logic. Five minutes later, after several backtracks and some good luck, they found the appointed place. As soon as they got out of the air-conditioned vehicle, a blast from the midday furnace hit their faces. But as strong as it was, it couldn't compete with the stench.

'Good Lord!' Webster held his nose. 'Whatever died was awfully big.'

Martinez was sweating profusely. But not just from the heat. He was visibly upset. 'This is terrible! We just saw the man yesterday.'

'Assuming it's him.' Webster mopped his face with the tail of his shirt. 'Y'all want to call it in to the local authorities?'

'Shouldn't we check it out first?'

'My nose already did that.'

Martinez gave him a look.

Webster shrugged carelessly. 'Go ahead.'

'By myself? Suppose there's someone lurking in the back?'

Webster grimaced. 'You just want me to puke.'

'Stop being such a wuss.'

'Them's fightin' words.'

'Good. Let's go.'

The two of them trudged through the detritus of dried leaves and dead foliage, feeling the crunch under their shoes. The fumes grew stronger and more organic – the putrid stink of rotted flesh and waste. Dense clouds of black flies swirled about their faces, their hums intoning like a monk's mantra. Webster swatted them away from his face.

The door to Tarpin's cabin was partially open. Martinez pulled out a handkerchief, wrapped it around his hand, and gave the portal a sizeable nudge.

More flies rose up along with other creepy-crawlies – bees, wasps, mosquitoes, gnats, mites, spiders, beetles, and silverfish. A veritable bugfest of black and silver winged things as well as slithery creatures gorging themselves on flesh, bone, and blood. A large brown rat scampered across the wood-planked floor. Among the drones of the vermin and the odor of putrefaction lay Tarpin in a black-veined, maroon pond of sticky, coagulated blood and sera. His eyes were open; his mouth was agape, maggots wriggling through the open orifices. His hair was matted and wet, a natural breeding ground for anything with six legs. He was fully clothed. He had been shot in the head.

Pulling out a camera, Martinez started snapping pictures. Webster rocked on his feet, sensing electric flashes and sparkles dance through his once perfect vision. Abruptly, he excused himself.

Martinez watched him go. At least Tom had the smarts to lose it away from the crime scene. It would have been very unprofessional of him to contaminate the evidence.

Oliver parked his butt on a hard folding chair and slung his head back. Talking to the ceiling even though there were three other people in the room. 'Every time we get a suspect, he winds up dead.'

'That's the good news,' Marge responded. 'It means we have very few people on our wanted list left to investigate. The bad news is if we strike out with them, we're screwed.'

Oliver sat up, took off his jacket, then loosened his tie. 'Doesn't this place believe in air-conditioning?'

'It works great in the winter.' Decker wiped his face

down with a handkerchief and tossed a manila envelope to Oliver. 'Your passport, Detective. Dr Estes is expecting you and Marge in an hour.' He looked at his detectives' faces covered with sweat. 'If you leave now, you'll have plenty of time.'

Oliver took out the warrant. 'How'd you pull it so fast?'

'I've got connections in high places. Also, Tarpin's death sped things up.' Decker had taken off his jacket but had kept his tie knotted. He had large, wet ellipses under his armpits, and his neck was bathed in perspiration. Marge and Wanda wore short-sleeved blouses, but their armpits were damp as well.

Marge checked her watch. 'What time's the funeral?'

'Six o'clock.'

She frowned. That gave her and Oliver just a little over three hours to make it into Beverly Hills, root through the Baldwin files, and make it back into the Valley. As it stood, they were looking at fifty minutes of absolute travel time, more actually because peak commuter time was just around the corner. 'We're not going to make it.'

'You're excused. This new homicide changes things.' Decker looked at Wanda. 'What do you have?'

She bit her lower lip. 'It isn't looking good, sir. The PEI office was completely cleaned out. Not a scrap of paper to be found.'

'What about the furniture?' Marge asked.

'It was still there,' Wanda said.

'That makes sense,' Decker said. 'You take off quickly, you don't take furniture.'

'I sent a tech over there to dust the place,' Wanda said.

'What do you hope to find?' Oliver challenged.

'I don't know what I *expected* to find,' Wanda answered. 'But what I got was surprising. The walls and the furniture were basically free of prints.'

'Basically?' Oliver asked.

'We pulled up about a dozen fingerprints . . . a couple of palm prints. Way less than expected.'

Decker said, 'Someone wiped down the place before he cleared out.'

Oliver said, 'You mean Darrell Holt wiped the place before he cleared out.'

'Yes, that is what I mean.' Decker took out his pad and paper. 'Put the prints into the system. Let's see if it spits back anything.'

'That'll take days,' Oliver answered.

'Are you going anywhere?' Decker retorted.

'I'm only lamenting, Loo. So much for a quick solve.'

'I lament with you, Scott.' Decker tried to clear his brain. 'What do we know? We know that the Baldwins were Holt's therapists. According to Tarpin, Holt wasn't one of the Baldwins' success stories. We also know that Tarpin was involved with Holt and PEI. That's what we know.'

Oliver said, 'So if Holt's the perp, we've got to ask ourselves what would Holt have to gain for whacking the Baldwins and Tarpin?'

Decker said, 'You forgot about Ernesto.'

'I think he was wrong place, wrong time.'

'You think so?'

'I think so.'

'Okay. We'll assume that for the moment, although I'm not convinced. But if it were the case, what would be Holt's motivation for wanting the Baldwins dead?'

Wanda said, 'Maybe the Baldwins had something on him?'

'Holt wasn't running for Congress,' Oliver answered. 'What could they have had on Holt that would have been more embarrassing than his association with PEI?'

'Maybe something from his therapy days?' Marge suggested. 'A weird sexual proclivity that wouldn't play well with PEI?'

'Like he likes little boys?' Oliver asked.

'Or how about little girls?' Wanda said. 'Tom said the girl who was working for him was definitely jailbait.'

Oliver considered some theories. 'Maybe it was the other way around. Maybe Holt was blackmailing the Baldwins using Tarpin as a go-between. Maybe that's why the Baldwins kept a racist like Tarpin on for so long.'

Marge said, 'Scott, if you're squeezing money out of someone, you don't want them dead.'

'So maybe the Baldwins got tired of being blackmailed,' Oliver answered. 'Maybe they were going to expose Holt. So Holt killed the Baldwins to shut them up.'

Decker asked Wanda, 'Any set amounts of money going out of the Baldwins' bank accounts on a regular basis?'

'Yeah, like every dime.'

'The payoff for blackmail?' Oliver asked.

'Or they just spent a lot of money,' Wanda said.

Decker answered, 'What could Holt have on the Baldwins that would make them susceptible to blackmail?'

'Maybe the Baldwins were racists in their younger days. If they had been like ex-PEI members, that wouldn't look good with their current clientele.'

'They've been in practice over twenty-five years,' Decker pointed out. 'Long before the inception of PEI.'

'So maybe Holt found some other skeleton in the Baldwin closet via Tarpin.'

'What kind of a skeleton?' Decker asked.

Oliver shrugged. 'Well, what were the Baldwins noted for? Taking bad, rich boys and putting them into their high-priced camp instead of real punishment from the schools. In Ernesto's case, camp instead of jail. Maybe the Baldwins gave a kickback to each kid sent their way by a judge, or by a school. Or maybe Holt found out that the Baldwins were using insider's information with the standardized tests. Maybe Tarpin knew about the schemes and passed the information on to Holt.'

'Why would Tarpin do that?' Marge asked.

'Because Tarpin believed all that PEI crap,' Oliver said with animation. 'The two of them used the money to further PEI's crazy philosophy.'

Wanda broke in. 'Scott, PEI was a rinky-dink operation. If Holt was getting blackmail money, he wasn't using it for PEI in a big way.'

'Well, then, maybe PEI was a front to launder blackmail money into their personal accounts.' Oliver smiled. 'That sound good?'

'In theory,' Decker said. 'But I came back from the murder scene about forty minutes ago. Tarpin was living in a basic one-room cabin. Holt rents a one-bedroom unit just north of Roscoe Boulevard. They don't appear to be living a profligate lifestyle.'

'Holt's apartment has been cleaned out,' Wanda added.

'You mean Holt cleaned out his apartment,' Oliver said.

'Whatever,' Wanda answered. 'The place is empty. We're in the process of checking out Holt's parents . . . his father. He's a local. According to the senior Holt's secretary, Darrell's mother is long gone – maybe not dead, but out of the picture.'

'Where is the father now?' Decker asked.

'Eight miles high in transit.'

Oliver said, 'What about the girl? The jailbait?'

'Erin Kershan,' Wanda answered. 'The address I pulled off her driver's license doesn't exist. I'm thinking that maybe she lived with Holt and was a runaway. I'm in the process of checking the data banks.'

'So you think she's in on it?' Oliver asked.

'She's awfully mousy . . . seemed pretty harmless when Webster and Martinez interviewed them months ago.' Wanda shrugged. 'But you know young girls. They get swept away. Maybe that's what happened . . . she got swept away with Holt and the entire PEI movement. So yes, I'm hoping that she's involved. Because if she isn't involved – and Holt is – that's not good. We don't want her turning up as victim number four—'

'Five,' Decker corrected. 'There's Ernesto.'

'God, this is terrible!' Marge was upset. 'How many dead bodies are going to turn up before we solve this thing?'

Oliver said, 'It's not helping L.A.'s crime statistics, that's for sure.'

Decker didn't bother to chastise him. Being cavalier was how Scott dealt with the atrocities. Suddenly, his tiny office started to drop in temperature.

Oliver dabbed his brow with a Kleenex. 'Feels cooler.'

Decker said, 'I think the air conditioner kicked in.'

Marge was glum. 'Nice to know that something's being productive.'

Decker said, 'You two better get going over the hill. Until we hit on something, I want you to go through every single file.'

Another all-nighter. Oliver said, 'Can we break for dinner?'

'You can order takeout and bill it to the department,' Decker answered. 'As soon as Webster and Martinez are done with Tarpin's crime scene, they'll come over and join you. Wanda, you keep searching for Holt and Kershan. Also, keep going through the Baldwins' phone records and bank accounts. Maybe something will turn up.'

'Yes, sir.'

'Tom said that the meat wagon picked up Tarpin's body about twenty minutes ago. I'm pushing the pathologist to do the autopsy . . . at least to get the bullet out and send it over to ballistics.' Decker stood up and straightened his spine until he was all of his six-foot-four-inch, 220-pound frame. 'I've got to clean myself up. Don't want to go to a funeral smelling like a hamster.' He shook his head. 'Although I suppose no one will notice.'

27

Pulling out of the parking lot, Marge went east until she hit the 405 South, the ultimate destination being the Baldwins' main offices in Beverly Hills. A quick solve was drifting out of reach, and though she never expected a cakewalk, a suspect to lean on would have been nice. She dealt with the disappointment by concentrating on her driving. Oliver, unusually quiet, busied himself by reading the reported incidents that flashed across the cruiser's monitor.

Twenty minutes later Oliver spoke, a bit startled by the sound of his voice after riding in a protracted silence. 'There's a hot domestic in Brentwood.'

'We're far from Brentwood.'

'I'm not saying to go there.'

'So why mention it?'

'Because I was wondering what the rich fight about.'

'You can't be serious.'

'I am serious.'

'Scotty, look at your own divorce.'

'My infidelities were an escape from my ex's complaints about always being broke! I may have been a prick in the bed department, but I wasn't a reckless spender. If I had money, it would have been different.'

'Think so? I bet you would have fought about how to spend it.'

Oliver didn't deny it. She was probably right. 'I should have had such problems.'

Marge glanced at him with sympathy. Although Oliver was dating his usual young bimbos, the young Ms Decker was still on his mind. Cindy had knocked the wind out of him, and he had yet to recover. He fidgeted in his seat, a man angry and anxious. That meant he was serious. That meant he'd do a good job.

'What do you mean go through *all the files*?' Maryam Estes was blocking the door with thin, silken arms, the bronze-colored extremities holding dozens of silver and gold bracelets and bangles enveloping her limbs clear up to her biceps. 'You can't intrude on their confidentiality. These are current cases!'

'The warrant specifies *all* cases that had been handled by the Baldwins,' Oliver stated. 'And it's printed in English, Ms Estes, which is your native language—'

'I don't appreciate your snide remarks at a time like this!'

'You can be as outraged as you like,' Marge said. 'Just let us do our job.'

Oliver said, 'That's your cue to get out of the way.'

'I will not!'

A staring match went on for several seconds. Oliver debated calling in the proper authorities to have her physically removed. If they did it themselves, they'd open themselves up to charges of police brutality. But time was ticking away. Oliver reached toward her and tickled the pits under her sleek arms. As she involuntarily retracted, he ducked and went inside.

Pragmatism was always a good ally.

Maryam stomped after him, then marched ahead of him, glancing over her shoulder with hot, angry eyes. 'I am going to report you to your superiors.'

'I believe you, Doctor.' Oliver tried not to ogle her shapely ass. Not that he could see the outline all that clearly, because her dress was A-line. But it was red and it was sleeveless and that made it sexier than hell. Her hair had been pulled back into a bushy ponytail, showing off an oval face with mocha skin, slightly bumpy from a few acne marks. The imperfection only made her that much more attractive. Of course, her deep brown eyes and mother-thick red lips didn't hurt, either. The nostril pierce, as small as it was, still bugged him. But hey, you can't have everything.

For a brief moment, Oliver flashed on Cindy, probably because of Maryam's forceful personality. He missed her in ways he dared not admit to anyone, least of all himself. But there were times when he lay alone at night in his bed, just thinking . . . He had summoned up the nerve to call her several days ago, suggesting a friendly, nonpressured dinner. To his surprise, she accepted. That was supposed to have taken place tonight, but Tarpin's murder changed all that.

Marge spoke to him behind the fast-paced Maryam. 'We look for Holt first?'

'Yeah.'

Marge stopped abruptly. 'He's not a current patient, and we don't know the Baldwins' filing system. How about we try a truce?'

'Be my guest. I'm never one to anger beautiful ladies.' He reviewed some options mentally. 'How about if I go through the desks in their offices first while you ask her about the files? Plus, dealing with Holt may work to our advantage because he's not a current patient. She may have fewer problems with confidentiality.'

Marge jogged to catch up with Maryam, and tried out empathy. 'Please wait a moment, Dr Estes. Let's talk this out.'

'There's nothing to discuss.'

'There's a lot to discuss. Don't you want to hear about it?'

No response, but Maryam halted in her steps. Folding her arms across her chest, she tapped an open-toe sandal, the red nails going up and down, up and down.

'First of all, I'm very sorry. This must be awful for you. Not only the Baldwins, but Mr Tarpin as well. You can see why we feel there's some urgency here. We're doing this job first and foremost for your protection.'

Maryam stopped tapping. '*My* protection?'

Marge tried out a wide-eyed look of surprise.

'Doctor, don't tell me you haven't thought about it. First it's your bosses, then it's Mr Tarpin. Right now, we consider you at risk.'

Maryam was taken aback. 'No one is out to get me.' Her voice wavered. 'Why would someone be out to get me?'

'Why would someone be out to get Merv or Dee Baldwin? Or Hank Tarpin?' It was time for Marge to make her pitch. 'I believe the answer is in those patient files.'

'I don't agree.'

'With what?'

'That someone is out to get *me*! It doesn't have to do with the practice. It has something to do with the nature camp – probably because of that . . . that . . . *man*!'

'Tarpin?'

'Exactly!' She was trying to convince herself as much as she was trying to convert Marge. 'The camp wasn't my bailiwick. As I told you the first time, I primarily worked with Dee, doing testing and relaxation therapy for anxiety disorders.' Her jaw tightened, but now her eyes were nervous. 'I actually had very little to do with Mervin. And *nothing* whatsoever to do with Hank Tarpin!'

'You didn't like the man,' Marge stated.

'What in the world was there to like about him? He was a racist pig!'

'He made comments to you?'

She slammed her lips shut. 'Not directly.'

'How about indirectly?'

'No,' she admitted. 'But he was associated with that vile hate group.'

'The Preservers of Ethnic Integrity?'

'So you know about it.'

'Yes, Doctor, we do. Did Tarpin ever talk to you about it?'

'No, *he* didn't. But that freak that Tarpin brought around sure spoke his mind!'

'Darrell Holt?'

Maryam was shocked. 'Yes. Darrell Holt. Exactly! How did . . .'

'What do you know about him?' Marge tried to hide her excitement.

'What do *you* know about him?' Maryam retorted.

Turning a question into a question. Marge kept it short. 'He was the local head of the Preservers of Ethnic Integrity.'

'That little freak had the nerve to insinuate that I acted like I did because I was ashamed of my heritage. That to get in touch with who I am, I needed to figure out what I was. As if you can hide being African-American. I am very proud of who I am and want my people to see me as a role model of what they can become. I was never so insulted in my life. I would have kicked him out on the spot, but then Dr Baldwin walked in and the three of them went into the doctor's office.'

'When was all this?'

Maryam took a moment before replying. 'About six months ago, I think.'

'What did the three of them talk about?'

'I have no idea. I was so unnerved by the conversation that I went out on my lunch break!'

'Did you talk to Dr Baldwin about it?'

She lowered her head. 'No! I only spoke to that little freak the one time. I didn't want to make a big deal out of it. But I did tell Tarpin not to bring him around when I was here.'

'So Holt came around often?'

'Not often at all.' Maryam hesitated. 'I saw him maybe three times in my eighteen months here.'

Three times. More than just an accident. Marge said, 'How did Tarpin respond when you asked him not to bring Holt around?'

Maryam waited. 'Actually, he sort of apologized for the freak's behavior. He claimed that Holt was a bit outspoken but had his good points.'

'What kind of good points?'

'I never asked because I didn't care.'

'Why do you think Holt was meeting with Baldwin?'

The question made her anxious. 'I couldn't imagine why. Except that Dee often . . . extends herself to disturbed people. She's very ecumenical.'

'*Dee* was ecumenical,' Marge said.

'Yes. They both were.'

Marge regrouped her thoughts. Every time someone spoke about 'Dr Baldwin', Marge assumed it was Mervin – a holdover from growing up a military brat. 'Doctor' always meant a man. 'So it was *Dee* who met with Tarpin and Holt?'

'Yes, didn't I say that?'

'You didn't specify which doctor,' Marge told her.

'Did you know that Darrell Holt was a patient of Mervin Baldwin's?'

Her face darkened. 'Who told you that?'

'Tarpin did,' Marge answered. 'Tarpin claimed that Holt saw Dr Baldwin about eight years ago.' She made a face. 'He also didn't specify which one. In either case, Holt doesn't appear to be a success story.'

Maryam said, 'What school did he go to?'

'What *school*?'

'College. Do you know if Holt attended college?'

'Supposedly, he went to Berkeley. Why do you ask?'

'Because maybe Holt didn't see Merv for behavioral problems. Maybe Holt saw Dee for college counseling. And if he got into Berkeley, then maybe he was a success story.'

Defending her bosses to the end. Marge said, 'I was led to believe Holt was seen for behavioral problems.'

'Well, then, you know more than I do.'

'Why don't we find out?' Marge suggested. 'Why don't we start by looking up Holt's file?'

'From your questions, I take it you have grave concerns about Darrell Holt.'

'Yes. Don't you?'

Now Maryam really looked worried. Her hand went to her throat. Suddenly, she appeared small and vulnerable with her bare arms and painted nails.

Marge said, 'Maybe we should look at Holt's file?'

Maryam nibbled a hangnail. 'Follow me.' Taking out a key, she unlocked a door that led into a six-by-eight windowless room illuminated by fluorescent light. It was lined with metal file cabinets. 'This is where we keep our former clientele information.'

'Lots of files.'

Maryam didn't respond. She jerked open the appropriate drawer and started sorting through the multitudes of Pentaflexes. Within minutes, she pulled out a skinny folder, then yanked the papers from the folder, flipping through the pages – three or four of them. Then she went back and started reading in earnest, heaving burdensome sighs as punctuation. Her hands were shaking.

'May I see the notes?' Marge asked.

'There's nothing much in here, Detective.' Maryam seemed reluctant to let go. Perhaps she was hoping that the notes contained a magic bullet. 'These diagnoses . . .' Another sigh. 'They're interchangeable with those of the thousands of other teenagers that have passed through these portals.' She hit the pages with the back of her hand. 'Holt was seen by Mervin. He seemed to be a hostile teenager exhibiting oppositional behavioral problems. He also had an unresolved oedipal conflict with his father, stemming from his mother's absence. Being as he was of mixed blood, he suffered with identity crises . . . and he had the *nerve* to accuse me—'

'May I *see* the papers, please?'

Maryam looked up; her face was covered in sweat.

Marge took the papers. 'Maybe you should sit down, Doctor.'

'Perhaps that would be . . .' There was a small folding chair in the room. Maryam plunked herself down and dropped her chin to her chest. 'I think I'm overreacting. I'm very suggestible.'

'It's totally understandable,' Marge said. 'Give me a moment to look at these papers, all right?'

As Marge scanned the notes, she realized that Maryam had been improvising. Baldwin didn't believe in complete sentences, using abbreviations whenever he could. There were more single words and fragmented phrases than actual sentences. The first page was more like an appointment sheet, dates written in the left-hand column on grid-lined ledger paper. What looked like check numbers and the abbreviation FF were written in red ink after each date. No monetary amount was recorded, however. Several of the lines were inscribed with the word 'progress', but several others were marked with the word 'regression'.

The actual notes were penned on blank sheets of paper. The first was titled FAMILY HISTORY – written in block letters with a red, felt-tip marker.

> *Intake by Father. Mother AB 'out of picture by age ten' as quoted by F. Refuse to talk about it. Only child of Preston and Myna Holt. Accord to F, FT baby with norm Apgar, but F doesn't know. Speaks of precocious child but F doesn't know milestones . . . walking, speaking, toileting. Bhav problems started at 10, progressed into adolescence. Concomitant with AB of Mother?*
>
> *F: cold, distant . . . very wealthy!*

Marge said, 'He mentions that the father was rich.'

'Let me see . . .' Maryam read the notes. 'In this context, I believe Dr Baldwin was presenting a psychological profile of a man more concerned with money than with his child.'

'It doesn't say that,' Marge said.

'That's because you have to know how to read between the lines!'

'If you say so.'

Marge read on to page two. More dates and check marks and FF. Some diagnostic notes: *Hos & Ang, unre ID crises with mix-race – M ½ black, unre OE con, origin; bad breast. Mother ???? Deserted or removed ????* She pointed the abbreviations out to Maryam. 'Translate for me, please.'

Maryam sighed again. 'Hostile and angry, unresolved identity crises – mother was half-black, unresolved oedipal conflict stemming from a bad-breast mother – that's a Freudian way of saying a cold, unresponsive mother.'

'What does Baldwin mean by "deserted or removed"?' Marge asked. 'Did the father kick the mother out or something?'

'I couldn't tell you,' Maryam stated. 'Obviously, this was something that Dr Baldwin was dealing with Darrell about.'

Marge said, 'Is it unusual that the father refuses to talk about the mother?'

'Lots of men have communication problems. Usually . . .' Maryam made a face. 'When a party is that resolute in his or her silence, it obviously means the situation was very, very painful – beyond the usual stress of divorce.'

'An affair?'

Maryam shrugged.

'Did the mother suddenly desert the family?'

'I couldn't say. But it was obviously very traumatic for the father.'

Marge turned back to the ledger page. 'What does FF mean?'

Maryam blushed. 'I think it means full fee.'

She thinks.

'That would make sense,' Marge said. 'It goes along with Mervin stating that the father was wealthy.'

Maryam looked away, not wanting to deal with the implications.

The next page of notes was more like scribbles, taken at varying times in different colored pens: *Anti-S bH shown by W, DU, isolation, long hours at the computer. Extreme oppositional behavior!!!!! Perfect for nature camp. Tkd to F: agreed for June session, FF.* Again, she showed the page to Dr Estes. 'What's this stand for?'

The doctor looked at the chart. 'Anti-S is antisocial. W is withdrawal. DU is drug use.'

'And what is oppositional behavior again?'

'Acting out,' Maryam stated. 'Darrell Holt had a big behavioral problem.'

'And we're back to FF again. This time Baldwin appears to mean that the father was willing to pay full fee for the camp.'

'Why are you begrudging Dr Baldwin's right to make a good living?'

Marge didn't push it. 'I'm sorry if it appears that way. I'm just trying to understand the man—'

'He was not in it for the big money. He could have

made far more bucks doing the radio and TV talk-show circuit, but he refused to play that game because he and Dee felt it was unethical!'

Marge tried to appear convinced. Another page of notes with more abbreviations. An appointment set up to talk to the father about the nature camp.

On the last page – dated six years ago – the heavy block letters had been replaced. She noted the word 'Harvard' scrawled across the page. Under it was a complete sentence: 'SAT review set up for Saturday the 15th.' She showed the sheet to Maryam. 'The handwriting changes.'

'It's Dee's. Obviously, she did some college counseling and test review therapy with Holt.'

Marge said, 'And Dee set up a test review with him on that Saturday?'

'Yes, it seems like it.'

'What exactly is test review therapy?'

'A simulated SAT test. Then they go over the answers together, figuring out the best way to approach each question. It's basically a one-on-one SAT review course.'

'There are courses on how to take the SAT?'

'Yes. As I recall, you spoke about having a daughter? You'll know about these things later on.'

'What kind of questions do you ask?'

'Questions that Dee felt might be representative of the test.'

'Where'd they get the questions from? Past tests?'

'Some from past tests to be sure. But that's not enough because everyone has access to past tests.

Mostly, Dee formulated her own questions, based on her extensive knowledge of test-taking skills. Her seminars are designed not only to give her patients maximum exposure to typical test questions but also to teach a student how to take the test with minimum anxiety for maximum performance. And lest you scoff, take a look at Dee's results.'

'I'm not scoffing at anything,' Marge said. 'Lots of pressure, right? To perform well on these tests.'

'Unbelievable. Some of it is self-generated, but lots of it comes from the parents. They are vicious when it comes to their children. You'd swear that it was they who were applying. If their children don't get into the prescribed school, they take it as a failure on themselves.'

'Why?'

She sighed. 'Because . . . unfortunately . . . they see their children as a reflection upon their own status. Lots of these parents didn't go to any of the Ivies. So they want something better for their children. And those that did go, they feel their children should continue the legacy.' She licked her lips. 'It's a bit intense—'

'It's nuts!' Marge said. 'There's life beyond college.'

'Not in this fiercely competitive world. You need an edge.'

'And this is what Dee Baldwin was selling?' Marge asked. 'The edge?'

'She wasn't selling anything! She was just helping kids reach their maximum potential!'

'You know what happens to a machine that runs full tilt?'

'People are not machines!'

'But they do burn out. How much do these parents pay to get the edge?'

'They pay for the therapy and for the tutelage. It varies from child to child.'

'About.'

'Three-fifty an hour. About what lawyers make, and they do a hell of a lot more good than attorneys.' She kneaded her hands. 'It's not an easy task – fitting each child with the right university. Sometimes parents are insistent even if the odds are bad. You do your best with whatever raw material you have. Sometimes parents want miracles.'

'And what happens when they figure out you're not a miracle worker? What happens to those cases?'

There was silence. Then she said, 'Dee had a good success rate. She could always point to that.'

'Dee scribbled the word "Harvard" on Holt's chart. But Holt went to Berkeley,' Marge said. 'Does that mean he didn't get into the college of his dreams?'

'I have no idea.' Maryam hesitated. 'Berkeley is a top school.'

'It's not Harvard—'

'Actually, it's better than Harvard in some departments.'

'But it doesn't have that same . . . cachet, correct?'

'Only if you're very narrow-minded.'

'Or an angry, hostile teenager.'

'You're actually suggesting that Holt killed the Baldwins because he didn't get into Harvard *eight years ago*?'

The nagging question: If Holt wanted vengeance, why did he wait so long? 'Does the name Ricky Moke sound familiar to you?'

She thought, then shook her head. 'No, I can't say that it does.'

'Can you check to see if Baldwin has a file for him?'

'With that warrant, I suppose I don't really have a choice.'

'No, you don't, but I'm being polite.'

Maryam looked down. 'At least you're honest. How old is he?'

'I don't know . . . probably around Holt's age.'

'A past patient?'

'I'd assume so.'

Maryam opened the appropriate drawer and sifted through the folders. 'I'm not finding anything. Let me check again.' A few moments passed. 'Sorry. Nothing. Could he be a current client?'

'Let's check it out.'

The two of them left the small closet and walked back over to the Baldwins' plush, oversized office, the huge double desk acting as its centerpiece. Lots of care had been taken in decorating it. The rose tint in the sofas matched perfectly with the rose upholstery of the stuffed chairs. The tables were adorned with the perfect accessories. Even the landscapes looked to be color-coordinated.

Oliver, who had been sitting at Mervin's side of the partners desk, looked up as soon as the women walked in. He raised a single eyebrow.

Marge picked up on it. 'Find something interesting?'

'*Really* interesting. Guess who was on Dee Baldwin's payroll?'

'Darrell Holt,' Marge said.

'Darrell Holt?' Oliver's response was a question.

This threw Marge off kilter. 'Not Darrell?'

Oliver shook his head. 'Ricky Moke.'

Maryam was perplexed. 'Who on earth is Ricky Moke?'

Marge slapped her forehead with her palm. 'He's Darrell Holt, that's who he is.'

28

Architecturally, the church had been built with light and air in mind – a vast, vaulted ceiling combined with lots of windows and an enormous domed stained-glass skylight. But even with the space and the light and the air-conditioning going full force, the sheer density of human flesh made the sanctuary unbearably hot. Of course, the suit and tie didn't help. Within minutes, Decker was as wet and limp as a discarded bath towel.

He stood at the back in a standing-room-only capacity crowd, preferential seating having been given to the relatives and friends of the Goldings. The coffin, draped with a beautifully ornate, embroidered spread, lay atop the stage, surrounded by wreaths of white blooms – lilies, carnations, gardenias, and roses. The choir stood on risers in front of the stage, draped in satin robes of red and white. They sang hymns that Decker didn't recognize, but this was a Unitarian church, and the liturgy was different from that of his

Baptist upbringing. The harmonies rang out in the cavernous acoustics – haunting and beautiful. If there was a heaven, Ernesto was definitely there.

The weeping was audible; the sobbing echoed off the stone walls and filled the empty space. The family was seated in the front row, a trio in black. Decker had only caught a glimpse of them as they walked down the aisle, and only because he was so tall. There was Jill – so tiny and frail – limping as if her hips were in tremendous pain. It was as though the pelvic bones that bore her son had betrayed her. Carter was hunched over and shuffled alongside his wife like a crippled old man. Karl, the surviving brother, had aged in just two days. The three were holding on to one another, clinging for life while huddled as if on a life raft.

The minister talked of Ernesto's glowing years cut short by a terrible fate. That it was up to them – the congregation – to come together and help lead Jill and Carter and Karl out of the valley of darkness and into the spirit's light. But it would take time – months, years, decades, and maybe never – but they, the community, must never stop trying. Never turn their backs; never forget the wonderful human being that was Ernesto Che Golding. He urged the family to make a commitment to life.

Then the minister talked to the parents directly, offering them personal words of solace. Next came Karl – the survivor's role is the most difficult. He blessed the boy and told him to try to get on with his life, to remember the joy in Ernesto and live that joy. That would be the best memorial to his brother. Do not let the death of one son become the death of two sons.

Decker had seen that all too often. Death murders more than one victim. The preacher had to have been in his fifties – squat and round, and unprepossessing physically, but he had a definite presence. He had a knack of speaking intimately to the family, yet his words could be heard clear to the back of the sanctuary. As he spoke, the weeping rose and fell in pitch like waves tossing on the shoals.

To pass the time, Decker looked for familiar faces. There was the mayor, a state senator, several state and national congressmen. The captain and the commander of police were sitting behind the politicians – an appropriate fit. The local news networks had set up cameras on the aisles. Farther down the rows of pews sat Lisa Halloway, her hands shaking, her face covered with tears. Headmaster Williams was wiping his eyes. Jaime Dahl was weeping openly. All of his classmates . . . all of them the same ages as Decker's own sons. Ruby Ranger had decided not to make an appearance. But then again she could be in the church. He only knew her by snapshots.

Decker had a lump in his throat. His eyes ached along with his head. His heart began to bang in his chest. He was melting in the heat, and his feet were sore from standing. His brain began to ring – loudly. Then he realized it was his cellular phone.

Embarrassed, he made a quick exit and answered it on the fifth ring.

'Decker.'

'It's me.'

Me was Marge. Decker said, 'What's up?'

'Where are you?'

'I'm at the funeral.'

'How much longer?'

'I don't know. What do you have?'

'Lots of things. You should come down here.'

'Why? Do you have something on Holt?'

'Both Holt and Ricky Moke. Holt was involved professionally with Dee Baldwin. Dr Estes saw them together in her office, along with Hank Tarpin. But get this. It was Ricky Moke who was on the Baldwins' payroll.'

The light went on. Decker said, 'They're the same person.'

'Well, we're all thinking along the same lines.'

'Were Moke/Holt and Dee Baldwin only involved professionally?'

'That's still sketchy at this point. That's why you should come down here.' She gave him a brief recap of her conversation with Maryam Estes.

Decker said, 'So it looks like Scott was right . . . the Baldwins had some insider's info with the standardized tests.'

'Agreed. When do you think you'll be done?'

'I don't know. I have to show my face to the family.'

Marge sighed. 'Pete, maybe the appearance could wait. We're onto something.'

'No, it can't wait. First of all, being a father myself, it's the decent thing to do. I've got to express my condolences, and it has to be done personally. Secondly, if we're totally off with this Moke/Holt thing,

I'm going to need the Goldings as the case progresses. I'm not about to squander goodwill. I'll be out as soon as I can.'

'You're getting soft in your old age.'

'It's one of the luxuries, Dunn.' Decker cut the line, then called Martinez on his cell. 'Are you still at the crime scene?'

'We're about to merge onto the 215,' Bert answered. 'I thought you wanted us to help Marge and Oliver out?'

'I want you to track down Darrell Holt's father. See if his plane landed and interview him ASAP. Maybe he'll have a clue as to where Darrell is.'

'I thought Wanda was on that.'

'I want Homicide on it. We need a fix on Darrell Holt, and we need it right now.'

Martinez recognized the urgency in the Loo's voice. 'We're on it. I'll report back as soon as I have something.'

'Do that.' Decker hung up. As hot as it was outside, at least there was a discernible breeze. He took off his jacket and decided to wait until the remaining portion of the service was over. He found shade under some specimen sycamores and took out his notepad.

Jotting down bits:

Moke as Darrell. Same age, same school – Berkeley. Moke on the payroll. What could Moke do for the Baldwins? Moke investigated for hacking . . . Darrell as a hacker? What could Darrell hack into for the Baldwins? Get into the Education Testing Center and get copies of standardized tests before they were given. Dee paid Holt/Moke for this. Then she threatened to stop and Holt murdered them all? What about PEI? Tarpin and Darrell in PEI. Used hacking money to fund PEI? Personal gain? Tarpin lived like shit, so did Darrell?

The doors to the main sanctuary opened, but the people did not spill out. Solemn music could be heard; it was a slow, ponderous dirge. Minutes later, the coffin appeared, being carried out by six teenaged male pallbearers – classmates of Ernesto, maybe cousins. Big boys who had been openly crying, with their red eyes and runny noses and curled lips.

There but for the grace of God go I.

Right behind the coffin was Jill, held up by Carter. Karl walked behind his parents, looking like a bear awakened from hibernation. His eyes were darting about, refusing to focus. They swept over Decker's face, then did a double take. Then he mouthed the words clearly: *I need to talk to you!*

Wide-eyed, Decker suddenly straightened up, then held out his palms as if to ask, *When?* He took a step forward, but Karl shook his head ever so slightly, then mouthed the words – *At the house . . . in an hour.*

An hour was not nearly enough time to make a round trip from here to the Baldwin office. He might as well stay put. Decker retrieved his car and joined the procession heading for the graveyard.

The cemetery was fifteen minutes away, in the hills of the Valley, overlooking the smoggy basin. It took some time for all the cars to park and for the people to gather around the coffin hole. It was late, late afternoon, and because the sun was low on the horizon, the rays were intensely hot and glaring. Several times, Jill's balance faltered. Once, Carter swayed on his feet. As they lowered the casket into the ground, the weeping grew to wailing – loud and disturbing. The pain was so incredibly hard to bear, even for a seasoned pro. Friends and relatives took turns shoveling dirt atop the casket. This was not a Christian custom, having the mourners bury the body. But it was a Jewish custom not to leave the coffin until it is completely under soil. Since the church was Unitarian, Decker supposed that they took bits and pieces from every religion.

There they were – boys and girls, men and women who labored in the setting sun to bury their classmate, their friend, their nephew and cousin. Finally Karl stepped up and grabbed a spade, the big, broad shoulders shaking with grief as he threw clods of earth over his brother's casket. Sweating and shoveling over and over and over.

After a half hour, the grave was a mound of freshly turned soil. The devastated family returned to the hearse, and the procession descended the mountain. Car upon car, bumper to bumper. It took a half hour for Decker to get back onto the main road; another twenty minutes for him to find a parking space. He had to settle for a spot a block away from the Goldings' home.

People were tumbling out of the front door. Some were holding drinks, others were eating or talking. No one was crying; no one even looked upset. It could have been a party, except the conversation was subdued, lacking the lighthearted, tinkling laughter that usually accompanied the ingestion of alcohol.

Muttering several ' 'Scuse me's', Decker squeezed his way through the doorway, pretending not to see the dirty looks. They viewed him like he was a grizzly rummaging through the tents. Because the house had high ceilings, it was a din of echoes, noise, chatter, and intermittent sobs. Decker used his height advantage to see over the masses, but he couldn't find Karl. He did spot Jill, weeping into a handkerchief. He saw Carter shaking hands with the minister. They were about a hundred feet from where he stood, and to get to them, he'd have to wade through many beating hearts. He wavered, then pushed his way through.

Carter noticed him first, acknowledging him with a simple nod. Decker nodded back. There was a hesitation, then Carter spoke.

'Reverend, this is Lieutenant Decker . . .' Golding paused, his lower lip trembling, then he turned his head away.

Decker said, 'I'm in charge of the investigation.'

'Jack Waylen.' The reverend held out his hand.

Decker took it. 'You spoke from the heart.'

'It was from the heart.'

Decker turned his attention to Golding. 'It was a beautiful way to say good-bye to your son.' He sighed. 'I just wanted you to know that I'm available for you twenty-four hours a day.'

Carter closed his eyes. 'Thank you.'

'When things are quieter, will you tell your wife that as well?' Again Decker sighed. 'I'd tell her, but I think my appearance might upset her.'

'It would.' Carter clasped his hands together. 'Thank you for coming.'

The dismissal line. Decker was relieved. 'Again, my deepest condolences for your terrible loss.' He slowly turned and walked away. Moments later, he felt the presence of another body. The minister was at his side.

Waylen said, 'Do you have any idea what's going on with the murder?'

'I have ideas.' He faced the stocky man. 'But they're not for public consumption.'

'This case shouldn't drag on. It would do permanent damage to your image and to the morale of the community.'

'I'm doing my best, Reverend.'

'This isn't like The Order, Lieutenant,' Waylen said. 'This isn't some isolated sect. The Goldings are community people – loved and respected. There hasn't been a tragedy that has cut as deeply as this one since Dr Sparks was murdered six years ago. We need resolution, and we need it quickly if healing is to begin.'

Involuntarily, Decker bristled, not from Waylen's admonitions, but from hearing the name Sparks. 'We solved that one, we'll solve this one, too.' A pause. 'Anything else?'

Waylen said, 'If you want to tell me anything, I'm here to listen.'

'And if there's something you want to tell me, I'm

here to listen as well.' Decker looked him in the eye. 'You know how it is. Confession is the mainstay of both cops and priests.'

The minister's eyebrows lifted. He didn't have time to respond because Karl had materialized. Instantly, Waylen went to work. He hugged the boy and held his hand as he spoke. 'What can I do for you, Karl?'

'I'm okay, Reverend.'

'I am here for you. I want you to know that.'

'Thanks, Reverend.' The boy looked down and extracted his hand from the minister's grip. 'I appreciate that.'

No one spoke.

Karl wiped his forehead with a tissue. 'I'm tired.'

Waylen said, 'Maybe you should lie down, Karl.'

'I don't think I should leave my parents.' Karl looked beseechingly at Waylen. 'Could . . . could you attend to them for about a half hour? Just . . . just so I can change my shoes or—'

'Of course.'

He turned to Decker. 'Lieutenant . . .'

'Karl . . .' Decker answered.

'Maybe . . . you can bring me up some water?' the boy asked.

'Absolutely.'

'I'll do it,' Waylen interjected.

'Reverend, I think my parents . . . you should stay with them.'

'Go lie down,' Decker said. 'I'll get you the water.'

'Thank you.' Rapidly, Karl moved through the crowd, resisting contact with anyone. Decker retreated from the minister, then headed for the kitchen, until he spotted a table that held glasses of prepoured soda. He picked up a 7/UP and, drink in hand, he made his way to Karl's bedroom. The door was closed.

Decker knocked. 'It's Lieutenant Decker, Karl.'

Footsteps, then the deadbolt unlatched. 'Quick!' the boy said. As soon as Decker cleared the threshold, he secured the lock. 'I just . . . don't want to talk to anyone else.'

'I got you 7/UP,' Decker said. 'Is that okay?'

The boy threw himself on his bed, then turned so he was lying on his back and looking up at the ceiling. 'I'm not thirsty. I just wanted an excuse to get you up here.'

'Where should I put this?' Decker asked.

'I dunno . . . anywhere.'

Decker put it down on his desk. The room had been cleaned up since the last time he was here, straightened to the point of sterility. 'How are you holding up?'

Karl didn't answer. Decker pulled out the desk chair and waited.

'I want to kill someone,' he announced.

'Anyone in specific?' Decker asked.

'I'd say my brother, but he's already dead.' The seconds ticked away. 'For a smart guy, he was stupid when it came to girls.'

'Most teenage boys are.'

'No, I mean real stupid. He had a nice girlfriend, but he dumped her.'

'Lisa Halloway.'

'Yeah, Lisa,' Karl answered. 'Lisa was pretty, smart,

and she was nuts about him. I think they were even doing it. I can't figure out why . . . no, I take that back. I know why he fell for Ruby Ranger.' Abruptly, the sixteen year old sat up, then reached under his mattress, fishing out a package. He tossed it to Decker. 'Last night, I couldn't sleep. I started cleaning up my room . . . 'cause . . . I dunno . . . I had to do something. I found them under my mattress. Ernesto must have hid them there.'

'You read them?'

'Yeah, I read them.' He wiped his eyes. 'Something weird was going on with the Baldwins. They were doing something they shouldn't have been doing, and Ruby was in on it. I have a feeling she was blackmailing them. I think Ernesto knew about it, too.'

Decker regarded the letters – three of them and no return address. The postmarks were from Oakland, dated five, three, and two months ago. 'Do you mind if I read them here? Every minute matters.'

'Sure, go ahead.'

Decker started with the earliest one – dated right after the vandalism episode. No date on the letter itself. He read.

Hey Italian Stallion:

Believe it or not, the discipline queen has a few misguided feelings, one of them includes missing you on some carnal level . . . specifically your delicious cock. Just thinking of it makes me all wet and ready, not to mention the fact that I just adore a man in a uniform. I wonder what little Lisa would think of my sucking and slurping with copious amounts of cum on my face . . .

Decker scanned down until he found something of substance.

Hope Dee Bee and hubby aren't being their usual sanctimonious assholes. If they give you any kind of 'tude, just remind them that you're the favorite of Ruby's boy toys, and that should shut them up. Since I know the system, lover boy, I am a dangerous person. You should remember that. What we do in the sack is one thing. Outside the physical, it's each body for itself.

The letter was unsigned. But it had the advantage of being handwritten, rather than typed or taken off E-mail. If Alice Ranger had copies of Ruby's handwriting, they could do an analysis to make sure it matched. Also, they had a postmark – not a recent one – but maybe it would help locate the errant woman.

He said, 'Have you any idea what system she's talking about?'

'No idea,' Karl said. 'But she mentions it several times. Obviously, Ernesto knew what she was talking about because she didn't explain it. Read on.'

Decker did. The next letter was postmarked two months later . . . about a month before Ernesto was due to graduate.

Congrats about getting into Brown – as if I didn't

know you'd do it. Lucky for you that your daddy had influence and bread to pay off the judge and seal the fact that you are a very, very nasty boy who likes doing very, very nasty things.

Then she began to get explicit again, describing sex acts in gross detail. Decker had seen the most outrageous of things. But even so, the sheer sexual content – its rawness and rudeness – made him squirm. He knew that he'd have to read it all to see if something was encrypted in it. But for now, he skimmed the smut until he hit the last paragraph.

I cannot believe that you are actually thinking of going to that camp. It's only been two months and already you're softening like butter in the sun. Are you out of your mind? Influence is only good, lover boy, if you use it. You know you can get out of it. If you just hint at knowing the system, they'll fold like a bad poker hand. I'm not saying you tell them outright . . . that could be tricky. But surely, a guy with such a terrific prick and all that debate team experience should be able to be subtle enough about it. They'll know the score. The camp is pure shit, and Tarpin is a fucking Marine, for God's sake! You can't be weakening that fast. Maybe I'll have to come down and give you a tune-up. Just suck you dry until you remember that you make the rules, not them. If you firmly subscribe to that, you will get places. If you don't, you're sunk. And that would be a waste of a glorious set of six-pack abs not to mention a fine specimen of a cock.

Again it was unsigned. Decker folded the paper and put it back into the envelope. 'What do you know about the Baldwins?'

Karl shook his head. 'I was never in therapy with them. I've never been in therapy, period. I'm just Karl . . . the dumb jock who doesn't cause any problems. Ernie was the golden boy. Brilliant but screwed up . . . like a good genius is supposed to be. Me, I'm simple. I'm starting eleventh grade. If things progressed like they were supposed to, I would have seen the Baldwins for college counseling in a year. All the twelfth graders at Foreman Prep see the Baldwins. It's like a ritual.'

'A ritual?'

'It's getting with the program, Lieutenant Decker. We all go to the same schools, do the same activities, play on the same soccer teams, go to the same summer camps, go to the same parties, make it with the same girls, and when it's time, we all see the Baldwins. It's like the parents are afraid to break rank. Because that means that maybe someone else's kid has an edge over your kid. I love my parents. I think they've got a lot of . . . you know . . .'

'Integrity?'

'Yeah, integrity. But even they fall into traps. They say it's because they want the best for us. That's true, but also, they don't want us to look dumb to their friends. It would be embarrassing if we failed. So that's where the Baldwins come in. They prevented parents from being embarrassed. We usually got into the schools we picked, because the Bees had this knack of matching the right kid with the right school and making everyone feel happy about it. That was the point of seeing them for counseling.'

'Anyone ever hint that they did illegal things to get the kids in the right schools?'

'No. These letters were the first I've heard of it. But let's face it. People look the other way if they get what they want. What kind of illegal things do you think they might be doing?'

'Maybe they had some kind of jump on the SAT.'

Karl looked blank. 'Jump?'

'Insider's information. Maybe they knew the SAT questions in advance?'

'Beats me,' Karl answered.

Decker said, 'I'm just wondering if that's the system that Ruby's talking about. That they have inside information.'

'You'd know more about that than I would,' Karl replied. He lay back down on the bed. 'I'm real tired.'

Decker knew he should leave. But this was a one-time opportunity. He tried a different approach. 'You mentioned going to the same parties. Did Ernesto ever take you to any of the parties he went to?'

'You mean the raves?' Karl blew out air. 'Sure. Unless you were a nerd or a wuss, everyone at Foreman went to the raves. I'd go just to be seen. But I don't like them. I don't do drugs. If you don't do drugs, there's nothing to do. It's boring to watch people getting stoned or cracked.'

Karl wasn't the dumb jock when it came to important

things. Decker said, 'Did you ever meet any of Ruby's friends?'

'Ruby didn't come with her friends. I don't even think she had friends. I only saw her a couple of times with her brother, Doug the pothead.'

'So she wasn't a regular?'

'Nope. But she sure attracted attention when she came. She was really hot looking. I didn't like her, but I understand why Ernesto did.' He shook his head in wonderment. 'If she did *half* of what she writes about, I'd cut off my left nut to spend a night with her.' He scrunched up his brow. 'Well, maybe not my nut.'

'I understand what you're saying.'

'All the boys had the hots for her. Only Ernesto was brash enough to go up to her and attempt conversation. Like really talk to her. Mostly, she just talked and guys listened. Like hung on her every word . . .' Abruptly, Karl stopped talking. His eyes went to Decker's face, then he averted his gaze.

Decker said, 'I know that my son went to some of the parties.'

'Not for a long time.' Karl couldn't look at him. 'Really. I haven't seen him in about a year. He was real smart, you know. All the girls liked him.'

'Except Ruby,' Decker said.

'Oh.' Karl blushed. 'He told you about that?'

Decker nodded.

'Yeah, it was pretty nasty. It was Ruby's fault. She kept sticking it to him. And Ernesto was kinda pushing her on. Finally, Jake had enough. He got her good, but it was real ugly. Actually, I think that was the last time I saw him.'

Consistent with what Jacob had told him. Decker had one more letter to read. 'Just let me finish this letter off and then I'll leave you in peace.'

'All right.'

The poor kid sounded so tired! Decker skimmed the contents of the letter, noticing that the tone had changed – more veiled warnings than sex.

If you're going to be part of the cabal, you've got to know what you're doing. If it's obvious that you'll break, it's not going to carry weight. You need to walk the walk as well as talk the talk. It probably would be best if I came down for a show and tell. In the meantime, you shouldn't talk because people might take it the wrong way. The Bees can be had, but they're not total morons. You've got to tread gingerly, or not at all.

The more I think about it, the more I think I should come down. It's getting boring up here. I've run through about twenty men – all of them rich dot-com nerds and over forty. It's nice because they take me places, buy me meals, and I get all the pills and ciggies I can jack. But I miss your young, studly prick. I need it inside of me. So yeah, maybe I'll come back down and we can work the details out before you're shipped off to Auschwitz West. Because it's clear to me that we need to talk.

Decker reread the last two paragraphs. Now it appeared

that Ruby was in Los Angeles. Or maybe at least, she had *been* in Los Angeles. He looked up at Karl. 'Ernesto was up to something.'

'Yeah, he got in over his head, the dumb fuck!' Karl closed his eyes. 'I loved my brother, you know.'

'I'm sure you did.'

'I admired Ernie a lot. But he had this way of being arrogant . . . it could really make you feel small. Ruby was the same way. Do you think she did it?'

'She certainly hasn't been ruled out,' Decker said. 'Any idea where she might be?'

'No. She never talked to me, Lieutenant Decker. Never said anything nice to me, never said anything mean to me. She didn't even waste her time sticking it to me like she did Jake. I was just this . . . nothing to her. As far as she was concerned, I didn't exist.'

29

'We finally tracked down Darrell Holt's old man,' Martinez said. 'Philip David Holt. He just got back into town about three hours ago, according to his private secretary, but he's willing to meet with us. He lives in one of the high-rises in the Wilshire Corridor. His unit takes up the entire twelfth floor.'

'What does he do?' Decker asked.

'Investment banking/money manager,' Martinez answered. 'His main offices are in Encino and Beverly Hills. Does the name Holt Investments sound familiar?'

'No, but I'm not in the league where I need a money manager.'

'You probably wouldn't know him even if you were in the league. He runs one of the largest West Coast mutual funds for African-Americans. He manages assets of close to a billion dollars. That's a billion . . . with nine zeros.'

'Okay, I'm impressed.' Decker shifted the cell from

one ear to the other. 'Does his clientele imply that Mr Holt is African-American?'

'Darrell says he has black blood in him, so I'd say that's probably a good assumption.' Martinez paused. 'He didn't really look African-American to me. Darrell's lighter than I am! And I'm not all *that* dark.'

'When did he say he'd meet with you two, Bert?'

'I told him we'd be there in about an hour. We're still in the Valley.'

'So he's home now.'

'Yes, he's home.'

'Okay,' Decker said. 'This is the deal. I'm already on the 405, almost at Sunset.'

'So you're right around the corner,' Martinez said.

'Yes, I am. Give me the gentleman's phone number and I'll give him a call. In the meantime, since you did such a good job with locating evasive people, I want you to go back and pump Alice Ranger. I need to find out where Ruby is.'

Silence on the line.

Then Martinez said, 'I really don't like that girl.'

'You're not alone. But this isn't about congeniality. Just do the job.'

First, Decker had to get past the doorman whose uniform resembled that of a bandleader. Then he had to get past a desk clerk in a three-piece suit. Then an elevator operator – uniformed *as well as* white-gloved – took him up to the twelfth floor. The doors parted, and Decker stepped into a hallway that snaked right, then left. He walked about fifty feet until he came to a set of brass doors. He rang the bell and a tuxedoed butler answered the chimes. Once the man had been tall, but age had stooped his shoulders. He was hollow-cheeked with milky gray eyes and a complexion the color of a dull penny. His head was bald except for the curly pewter hair that neatly ringed his scalp in back – from one ear to the other.

Beethoven's Pastoral Symphony could be heard in the background. Decker held out his badge. 'Lieutenant Decker from the LAPD. I believe Mr Holt is expecting me.'

The butler moved aside. 'Yes, sir. Come in.'

Upon entering, Decker was immediately hit with a sense of flying, then falling, because he faced a wall entirely constructed from glass. With no framework around the panes, it appeared as if he were stepping directly into the ethers of city lights. The great room's ceiling was high – at least twelve feet – with coffers and carved beams. The floor was polished black granite, covered with Persian rugs that had enough wear on them to look valuable. The furnishings, upholstered in lamé fabrics of bronze and silver, were sinuous shapes, oversized enough to fill the space, but not bulky enough to overpower it. A floor-to-ceiling granite fireplace took up a second wall, and a third was hung with enormous oil canvases – de Kooning's squiggles, Motherwell's abstracts, Bacon's distorted bodies, and a single Jackson Pollock number that dripped red.

Inside, the music had become louder . . . loud, actually. The symphony was still on the first movement, and Decker could picture little satyr centaurs chasing nubile female centaurs. As a young man, he had taken Cindy to see *Fantasia* at least twice.

'This way, this way.' The butler beckoned.

Down a foyer, passing another room that was almost identical to the first one. Same ceiling and floor, the same suspended wall of glass. But this spacious region held a smaller fireplace that shared the wall with a space-age entertainment unit. A built-in wet bar serviced the thirsty on the opposite side of the territory. In the center stood a grand piano, hood up and gleaming black.

Opposite the entertainment room was the dining room that held a black lacquer table with seating for eighteen. The same all-glass view except it was a different part of the city. The table had been set, complete with layers of dishes, shiny silver, and crystal stemware for white and red wine as well as for water. Not a speck of dust marred the table dressing. It was as if Holt were expecting the dinner party any moment, except there were no kitchen smells, no sign of life, period.

The butler bade him forward until the hallway ended in double brass doors. The butler pushed a button and they were both buzzed in.

The master's bedroom suite appeared to be a thousand square feet, having the same views and more artwork. A self-contained unit, it had its own mini-kitchen complete with fridge and stove as well as its own entertainment unit. It had couches and chairs and loveseats and chaises. But its centerpiece – literally in the center – was a platform king-size bed topped with a brown suede cover. King-size suede pillows leaned against an ebony headboard. Against the pillows lay Holt, clad in blue silk pajamas. They hung on his thin frame. His mocha-colored face was small and round, the skin stretched over prominent cheekbones and a wide-bridged nose. He had dark brown eyes and black hair that was cropped close to the scalp. Fuzzy socks were on his feet. Around him were piles of papers, two laptop computers, several cell phones, one plugged-in land phone, and an electronic ticker-tape machine – neon green symbols flying past Decker's eyes.

'Foreign markets.' Holt typed as he spoke. He also had to scream because the music was so loud. 'God made twenty-four time zones so that there would always be some stock market to watch.' He looked up and smiled. 'I'm being humorous. Have a seat, Lieutenant Decker. You don't mind if I work while we talk? I'm quite adept' – type, type, type – 'at juggling multiple tasks. Besides . . .' A cell phone rang. He answered it, whispered orders, then hung up. 'I don't think we'll have a lot to talk about.'

'I can barely hear you.'

'I can hear you just fine.'

The man had no intention of turning the music down. Decker yelled, 'Can I sit on the edge of the bed?'

'Certainly.'

Magically, the music dropped a notch. Surprised, Holt looked up and saw the butler a few feet from the entertainment area. Holt was about to speak, then thought better of it.

The butler said, 'Anything I can get you, sir?'

'Uh, yes, George. Two teas . . .' To Decker, 'Is tea all right?'

'It's fine.'

'Earl Grey, George. Decaf please. It's late-ish, isn't it? I have no idea what time zone I'm in. But I see it's almost dark. What time is it?'

'Eight-thirty, sir.'

'Throw in a couple of butter cookies.' Holt continued to type on his laptop. 'Tea and butter cookies. Excellent.'

'Very good, sir.'

The double brass doors opened, then closed.

'No, I don't know where . . .' Holt typed vigorously. 'Yes! Let me . . .' Again he typed and waited. 'Just a moment. I want to make sure this order goes through . . . There. Very good. I don't know where Darrell is, Lieutenant. I've completely lost track of him. I haven't seen him in a good three to four years. At one time, he did have a trust account, so I could suggest tracing him through the bank. But I believe he had gone through it as of a year ago.'

'So you last had contact with him four years ago?'

Holt took another phone call, turned, whispered, clicked off that cell, then took another call. Whisper, whisper, whisper. He typed, called, then whispered, then typed some more. Several minutes later, he said, 'Yes, I believe it was that long ago. Right when he came back to Los Angeles from up north. When he started getting involved with that ridiculous supremacist group.' A laugh. 'Darrell is a light boy by African-American standards. But the child is not white, that's for certain.'

'From what I understand, he never claimed to be white. He told my men that he was Acadian.'

'Oh, that's a good one.' Another laugh. 'Darrell the Cajun. My, my. Darrell has reinvented himself many times over. He is not Acadian although his mother was from Louisiana. What Darrell is . . . is a little psychopath. Not surprising considering his genetics.' He looked at Decker. 'Hers, not mine.'

'His mother.'

'His mother was a slut.' The nostrils fumed. 'I'm not even sure Darrell is mine. But I took him on as if he were such because . . .' He paused, typed furiously, then resumed conversation. 'Because I felt I had no choice. I was too ashamed and too embarrassed and too stupid and too enthralled with the woman's sexual prowess to question. And some humanitarian part of me felt sorry for the little bastard. Maybe he was mine. Whatever seed penetrated that woman's ovum produced an offspring that had some smarts. The boy is not stupid. Just amoral . . . and lazy. Very, very lazy. He wanted all the trappings . . .' Holt swept his hand across the room. 'But never lifted a finger to work for them.'

'Has he called you within the last four years even if he hasn't seen you?'

'Maybe. I certainly haven't talked to him. He'd only want money so why bother speaking to him? But you can check the phone records if you'd like, Lieutenant.'

'Any idea how he's been supporting himself?'

'He's twenty-four and computer-savvy.' Holt checked

the electronic ticker tape. 'Very, very good. What were we talking about?'

'How Darrell is supporting himself.'

'The boy has skills. He had two years in Berkeley. Not to mention the fact that he is highly manipulative. I don't fret for him.'

'Do you know if he held down any kind of a job?'

'No, I do not.'

There was a knock at the door.

'Ah, the tea.' He reached around and pushed the buzzer. The double doors opened. 'Just in time. Can you pour for us, George?'

'Certainly, sir.'

'George, maybe you can help the lieutenant out. He wants to know about Darrell.'

The old man stopped pouring for a moment, then continued. 'Yes, sir?'

'Have you seen him lately?'

'No, sir.'

But the hesitation told Decker a different story.

'Any calls from the lad?' Holt asked his butler.

'No, sir.'

Holt held up his hands. 'If George isn't aware of Darrell's whereabouts, then no one is. Darrell always liked George, isn't that so?'

'I would hope so, sir.' George handed Holt a gold-rimmed china teacup, then served an identical one to Decker. As soon as he was relieved of the cups, he passed around a tray of butter cookies. Holt took two, but Decker declined.

'Oh, do take a cookie, Lieutenant,' Holt advised.

'Life needs to be sweetened from time to time.'

'The tea is fine, sir. What else can you tell me about Darrell?'

'I told you everything I know about him.' He smiled. 'He's a psychopath. There is nothing else to tell. George, do you have anything to add?'

'No, sir.'

'When was the last time you talked to him?' Decker asked.

'Years ago.'

'How many years?'

'I believe I stopped talking to him when he got involved with that crazy group.'

'Preservers of Ethnic Integrity?' Decker said.

George made a face. 'Nothin' but a bunch of lunatics.'

'Well spoken,' Holt agreed.

'Anything else I can get you, sir?' George asked.

'No, George, I'm fine, thank you.'

George left. Decker waited a few moments, then rose from the bed, still holding the teacup. He took a card out of his pocket. 'You will phone if he contacts you?'

'Of course.' Holt looked up from one of his laptops. 'What did he do, by the way?'

'I can't say, Mr Holt. It's an ongoing investigation.'

'Then remain tightlipped if you please.' Holt typed away. 'Whatever you think he did' – type, type, type – 'I'm sure he did it.'

Decker waited. Then he said, 'I'll just close the door behind me.'

'Fine, fine. Take a butter cookie on the way out.'

'Thank you.' Decker opened one of the brass doors and shut it softly. The teacup in his hand gave him the perfect excuse. Quickly, he walked down the hallway, passing the entertainment/piano room and then the living room, on to the other side of the house, where his journey ended with another pair of brass double doors. Decker rang the buzzer and a moment later he was allowed to walk into a cavernous kitchen. It held black and white lacquer cabinetry – smooth doors without handles. There was an eight-burner Wolf range in the center with a slab of metal suspended from the ceiling to act as an exhaust vent/hood. Even in the off position, the range emitted a sizeable amount of heat. The countertops were fashioned from jet-black granite and were completely empty – devoid of any appliance, breadbox, canisters for flour or sugar, flowers, knick-knacks, cookbooks, or anything a human being might use in the process of cooking – *except* for a block of steel-handled knives. About as homey as the county morgue.

George stood in front of a stainless-steel sink, rinsing out the teapot. Slowly, his bent, arthritic hands turned the china over and over. He spoke with his eyes on the water. 'He wasn't all bad.'

'I'm sure he wasn't,' Decker said. 'There's always other sides.'

'He had it tough. A tough father, a bad mother. He had it tough, Darrell did.'

'How long have you been working for Mr Holt?'

'Sixty years.'

Philip Holt looked to be in his early fifties. Decker

said, 'You worked for Mr Holt's father, then?'

'Yes, sir. Ezekial Holt. A smart man, Mr Holt was. And a good man, but he had his problems. He spoiled that boy rotten. Both him and his mama – Inez. They spoiled that boy.'

'Spoiled Darrell?'

'No, spoiled Philip. When Philip married that woman, Inez was tore up from limb to limb. She could tell that that woman was no good from day one. But Philip wouldn't listen to his mama. Philip . . . he just saw what he wanted to see.'

'Did Philip have words with his parents about the woman . . . what was her name?'

'Dorothy. Everyone called her Dolly Sue.'

'What happened after Philip married Dolly Sue?'

'He had words with both his mama and his papa. Both were against the marriage. The woman was bad from day one.'

'Promiscuous,' Decker said.

'She liked all the boys – and had them, too. Her with her pretty blue eyes and corn silk hair. Acting all flirty. Talking with that Southern talk. Philip couldn't help himself.'

Blue eyes, blonde hair, Southern talk. Decker said, 'She was white.'

'Yeah, she was a white woman. Philip met her when he was down in Shreveport, doing some work at the college. She worked at the college as a secretary. As soon as she found out that Philip had some money from his papa, she took him into her bed. After that . . . psssss . . . can't fight that kind of temptation.'

'Philip's father had money?'

'For a colored man, Ezekial had lots of money. Y'see, he was a trucker for Coca-Cola in Atlanta, Georgia. Every penny he got, he put into the Coca-Cola stocks.'

'That was very forward thinking.'

'It wasn't Ezekial's thinking. Ezekial did it to impress a white girl he liked. Y'see, her brother . . . he was buying up the stock. So Ezekial did the same thing. But back then, it was hard for a colored man to buy stock. No broker would see to the Negroes. So the white boy did it for him. Told him it would make him money. Ezekial bought the stocks for pennies during the Depression. He did real well.'

'A white boy bought stock for Ezekial and put it in Ezekial's name?'

'Yes, sir, he put it in Ezekial's name. That boy was a fine white boy. He did right by Ezekial. Not all white people hated the colored. Most did, but not everyone.'

'Interesting.'

'After the war . . . in the fifties . . . Ezekial bought himself a fine house in Atlanta in the old colored area. A big house. And he still had stock left over. Philip grew up like a rich boy. Got hisself a good education. Went to the university. That boy got *everything* he wanted. Trouble is, he wanted things that weren't good for him. Now remember, this was the sixties. The black man started getting power . . . started getting a taste for things that he shouldn't have no taste for. The white girls were giving it to them in free love. It made the black man think he was one of them. It was disgusting.'

George shut off the water and dried the pot. But he didn't turn around.

'That was Dolly Sue. Free love to the black man . . . to everyone. She was no good.'

'How long before Philip realized that Dolly Sue was no good?'

'Soon.'

'How soon is soon, sir? A year? Two years?'

'Third year, Christmastime.' He stowed the pot in one of the black cupboards. 'He and Dolly Sue were living here in Los Angeles. They went home to see the folks for the holidays.' He turned to face Decker. 'I'll take that cup from you, sir.'

Decker handed him the teacup. 'What happened?'

George pivoted around and turned on the water. 'He found her in bed with another man.'

Decker made a face. 'Another man?'

'Yes, sir.'

'May I ask who?'

George lowered his head. 'I'm ashamed to say it, sir.'

Decker grimaced. 'Philip's father?'

'Yes, sir.' George's black complexion had taken on a rosy hue – like a Bing cherry. 'Philip and Inez was supposed to be out Christmas shopping. But Philip came home early 'cause he wasn't feeling well. He caught them, he did. Ekezial . . . he threw himself on his son's mercy. Philip was a spoiled child, but he was no monster. He forgave his father and promised he wouldn't say nothing to his mama. Of course, he wanted to end it with Dolly Sue. But a month later, she told him she was in the family way.'

Silence.

George said, 'No one knows who the real papa is, sir. They both had her, so it could have been either one. Inez . . . she never did find out. And Philip . . . he tried, sir. He tried to make it work. But the woman wouldn't quit her flirty ways. When she had the second baby, Philip had suspicions. The baby was much too dark.'

'The baby was too dark?'

'Yes, sir. Philip wasn't dark because his mama wasn't black. She was Mexican. And Dolly Sue was white. The baby was like pitch coal. Even so, Philip tried, sir. For four years, he let that little mongrel call him Papa. But in the end it was too much for him. He made the mother put the baby up for adoption.'

Decker licked his lips. 'Did she do it?'

'Yes, sir, she did. She didn't want to lose Philip, and she didn't want to lose Darrell. She was nothing and had nothing without them. So she put the baby up for adoption.'

'She actually put her own child, whom she had raised for *four years*, up for adoption.'

'Yes, sir.' George shook his head. 'It was sad, sir. I felt sorry for the woman, but she had it coming. She had no right bringing a bastard into the house and palming it off to be Mr Philip's. The one I really felt terrible for was Darrell. That little boy was Darrell's brother. It broke his heart to see him go.'

Decker tried to keep anger out of his voice. 'I would imagine that would be traumatic.'

'It wasn't that Philip didn't try.'

'Just a rotten situation,' Decker said, attempting to ease the old man's guilt.

'Exactly, sir.' Another sigh. 'And even that didn't work. She still wouldn't quit her flirty ways. So finally, Philip kicked her out. Gave her some money on the condition that she just pack up and leave. Darrell was ten. But even at ten, the boy cried a mountain of tears. Mr Holt, he couldn't take it. He brought me from his pappy's home to take care of Darrell. I was the one who held the child at night.'

'And even with everything, he kept Darrell. Why?'

'The boy was his own flesh and blood – maybe brother or maybe son – but he was flesh and blood. When he kicked that woman out, Philip told his papa that he couldn't raise Darrell alone. I came over and started working for Mr Philip.' George placed the teacup on the stark, granite counter. 'She died a few years later . . . after Mr Philip kicked her out.'

'How'd she die?'

'Something with an infection and gangrene . . . had her leg chopped off. It was real sad. Mr Philip paid for the cremation. Felt it was the right thing to do.'

What a sport, Decker thought. Yet who was he to judge? Then he thought, why shouldn't he judge? He took care of his daughter after his divorce, he took care of his wife's sons, loved them and raised them and treated them as if they were his own – they were legally – at great cost to his own psyche. Damn right, he could judge.

'And the baby brother?' Decker asked. 'What happened to the little boy?'

George shrugged. 'I don't know, sir. Darrell . . . he once told me that the boy died. Then he told me the boy was alive and adopted by a real, rich family. Then he told me that the boy was a Black Muslim. He makes up stories, Darrell does. He's always made up lots of stories.'

Decker nodded. 'Thanks for the tea, George.'

'You're welcome.' Finally he turned to Decker. 'Don't be thinking too badly about Darrell. He had it rough.'

'I can see that.' Decker tapped his foot. 'When was the last time you've heard from Darrell, George? This time I need to know the truth.'

'Three days ago,' the butler admitted. 'The boy wanted money . . . like Mr Philip said.'

'Did you give him money?'

'Four hundred dollars . . . from my savings. It wasn't smart, but like I said, the boy had it rough.'

'Any idea where he might be?'

'No, sir. Before three days ago, I didn't see him in three years.'

'How did he appear? Nervous or calm?'

'He was jittery. I just thought that he was nervous to get out before his papa came home. I tole him he could stay the night . . . that his papa wasn't coming home. But he just took the money and left.'

'Didn't say anything to you?'

'He said "Thank you, George. Thank you, very much. I love you." ' The old man's eyes watered. 'I do believe he meant it.'

'I'm sure he did.' Decker hesitated, then said, 'By the

way, this lost brother of Darrell's . . . was his name Richard . . . Ricky for short?'

George went wide-eyed. 'How'd you know that?'

'A guess, sir.' Decker patted the butler's rounded shoulder. 'An educated guess.'

30

Decker looked up from Merv Baldwin's computer. 'How many years was Moke on the payroll?' he asked.

'Officially?' Oliver put down one accounting ledger and picked up another. 'I've got six checks made out to him, the earliest one dating three years ago.'

'For how much again?' Decker asked. 'Five G's per check? Don't look at me like that, Oliver. I've got a lot on my mind.'

Oliver tried to soften his sneer. 'The first one was for fifteen hundred, then two, then twenty-five, then five, then seventy-five. The last one was ten grand. That was dated six months ago. Maybe Moke had asked for even more and Baldwin finally balked.'

'You're talking about the female Baldwin, right?' Marge was seated in front of Dee's computer. 'She wrote the checks to Moke.'

Oliver said, 'Yeah, I'm talking about Dee.'

'But Dee didn't write most of the business checks,' Decker said.

'Correct,' Oliver said. 'Merv did most of the accounting—'

'Correction,' Maryam Estes broke in. 'The accountant did most of the accounting. Merv just signed the checks.'

Decker looked at her. 'How do you know that?'

She moved her head back and forth in twitchy little motions. 'I had a couple of questions about my salary check. Merv told me to take it up with the accountant.'

'What kind of questions?' Marge asked.

'It was nothing serious. Dee forgot to pay me for a few extra hours when I filled in for her in group therapy. She wasn't the best bookkeeper in the world. So I went to Mervin about it. It was all straightened out very quickly.'

'Who signed your salary check?' Oliver asked.

'Dr Baldwin . . . Merv did.'

'Even though you worked mainly for Dee,' Marge commented. 'See, that's my point. Merv did most of the signing, but not when it came to Moke. Dee took care of Moke. I think she was the one who hired him on. She may have even kept her husband in the dark about him.'

'All the checks were drawn from the same account,' Oliver told her. 'So even if it wasn't Merv's idea to hire Moke, he should have known what was going on. The checks were for large amounts.'

Maryam gave out an exasperated sigh and stuck a

novel in front of her face. Decker smiled at Marge, who smiled at Oliver. They had spread out over the entire office. The Baldwins' partners desk was filled with patient files, stubs, ledgers, appointment books, and piles of papers. Oliver was doing the scut work, sorting and collating all the loose pages, Marge was at the computer, sifting through Dee Baldwin's electronic files, and Decker was scrolling down files in Merv Baldwin's desktop.

Meanwhile, Maryam made a weak stab at distancing herself, pretending to be either reading or doing her own paperwork. Her cell phone was ringing so much that Marge had asked her to turn it off. Every so often, Oliver stole a glance at the psychologist's face. She was nervous and taut, not an ounce of slack anywhere on her face. She spoke up frequently, especially when she felt her bosses were being unfairly attacked. Oliver had dropped hints about the length of the investigation, inviting her to go home. But she clearly had a mission: to protect the Baldwins' previously unblemished reputation.

Both Oliver and Marge had tried to stay clear of her. The Loo, on the other hand, seemed impervious to her brittleness.

'Your bosses weren't very organized,' he had complained.

She had glared at him with wet eyes. 'I'd pass on the message except I doubt that it would do any good!'

Decker stared at the blinking computer icon. The files were mundane – business spreadsheets and patient notes. Marge was right about one thing: Moke did seem to be Dee's responsibility. He had yet to find anything on Merv's file as to what Moke was being paid for.

He looked up from the monitor. 'The checks started three years ago. Holt came on with PEI about four years ago. So they took about a year to develop whatever racket they had going.'

Maryam couldn't contain herself. 'You're wrong!' She had colored with indignation. 'You are so way off—'

'Nah, not way off,' Decker answered. 'Darrell Holt/Ricky Moke was either blackmailing Dee or doing some kind of illegal service for her or both. And if Holt was blackmailing, it implies that the Baldwins had done something bad. And you already know what my guess is, so I won't bother repeating myself.'

'For the fiftieth time,' Maryam said, 'you can't hack into the Educational Testing Services to get advance copies of the SATs or any other test. They have their own nerve center that is not connected to anything on-line!'

Decker said, 'And for the fiftieth time, I'm saying that there was probably an ETS insider who's downloading from the nerve center onto either the Baldwins' computer system or maybe Holt's computer system.'

'You've gone through the files—'

'Not all the files.' Marge sighed.

Decker said, 'Besides, we're not a professional hacker.' He blew out air. 'Maybe we should just take all this equipment back to the stationhouse.'

'There are patient files in those computers!' Maryam protested. 'Your search warrants allow you to search, not to steal. This is an incredible invasion of privacy—'

'Doctor—'

'Why would the Baldwins do that?' the psychologist cried out. 'Risk everything that they had worked for? You know the Baldwins' success record started way before three years ago! They've maintained a lead in the field of test preparation for at least ten years!'

'Competition is fierce,' Marge said. 'You said that yourself.'

'Competition among students, not among psychologists. The Baldwins were in a class by themselves. Your assumptions are . . . you don't even know that this Moke and that horrible man Holt are the same person.'

'How much do you want to bet?' Marge spoke dryly.

Maryam rolled her eyes. 'That's very juvenile.'

'Wanna know my opinion?' Oliver said.

'I suppose I'm going to hear it whether I want to or not.'

'Dee needed to stay on top of this testing thing because she needed to charge top dollar.' Oliver picked up a stack of papers – credit card bills. 'The woman had good but expensive tastes. There are charges from Gucci, Tiffany, Armani, Valentino, Escada, Zegna . . . that must be for the mister—'

'Not to mention the remodel on their house in Beverly Hills,' Marge added. 'And the ten grand a month to rent a beach condo.'

'So where are these mysterious SAT files?' Maryam asked. 'You have no evidence!'

'We'll find them,' Decker muttered. 'Maybe not me,

but someone will. Even if they had been erased, there are thousands of ways to retrieve them. Well, maybe not thousands—'

'You don't even know what you're talking about!' Maryam chastised.

'Neither do you,' Decker retorted. 'If Dee Baldwin was paying someone to hack into private files, you'll be lucky if you get out of this without your reputation besmirched. You might want to consider hiring a mouthpiece. You're part of the practice, Doctor.'

Again, tears pooled up in Maryam's eyes. 'I can't believe it.'

'Just trying to be helpful.'

'Well, you're not!' Maryam buried herself in a book, but her shaking leg indicated that she was anything but calm. Finally she put down the novel. 'I'm going to take a walk. I'll be back in five minutes.'

Decker nodded.

In a huff, she left the office. As soon as Marge heard the door slam, she sighed in relief. 'Thank God!'

'Don't bother,' Oliver said. 'She's probably hiding behind the wall, trying to eavesdrop.'

'You think so?'

'Go check it out.'

'Ah.' Marge waved him off. 'Let her listen in.' She slid back into the desk chair and rolled backward a couple of feet. 'You know, Pete, after hearing George's story, I kind of feel sorry for Holt.'

'Even if he's a mass murderer?'

'Yeah, well, maybe not.'

'If it's even true,' Decker said.

Oliver looked up. 'I thought you said the old man seemed honest.'

'He did,' Decker said. 'Now I'm just wondering if he's maybe exaggerating. You know, trying to create sympathy because he knows that Holt's in deep water.'

'Doesn't seem like it would be too hard to check out George's tale,' Oliver said.

'How?' Decker asked. 'The mother is supposedly dead. Who knows what happened to the kid?' He rubbed his forehead, feeling a headache coming on. 'I suppose we should concentrate on finding Holt first.'

Marge said, 'I sure hope we're right about this . . . about Holt and Moke being the same person. If not, we're gonna look awfully stupid.'

Oliver said, 'These letters that you got from Karl. Are you sure they're legit?'

'I don't know why they wouldn't be,' Decker said.

'Whole thing could be a setup,' Oliver said. 'Maybe Karl did it and is framing Ruby Ranger.'

Decker did a slow burn. 'First off, Karl hated Ruby. Secondly, why would he kill his brother?'

Oliver shrugged. 'Okay. So maybe he doesn't know who killed his brother, but he's framing Ruby because he hated her.'

Decker hedged. 'The kid isn't that Machiavellian.'

'What about Ernesto?' Marge asked. 'Was he in on the scam?'

Decker said, 'I'm not sure. All of Ruby's letters to him held veiled threats or worse. It's possible Ernesto may have had a change of heart and was thinking about blowing the whistle on this entire thing. And that's what did him in.'

'So this kid, who vandalized a synagogue and painted swastikas, had this big change of heart?' Marge was dubious.

'I talked to Ernesto a few times,' Decker said. 'He was riddled with guilt about the incident. That combined with Ruby warning him not to do anything he might regret . . .' He mulled over ideas. 'Maybe that's what he was doing in the tent at three in the morning – talking to Merv Baldwin, giving the doc the lowdown on his wife's scam—'

Oliver blurted out, 'Or threatening to go to the police if Merv didn't pay him hush money.'

'And that's why Holt popped them all?' Marge made a face.

'Why not?' Oliver said. 'They were all a threat to him. They knew about Holt's scam.'

'Then that would mean that Ruby Ranger's a threat as well,' Marge said.

'Unless she's in on it,' Decker said.

'So how did Holt and Ruby Ranger hook up?'

Decker said, 'They were both up at Berkeley at the same time.'

Oliver said, 'Holt's older, right?'

'Two years,' Decker said.

'So Darrell has been in L.A. for the last four years. They only had a year up there in common.'

'Maybe they met down here,' Marge said. 'Didn't your son say something about Ruby being interested in Nazis or supremacist groups?'

'She made comments about Hitler being a hero or something. I don't remember the exact words. Could be she once flirted with PEI.'

Oliver broke in, 'This is what I don't understand. How can Holt be a mouthpiece for a group that basically fronts for white supremacy when he's part black?'

Marge said, 'Holt hated his black father because Daddy sent away his mother and brother. So Holt denied his black heritage and identified with the victim – his mother – who was white.'

'Not at first,' Decker said. 'He was a typical Berkeley radical.'

'But he went through a big metamorphosis. In the end, he sided with Mommy because she was the underdog, and Dad was a bastard.'

'I didn't say his father was a bastard.'

'You said he was a schmuck,' Oliver added.

'Yeah, but his wife might have been horrible, too.'

'Maybe bad as a wife, but maybe she was a good mother. And Darrell really never got a chance to find out who she was, because she and Darrell's brother were exiled.' Marge rolled herself back to the computer. 'You like my explanation? I've been working it over in my mind for the last hour.'

'Freud would be proud,' Decker said.

'No, really.' Marge was emphatic. 'Doesn't it make sense?'

'It floats my boat,' Oliver stated.

Decker said, 'We're never going to be able to break all these files here. We need professionals.'

'I second that,' Marge said. 'But she's not going to let us take the computers unless we invent a good reason to do so.' She thought a moment. 'We need Holt. You don't think the father was holding back?'

Decker shrugged. His cell phone went off. He pushed the green send button. 'Decker.'

'Erin Kershan's real name is Erin Beller.' Wanda's voice was filled with excitement. 'She's a fifteen-year-old runaway from Scarsdale, New York. Her parents have been looking for her for six months. She's run away before but only for a week at a time. This last time, she flew the coop with some lowlife biker that she had met in Woodstock, New York, while on a family vacation.'

'Any clue as to where she might be right now?'

'Yes. They have relatives here in L.A. – in Brentwood. Relatives they don't like.' Wanda gave him the address. 'The Bellers had called the Frammels – the Brentwood relatives – just to let them know that Erin was missing and would they please call if she showed up. Of course, the Frammels said that they would contact them if she showed.'

'But so far there's been no contact.'

'Exactly. But lack of contact with the parents doesn't mean that Erin isn't there now.'

'And you did instruct the Bellers not to call their relatives in Brentwood.'

'Yes. I did. I told them that if they gave Erin a heads-up, both of us would lose her. The parents didn't like it – they want to talk to her – but they're cooperating for now.'

'I'm not too far from Brentwood,' Decker said. 'Maybe I should pay them a *surprise* visit.'

'I think that would be a very good idea, sir.'

Alice Ranger was as thin as ever, her face made even more severe by layers of foundation that gave her a ghostly appearance. The makeup looked newly applied, as if she were planning on going somewhere. If that were the case, she gave no indication of being in a hurry. On the contrary, she acted welcoming, as if the visit from Martinez and Webster were a social call. A brown knitted pantsuit hung on her bony frame; her feet were bare with toenails painted egg-plant purple.

'Come in, come in.' Acting like old friends. 'Would you like something to drink?'

Webster shook his head, but Martinez told her that water would be nice. He came from a culture that considered it an insult to refuse hospitality.

Alice regarded him with displeasure. Trying to stand in one spot, she teetered on her feet. 'Only water?'

'Water, juice, a Coke . . .'

'How about a rum-and-Coke?'

'No, thank you.'

'Don't be shy.'

'Then how about coffee?' Martinez asked.

'Coffee?' She was incredulous. 'It's well into the martini hour, Detective.'

'Thank you, but I'd still like coffee. How about making up a pot?'

'A whole pot?'

'Yeah. Tom'll take a cup. And you'll join us, of course.'

Alice made a face. 'You want me to drink coffee?'

'Yeah. Go make up a pot, Mrs Ranger.'

'All right.' It took her a while to focus. 'I'll get you coffee.'

'Thank you.'

'Be right back.'

'Okay.'

'Don't go away.'

'No, we won't,' Webster said.

'Hey, you can talk,' Alice sniped.

'Yes, ma'am, I can talk.'

Alice's smile was loopy. 'Be right back.'

'Yes, ma'am.'

Finally she left. Martinez gave a quick once-over to the living room, hoping to glean some information about the family from the furnishings. Unfortunately, the decor was a vast snowscape of white carpet holding thick blobs of cream and white furniture. The art that broke up the vanilla walls was drab and shapeless, the coffee and end tables were as empty as the desert plains. No photos, no vases or bowls or plates or displays. No TV or entertainment unit, either. But there was a well-stocked, mirror-backed, granite-topped wet bar that took up half the room.

Webster had followed the arc of Martinez's eyes, seeing them light on the bar. He whispered, 'How much vermouth do you think is in that woman's liver?'

'That's between her and God. Our job is to get her reasonably sober enough to make sense.'

'It's going to take more than coffee to do that.'

'Then we'll have to take our time.'

'How 'bout I peek upstairs on the off-chance that Ruby's there?' Tom suggested. 'Could be the reason why the mother is so soused.'

'You know, it's a good idea,' Martinez said. 'Even if she's not up there, you can snoop around the room. I'll stay here. If she comes back and wonders where you are, I'll tell her you're in the bathroom.'

'Yeah, I think she likes you better than me anyway.'

'That's because I smile when I talk to her.'

Webster nodded, stood up, and quietly made his way up the narrow staircase, remembering that Ruby had hibernated on the third floor, her space being more an attic than a room. When he opened the door, he slumped with disappointment. All of Ruby's influence had disappeared, and in its place was an insipid guest room. It had ivory walls, a blond oak-planked floor, a Persian-style rug, and a double bed dressed with a dusty rose comforter and a matching quilted head-board. Crammed into the square footage were also a TV sitting in an oak bookcase, and a couple of night-stands. Harmless, characterless. Ruby hadn't been there for a long time.

Out of habit or boredom, Webster went through the drawers, checked under the bed and furniture, slipped his hand under the pillow, lifted up the covers, stuck his arm between the mattress and bed frame. And what did he expect to find? A gun? A hidden computer file? A stash of money or drugs?

All he found were a couple of dust balls.

By the time he made it back down, Alice had returned with the coffee.

'Did you get lost?' she asked him.

'Just looking for the little boys' room.'

'On the third floor? Ever hear of a powder room?' She rolled her eyes. 'You were snooping.'

Webster smiled boyishly. The woman wasn't as pickled as he had thought.

Alice said, 'You won't find anything of hers in it. I redid the place. Never felt so good about anything in my life. Clearing out her garbage was instant therapy. That girl has been trouble from day one.'

'In what way?' Martinez asked.

'What way?' Alice shook her head. She had returned with a glass of something amber and iced in a crystal tumbler. 'Lying, drinking, stealing. And those are her good points.' But her face held tremendous pain. 'You know, it's getting there that's so hard. Once you make the commitment to separate, the rest is easy. I should have done it a long time ago.' She moistened her lips with her drink. 'Now that she's gone . . . it's calmer. Things don't bother me too much. Even his tramps.' She cocked her head at nothing in particular. 'Nah, even *he* don't bother me.'

'He' was obviously the husband.

'When was the last time you saw Ruby?' Webster asked.

'When was the last time you saw her?' Alice parried. 'That was my last time.'

'That was about six months ago,' Martinez said. 'She hasn't contacted you since then?'

'Nope.'

'Not even to say hello?'

'Especially not to say hello.'

'How about for money?'

'Nope. Although if she did contact me, it would have been for money. Nah, I haven't heard from her. Ruby has been flush the last couple of years. Probably whoring. Or stealing. Or even dealing.'

'How about computer hacking?' Martinez brought up.

'What?'

'Playing with computers.'

'Yeah, Ruby used to do that a lot.'

Webster said, 'I didn't see her computer up there.'

'She took it with her.'

'What did you do with the belongings she left behind, Mrs Ranger?'

'Threw them away. I would have burnt them in the fireplace – you know – to make a statement. But then I was afraid I'd set off the smoke alarms.'

'Did she leave any disks or CD-ROMs behind?' Webster threw in.

'Nothing that I took notice of.' Alice swirled the ice in her drink. 'I bought her a laptop. A state-of-the-art Toshiba. It put me back almost eighteen hundred dollars. God, was I a sucker.'

'So whatever was left over in the room,' Martinez said, 'you threw it all away?'

'Threw it away, gave it away. She had an old Nintendo game system. I gave that away to Goodwill. I also gave away her bed, her furniture, her old TV, and the clothes she left behind. As far as I'm concerned, that girl is my daughter only on her birth certificate.'

Webster said, 'You're angry.'

'Furious.'

'Do you know if she was doing anything illegal?' Martinez asked.

'She was doing drugs.' Alice shrugged. 'That's illegal.'

'What kind of drugs?'

'I don't know . . . I never asked. She's been doing them since she was fourteen. Nah, I don't know for certain that she was doing something real bad. But she hung in bad company.'

'Like who?'

'She brought home strange boys. The last one was really spooky. A black boy. Light skinned but you could tell it anyway.'

'Darrell Holt?'

Alice thought a moment. 'He never did say his name. She brought him by twice. I put my foot down. I said no bringing boys up to your room. She spit in my face and told me she'd eff whoever the eff she wanted to eff.' The woman sighed. 'I shoulda kicked her out.' Tears. 'But it was my own daughter.'

'Did she come home with any other friends?'

'Once or twice she brought up the boy who was in the papers.' Alice's eyes darkened. 'The one that was . . .'

'Ernesto Golding,' Martinez filled in.

Alice made swipes at her cheek. 'What happened?'

'That's what we're looking into,' Webster stated.

'You think Ruby had something to do with it?'

'You tell me,' Martinez answered.

'How should I know? I never had any idea what that girl was doing.' But her eyes told a different story.

Martinez pressed her. 'Did you ever meet Ernesto?'

Slowly Alice nodded. 'Once. He came here waiting for Ruby. She never did show up.' She opened and closed her mouth. 'He made an attempt to be civil. I thought that was nice.' She got misty-eyed. 'Ruby . . . she was bigmouthed, but she wouldn't . . . she couldn't have . . . you know.'

They knew.

'Ernesto . . . he was okay.' Another sip. 'He was Ruby's flavor of the month. She was probably using him. But using people is one thing . . . The other thing . . . she wouldn't . . .' But the woman did not sound convinced. 'She wouldn't do that!'

'You mean murder?' Webster filled in.

Alice grimaced. 'My daughter is not a killer!'

Obviously, the woman, as much as she was proclaiming not to care, couldn't wipe her hands of her own offspring.

Martinez spoke in a soft voice. 'You tried.'

'Yes, I did,' Alice agreed. 'I tried very hard. But very hard wasn't good enough. I tried but I still failed.'

'Any idea where she may be?'

'No, but if you find her, tell her she owes me money for junking her stuff.'

Webster said, 'Mrs Ranger, would you happen to have an old phone bill from when she was living at home?'

'Probably.'

A long pause.

'You think you can look it up for us?'

'Now?'

'Yes, now,' Martinez said.

'It could take a little while.'

'We can wait.'

Alice stared at her drink. 'She's in big trouble, isn't she?' There was a long pause. Then she whispered, 'Is she in danger?'

Martinez shrugged but didn't answer. Alice felt herself shudder. It was always what wasn't said that scared her.

31

The house was situated on the side of a mountain, one of those places precariously perched on concrete reinforced stilts and built by optimists who denied earthquakes happened in Southern California. It was dark outside, so it was hard to tell the color of the exterior, but it looked to be tan and white stucco spruced up with white gingerbread. Since it was a two-story split-level, most of the physical structure remained hidden, the majority of the edifice having been bolted and carved (hopefully) into the rocky hillside. The appeal of these domiciles extended beyond the thrill of danger: the homes had tremendous views of the verdant canyons and the glittering city lights beyond.

Since the house was gated, Decker had to ring to get in, but suddenly announcing himself as a police officer would ruin the element of surprise. He looked around. Behind the metal barrier was a small blip of asphalt driveway holding a lone black Mercedes. Outside the gate, resting on the fold of a mountainous curve, were an SUV and a three-year-old Mustang.

Decker rang the bell. A woman, talking through a squawk box, answered his page.

'Yes?'

'You own that orange Mustang parked outside?'

'Who is this?'

'We're about to tow it away. It's got four unpaid parking tickets.'

'What? Hold on! Justin! Come here this instant! There's a man—'

'I'm towing the car now.'

'Hold on!'

'Can't do that,' Decker said. 'I've got a job to do.'

'There's a mistake—'

'No mistake. Some of the tickets are over a year old.'

'Wait! Don't tow the car. Just hold on!' She screamed, '*Justin! Get over here right now!*'

Purposely, Decker didn't answer. A moment later the gate began to swing open. Light spilled out from the front door. A woman came running after him. 'Excuse me! Who are you?'

She was knife-edge thin and looked equally hard. A pinched nose, hollow cheeks, a strong chin, a shiny white forehead with straight black hair sprayed stiff and combed straight back.

'Just what do you think you're do—' Panting, she glanced about with jerks of the head. 'I don't see any tow truck.'

Decker took out his ID and badge and showed it to

her. 'That's because there is no tow truck. I'm the lead investigator on the Baldwin murder case. And I bet you know why I'm here, Mrs Frammel.'

Panicked eyes went from the ID folder to Decker's face, then back to the badge. 'I . . . I want to—'

'Let's take it inside. No reason for the entire neighborhood to hear us.' Decker began to urge her forward by her elbow, but she resisted.

'You'll have to come back when my husband's home.'

'You're harboring a fugitive wanted for murder,' Decker replied. 'I think not.'

Again the woman was stunned. 'Wanted for . . . no, no, no, no, no. You've got it all wrong.'

'So let's go inside, and Erin and you can explain it to me.'

At the mention of her niece's name, the woman winced. 'God damn it! How do I end up in these situations?'

'Let's go inside.'

'How do I know that badge is real? How do I know you're not going to attack me once I let you inside?'

'Because I would have attacked you by now.' Decker sidestepped her, jogged up to the front door, and pushed it open. Walking in, he took two steps down, his feet sinking into deep-piled gray carpet, his eyes drawn to the glass wall before him.

The view was breathtaking – a stunning panorama of twinkling, multicolored lights. Below the switchboard sky were long stretches of onyx black that probably held the wooded copses seen only in the daytime. The room held modern furniture in vogue about fifteen, twenty years ago – sling-back leather sofas and chairs, chrome and glass tables. A stone wet bar sat against one wall; a stone fireplace stood on the other. Resting above the mantel was a tremendous, unframed canvas of some kind of leaping animal. It could have been a deer, a cougar, or even a Matisse-type dancer.

'Where is she?' Decker asked.

'I want to call a lawyer.'

'You could do that. But it might make things worse for you. Because if you call a lawyer, then I'll have to do things like . . . officially arresting someone. But sure, go ahead.'

The woman tapped her toe. 'I want to call my husband.'

'Sure, call him.' Decker looked at his watch. 'But I'm on a tight schedule. If I can't conclude the interview here, I'm going to have to haul Erin down to the stationhouse. The one where I work . . . in the Valley.' His eyes went back to the view. 'You can meet us there if you want.'

'At least let me call my sister.' A pause. 'That would complicate things.'

'You know your sister.'

'It's not my sister who's the problem, it's her husband. If he were any more of a fascist, he'd be a Nazi. And that's a pretty good trick because he's Jewish.' She rolled her eyes. 'Not that I'm anti-Semitic. He just happens to be a prick.'

'There's usually one in every family. I'd like to talk to Erin now.'

'I *knew* this was a bad idea, taking her in. She just looked so . . . scared.'

'I'm sure she is scared. That's why I'd like to talk to her.'

She kneaded her hands. 'I don't know . . .'

Talking more to herself than to Decker. He said, 'While you decide, I'll look around in the meantime.' He started down a long foyer that was covered with the same plush carpet. The pile was so soft, it was almost like wading in muck.

The woman came after him. 'You can't just . . . Goddamn! *Justin, turn down that awful music!*'

There was no discernible decrease in volume. To Decker, she shouted, 'Now, you stay right where you are. I will not let the police bully me or Erin or anyone. That poor girl has gone through enough.'

Decker walked back into the living room, away from the noise. 'So tell me about it.'

The woman's lips shut.

'Mrs Frammel, my coming here may have been the best thing for your entire family. Somebody – or bod*ies* – has killed four people in two days. Given the numbers, I don't think he or they would hesitate at killing four more.'

She shuddered. 'That's a horrible thing to say.' She brought her hand to her throat. 'You're being deliberately cruel. Just like my brother-in-law.'

'I'm not being cruel, I'm trying to emphasize the gravity of the situation.'

The woman wrapped herself in her arms. 'She isn't in any of these rooms.'

Decker studied Mrs Frammel's face – guileless, worried, and concerned. 'Where is she?'

'Why should I trust you . . . what's your name again?'

'Lieutenant Peter Decker. It's on the front page of the paper. I'm quoted regarding the death of Dee Baldwin. Where is Erin, ma'am?'

The woman hesitated. 'We have a cave . . . down below. My husband . . . he wanted to be more . . . in touch with the elements. He excavated this room from the wall of the mountain.' She made a face. 'It's his pride and joy. He did it all himself. But it isn't up to code.'

'I promise I won't report him to the building commission. How do I get down there?'

She told Decker to follow her. She led him into a wide, open caterer's kitchen, filled with stainless steel appliances, stainless countertops, and white, lacquered cabinetry. In the middle sat a leather and steel dining set, the table being round and balanced on a pedestal that looked more like a giant spring than something designed to support. The chairs had black leather seats and were also balanced on spring-looking bases. Perhaps if one bounced hard enough, one could catapult across the room.

'This way,' the woman told him.

'Thank you, Mrs Frammel.'

'Doreen.'

'Thank you, Doreen,' Decker repeated.

'I suppose I should answer "you're welcome", but I don't know if that would be answering truthfully.' She sneered. 'God, why does he play that music at ear-splitting level?'

'To annoy you.'

'Well, it's working.' She opened a drawer and took out a key. Then she brought him into the service porch. A Miele washing machine was tumbling wet, soapy clothes. Doreen stared at the rotary drum for a moment. 'Sometimes I think it's better than network TV.'

'It's certainly more dynamic.'

Doreen managed a small grin. 'She's a real screwed-up kid. I'm the first to admit it. But she doesn't deserve to go to jail because she, like my sister, has lousy taste in boys.'

'Lousy taste isn't punishable by imprisonment. But aiding and abetting a criminal is.'

'She's stupid,' Doreen insisted. 'Cut her slack.'

'Why don't you let me talk to her first?'

The woman rubbed her eyes and unlocked a door. She flicked on a wall switch, and a beam of narrow yellow light revealed a narrow staircase. 'Watch your step, watch your head. I hope you're not claustrophobic.'

'No, I'm not.'

'Then you're one step above me. I hate this. Frankly, I think my husband's crazy.'

The steps going down were wooden and rickety and too small for his feet. Decker had to tiptoe on a few of them. He also had to stoop to descend the steps. By the time he was close to the bottom, he was almost entirely bent over. The passageway ended in another door. Heavy metal music escaped from the rocky walls. It was muted, so all Decker could hear was the thumping of the bass line.

Doreen knocked. 'Erin, honey, open up, it's me.'

No answer.

She knocked again. 'Erin?'

Nothing.

'Come on!' She pounded.

Suddenly, the music turned softer. The door opened. The kid's eyes did a quick assessment; she decided that slamming the door shut was her best bet. But Decker had anticipated her actions. Positioned well, he leaned forward, taking the brunt of the force on his shoulder – the one *without* the bullet scar. At the same time, he threw his weight onto the swinging slab of solid wood, and the door flew back open.

He went inside. He could stand up straight, but barely so. At certain points, the cave-room ceiling brushed against his hair, making it not more than six-five or -six.

Decker concluded that Mr Frammel must be a short man.

The niche was big enough – about two hundred square feet. The floor had been finished with cork tiles, but the walls had been blasted from the raw mountain, giving the room a primitive caveman-era look. Any wall that wasn't rock was glass. At one point, the room had been constructed to look as if the floor dropped out from under one's feet, giving one an off-balance feeling of floating or falling – disconcerting but original, he gave Mr Frammel that much.

The space held a bed, a TV, and a desk with a computer, modem, phone, and fax. There was a book-shelf that held more videos than novels, but there were some paperbacks, almost all of them in the true-crime genre. Lurid cases. Decker remembered some of them. He wondered if Mr Frammel had hidden whips and chains somewhere.

Erin had locked herself behind a door – presumably the bathroom.

Decker turned off the blaring stereo. 'Come on out, Erin. I'm here to help you.'

'You're part of it. Go away!'

'Part of what?'

'His worldwide alliance – the New World Order.'

'I'm not part of anything.'

Erin was silent.

Decker thought a moment. 'All right. If you feel safer talking from behind the door, then that's okay with me. Just talk to me, okay?'

Several moments passed, then a full minute.

'Aunt Doreen?' The voice from behind the door was tiny.

'Yes, I'm here.'

'I'm sorry.'

'It's okay, darling. Come on out. He's . . .' She glanced at Decker, her expression sour. 'I think he's here to help.'

'You think?' Decker whispered.

She snarled back, 'I don't know who the hell you are.'

'Aunt Doreen?' she bleated.

'Yes, Erin. What? Come out, okay?'

The woman was growing impatient.

Decker whispered, 'Maybe you should call up your husband or your sister.'

'And leave you alone with her?'

Decker took a step forward until he was almost chest to chest with the woman. 'And you really think that you could protect her against me?'

She swallowed hard.

Decker stepped back. 'I'm on the right side. Go make some phone calls to the police if you don't believe me.'

The woman hesitated.

'Aunt Doreen?'

'What, Erin?'

'Do you think it's okay?'

A sigh. 'Yes, honey, I think it's okay. I think it's time we tell the authorities.'

Seconds passed . . . then the door opened.

32

The girl was a stick figure: one-dimensional arms and legs with almost no body. She had thin brown hair – long and straight and dull. Wide waiflike brown eyes were set over small lips. Her nose was red and dripping. She wiped it with a bony finger.

'She has a terrible cold,' Doreen said.

'Go upstairs, Mrs Frammel,' Decker told her. More force was in his voice. 'We'll be fine.'

Doreen looked at Erin. The young girl nodded.

'I'm leaving the doors open,' Doreen announced. 'Shout if you need anything.' Then she started the journey up the steps. Decker waited until he heard the footsteps recede. Then he sat on the edge of the bed. She was sitting on the opposite corner, legs tucked under her wasted body, head against propped pillows.

Decker pulled out his notepad and a small tape recorder. 'Do you mind?'

She shook her head.

'I need you to talk, Erin. The recorder doesn't pick up head movements.'

'You can record it. I don't care.'

'Good.' Decker adjusted the volume, then set the machine in the middle of the bed. 'How long have you been using?'

Erin's eyes jumped around, landing on the machine.

Decker said, 'I'm not going to bust you. I'm just curious.'

'I dunno. Over a year.' She rubbed her nose, then got up and closed the door. She plopped back down onto the bed, bouncing the tape recorder as she did so. 'That's why I stayed with Darrell so long. He supplied me.'

'What happened to the biker you took off with?'

'A real bummer.' She straightened her spine. 'I thought he was gonna be my meal ticket . . . but then he made me work for it.' Her mouth turned downward. 'Asshole.'

'What about Darrell?'

'He's an asshole, too. A sick puppy, but so are most guys. But he didn't make me work for my shit. All I had to do was give him what he liked, the way he liked it. Sex games – him and her.'

' "Her" is Ruby Ranger?'

She nodded.

'What kind of sex games?'

She shrugged.

'Did he take movies?'

'None that I saw.' She sniffed deeply. 'The two of them . . . they liked to pick up teenagers at a party . . .

screw them . . . mess with their heads. That's what they really liked to do . . . mess with their heads.'

'How'd you meet him?'

She scratched her scalp with a dirty nail. 'The biker that I went off with ran with a pack. The leader gave me to Darrell for money. Weird. Like they sold me for a grand or something.'

'Sold you?'

'Yeah, but it turned out okay. I didn't have to turn tricks.'

'What *did* you have to do?'

'Just play their little games . . . get tied up and scream a lot . . . you know, act like I was scared.' She made a face, stuck out her tongue. 'Stupid, but it beat the hell out of turning tricks. I think I could have made the break – Darrell wouldn't have hunted me down – but I decided to stay. It was better than home.'

'Your home life was that bad?'

Her face turned hard. 'My parents are assholes. My mom's this perfect soccer mom who won't stand up to my dad, who's a super asshole. My sister's the princess. I'm the dumb one in the family. Me, I could never do anything right. It was all about how stupid I was, how ugly I was, how I wouldn't ever be anything because I was stupid and ugly . . .' There were tears in her eyes. 'He never trusted me. He always went through my drawers. At first, he didn't find anything, because I didn't do anything. Later on, he found my stash. He locked me up in a place for users. God, I was only smoking pot, and he acted like I was this strung-out H addict. So he sent me away to the school for fuckups. I ran away. After that, he said he was sending me to reform school or juvenile hall or something even more shitty than the fuckup school. I told him over my dead body. And then I slugged him. Then he slugged me back. I fell and hit my head. The asshole almost put me in the hospital.'

'Why didn't you report him?'

Tears fell from her eyes. 'He has connections. The easiest thing to do was to take off. My mother was really mad that my father hit me. Of course, she wasn't mad enough to throw him out. Instead, she suggested we all go away for a little time out. So we went to Woodstock. That's where I met Brock.'

'The biker.'

She nodded, then slumped back down in the pillows.

Decker tried to be objective, but it was hard. All these wounded lives.

She went on. 'Darrell was a perv, but at least he didn't hurt me. And he gave me junk. He could afford it. He was always flush.'

'The Baldwins paid him well?'

She shrugged.

'What did he tell you about them?'

'Not much. I didn't ask questions about things that weren't my business.'

'What was your business?'

'Mostly I helped Darrell at PEI. At first, I thought he was a lunatic, but I didn't care 'cause he was giving me money. Then after a while . . . I don't know . . . I got into it. Darrell started making sense. Especially the stuff about the Jews controlling everything. Because when you got a father like mine – the most controlling asshole in the world – it's easy to believe that. That's what Darrell and I really had in common. We both hated our fathers!'

Somehow it always boiled down to bad parenting. Which made Decker feel queasy. Sure, there were lots of other explanations for Jacob's rebellious behavior – the loss of his father at a young age, the molestation, the remarriage of his mother, a new baby, and his innate temperament. But did Decker do all he could have done to get the boy through it? All those nights working instead of taking care of business at home.

Erin continued. 'After a while, I got into it . . . the whole PEI philosophy. He told me he got most of the ideas from some genius guy named Ricky Moke. I'm not the sharpest knife in the block, but it didn't take long for me to figure out who Moke was. But I went along with it anyway. That was Darrell's thing – different identities. He had a million of them. Most of them came out in his sex games.'

'When did Darrell use the name Darrell Holt, and when did he use Ricky Moke?'

'Ricky Moke was his baaaad boy.' She leaned forward and grinned knowingly. It made her look years older and decades harder. 'He actually became this Ricky guy with separate identity pictures, a Social Security card, a *graduation* diploma. God, that was real impressive to me. I told him to get me one of those. It's like Darrell cut himself in two. As Darrell, he was the political activist. Sometimes it was real weird because Darrell would talk about Ricky like Ricky was another person. A real nother person. Like they were really two people—'

'I get it.'

'And he'd say things like . . . like although he admired Ricky, he didn't like him because Ricky was doing illegal stuff like hacking and bombing and being a sexual pervert. Tell you the truth, I liked Ricky better than Darrell. He was more exciting. Ricky's wanted by the FBI, you know.'

'For computer hacking.'

'For hacking and for bombing.'

'I haven't found the bombing to be true.'

'Yeah, look again. I wouldn't put it past Ricky.'

'Ricky *is* Darrell, Erin.'

'I know,' the teen answered. 'But they've been two separate people for so long, it's hard to think like that. Darrell . . . he's an alien, but he's brilliant.'

'So I've heard.'

'Why should you doubt it? Most pervs are brilliant.'

'No, Erin, that's not true. There are many stupid perverted people.'

'Not the ones I know.'

'That may be. But I'll tell you something. The smart ones are often the most dangerous, because they are able to plan their crimes. These murders didn't happen at random. They were planned, and we both know who planned them.'

Water pooled in her orbs. She didn't answer him.

Decker said, 'I need you to tell me where Darrell is.'

'I don't know—'

'Yes, you do know!'

But she denied it with a fierce stare and a shake of the head. '*No, I don't know!* Darrell's a survivalist, in case you forgot. He was in Old Man Baldwin's camp when he was sixteen or seventeen. He hated it, but he did learn how to survive in the wilds. What he didn't pick up from camp, he learned later from Hank Tarpin after Darrell joined PEI. Darrell's been going in and out of the woods for years as Ricky Moke. He claims he's got all these little campsites all over the state. He could hide out for ever. You'll never find him. The FBI hasn't.'

'Can you give me a guess?'

'Nope. And if he called the apartment to say where he was going, I didn't get the message. Soon as I heard about Ernesto and the doctor getting whacked, I took off.'

'The unit number you gave us was bogus. Where were you living?'

'With Darrell.'

'And it didn't bother you that Darrell hadn't come home that night?'

'Nah. Lots of times he was out all night.'

'Doing what?'

'How should I know?'

'Guess.'

'Maybe with Ruby.'

'And where does Ruby live?'

'Beats me.'

Decker thought a moment. Something was off. At the time of the synagogue vandalism, Ruby was living at home. Then she moved back up north. Wanda had given him the former listing. But then she disappeared and presumably came back down to L.A. So where did she reside?

Alice Ranger swore that she hadn't seen her daughter in months. The empty room seemed to bear that out. And Wanda had yet to find a temporary address for Ruby. She had checked with the DMV, the DWP, the gas company, local credit-card companies, Ruby's former bank . . . No new address had popped up. So now Decker was beginning to think that maybe Ruby had a Ricky Moke-type alias as well. Both of them – Darrell and Ruby – knew how to manipulate the Internet. They could enter any world from thousands of miles away under hundreds of different aliases. It made for a vast arena for potential crime that was staggering.

Erin was talking.

'. . . stuffed all my shit into a paper bag and came here. I never did tell Darrell my real last name. But I know he could have found out if he wanted to.' She bit a nonexistent nail, her fingertips being raw and red. 'Do you think he'll come here?'

'The thought has crossed my mind.'

'This place is patrolled, you know. But the guys don't look too scary. I could probably take 'em down if I had the weapons.'

Decker's eyes went to Erin's young face. The steely way she had spoken those words had sent a chill down his spine. 'I'll put in a call to West L.A. police for protection. They'll send over some cruisers to keep watch until we can sort this out.'

'That's good. I wouldn't want anything bad to happen to my aunt. She's the only person in the world who has ever been *nice* to me.'

Stated so plaintively. She was a broken soul, but that didn't mean she was harmless. Street junkies – especially young ones who have experienced so much rough trade in so few years – were notoriously unpredictable.

'So even when Darrell was living with you, he stayed out all night?'

'Sometimes.'

'Ever tell you about it?'

'Nope. I just assumed he was with Ruby, doing their thing.'

'And you didn't care what Darrell was doing?'

'You mean, was I jealous?' She laughed. 'I didn't care as long as he was nice to me.'

Nice, as in supplying her habit. He said, 'I was thinking more like the illegal things. Weren't you worried about the police catching up with you?'

'A little. Still, it was worth the free junk.' She rubbed her nose. 'Think I should get tested?'

'For AIDS?'

'Yeah. When I started living with Darrell, he made me get tested. I was negative. I've only done it with, like, three other guys since then. Think I should get tested again?'

'It's a good idea.'

'Yeah. I thought so.' She sniffed. 'You're gonna take me into, like, custody, right?'

'Right.'

'I gotta get a lawyer, right?'

'Right,' Decker said. 'If you can't afford one, we'll get you one.'

'My parents are flush. They'll hire me out someone.' She looked at him. 'What about my jones? I'm not going cold.'

Barking orders as if she had a choice. But why rile her up? It would just make it harder to get her in. 'If you cooperate, I'll try to get you into a hospital under a doctor's supervision.'

'You mean like methadone?'

'*If* you cooperate,' Decker stressed. 'A couple more questions, Erin. Did you ever meet Ernesto Golding?'

She didn't have to think about the answer. 'Long time ago. Ruby brought him over to PEI a couple of times. Right before he trashed the synagogue.'

'Did you know that Ernesto was going to trash the synagogue?'

'You mean like before he did it?'

'Yes, that's what I mean.'

'No, I didn't know before . . . just afterward. Because it was all over the news.'

'Erin, I think Ernesto had help in that crime. What do you think?'

'I dunno.'

'Help like in Darrell Holt help.' He looked at her. 'It'll help you to tell the truth, Erin. Help you inside your heart, and help you with the law.'

'Far as I know, Darrell wasn't part of the synagogue mess.'

Decker smoothed his mustache. 'How about Darrell as Ricky Moke?'

'Nah, not him either.'

Decker studied her. 'You honestly think that Ernesto vandalized the synagogue all by himself?'

'I dunno. All I'm saying is Darrell didn't do it. Or Ricky. Or me.'

'What about Ruby Ranger?'

She shrugged. 'Nah, Ruby would never do it. Might break a nail or something. The girl never got her hands dirty. But I could see her manipulating Ernesto by using sex as a reward. That's what they both liked to do . . . manipulate people.'

She looked down, her face reddening. Decker asked her what was on her mind. After more prodding, she finally spoke. 'I was just surprised about Ernesto's murder. It was . . . a shock.'

'You had no idea?'

'*No!* It freaked me out, man.' She sounded genuine. 'I thought he was—' She stopped herself.

'Part of the Baldwin scam?' Decker filled in.

'I was gonna say "I thought he was one of us," ' Erin answered. 'I don't know if he was popped on purpose or he was just in the wrong place at the wrong time.'

'What do you think?'

'I know that Darrell was real mad about the temple thing. But then after Ernesto confessed, I thought it was . . . over.'

'Why was Darrell mad about the vandalism?' Decker asked. 'I would think it would fit into his grandiose image of himself.'

'It brought the heat to PEI,' Erin stated. 'The last thing Darrell wanted was to be noticed, because he had this thing with Dee Baldwin . . . the test thing.'

'Tell me about that.'

'I don't know about it.'

Decker glared at her. 'We could keep talking here . . . or I could take you down to the stationhouse.'

'You're gonna do that anyway.'

'True. But down there I won't be the only one who'll be talking to you.'

'What is it? A torture chamber or something? I've had worse.'

'Suit yourself.'

'What did you ask me about?'

'What do you know about the Baldwins?'

'This is just . . . guessing kind of, okay?'

'Okay.'

'Okay.' She sat up. 'From what I could figure out, I think the old lady was paying Ricky Moke money to hack into the test center to get advance copies or questions of all the college tests or something like that. He had this whole network thing because you can't get the stuff just by hacking, 'cause they have protection things like firewalls . . . which isn't a problem for Ricky. But apparently the testing center has its own computer that isn't connected to anything on-line. But Ricky had this whole thing of people he knew. I think someone was bought off.'

'How did Hank Tarpin fit in?'

'He was with PEI.'

'He was also employed by the Baldwins.'

'Yeah, he was the head guy at the nature camp.'

'Was he involved in the hacking scheme?'

'I dunno. Why don't you ask him?'

Was she serious? Decker said, 'I would except he's dead, Erin.'

The girl blanched like boiled cauliflower. 'Oh!' She stuck the raw fingertip into her mouth. 'Oh God! When?'

'We found him about six hours ago. It's been on the news—'

'Who the hell has been watching the news!' Abruptly, she jumped up and started to pace while nibbling on her thumb. 'Man, he's covering all bases, isn't he?'

'Let me ask you again. Was Tarpin part of the computer hacking—'

'Are you kidding?' she broke in. 'Tarpin was a dweeb. He was paranoid about anything that had to do with the twentieth century!'

She stomped back and forth in front of the picture window. One wrong move and she'd be free-falling several hundred feet.

'Sit down, Erin,' Decker ordered.

The teen didn't seem to hear him. 'Hank was pure PEI – things should go back to the good old days when the white man was the strong, all-powerful but benevolent father.'

Decker got up and grabbed her arm. Instinctively, Erin flailed in his grip. He said, 'I'm worried that you're going to have an accident. You're awfully close to the window.'

She looked around, realizing she was inches from the

glass wall. 'Oh . . . okay.' She sat back down. 'It's tempting, you know. Just take the plunge.'

His mind flashed to his own daughter hurling over the mountainside. Instantly, his heart was hammering.

She's fine, he told himself. *Doing her thing over at Hollywood and doing it well. As a matter of fact, she's* way more *fine than you are*. 'There are people you can talk to after we clear up this mess.'

'Yeah, shrinks. No thanks!' She let out a bitter laugh. 'Look what happened to the Baldwins.'

'And you don't think Tarpin had anything to do with the hacking scheme?'

'No. The Tarpin I knew had this weird code of honor – like it was okay to hate as long as you were honest about it. Maybe it was something he learned in the Marines.' She looked at Decker. 'Hank was in the Marines.'

Decker knew. But Maryam had seen Holt and Tarpin go into Dee Baldwin's office about six months ago. If Tarpin wasn't a part of it, what had that meeting been all about?

'Tarpin . . .' She took in a deep breath and let it out. 'He had some kind of argument with Darrell around the time of the vandalism. When was that? About six months ago?'

'About.'

'I just caught the tail end of it.'

'What was it about?'

'Something having to do with the direction of PEI.' She tapped her foot. 'You know, it was Tarpin who introduced Darrell to Dee like three, four years ago.'

'No, I didn't know that,' Decker said.

Erin became animated. 'PEI was going under, and Darrell needed money to keep it going. So Darrell went to Hank, and Hank convinced Dee to give Darrell a job. She brought him on to do computer work because she didn't know shit about computers. Darrell told me that at first she gave him just secretarial stuff. Then Darrell and Dee got to know each other . . . pretty well, in fact.' Her smile became a leer. 'One thing led to another with work and with play.'

'Who suggested breaking into the testing center?'

'Probably Darrell. But I don't know that. All I know is that Hank was upset with Darrell. He was saying things about Darrell compromising PEI's integrity and hurting the Baldwins. Darrell kept saying that it was Dee's idea, so he should just shut up.'

'So Tarpin liked the Baldwins?'

She rubbed her nose. 'Tarpin liked the boys . . . not to fuck them, but he liked doing the camp thing. He liked to play Mr Marine. I don't think he'd hurt any of the boys, including Ernesto. And I can't see him whacking the Baldwins.'

Decker formulated ideas. Had Tarpin threatened to expose the hacking scheme? Was that why he was murdered? If so, it had taken Darrell six months to do it. And then there was Ernesto. How'd he fit in? Decker asked Erin for her opinion.

She looked down at her lap. 'Once . . . when Darrell thought I was sleeping, I overheard Ruby telling Darrell things . . . that Ernesto was a problem.'

'A problem . . .' Decker waited until he could make eye contact with the girl. A hard stare. 'What did he say to that?'

'Maybe he said something like "Take care of him." '

Take care of him.

'And what did that sound like to you, Erin?'

The teenager didn't answer.

The little psychopath! She knew all along. Decker said, 'Didn't you just tell me that Ernesto's death came as a shock to you?'

'It did!'

'Then I'll repeat my question. What did "Take care of him" mean to you?'

She began to cry. 'I didn't *know* Ernesto was going to *die*!'

'But you knew it wasn't going to be good—'

'I thought Darrell was just . . . being cool or something.'

'To whack someone is to be cool?'

'You're putting words into my mouth!' She was sobbing by then. Decker let her go on for a while. Then he said, 'So Ruby set Ernesto up?'

'How was I supposed to know? I'm just this dumb junkie living from fix to fix!'

A dumb, psycho, *lying* junkie, Decker wanted to add. He shut off the recorder, leaned forward, and grabbed the girl's shoulders, his eyes staring into her blank pupils. 'Erin, where can I find Darrell?'

'I don't know,' she whimpered. 'I swear.'

Decker let go of her arms and backed away, giving her some breathing room. His eyes continued to bore into hers. 'Give me *an idea*, little girl! Something! *Anything!*'

'He's probably hiding in the hills somewhere between Santa Barbara and Orange County. I don't think he's left Southern California.'

'Narrow it down!' Decker ordered.

'*Stop yelling at me!*' she screamed.

'What's going on down there?' a disembodied voice yelled down. Doreen to the rescue. 'I'm coming down right now!'

Decker glared at Erin. 'You're in trouble.'

'I don't know where he is!' she bleated. 'Go lean on Ruby Ranger, why don't you? She's known Darrell a lot longer than I have.'

Doreen appeared. 'The questioning is over!'

'Fair enough. I'm taking her in.'

'What?' Doreen was outraged. 'You can't.'

'I can and I will. You can come along. As a matter of fact, it would be good if you came along.'

'I have kids here!'

'So don't come.'

'So you're just going to arrest her?' Doreen asked.

'Take her in for questioning,' Decker corrected. 'Actually, I'm not going to take her in. I'm going to contact a female juvenile officer from Detectives to bring her in. It'll take about an hour.' To Erin he said, 'You have time to change and wash up if you want.' *Give yourself a final fix* was the nonspoken message. 'But you can't lock the door to the bathroom. If you do, I'll break it down.'

'Why?' Doreen asked.

'Policy,' Decker said. 'I need to keep an eye on her.'

'I *cooperated* with you,' Erin said sulkily.

Decker snapped back. 'That's why I'm letting you go to the bathroom, Erin.'

'Okay. Then maybe I will . . . go to the bathroom.' Her eyes met Decker's. 'They're probably together – Ruby and Darrell – but not the way you think.'

A sly smile spread across her face. Decker wanted to smack her. Instead he said, 'Erin, this isn't a game. You are in trouble. If I find out you're holding back, I will not only *nail* you legally, but you can forget about a hospital—'

Doreen blurted out, 'That's enough!'

But Erin spoke anyway. 'I told you I don't know where he is.' A hesitation. 'I'm fucking *scared*, you know!'

'You should be!' Decker answered. 'You remember the things that happened at your stay in rehab. Do you think jail without medical care is going to be better?'

'You're threatening her!' Doreen yelled.

'Telling her the facts.' Decker's eyes bored into Erin's. 'Help me and I'll help you. Makes your life easy.'

'I don't *know* where they are,' Erin repeated. 'I'd have no problem telling you, but I don't know!'

'You're repeating yourself. Tell me something new.'

'Okay, okay . . . uh, hey, how about this. Darrell considers Ruby's mouth a problem.'

Decker took this in. 'That's good. How big a problem?'

'A real, real big problem.' Out came the grin. 'She

was part of Darrell's operation. Now Darrell has to move on. So she's a problem.' She snapped her fingers several times. 'What's the word he used? A libility?'

'Liability,' Decker corrected. 'How much of a liability?'

Erin looked the other way. 'Something that has to be taken care of. Darrell doesn't like things hanging over his head. He likes . . . permanent solutions.'

'Meaning?'

She extended her first two fingers to form the barrel of a gun, then pantomimed the shot using a thumb for a trigger. Her grin turned into a savage smile aimed right at her aunt. 'What the hell! I hated the bitch!'

33

He was one of those old men who had that incongruous young man's hair – thick and luxurious except it was as white as Crisco. Way back when, he must have been a genuine blond. With his pale blue eyes and his pallid complexion, he could have easily passed for one of Hitler's Übermenschen. Perhaps that was why he lasted so long before he was crammed into a railroad car and headed toward certain death. His existence was a testament to miracles.

Having lived a long life, Oscar Adler wore the battle decorations of age, face and hands riddled with liver spots. His forehead held several shiny pink depressions – scar tissue left over from the removal of growths. Rina's father had had several basal-cell carcinomas removed from his face because he was also very fair. Both of her parents were light-complexioned and light-eyed, but her mother had always made a point of wearing a hat when she was in the sun. It had paid off. Mama had beautiful skin.

Oscar was older than both Mama and Papa. His cheeks clung to the skeletal structure underneath as tightly as a rubber mask. His eyes were sunken and framed by jaundiced folds of skin, the irises almost pinpoints under thick glasses. Remarkably, he still had his own teeth even if some of them were chipped, and all of them were as yellow as egg yolks. Rina knew about his teeth because Oscar was smiling as he slurped soup.

The man had a hearty appetite. He had managed to get down an entire rib of flanken. On the downside, he coughed back a third of it.

'You're eating too fast,' she scolded.

'Nyaaah,' he answered back.

'You're taking too big bites—'

'A *bissel fleisch*.'

'Not a *bissel*. *Asach*. Too much.'

He waved her off and tried to wolf down another piece of meat. Again Oscar started hacking. Rina gently patted his back. 'Are you okay?'

'Yeah, yeah—'

She picked up the spoon. '*Esse de kraut*.'

'No protein in the cabbage.'

His voice was high. He had to strain to get the words out of his larynx.

'But lots of good vitamins,' Rina told him. 'And it tastes good, right?'

Oscar didn't answer.

'Right?'

'Right, right. You don't have to talk Yiddish to me. I know English.'

'You were talking Yiddish to me.'

'A *bissel fleisch* isn't Yiddish.'

'Oh. Then what language is it?'

'It's . . . an expression.'

'An expression in Yiddish.'

'It's . . . English. *Bissel* is English.'

'Only if you're selling carpet shampooers.'

They were sitting in the rest home's common dining room. Eighty Jewish people over eighty years of age, the vast majority of them women. Some of them could have been beauties in their youth – the features were even and placed geometrically on the face – but the passage of time had dumped them into the category of 'elderly'. Which carried with it a certain amount of relief. Certainly for women the pressure was off. They didn't have to worry about that extra piece of cake. If they ate and kept their weight up, that was a sign of good health. Not surprisingly, there was a wide variation in personal appearance. Some women were dolled up with makeup and jewelry, but others, and not necessarily the older ones, were content in housecoats and mules.

This is me in fifty years, Rina thought, *if I'm lucky*. No matter how important the present appeared, it soon turned to the past, and that was the eternal cycle. The perpetuity of life made her smile. Rina had witnessed too much untimely death to be depressed about aging.

Rina smoothed her red cotton skirt and hiked up the sleeves of her white blouse to her elbows. There was some air blowing, but it felt tepid. Too much of a cold breeze wouldn't do well in the crowd with weak bones and swollen joints. So Rina tolerated the heat with understanding, happy that she was one of those lucky people who didn't sweat much. Twenty tables were scattered about the room awash in fluorescent light. A couple of window shades were open, allowing Rina to catch a glimpse of the moon and stars. The checkered linoleum floor was discolored but clean; the walls had been recently papered with a rose-on-a-vine pattern. White-uniformed Hispanic women wheeled carts in between tables and doled out the soup of the day: chicken noodle.

This created a problem.

At first, the kitchen refused to allow Rina to serve her soup to Oscar, not due to health reasons – she had purposely made it without salt – but because the dietitian was afraid that Rina's potage – thick and meaty – would start a rebellion among the residents. So Rina offered to serve it to Oscar in his room. But that wasn't acceptable, either. What if Oscar choked? (Apparently Oscar gagged a lot.) So then Rina offered to sit with Oscar out on the facility's patio. Again she was refused.

After twenty minutes of begging and cajoling, the dietitian finally relented. Oscar could consume the soup in full view of the other diners.

This wasn't sitting well with them. They eyed the food enviously. And it didn't help that Oscar kept smacking his lips – accidentally on purpose.

'It's good,' he announced.

'Of course. It's homemade.'

'Not all homemade cabbage soup is good. Sometimes it's greasy.'

'Not mine.'

'No, yours is not greasy.'

'Thank you.'

Oscar nodded, his head looking like a cotton ball waving on the stem of his scrawny neck. He wore a short-sleeved blue-and-red-striped shirt and tan slacks. His bony elbows were sharp enough to be lethal weapons. He ate noisily until the bowl was empty. He pushed it in front of Rina.

'You have more soup?' Oscar demanded.

'For tomorrow.'

'Why tomorrow?'

'The dietitian set a limit on just two bowls.'

'Why?'

Rina shrugged.

'I'm hungry now. Give me more soup.'

'I can't do that. She told me two bowls. If I don't listen to her, she'll throw the rest of the pot away.'

'Why two bowls?'

Rina leaned over. 'I think the others are jealous—'

'Nyaaah.'

'I think you can have some of the regular dinner if you want.'

'Nyaaah.'

'Do you want to go up to your room, Oscar?'

He thought a moment, then shook his head.

'Should we take a walk?'

Again the headshake.

'So we'll sit here for a while?'

This time he nodded. One of the servers was a young Hispanic named Yolanda. She offered Rina something to eat.

'Just a cup of tea when you get a chance,' Rina answered. 'You want tea, Oscar?'

'Tea is good.'

'Two teas.'

'Oscar likes his with honey,' Yolanda said. 'How about you?'

'I'll take honey,' Rina answered.

'Give me a minute.'

'Take your time,' Rina told her.

Oscar picked up the bowl and ran a finger around the inside rim, collecting a bit of the puree on the bony tip. He licked it eagerly. Rina sighed, snatched up the bowl, and stood up. 'This is ridiculous.'

Oscar looked upset. 'Where are you going?'

Like a kid who had done something wrong. 'I'm getting you more soup.'

She marched into the kitchen. After ten minutes of finagling, she returned with half a bowl. 'They are *tyrants* in there.'

Oscar nodded. 'See what we have to put up with?'

It came out 'See vat ve haf to put up vit?'

Rina said, 'Of course, they can't go around letting everyone eat whatever they'd like.'

'Why not?'

'There are a lot of restricted diets here.'

'That's not my problem.'

'It's somebody's problem,' Rina insisted.

'Somebody's, yes . . . not mine.' Oscar emptied the half-bowl. 'Now I'm finished. Thank you.'

'You're welcome.'

'You are a friend of Georgia's?'

'I know Georgia, yes.'

'Are you nosy like her?'

'I take exception to that. Neither Georgia nor I are nosy . . . just curious.'

'Nyaaah. You come to pester me. Why you think you can bribe an old man with soup?'

'I have confidence in my cooking. My mother is an excellent cook.'

'So your mother is alive?'

'Both my parents. My mother is seventy-seven, my father is eighty-two.'

'Youngsters.'

'I'll quote you on that.'

'Where were they born?'

'My mother was born in Germany, my father is Hungarian.' Rina paused. 'Actually, my mother is way more Hungarian than German. She moved to Budapest when she was eleven. Her mother died before the war in some kind of tragic accident. She doesn't like to talk about it.'

'I don't blame her.'

'Neither do I,' Rina said. 'Still, it's a shame. She has unique knowledge of family history that she's not going to pass on. It'll be lost for ever.'

'Some things are better lost,' Oscar commented.

'I suppose.' But Rina's facial expression belied her words.

'Why is the past so important?' Oscar said grumpily. 'We say we learn from the past? We never *learn* from the past.'

'I don't know if that's totally true.'

'On good days, when my eyes can see, I read the paper. Then I wonder why I do it. The killing still goes on.'

'True.'

'The past . . . Hmmmph!' He waved twiggy fingers. 'Nothing! Empty space.'

'That's how my mother feels. But sometimes I think it eats away at her. Maybe if she faced it—'

'Nyaaah. She faces it. I know. It comes back in nightmares. Terrible, terrible dreams. Dreams you don't talk away, dreams you don't psychoanalyze away, dreams that aren't helped by sleeping medicines. They are dreams that haunt for ever. It's terrible enough that it happens in sleep. Why do I have to think about it when I'm awake?'

Rina conceded that he was making valid points. Then she said, 'I don't know about you, Oscar, but maybe if my mother talked about them during the day, she wouldn't have the nightmares.'

'No. You are wrong. Then she thinks about it in the day *and* has the bad dreams at night.' Oscar was breathing hard. 'What camps were they in?'

Said so matter-of-factly as if asking what state they were from. 'Auschwitz. My father was at the Jewish side, but my Jewish mother was at the goyish side – Monowitz.'

Oscar looked blank.

'The labor part of the camp.' Rina bit her lip. 'My mother has dark hair but light skin and blue eyes—'

'Your mother passed for one of them?'

'I think the Kommandant wanted her to pass. She was stunningly beautiful. He . . . liked her.'

'Oy.'

'Her looks probably saved her life. All her girlfriends went to the Jewish side – to Birkenau – and all of them were murdered. Also, because she spoke German, she had the definite advantage over the Hungarian girls. He put her to work in the kitchen. It was a horrible existence, but she didn't starve. That's how she met my father . . . she sneaked food to the other side. My father was the "food runner" for the men's side.'

'She would have been shot if she was found out.'

'Yes, she has some stories. She was very scared. She always told me the hardest part was taking the first step. After that, it was almost habit.'

'She's a hero.'

'I think she was just in love. Papa was very handsome – even at one hundred and ten pounds.' Rina smiled. 'She considered herself one of the lucky ones. She had bread and soup and an occasional bone to gnaw on. She had clean water and though they cut her hair off, her scalp was lice free except in the heat of the summer. She has often said that she felt like a queen compared to the Jewish inmates. I don't know how they survived.'

'You do what you must.'

Rina shrugged.

Oscar's eyes darkened. 'You can see why it is hard to talk about it.'

'Yes, of course. It's strange. My mother can talk about the Holocaust. It's just her mother—'

'But some people can't talk about it. And you must respect that.'

'Absolutely.'

'So . . . I say thank you for the soup . . . and good-bye.'

Rina couldn't hide her disappointment. But she wasn't about to stir up a hornet's nest without the man's permission. 'Maybe I'll come next week, Oscar, and visit you again.'

'You'll get the same answer.'

Rina smiled. 'You enjoyed the soup so much. Next time, we'll sneak it up to your room.'

'You think you get me alone, I'll talk?'

'No. I'm thinking maybe we'll avoid the hostile looks.' She gave his hand a gentle squeeze. 'Bye.'

But Oscar didn't let go. Tears formed in his eyes.

'It's okay,' Rina said. 'Oscar, I'm not upset. Please.'

The eyes remained wet, but the drops refused to fall. 'Why you do this?'

Rina just shrugged.

Oscar snarled. 'Give me the name.'

'Yitzchak Golding.'

He thought a long time, then shook his head. 'No.'

'Well, then, that's that. I'll still come and visit you—'

'You have to remember . . . they killed people every day. At most, you work a week and then you are shot or gassed. Turnover . . . always new Jews coming in to kill. Even the regulars . . . no one lasted more than a few months. Almost a million Jews in one graveyard. Bodies on bodies. All of them . . . lost . . . forgotten.'

'Not forgotten,' Rina said. 'They'll never be forgotten. Jewish law won't allow it. You know *halacha* . . . finding the unknown body that has been murdered within the city limits. The *chok* about the red heifer.'

Oscar looked blank.

'It's right from the *Chumash*. If you find a dead body within the city, and no one claims responsibility for it, the entire community is responsible. And it is up to the community to give that body a proper burial. That's all I'm trying to do, Oscar. Give this man a proper burial.'

'I do not know the name. Who is he to you?'

'I'm doing someone a favor. Not because he's a friend, but because he's a parent. His son was murdered, Oscar.'

'Ach! That's terrible!'

Slowly, Rina told him the story. Midway through, Oscar closed his watery eyes. But Rina could tell that he was still listening and listening intently. By the time she was finished, most of the room had been cleared of its diners. Her voice seemed louder, so she dropped it a notch. 'I have a picture of them . . . all of them. It was given to me by the man's son. Carter Golding—'

'What kind name is Carter?'

'A goyish name. His mother wasn't Jewish.'

'So he's not Jewish. Why you help out a goy when there are so many Jews?'

'He's a parent.'

The old man beckoned the snapshot with a crooked finger. Rina pulled it from her purse and showed it to him – grandfather, father, and two smiling sons. Oscar stared at the generations of Goldings. She offered to let him hold it for a closer look. He took the four-year-old snapshot with hands that had a Parkinsonian tremor.

'Yitzchak is the elderly man.'

'I know. I'm not stupid.'

The feistiness was back. That made Rina happy. 'I'm not implying—'

'Nyaaah,' Oscar sneered. 'You want to know who he looks like to me?'

Rina was excited. 'Who?'

'He looks like an old man I never met. Take it back,' Oscar said. 'It won't help if I look longer.'

Rina took the picture and held it between her fingers. 'Oscar, can I ask you one last favor?'

'Ask.'

'Do you remember . . . about six months ago a *shul* in the Valley was vandalized?'

The old man's eyes clouded. 'Maybe.'

'That was my *shul*.'

'Oy vey.'

'The person who admitted to the crime,' she gave Oscar another look at the picture, 'it was this boy . . . he was also the one who was murdered.'

Oscar stared at her. 'I am confused. It is this boy who thinks that his grandfather . . . Maybe you should start over.'

'I will, but maybe we should move to a little more private place.'

Oscar waved her off. 'Why you help the parents of such a bad boy?'

'Troubled—'

'Bad.'

'Troubled,' Rina insisted.

'Bad and troubled. The two go together.'

Rina went on. 'When the boy vandalized the *shul*, he left old black and white photographs. Apparently, he had lots of photographs – bad photographs of dead bodies. But they looked different from the ones I've seen before.'

Oscar waited.

'We've all seen the piles . . .' Rina had to turn her head. It was painful to look in the old man's eyes. 'These were all individual pictures – of Jewish men and Jewish boys.' She felt her throat clog. 'Very focused, very clear. That's what made them so awful to look at.'

Oscar was silent.

Rina was supposed to ask if he would look at them. But she couldn't get the words out. 'I don't know.' She squeezed his hand. 'I should be going.'

'You want that I look at them?'

'No . . . no, you shouldn't.'

'These pictures . . . the bodies . . . they are naked?'

Rina thought a moment. 'Some are, some aren't.'

Something shone in Oscar's eyes. 'Let me see that picture again – of the old man and the young boys.'

Rina gave him the snapshot. This time Oscar studied it for a very long time. 'This boy . . .' He pointed a crooked finger at Karl Golding. 'I know him.'

Rina was puzzled. 'Oscar, he's not the one who died.'

'I didn't say he was. I said . . . I know him.'

'How?'

He wagged his finger at her as he thought. 'These

pictures left behind. No piles, right? It was one body in a picture.'

'Yes, exactly. What?'

'This boy . . .' Again the finger wagged. 'If you give him . . . four, five years. Maybe, just maybe, he is the boy with the camera. The Polish boy. About . . . sixteen. Not a village boy, a city boy.'

Rina was stunned. But, of course, that made total sense. If Oscar were to remember anybody, it wouldn't be the face of an old man who called himself Yitzchak Golding; it would be a young face that had been etched in Oscar's mind some sixty years ago. 'You remember a boy with a camera?'

'Yes, there was a boy with a camera. He takes pictures maybe one week before the camp burns down.'

Rina pointed to Karl. 'He looked like that boy?'

Oscar nodded.

'Not this boy.' She showed him Ernesto.

'No, this one.' Again he had pointed to Karl.

Rina said, 'A Polish boy. Who was he?'

Oscar shrugged. 'A boy with a camera. So I think he had money. I think his father was big in the *Polnische Polizei*.'

The Polish police. Rina nodded. 'Can you tell me anything else about him?'

Again the finger started wagging. 'He took pictures through the fence . . . It was electrified, the fence. If you tried to escape . . .' He loudly clapped his hands. 'Like a mosquito on a lamppost. You could hear them frying . . . smell it.' He covered his mouth, then dropped his hands. 'So he didn't touch the fence. You have the black and white bad pictures?'

Rina nodded.

'Show me one.'

Rina rummaged through her briefcase and pulled out the least offensive one she could find: a bony old man who looked like he was sleeping in striped pajamas.

Oscar studied the picture. 'Yes . . . yes. You see these light lines? That's the fence. That is the fence!'

Rina covered her mouth and nodded. 'Yes, I see.'

He handed the photograph back to Rina. 'I don't know the boy. Some people talk to that boy. Some tell the boy to take their pictures. One man . . . he brings his dead son . . . let the boy take picture. Me?' He shook his head. 'I say nothing to him.

'He comes for five, ten minutes, takes pictures, then he hides back in the forest. You don't stay near the camps too long. You get shot.' Oscar scrunched up his forehead. 'He brought bread . . . not real bread, most of it was ersatz . . . sawdust . . . but better than what we had. He takes it and squeezes it into little balls and throws them through the spaces in the fence. Never missed once. Good arm.' He nodded with admiration. 'A dangerous thing to do. If it hits the fence, it sets off the electricity. Then the guard is warned what is going on. He never missed.'

Tears were streaming down Rina's face. 'He gave you food?'

'Tiny balls of bread – half bread. And bits of carrots and turnip. And once . . . tiny wild strawberries. Do you know how much of a luxury that was? Strawberries? Warsaw had nothing! For him to have strawberries . . .

and afford to give them away. Oy vey, he was a very rich boy. The boy with the camera who throws at us bits of food.'

'Did he speak to any of the inmates?'

Oscar thought, then shook his head. 'No, he never said a word. Just took the pictures. Maybe he wanted to laugh at the dead Juden after we were all gone.'

'Or maybe he wanted to remember. He couldn't have been that cruel if he gave you food.'

'Maybe he liked seeing the Juden act like animals – like feeding animals in the zoo. Still, we act like animals, clawing at the ground to find the bread balls or bits of turnip.'

'If he had wanted to cause you trouble, he would have hit the fence at least once. He wouldn't have thrown a hundred percent, *nu*?'

'You want to see good in him.'

Holding back tears, Rina nodded. 'Yes.'

'That is nice.' Oscar shrugged. 'Tiny balls of bread. It tasted like . . . as good as your soup.'

'That's some compliment.'

'Yes, it is a compliment.'

'Should I show you more pictures that were found in the synagogue? Maybe these were the pictures the boy took?'

'You say they are only of dead people?'

'I don't remember, Oscar. Maybe some of them were alive.'

'No matter. They're all dead now.'

'Maybe he took your picture.'

'If he did, I don't want to see it!' He spoke with

volume and force. Then he exhaled, deflated, as if his lungs had no more capacity to breathe. 'This boy . . . maybe he wanted to help. Maybe not. But even if he did want to help, he was not a big hero. Nothing like that.'

There was silence.

Oscar said, 'At most, he was a small hero.' The old man let go with a lemony smile. 'Still, a small hero is better than nothing.'

34

It was going to be an all-nighter, so Decker decided to put in an appearance at home. Pulling into the driveway, he saw that the living room windows were dark, meaning that his family was out, doing their own thing without him of course, and he could have just as well stayed in the office. The realization that he wasn't needed or missed drew mixed emotions. He felt hurt, but at least his loved ones could function without him – a meager bit of comfort. Since he was home, he decided to freshen up with a quick shower and a change of clothes.

As soon as he stepped inside, he noticed that the house wasn't entirely dark. There was a light on in Jacob's room . . . no noise coming from the stereo. No conversation, either. That made his stomach turn.

Anytime the house was too quiet, and Jacob was alone, Decker held this nagging suspicion that something illicit was going on. As much as he proclaimed his confidence in the kid, he couldn't bring himself to trust him totally.

He tiptoed over to the room, listened for a minute. Nothing. Then he knocked on the door.

Immediately, Jacob told him to come in. Decker hoped the kid hadn't heard him whoosh out an exhalation of relief. Wearing a black leather yarmulke, Jake was sitting at his desk, bent over a tome of the Talmud, concentrating as he read the Aramaic text. Then he looked up.

'Hi.'

'You're home alone?'

'Hannah's here.'

'Oh.' Decker listened, perceiving just air. 'I don't hear the TV.'

'It's after nine, Dad. She's asleep.'

Guilt stabbed his innards. 'That would make sense.'

'Want me to check in on her?'

'I'll do it.' But Decker didn't leave right away, transfixed by his stepson's aberrant studious behavior. 'I thought it was summer.'

'I'm trying to catch up before I go to yeshiva. I don't want to look too stupid.'

'That would be impossible.'

'You'd be surprised. Amazing. The more you study, the more you know.'

'Truisms work.'

'Sammy and I have been learning together for the last two hours, but then a friend called him. I told him to go out. He was looking a little pale.'

'You didn't want to go?'

'Someone has to be home for Hannah. Eema's at some old-age home, talking to a camp survivor. She actually offered to come home early so I could get out – I think she's worried about me becoming too serious, if you can believe that. I told her I was okay. This visit seemed important to her for some reason. Besides, I don't mind a little quiet time. Things have been hectic enough around here.'

Decker kissed the top of his head – his yarmulke. 'I'm sorry, Jacob.'

'S'right.' He stood up. 'You're exhausted. There're leftovers. Can I fix you up a plate while you shower?'

'Sure.'

Without another word, Jacob went to the kitchen. Decker peeked into his daughter's room, seeing not much more than orange ringlets on a pillow. He tiptoed over. She was breathing deeply, slowly, the coverlet moving up and down in languid, rolling waves. She smelled of shampoo and fabric softener. He smiled, always surprised that such a miracle could emanate from his loins. He left the room with an ache in his heart, then undressed, plunging into the hot needles of a brief shower. After changing into clean clothes, he went into the kitchen and was greeted by white meat turkey, mashed potatoes, and limp broccoli, but a fresh salad. His stepson was dressed in a black T-shirt and black pants. Once upon a time, Jacob was all skin and bones. He still had that long, lank look, but weight lifting had given him a chest and arms, and a good set of stomach muscles. He was a kid on the brink. A year or two more of maturity would put him right up there with James Dean in the heartthrob department – an angry young man with fierce blue eyes and a perpetual sneer. What made him really dangerous was his brainpower.

'Sometimes you're a real wonder.' Decker ate with gusto.

'I can warm up grub with the best of them. Do you want coffee?'

'I'll make it.'

'No, I can do it, Dad. It's not a problem.' As Jacob made coffee, he noticed his stepfather had finished his meal. 'There's more if you want.'

'No, I'm stuffed.' He sat back. 'I ate too fast. That's not good.' He sighed. 'Someday I'll retire.'

'Sure you will.' Jacob watched the coffee drip. 'Did you go to Ernesto's funeral?'

Decker nodded.

'Pretty emotional, huh?'

'Very.' He looked up, started to talk, then thought better of it.

'What?' Jacob asked.

'Never mind.'

'No, what?'

Decker rubbed his forehead. 'You didn't know any of Ruby Ranger's friends, did you?'

Out came the sneer. 'No. But I knew plenty of her enemies. Everyone hated her.'

'You don't know anyone she'd run to if she were in trouble?'

Jacob sat down. 'What's going on? Is she in trouble?'

'I think so.'

'Doesn't surprise me. She's a very bad person.'

'Maybe it's coming back to haunt her. I think she's in physical danger. She's missing, and no one knows where she is. If you know any friends who might be hiding her, I'd like to hear about it. Be nice to know that she's alive.'

Jacob blanched. For a brief moment, Decker entertained the thought that Jacob had something to do with her disappearance. And although that was absurd, Decker had a sinking feeling that he had touched upon something. He continued to examine the boy's face. 'Do you have something you want to tell me?'

Jacob was silent, but unnerved.

'Jacob—'

'Nothing!' He turned his face away. 'I don't know anything!'

Decker didn't have time for niceties. 'Stop lying, damn it! Jacob, she's in trouble. *Spit it out!*'

'I don't *know* where she is!' Jacob screamed. 'Why the hell do you always assume the *worst* with me! I'm not a total fuckup! And *fuck you*, if you think I am!'

Without thinking, Decker slapped him across the face, hard enough to snap the kid's face back; hard enough to leave a sizeable palm print. 'Don't you ever, *ever* speak that way to me!'

The boy's eyes smoldered as he held his stinging cheek, glaring with hatred at his stepfather. 'I could report you to the authorities.'

'Go right ahead, big shot! I'll give you the goddamn number!'

Tears formed in the bright blue eyes. 'How come you can swear and I can't!'

'Because I'm a parent and I'm a hypocrite.' Decker leaned over, grabbed the boy's chin, and bored into his eyes. 'She's either a perpetrator or a victim. Either way, she's in deep shit! *What* can you tell me about it?'

Jacob jerked his face away and looked down, still holding his cheek. 'I don't know where she is!'

Decker was silent. Then he spoke softly. 'But you know something.'

It took a while for Jacob to find his voice. It was hidden somewhere between embarrassment and rage. 'You remember that I . . . I told you that I got into a hassle with her at a party—'

'You told me that you threatened to kill her.'

Jacob nodded. 'Sort of.'

'Go on!'

'After I . . . we had words, I stormed out of the house. I don't even know what I was doing there in the first place. It was a couple of weeks after you caught me with Shayna. And I had promised you that I'd stop using. And I *wasn't* using. I didn't even want to go to the stupid party. But then Lisa called me up . . . told me she was invited but didn't want to go alone. I was still really angry.' A sigh. 'I sneaked out. I didn't ask Sammy for help, but I knew he would cover for me if he had to.'

So tell me something fucking new, Decker thought. He clasped his hands together to prevent himself from lashing out. He wanted to throttle the boy. Just take him by the shoulders and shake him to death. Instead, he reined in his anger but not impatience.

'Speed it up!'

'I'm getting to it. This is very hard!'

Decker swallowed, counted to five. 'Go on.'

'Anyway, I bolted. Just started walking, swearing that this was it. Never again, never again, never again! And I really meant it. Suddenly, Ruby caught up with me, grabbed my arm, and told me to slow down . . . that she wanted to talk to me. It was like her whole attitude changed – totally. Completely different. Like two separate people. It was weird.'

And eerily familiar. Both of them – Darrell and Ruby – masters of different identities. 'Keep going.'

'We started talking. We talked for about twenty minutes outside the house . . . about two houses away actually. Then she asked me to take a ride with her . . . just to talk.'

'And did you?'

'Not right away. First, we went to her car and talked there.' He looked away. 'Just talking.'

Decker gesticulated for him to quicken the pace.

'She had pills.' His eyes started watering. 'I know I'm weak. It totally sickens me how weak I am. But that's not the point right now. We both got totally wired . . . blitzed.'

'What did you take?'

'Some kind of stimulant . . . uppers. After a few minutes, things began to happen.'

Fury coiled up inside Decker's chest. He clasped his hands tighter. 'What kind of things?'

'Amorous things.' Jacob couldn't look at him. 'I was high and so was she. She started touching me. She knew what she was doing. I got incredibly turned on.' He whispered, 'I don't have to spell it out for you, do I?'

'You had sex.'

'It's more complicated than that. She started the car and took me somewhere – I guess we were driving for about ten, fifteen minutes . . . it's hard to get a time frame because I was so high and so aroused. We couldn't have gone that far from the party, but it was somewhere pretty isolated, deep in the hills. She took me to this shack of a house . . . a place she'd obviously been before many times.'

For the first time, Decker could see the point of the confessional. She took him somewhere. *To a location!*

Erin's words: *He's probably hiding in the hills somewhere between Santa Barbara and Orange County. I don't think he's left Southern California.*

A location.

Don't rush him, don't rush him, don't rush him. He'll remember better if you don't rush him.

Jacob dropped his hand from his cheek. The palm print had darkened. Decker felt shame coursing down his spine, but he didn't dare interrupt. He watched his stepson drum the kitchen table.

'Nothing much inside,' he said. 'Just a big room with a big bed. She had a closet filled with things – costumes.' He licked his lips. 'Things for her fantasies.'

Decker waited.

'She had horrible, horrible, *horrible* fantasies.'

'What kind of fantasies?'

'She wanted . . .' He buried his face in his shaking hands. 'She wanted to dress me up in a costume. She said it would really turn her on and make it really great.'

The boy had turned ashen. He dropped his voice to a whisper.

'It was an SS officer's uniform. It might have even been the real thing.' He squeezed his eyes shut. But tears leaked out anyway. 'She had it all – the leather whips, the boots, the ropes . . . she wanted me to pretend like I was . . . you know . . . one of them. She told me to speak to her in German. For some reason, she thought I knew German. Why the hell would *I* know German?'

He paused.

'She . . . she wanted me to tie her up. She wanted me to slap her . . . whip her. She wanted me to . . . to pretend to rape her. She said that's how she got off.'

No one spoke. And now Decker understood where Ernesto's fantasies were coming from . . . that combined with his grandfather's vague origins. What vile seeds had she planted in that poor boy's head? What had it done to his stepson's fragile psyche? The seconds dragged on to infinity. Decker felt his whole body shake, felt his heart coming through his chest. He covered his mouth with his hand.

'Did you do it?'

Jacob shook his head in protest. 'I was drugged, but . . . something primal . . .' Tears poured down the boy's face. 'I suddenly got viscerally ill. From intense arousal to utter nausea in like one breath. I thought I was actually going to die. I saw the grounds of the earth opening – like Korach in the desert – and had this vision of me falling down and down and down . . .'

A long pause.

'And . . .' Decker said.

Jacob wiped his eyes and forced himself to look at his stepfather. 'It gets confusing for me here . . . because I was really doped up. I must have made tracks . . . and pretty quickly because she was out of breath when she caught up with me. We were outdoors, in the middle of nowhere. At least, I had no idea where I was. Ruby was a mess – horrible. She apologized profusely. It threw me off. I'd never seen her so upset before. She said she was just playing a little game. That she had played the game other times with other guys and they all loved it. She just wanted me to have some fun with her. She was trying to . . . loosen me up. Then she said she was sorry that I got so mad. She became very contrite. She started to cry. She kept crying and crying and crying. She wouldn't stop! At that moment, I don't know . . . I felt *sorry* for her.'

Again, he blotted his wet eyes with his fingers – silent tears that reddened his pale blue eyes.

'I had no idea where I was, and she was so . . . distraught. I thought about . . . well, at least, maybe I should calm her down so she would take me home. Just end this hellish nightmare. I swore to God that if I ever got out of this mess, I'd take steps to clean myself up for good. Stop stealing, stop going to the parties, stop taking drugs, stop goofing off—'

'Jacob, this woman is missing—'

'I know I'm rambling,' Jacob whispered. 'I'm trying to cut it to the bare bones, all right?'

'Okay.' Decker leaned over and Jacob involuntarily flinched. Nausea swept through Decker's stomach, his dinner turning over in belly acid. He took the kid's hand and kissed it. 'Go on, son. It's all right.'

Jacob heaved his shoulders. 'We went back to the place. I tried to tell her that it was okay, that I wasn't mad, that we should both just go home.' He looked away. 'We started being physical again. I don't know how it happened.'

A long pause.

'We . . . had sex. Just . . . plain . . . no-frills sex. It was over in about . . . thirty seconds.' He faced his father's stern eyes. 'I was a virgin.'

Decker felt his heart beating so fast it took his breath away. The kid was in so much pain, all he wanted to do was hug him and make the agony go away. But he held back. 'Did she ridicule you?'

'No . . . just the opposite.' He pulled his hand away and touched his sore cheek again. 'It would have been better if she had. Then I could have hated her with a pure hate. Instead, she told me to lie still . . . while I was still in her . . . that I'd become aroused again in a few minutes, and the second time, it would last longer and it would be better. And that's exactly what happened.'

Decker ran his fingers through thick hair. 'Did you use a condom?'

'Yes.'

'You have to tell me the truth with this one.'

'Dad, I swear on Abba's grave—'

'You don't have to go that far,' Decker said. 'Where'd you get protection if this tryst was totally spontaneous?'

'I don't think the house belonged to Ruby. I think it belonged to a guy. He had a drawer filled with them. I think all the shit – all the stuff – the whips and boots and uniforms – I think it was his stuff, not hers.'

Darrell Holt's sexual hideaway. Decker said, 'What happened after the sex?'

Jacob said, 'We got dressed and she took me home. The ride was totally silent. Nothing. Not even a good-bye.' He blew out air. 'I never saw her again. Never talked to her, never talked to any of them really. It was over a year ago, and I swear I haven't touched anything stronger than an aspirin. I also swore off of girls until I'm . . . older. It was just . . . too easy. The whole thing scared me to death! In a way that you never could. Nothing like a brush with hell to make you feel suddenly grateful. Since then, I've been playing catch-up with my life and it hasn't been easy.'

'And you think that's where Ruby is? At this shack?'

He shrugged. 'Maybe.'

'You have guts, I'll give you that. You did the right thing by telling me.'

'I had no choice. We're all *Tslem Elokim* – created in God's likeness.' He smiled sadly. 'Guess the rabbis taught me something.'

Decker closed his eyes and opened them. 'I'm sorry I slapped you. It was reprehensible.'

'I lost my temper, you lost yours.' He gave another smile. 'I would have slugged you back, but you're bigger than I am. I'm pragmatic if nothing else.'

Decker got up. 'You need some ice for that cheek.'

'Why? Is there a red mark?'

'Yep.'

'A big one?'

'Huge.' Decker took out a cold pack and gave it to him. 'Here.'

Jacob put it on his cheek. 'I get hit with basketballs all the time. I'm always getting red marks and welts on my face because I'm so fair. It'll go down in a couple of hours. Don't worry about it.'

Decker was quiet, feeling drained and sick. He was at least five inches taller and outweighed Jacob by sixty, seventy pounds. He was not only a failure as a father, but also a failure as a human being. Still, he had a job to do, which he supposed made him a decent cop. One out of three, pretty good odds in baseball.

Jacob patted his hand. 'I mean it, Dad. It's okay. Don't worry about it.'

Decker said, 'Is there *anything* you remember about your location?'

'Yeah. That *was* the point of this whole awful thing.

As we were riding home, I saw a street sign – Herald Way. About five minutes, maybe ten minutes later we were back on Devonshire. If I were driving back then, I would have noticed more. But this was before I had my driver's license. I didn't know the streets like I do now.'

'How old were you?'

'About two months shy of sixteen. She was about twenty-two. Pretty heady stuff, huh. Obviously, she got off on younger boys – me, Ernesto, there were probably others.'

Consistent with what Erin had told him. Decker said, 'She took you somewhere in the mountains, but not far from town.'

'Yeah.'

'If I drove you around up there, do you think you might remember more?'

'Possibly.'

Decker stood up. 'Then let's go for a ride.'

'What about Hannah?'

'You know where Sammy is?'

'Yeah.'

'Call him and tell him to come home to baby-sit. This takes precedence.'

'I could call up Eema—'

'Don't do that!' Decker found his voice had risen. 'She'd kill me if she found out I was taking you house hunting for a maniac.' His eyes went to his son's cheek. 'She'd also kill me for other reasons. I'm a real jerk sometimes!'

'Join the club.' He got up from his chair. 'Forget it, Peter. I've been riding you pretty hard this last year.

Whatever went on here will stay between us.'

He called him Peter. The anger was still there. Decker said, 'While you're calling Sammy, I'll call up Webster and Martinez. I want some professional lookout riding with us. Besides, maybe they'll know where the hell Herald Way is.'

35

It showed up on the map as a tiny vein that bled into the mountains. According to the latest L.A. street atlas, Herald Way did boast a single listed cross street – a bigger road but only in the comparative sense – called Manor Lane. Bert Martinez drove; Tom Webster sat shotgun, with his hand grazing against the butt of his holstered gun. In the back, Decker was belted in, but kept leaning his body over his stepson, covering him like a woolen overcoat. The Valley daytime temperatures had reached triple digits, and the night remained warm and stuffy. Jacob was sweating under his father's weight.

'Dad, I can't breathe.'

'Stay down.'

'I am down! If I were any more down, I couldn't see out the window. That sort of defeats the purpose—'

'Slow down, Bert.' Decker looked around. No streetlights; it was dark, empty, and wooded. The organic smell of decomposing foliage was mixed with the pungent stink of skunk markings. The humid air rang with a chorus of insect mating calls, accompanied by hoots from the local owls. The traffic from the distant boulevard came off as a continuous purr. 'Okay, now stop here.'

Martinez put on the brakes. They were at the marked intersection.

'There are the street signs – Manor Lane and Herald Way.' Decker leaned over to the front seat and pointed out the windshield. 'It's right in the headlights.'

Jacob nodded.

'Do you remember this spot?'

The teen leaned forward as well. 'Yeah . . .' Jacob's heart was pounding. 'Yeah, this is it.'

'You're sure?'

'Yeah, I remember the way the signs pointed down . . . off-kilter. You know, I should sit up front – that's where I was seated when she drove me home.'

'I know. But the back is safer. You're right behind where you were, so your view is pretty much the same.'

'Yeah, but I don't have a view from the front windshield. It'll make a difference, Dad.'

'We'll have to forgo it. Which way from here, Jacob?'

'I . . . I'm not sure.'

'That's okay. Take your time.'

His stepfather's voice was soothing. Jacob's mind was a swirl of unpleasant memories. He did some hand gestures that simulated turns, but shook his head. 'I remember going down. So which way does the road rise the most?'

'To the left,' Webster answered.

'Then go to the left,' Decker ordered. 'Sit back and put on your seat belt.'

'All right, all right. Stop being such a mother hen.'

'If I were a mother hen, you wouldn't be here.'

Martinez turned left, dragging the Honda along a partially paved road. The shocks, even at the current crawl, protested with each bump, dip, and pothole. Gravel churned under the tires. Bert flipped the switch into all-wheel-drive mode. 'I knew this car would come in handy one day.'

'First time you've ever used it?' Webster asked.

'For mountain roads, yeah. My wife uses AWD when she goes out in heavy rain.'

'Anything look familiar?' Decker asked his son.

Jacob's eyes scanned the terrain of shapes and shadows. 'No. It . . . it all looks the same.'

'Don't worry. We're going on a long shot. Nothing is expected from you.'

Which was good because nothing was what he was going to get. Jacob swallowed hard. It was impossible for Peter to imagine how drugs could distort perception. But being stoned had its paradoxical effects. Some things from that night had been indelibly etched in his mind, as unique as his thumbprint. The eucalyptus tree, for instance, its trunk bent and cracked from what had been recent canyon winds. It had reminded Jacob of a hunchbacked crone holding a walking stick, a role he had cast for Ruby even after they had been intimate. Even as her life hung in limbo, Jacob couldn't help but demonize her.

His eyes scanned the clumps of mountainside, hunting for the unusual shape. During the summer, everything was in full bloom, the clumps of fertile fauna casting silhouettes against the charcoal sky. Branches danced in short breaths of wind. He hadn't told his father about the broken bough, because then Dad would have asked him every ten seconds if this one or that one was the correct tree. For the integrity of his own psyche, Jacob couldn't afford to make any more mistakes.

Where was that tree? Did it even exist?

The car inched along its path. Webster spoke. 'Is this place *on* Herald Way?'

'No, I don't think so,' Jacob answered.

'So we should be looking for a side street?'

'I guess.'

'Trouble is, there aren't any listed side streets.'

'I remember turning . . .' Jacob licked his lips, now cracked from habit and heat. He took out a stick designed for chapped lips and smeared it over the raw areas. 'It was a long time ago.' *And I was flying at mach speed.* 'It could have been just a twist in the road.'

'There are certainly enough of them,' Martinez said.

And then he saw the crone. Son of a gun, it was still there, walking stick and all. Jacob said, 'We're on the right pathway. That broken tree . . .' He pointed. 'I remember seeing that. I bet there's a turn—'

'There it is.' Martinez brought the car to a standstill. 'On the left.' The roadway wasn't much bigger than a hiking trail, but seemed wide enough to accommodate a car. In the gleam of the headlights, he could make out thin tire tracks – a lightweight motorcycle or a mountain bike. 'Should we go up, Loo?'

'We're getting into tricky territory.' Decker was staring at the narrow passageway. 'We've got to think about an escape route. If he came after us on a motorbike, we'd have some maneuvering problems.'

'But he'd be out in the open,' Webster said. '*We'd* be protected by the car.'

Martinez said, 'But he could also run rings around us, pick off a tire or two while we couldn't get near him. We should go up on foot.'

'Then we'd be sitting ducks,' Webster said.

'But if we take the car up, it would make noise,' Martinez countered. 'Talk about announcing your arrival.'

'Bert, if we go up on foot, *we're* out in the open without any protection.'

'There's plenty of coverage. And we have weapons. We're fine unless he lobs a grenade or has land-mined the place. Even then, we can call in for backup if the situation gets bad.'

Decker broke in, 'We're not here to initiate anything. That means no raids no matter how easy it looks. This is just a lay-of-the-land kind of thing. Then we call backup. What concerns me is taking Jacob up there on foot.'

'You need me,' Jacob said.

'I know that—'

'I'm not worried.'

'That's the problem. You should be.'

'Okay, then, I am worried.'

Decker tossed him a look. Jacob tossed him back a smile. 'How about some code names – Caleb and Joshua?'

'You're way too cocky, guy!'

Jacob grew serious. 'I want to redeem myself.'

Decker held his stepson's cheek. 'There's nothing to redeem.'

But Jacob didn't believe him. 'How about if we walk up a couple hundred yards, and I'll see if I recognize anything. How much trouble could that cause?'

'Plenty,' Decker said.

'First off, even if I find the place, Ruby may not even be there. Secondly, what's the point of being so close and not getting it perfect?'

'Your heart stays beating.'

'You're just worried about Eema.'

Decker smiled. 'True, but that's not the entire picture.'

Martinez said, 'Let Tom and me go up and have a look around. You can stay here with him—'

'But you don't know what to look for,' Jacob said. Without asking, he got out of the car. Decker dogged him immediately, grabbed his elbow. Then he put his finger to his lips. He whispered, 'We turn back when I say so.'

Jacob nodded, his chest tightening, his breaths rapid and hollow. The other two emerged, Martinez holding the flashlight as the quartet inched their way up the turnoff. It was nothing more than a rut cut into dense brush. Insects twittered, owls hooted, coyotes ululated.

Fifty feet up.

Towering trees framed both sides of the road. The

geography resulted in limited vision: it was hard to see anything that stood behind the leafy skyscrapers. The sky began to lighten, having turned from charcoal to steel as the moon began to rise, a semicircle of silver light.

One hundred feet.

Their footsteps were measured . . . deliberate, largely silent except for the accidental scrape against the ground. Any noise that they made was muffled handily by nighttime animal sounds.

Two hundred feet.

Martinez kept the light localized and on the ground, not wanting to give their presence away by inadvertently shining a beam in an unseen building window. The disadvantage was that he couldn't spot anything in the brush-covered mountainside.

Three hundred and fifty.

Decker's steps became halting, his attitude more hesitant as they walked up into the unmapped lane and farther away from the car. The tire tracks had all but faded . . . dissolving. Where did they go?

Four hundred . . . four fifty, and still no sign of any kind of outpost. Except for the serpentine passageway, there wasn't any indication of human habitation. Either the shack wasn't nearby or it was hidden within the overgrowth.

Five hundred feet up the roadway . . . about one-tenth of a mile. Not much in distance, a short jog to get back to the car. About ten seconds . . . maybe fifteen. A lot could happen in fifteen seconds. Images darted across Decker's brain, specifically, the inferno that had destroyed the Order of the Rings of God. How close had they been to that crematorium, saved by seconds from becoming ashes of death? The horrible snapshot became too strong a picture to stifle, even with the strongest of rationalizations. Decker's growing concern for his son's welfare outweighed a life *possibly* at stake. He had been holding Jacob's arm. He tightened his grip, causing the teen to jump.

'We're going back,' he whispered.

'What! Why?' the boy whispered back.

'Because we're too far out. Because I say so.'

'But we're almost there.'

Martinez entered the conversation. 'How much farther up?'

'I'm not sure, but I think we're close,' Jacob insisted.

'You think?' Decker shook his head. 'That's not good enough. You don't even know if this is the right turnoff.'

'No, it's the right turnoff. I'm positive.' Jacob regarded his stepfather's skepticism. 'I know I was stoned, but you notice things.' His eyes scanned the terrain. Then he squinted, jutting his head forward. 'Is that light up there?'

'Where?' Martinez asked.

Jacob pointed. 'See that speck of light about . . . I guess about a hundred yards to the right of that huge sycamore?'

Though his night vision wasn't perfect, Decker could discern faint illumination. He wasn't sure if it was light or possibly an animal with reflective eyes, shooting back beams in the darkness. 'Maybe there's something.'

'Y'all talking about the light over to the right and up?'

'Exactly,' Jacob said.

'About two o'clock,' Martinez said. 'I see it. What do you want to do, Loo?'

Decker said, 'I want to go back before—'

Suddenly, the dim light grew stronger and wider. There was no time to think . . . barely enough time to react. Decker threw himself atop his stepson, sending both of them belly-first onto the ground. Martinez, also a Nam vet, pulled Webster down as his own stomach hit the dirt. The bullets came by in a steady stream – *thwack, thwack, thwack, thwack* – whizzing past them over their heads. Remaining on his stomach, Decker dragged Jacob into the brush, keeping both of them horizontal as he moved.

Some things you never forget.

Seconds passed. Then the light disappeared. Nothing but darkness. Or maybe Decker just couldn't see anything because he was pressed against the ground and had no line of vision. His heart was flying out of his chest. He knew he was going to survive this one, not for his sake, but for Jacob's. The boy's chin had been scraped raw. He was shaken. Other than that, he appeared all right.

Martinez spoke first. 'Think he has an infrared scope?'

'Probably,' Decker said. 'He's a survivalist.'

'Then we're daylight,' Martinez said.

Decker said, 'If he can see us, that's true.'

'Then why isn't he shooting?' Webster said.

'Because he can't see us,' Decker answered.

Martinez said, 'Brush is thick out here. Loo, if you crawl downward staying inside the woods, you stand a good chance. You go with Jacob and I'll create a diversion.'

'You do that, you might as well put a bull's-eye on your forehead,' Decker said.

'So what now?' Webster asked.

Decker pulled out his cell phone. The signal was weak, but 911 was able to hear even through the static. 'We stay put and wait for fucking backup.'

Several patrol cars arrived minutes later, tires spitting out dust and gravel. Decker could see the cloud of grit even though the black and whites had settled down the road from their inconvenient campsite. The cruisers' immediate arrival, complete with sirens and lights, did not draw out gunfire, leaving all in a state of limbo. Was the shooter still in the house? Had he or she taken off? Maybe the shooter was just biding time, waiting to pick off someone who came into view. It could be that the cops had parked out of the shooter's line of view. The trick now was to get everyone down the road and safely inside the cars.

Decker whispered into the mouthpiece. 'There are four of us . . . five hundred feet up, on the right side of the road. How many cruisers do you have down there?'

'Two . . . a third pulled up. Now we have three.'

'Okay. Right now, don't do anything until we have more metal. You've got to call this in because I want a two-cruiser blockade at either end of the road, standard pattern, cars parked grill to grill. I'll also need a couple of cars to come pick us up. Hold off on the flying power until you've delivered us. When you have more vehicles, I'll give you further orders.'

Decker cut the line.

Jacob said, 'We're just going to wait here?'

'That's exactly what we're going to do. Am I smothering you?'

'Sort of.'

'Good.'

Minutes passed by. Distant plaints became loud wails. The road lightened, as light bars threw blue and red strobic blinks onto the dirt. And while the light gave Decker more visibility, it also made them more vulnerable. The phone rang.

'We've got six cruisers.'

Decker said, 'Keep two where you are, send two up the road, and two to pick us up. Stay on the line and I'll tell you when to stop. When you drive, lay low . . . literally. I don't know if you're in the perp's crosshairs, but let's not take a chance. From the sound of the shots, the perp's location is about . . . seven hundred feet up from where you are on the right side of the road. We all saw a light. I don't know if it came from a flashlight or from an electrical bulb. If it came from a flashlight, you've got a shooter on the move, so take precautions. If it came from an electrical bulb, we're assuming that there's some kind of outpost hidden behind the brush that has workable electricity. But we don't know where.'

'What kind of weapon do you think he used?'

'Sounded like semiautomatic. I heard about six or seven rounds.'

'We'll come get you.'

'Do that.'

From where he was, Decker couldn't see the cars, only the maraschino and aqua glow reflected from the rotating beacons. But soon he heard the motors kicking in, the grinding of the wheels. Seconds later, two vehicles came into eyesight, inching up the lane.

'I see you,' Decker said. 'Keep going . . . going . . . going, going . . . going . . . going. Okay, make a U-turn, pull to the right, and stop. Kill the motor and duck.'

The cars went silent.

'Good,' Decker said. 'We're directly to the right . . . not more than a hundred feet. Keeping your heads down, go over and unlock the passenger doors. Open them but just barely. I don't want him to see any kind of swinging door. Got it?'

'Yes, sir.'

He disconnected the phone. 'You want the top car or the bottom one, Bert?'

'Doesn't matter. Top one's fine.'

'Okay, we'll take the bottom one.' As soon as Decker detected the motion of an opening door, he spoke to Jacob. 'This is what you're going to do. You're going to keep your head down and crawl over to the bottom car, to the backseat passenger door. You're going to open the door very slightly, just enough to give you some space, then you're going to quickly slide inside on your belly. Don't close the door, because I'm going to be right behind you. Okay?'

'Okay.'

'Jacob, whatever skin is not covered by clothing has a good chance of being scraped raw. No matter how it feels, *stay down*. When you get inside the car, I want you to remain horizontal. Lie on the floor until I tell you differently. Don't even *think* about picking your head up and looking around. It's very important that you do everything I tell you.'

'I understand.'

'Make as little commotion as possible. And I'm right behind you.'

'I'll be fine.'

'Your uncommon optimism is refreshing.' He arched his stomach upward to give Jacob room to maneuver. 'Go!'

Jacob slithered out from under his stepfather and slunk across the forested carpet. He was wearing short sleeves and that was a big mistake. His arms became scratching posts for organic detritus as twigs, rocks, pebbles, leaves, pinecones, quills, and spiky seed pods abraded his skin and worked their way under his shirt, scraping his stomach. The worst were the tiny stones that got caught in his stomach hair, pulling it as he skulked across the dirt. His legs were okay. Thank God for Levi Strauss and high-top Reeboks.

He was supposed to be scared.

Instead, he felt exhilarated.

Peter always said that adrenaline was the ultimate rush. He was surprised by how unhurried he was, savoring every moment of the unknown. But too quickly, it was over. He reached up, stuck his fingers under the steel door frame, and gave himself just enough clearance to undulate stomach-down into the backseat floor. A moment later, Peter was on top of him. He was talking into his cell phone.

'You got the others? Good, get us out of here!'

The cars went down the hill. Decker waited until the car was parked behind the police barricade. Then he got up, opened the door, and got out, offering a hand. Jacob took it and was liberated seconds later. He squinted as he stepped into harsh illumination coming from dozens of headlights. Decker was already on the phone.

'I want three copters. I need light, and I need it now!' He turned to the first patrolman he saw. 'Take this young man home.'

'I don't mind sticking around,' the boy said.

'That's interesting, Jacob. Now get out of here.' He turned to Martinez. 'Let's get a team going.' He frowned. 'I suppose we need to find the place first.'

'Lieutenant Decker?'

Decker turned around. Sebastian Bernard – Bastard for short – a uniformed sergeant in his mid-forties with twenty years' experience. He was tall and bald and had a big mole over the right corner of his lip – a Cindy Crawford birthmark on steroids.

'Do you want to send a team inside?'

'Yeah, I'm working on that.'

'How many windows, how many doors?'

'Fuck if I know. We've got to find the place first. Then we've got to find out if anything's booby-trapped.'

'We can send out a dog. See what pops up. Or we can

lob in some smoke canisters.'

'But that'll make it doubly hard to see any booby traps.'

'I can get masks.'

'Masks will help us breathe; they won't help us see.' Decker rubbed his neck. 'Let's send some cruisers up, and I'll bullhorn them.'

'Can I come?' Jacob asked.

'No, you can't come!' Decker shot back. 'Are you out of your mind? What are you doing here?' Again, he turned to the uniform – a boy not much older than Jacob. 'Didn't I tell you to take him home, Officer?'

The patrolman blushed. Jacob came to his rescue. 'You know, I've been inside the place. At least let me draw you a map.'

Bastard turned to the teen. 'You've been inside?'

Jacob felt himself going hot. 'A long time ago.'

'Better than nothing!' Bastard waited.

Decker bit back annoyance at being bested. 'What do you remember?'

'I only recall one room.' His face took on more heat. 'You open the door and walk right into the bed. I recall a closet and a bathroom. Like I said, it was tiny. A shack.'

'What about a kitchen?' Bastard asked.

'I didn't see one. Maybe I just didn't notice it.'

'Windows?' Decker asked. 'How many?'

'Windows, windows . . .' Jacob tried to bring up an image. 'One on the front wall, next to the front door.' He fishtailed his hand back and forth. 'One on the left . . . no, right. One window on the front wall, one on the right as you walk in, on the left if you're inside. The closet door was on the left if you were facing the back wall.'

'So you remember only two windows?' Decker asked.

'And one in the bathroom,' Jacob said. 'Frosted . . . small. You couldn't climb through it.'

'And no kitchen,' Bastard reiterated.

'Not that I remember.' He thought for a few seconds. 'I don't think there was a kitchen. I think I remember a hot plate.'

'How about exterior doors?' Decker asked.

'The front door. And there was a door . . . next to the closet on the left.'

'Opposite the window?'

'Yeah. I think when I stormed out of the place, I must have gone out that way and walked straight into the mountains. There's absolutely nothing around.'

'Okay, that was helpful,' Decker admitted. 'Now get out of here.' To Bastard, Martinez, and Webster, he said, 'We find the place, surround it, bullhorn first. If there's no response, we'll lob in a couple of canisters of tear gas and see if that draws anyone out. If there's still no response, then we'll send in the dog and weapons team to make sure the son of a bitch didn't rig something on the doors and windows. If everything else is clear, we go in and see what we find. If the shooter's gone – and I'm almost positive he is – we'll have to do a grid search of the hills. As a matter of fact, we can start cordoning off the back area as soon as the copters get here and give us some light.'

Before Decker made it into the police car, Jacob

caught up with him. 'I know you're extremely busy. But I wanted to say bye.'

Decker's brain was buzzing with the immediacy. His eyes saw Jacob, but his attention was focused elsewhere. 'Thanks for your help, Jacob, but you need to go.'

Jacob smiled, but was dispirited by the response. 'I know. See you later. Be careful.'

Decker mussed his son's hair and slipped into the driver's seat of the cop car. By now the rutted pathway had become a parade of lights, a wall of vehicular metal. Recalling the approximate location of the pinpoint spot of yellow light – Decker used the sycamore as a landmark – he spotted the lean-to nestled in a copse of trees and scrub. It took about twenty minutes to get the cars in place, another twenty minutes to get the teams around the shack.

He tried the bullhorn. That proved to be nonproductive.

Next came the gas canisters shot through the windows. Glass shattered, spewing crystal shards and splinters into the night air. Smoke began to pour from the broken panes: dense, billowing gray clouds. Decker waited, but no one came through the doors. Maybe they were holed up in the bathroom. So he shot a canister through the small window in the bathroom.

Zero response.

With his recourses drying up, he sent in a weapons and bomb team to check the doors and windows for booby traps. After being given an all-clear sign, Decker masked up and charged through the front door. A wave of intense heat girdled his body and strangled his gullet. He felt his feet rock, unsteady as he felt dizzy . . . his head swimming in stars. He forced himself to breathe slowly and regularly.

Not too deep, not too shallow.

Because he wore a mask, his nostrils and mouth being in a closed environment, he could hear every gasp he took. He sweated profusely as he prowled.

Visibility was nonexistent. Between the heavy mask, the darkness, and the smoke, Decker couldn't see more than an inch in front of him. He turned on the flashlight, but all that did was turn the dark gray smoke into light gray smoke. He groped the wall for a light switch, but couldn't feel anything. His feet stumbled over something as he crept along. Abruptly, his legs hit something immobile and bulky at knee level, causing him to pitch forward, the flashlight slipping from his grip. He caught his balance, then bent down to feel what he had crashed into. His palms sank into something soft and bouncy.

You open the door and walk right into the bed.

He was feeling a mattress.

The flashlight had hit the floor, sending a murky beam straight up to the ceiling. The dust particles reflected the photons, casting the room in an eerie, postnuclear glow. He still couldn't see much. His fingers walked over the lumps of bedding, patting the blankets and sheets.

And then he felt something solid.

His heart slammed against his chest as he bent

down at the waist to see what it was, using his hands to ascertain a shape. He was touching a foot – still warm, but that was to be expected since it was sweltering inside. The foot was attached to a leg. He followed the leg upward and found it attached to a body. The nude body of a woman whose arms were tied to the bedposts. He bent over as far as he could, as close as he could, but smoke and smudge blurred the features. He could, however, smell the blood.

As he stood up, he felt his head go light, his balance beginning to sway. He took a few moments to find his consciousness and professionalism, and when he did, he leaned over the body and pressed his fingers into the soft spots of her neck.

He felt for a pulse, and snapped into action when he found one – medic mode.

Stop the bleeding, treat 'em for shock, get 'em to a chopper.

Except this wasn't Nam: this was L.A. in the twenty-first century.

They've got professionals for this, Decker.

He untied the bound wrists, picked up the mike, and called for an ambulance.

36

Hiding under the cloak of darkness, in a tangle of fauna, he was out there. Maybe he was nervous, reeking with the sweat of prey, or maybe he was smirking as he thought about the police spinning their wheels, traipsing over *his* chartered territory, playing a game of gingerbread man. Decker wasn't optimistic about success even as helicopter beams swept over the dense terrain, even as the cops with their handy-dandy flashlights scoured through bush and brush. There were just too many empty pockets in the hillside.

Still, Decker had to put on a show, otherwise Holt would be a definite lost cause. Maybe the display of manpower would prevent him from running full tilt. In the morning, with the help of sunlight and a fresh crew, perhaps someone would pull the sucker out from under his rock.

He told his people two rules.

Rule one: Don't get shot.

Rule two: Don't shoot – even if shot at.

Because probability dictated that friendly rather than hostile fire would be the greater enemy. After he doled out the assignments, the positions, and the individual search grids, he rechecked his own equipment. Finding everything in working order, he decided to survey the territory on his own – a foolhardy as well as foolish resolution. Not more than an hour ago, he had insisted that his people forage the mountains in pairs, admonishing them to stick closely to one another, because backup was the elixir of survival. Furthermore, Decker hadn't had to use his own endurance skills in over thirty years. But the voice of vengeance whispered its plaints: four human beings cut down by bullets, plus a girl beaten unconscious into a casserole of body parts.

He knew Martinez would have gladly gone with him. He knew that Bert – also a vet – had a good nose and a sixth sense for danger. But he didn't want to be responsible for Bert's welfare. Instead, he gave his detective temporary command of the operation. Martinez knew something was up.

'Where are you going?'

'Just having a look around. I'll be back in twenty minutes or so.'

'What do you mean look around? You're not going up there by yourself?'

But Decker was already gone, one hundred feet away, and pretending not to hear. He had his radio, his cell phone, a loaded gun, and a flashlight. Like a good Boy Scout, he was prepared.

The midnight air was saturated with the aroma of

wet wood, and mosquitoes. He fanned his face, redirecting a funnel of gnats as he swung the flashlight's parabolic beam over the forest floor. Each footstep announced his arrival with a crunch as the soles of his shoes turned fallen leaves into organic rot. At first, he could hear the other cops, but as he drifted away, delving deeper into a black fog of copse, the voices receded . . . the spots from their flashlights flitting like fireflies. Walking farther along . . . five minutes, then ten, then fifteen. The ambient sounds came from insects, a nocturnal conversation of tweets and clicks and clacks with an occasional nighttime birdcall cutting through the timbre. Far off, Decker thought he might have even heard toads croaking, something that hadn't reached his ears in a very long time. Noisy, but reassuring because utter silence is reserved for those in cemeteries.

Away from the prescribed perimeter, away from the action and the people, his mind raced in many directions.

In Nam, he had mostly done the pickup after Charlie had done primary damage. But there were a few times, mostly at the end of the tour when there was nothing but virgin recruits, where he had been elected point man. He had seen enough trailblazers come back with stumps for legs, and he didn't want to join the ranks, but what could he do? Leaving it up to the virgins would have guaranteed nails in the coffins. Panic had enveloped him, though he had tried hard not to show it. Thinking back, he guessed that he had achieved some success. Either that or the men under his command had been too scared to notice how out of control their leader had been.

Taking the men from point A to point B as Charlie tried to pick them off. Trying to clear the roads so troops could go through. The snipers were badasses, but they were not nearly as terrifying as the land mines. Something primal about an explosion in the vicinity of one's balls.

He realized he was sweating. Weird because the air had turned cooler, everything damp and slimy. Still, the mist felt good on his cheeks, washing the grime from the smoke-choked shack off of his face and neck.

Images dancing in his brain.

After they cleaned the blood off of Ruby's face, Decker could make out intact bone structure. Her cheekbones seemed whole, her mandible as well, although it was impossible to assess hairline cracks on physical inspection. Her upper jaw seemed all right except for a few cracked teeth. Her nose had been broken, her lip was split, and her eyes had been swollen shut. She'd be hurting for a while, but with time and painkillers, she'd heal and heal well if her parents' money hired the right doctor. Los Angeles was the capital of plastic surgery: capped teeth and rhinoplasty being so common as to be registered as mundane.

Her body had also suffered. The whip marks were visible as crimson snakes sidling through her back and abdomen. Welts and bruises had made a crazy quilt out of her thighs and chest. Her wrists and ankles had been bound when he had found her. Her hands had seemed okay, and although her fingertips had suffered from lack of circulation – pinkish white flesh holding nails polished glossy black – they'd probably recover. Her ankles had been tied with a thicker rope and her feet were bluish gray when Decker had loosened the restraints, but they had taken on a little color as they loaded her onto the gurney – a good sign.

As Decker swiped his forehead with the back of his hand, grit scratched his skin.

She was oozing semen and trickling blood from between her legs, suggestive of being penetrated by more than just a penis. As soon as the smoke thinned, the shack would be gone over, bit by bit, floorboard by floorboard. Lord only knew what they'd find. He thought of Jacob losing his virginity in that hellhole, and anger knotted his stomach. How could such a brilliant kid be so *stupid*!

Of course, intelligence was irrelevant when the groin was doing the thinking. And how common was that? There was never a man alive – gay or straight – whose dick hadn't gotten the better of him. Sometimes that wasn't a bad thing. His dick had led him to Rina. Still, it was his heart that had kept him there, blithely accepting things – like religion, car pools, and soppy movies – without rancor.

A sudden *snap* brought him back to planet earth. His heart drummed against his chest, and his senses returned to high alert. With self-contempt, he recognized that his mind had been wandering. Now how idiotic was that?

Standing stock-still . . . waiting it out. Sweat poured off his forehead and down his face. Without being conscious of the act, he had released his gun from his holster and had turned off his flashlight. The seconds passed. Turning his head slowly, his eyes scanned the shadowed area. Finally, he spotted it, a pair of fire-yellow orbs that were sizing him up. They looked to be bigger than those of an alley cat. Decker pegged the animal to be a large opossum or maybe a small coyote. The eyes retreated and disappeared.

He counted to sixty, stowed his gun back in its harness, turned on the flashlight, then resumed walking. The ground began to slope upward and, walking off-balance, he wished he had worn better shoes. Although they were rubber-soled, the upper portions were leather, not nearly as flexible as his New Balance high-tops. The search team's flashlights had receded to pinpoints of illumination as small as the stars above.

Although tense, he wasn't as nervous as he should have been, considering that he was basically lost. He had a compass. He had a radio. He could find his way back. But he had no desire to return to the fray, because the walk was restorative, helping him sort out his thoughts. He was careful where he trod, not because of land mines but because each step gave away his position. The abrupt sound had put him in attack mode. *He* had to be the hunter, Holt the prey. Any slipup could turn it the other way around. He waved his flashlight, the beam cutting a wide swath over the ground. He searched for recent footprints, a pile of leaves or clumps of dirt that might have been depressed or disturbed . . . a clue as to where Holt might be.

A good idea, but it was leading nowhere.

He continued hiking up the mountain.

His mind leaped back to Holt's childhood, how truly frightening it must have been for Darrell to lose his baby brother, the pre-schooler discarded like old clothes. If Philip Holt had been of stronger mettle, he could have adopted the infant as his own. Decker had raised Rina's sons as diligently as he had raised – or was still raising – his own daughters. Of course, her boys weren't products from an adulterous union, a living, breathing reminder that your wife had fucked another man. After Decker had found out about Jan, they had spoken briefly about reconciliation. Dead conversation – both saying things that neither believed. The bitterness that had followed surprised him. They had talked a good case about being adult, when in reality they had acted like children for many years. Even now, he couldn't stand to be in the same room with her.

He hiked another few minutes, then stopped. He was buried within the thicket, and he was *alone*. Picking up his handheld mike, he decided to call in to civilization, find out about the progress of the investigation . . . and that's when he heard it.

In an eye blink, Decker had gone into a crouching position behind a wall of brush.

He froze.

It was a low-pitched growl, so completely without tone that it sounded like a series of rapid clicks. Instantly, the air became stifling as perspiration shot out from his pores. For just a moment, everything went quiet and still. The seconds ticked on, and then a few brave crickets dared to chirp. But within moments, they were silenced.

Because there it was again – a menacing admonition.

I'm here. I belong and you don't. Don't fuck with me!

As hard as he tried, Decker couldn't see anything – no shape or form, just gray, blurry space. His quadriceps tightened from his awkward posture, immobilized halfway between kneeling and standing. He knew that within minutes, his muscles would start cramping. He resisted the urge to squirm, to adjust to a more comfortable position. Things that go bump in the night were very perceptive creatures.

Of all the things to run up against. But then why not? He was in their territory. He had trespassed and now someone was pissed. He considered the options. Wolves hunted in packs, but cats were solitary animals. The growl that had perked his ears wasn't from anything canine, so let's hear it for the evenly stacked odds. This was going to be a game of one on one.

Ten seconds . . . twenty . . . thirty and forty. A full minute passed with time moving *verrrry* slowly, as if on TST – treadmill standard time. Minutes were always protracted when jogging on that god-awful contraption, working up a sweat by going nowhere. (Wasn't that an apt metaphor for life?) Just the opposite happened in sex: the clock ran at warp speed.

Why was life so unfair?

It felt like an hour had elapsed although it was probably not more than a minute. Wild cats were naturally reclusive, and this mountain lion was no exception.

At least, he *hoped* there was only one mountain lion.

Because that's what was out there: a mountain lion, or a puma, or a cougar . . . take your pick. He didn't give a rat's ass about the official name. It was something savage. It was something with sharp claws and glinty teeth. It was a goddamn, motherfucking big cat, and it sounded goddamn hungry.

He considered shining the flashlight in the sucker's eyes, but nixed the idea. It might spook rather than scare the kitty.

Just wait it out.

Except that his thighs were starting to ache *real* badly.

The growl resurfaced a third time. Then a faint rustle, like it was nosing through the detritus. Decker tried to home in on the sound – in front of him but somewhat off to the left. With great caution, he lowered the handheld two-way radio to the ground, then managed to free up his gun.

Stooped over and shaking, with a gun in one hand and a flashlight in the other, he scrolled back to his childhood, specifically his uncle who had taught him how to hunt. Something about how animals detected an object in motion a lot easier than an object at rest. Something about animals not being exactly color-blind, but not seeing too well. So if you blended, you'd be okay.

He remembered his first kill. It had been a deer – a small buck whose newly forming antlers were still covered with fur. His uncle and father had slapped him on the back, but it hadn't sat well with him. And even though he pretended to be thrilled, and had eaten every bite of campfire-roasted venison, Decker never went hunting again. His baby brother, Randy, hadn't liked hunting either, although Randy was an avid bass fisherman. Everyone in Florida fished bass. Like the Dolphins, the Marlins, and insanity, bass fishing was a state pastime.

As Decker's eyes adjusted to the dark, his respiration slowed to a fast trot. With great care, he lowered the flashlight, then took the gun in a standard two-handed grip.

He held tight and waited.

More moments passed. He heard another murmur . . . the soft brush of leaves underfoot. Barely audible . . . whispered in an undertone. Then another growl, this one closer to a purr. This sucker sounded content. Or maybe that was wishful thinking. A couple of counts passed, then Decker heard padded footsteps moving very deliberately. He could decipher them – *cla-clomp, cla-clomp*. Something walking on all fours.

Then nothing.

Moments passed, then a minute.

Where the hell was the motherfucker?

Decker's lips were dry, his throat was sawdust. A violent urge to cough shot through his gullet, but he forced it back down, his eyes watering as he managed an arid swallow.

More sounds, but not footsteps. Decker strained to decipher them.

Something between lapping and slurping. The animal was drinking, though God only knew where it had found water. The ground underneath was hard and dusty; the foliage was kindling. Though the air was damp, it hadn't rained in months.

The lapping stopped, and in its wake came that dreaded silence. He had nothing but his breathing for company.

A sudden *snap* crackled through the air, sending a shiver down Decker's spine. Then a distinct crunching sound, jaws crushing hard matter, pulverizing it to powder. Snap, crackle, pop, but it sure as hell wasn't Rice Krispies.

He had interrupted someone's meal.

His thoughts went back to the pair of eyes, what he had thought was an opossum. Okay, that made sense. A big wild animal had made dinner out of a smaller wild animal. That was the natural order of things. Let the feline sate itself, because then it would move on. And then he could move on.

More gnawing . . . chewing . . . gnashing.

Another loud *snap* that startled him.

Just hang in there, Deck.

Lap, lap . . . slurp, slurp . . . lap, lap.

It was drinking blood . . . an awful lot of blood coming from an opossum.

More chomps.

An awful lot of eating, too.

Maybe it was a bigger kill. There were loads of deer in these parts. Stray dogs and wolves . . . coyotes.

The noises abruptly stopped.

The gait . . . *cla-clomp, cla-clomp*. Leaves and twigs broke underfoot.

Two flaming orbs peered out from the bush. A thin sliver of moonlight allowed Decker to catch a flicker of white fangs.

Don't make me do it, Kitty. I'm a dead-on shot!

Talking to himself and talking hype at that. He couldn't see anything well except the eyes. Wounding a wild animal was a course of last resort. Scaring it off was preferable. Without changing his carriage, he lowered one hand down to the ground, then finger walked until he felt the handle of his flashlight. Sweaty fingers gripped the metal, the moisture from his hands making it slippery in his hold. He placed it back on the ground, then coated his palm with dirt from the forest floor. He picked up the handle again . . . played with it until he had a firm grasp.

Slowly, he raised it to the level of the cat's eyes.

His finger touching the surface until he found the power button.

He turned the beam on.

Nothing.

Waved the beam a couple of times.

Seconds strolled by like sightseers.

Finally, the alien eyes withdrew from sight. He could hear the animal walking . . . walking, not running. But the sound was retreating instead of advancing.

That was a good thing.

Thank you very much, God.

He *benched* a quick *Gomel*, a prayer recited when delivered from danger. It was a supplication he had said before . . . too many close calls in his life. How long before his luck ran out?

Don't think about that now.

He waited. And waited and waited and waited.

Finally, finally, he allowed himself to stand upright. After that, he broke into a fit of coughing – horrid, dry hacking worse than anything he had experienced in his smoker days. His eyes became puddles of water, his nose spewed out mucus, spittle shot out from between his lips. Gun still in hand, he wiped his face on his jacket sleeve, then shone the beam back and forth at the previously occupied thicket. The illumination failed to elicit any response.

He went over to investigate the kill. He shouldn't have been shocked by what he saw, but the raw horror of it brought up a surge of bile.

The lower portion of the face was gone, leaving only the skull, the eye sockets, and a few scattered teeth. The cranium still had the hair attached – rich, brown, frizzy hair that now looked like a clown wig. The torso had been devoured down to the ribs, the body cavity completely eviscerated, leaving the hips and legs detached from the thorax. One leg had been eaten to the bone, the large femur still whole. The other leg, sitting a few feet away from the torso, was untouched, the limb still wrapped in denim pants, a high-back sneaker still on the foot. The ground was damp and sticky, but there wasn't much blood left in what once had been a body. The cat had slaked its thirst.

Decker inched backward, his nostrils assaulted by the strong stench of urine. Beside the pile of bone, flesh, and shredded fabric was a mound of feces, still warm and sending up condensation in the cooler night air – a wretched, fetid stink. Decker's throat gurgled. He moved several feet to the right and puked. Then he picked up his radio and connected through to Martinez. 'Found him.'

'Where?' The detective's voice was animated. 'Loo, where are you? Are you all right?'

'I'm fine.' He took a deep breath and let it out. 'I'm not sure of my exact location . . . somewhere northeast of the original grid. I'll wave my flashlight's blinking beam up in the air. Tell the choppers to look for it. They'll zero in on the site.'

'Do you need backup?'

'Nope. He's dead.'

'Dead?'

'Very much so.'

'Should I call the shooting team?'

'Not necessary. All I need is the coroner. Tell the doc to bring a body bag . . . and a small one at that.'

37

He wasn't sure what hurt more, his bones or his head, but it really didn't matter. Advil was all he had for relief, so it would have to do, although the pain was way beyond anything offered OTC. Decker was dirty and tired and sick to his stomach, and all he wanted to do was crawl into bed. On his desk were piles of paperwork. He told himself it could wait until morning, except now, it was the morning. As he slogged through sheaf after sheaf, writing until his hand cramped, he tried to sort out the salient data. But he was too spent to think.

Marge came in a little after seven. 'I'd like to see Vega off to school.'

Decker attempted to focus on her face. She came out as a blur of ash-colored flesh. 'Good idea. We'll talk later. Or even tomorrow if you want.'

'No, I'll come back around two. Will you be here?'

'I'll be here.'

She regarded his red and watery eyes. 'Maybe you *shouldn't* be here, Pete. Maybe you should go home, too. You're looking so bedraggled, you make Skid Row Sam look stylish.'

Decker looked at his wrinkled suit. 'If this was linen instead of wool, you'd think me very stylish.'

'It isn't linen, Pete.' She stared at his clothing. 'I don't think it's even wool.'

'It's a wool blend. Say you're sorry.'

'Ex-*cuse* me.' Marge dragged over a chair and sat opposite him. 'Don't you find the entire thing ironic?'

Confused, Decker waited for the right answer.

'The survivalist getting eaten,' Marge explained. 'How did *that* happen?'

Decker shrugged. 'Beats me.'

'Like . . . was it an exceptionally big mountain lion?'

'I don't know, Marge. I didn't get that close.'

'Because mountain lions don't take down full-grown men. They're usually content with dogs and children. If the guy was any kind of survivalist, he wouldn't have tripped up over a cougar.'

'Maybe Holt stank of fear. Animals can smell it, you know. And even with Holt being a stone psycho, anyone would be a tad edgy with half of LAPD looking for him. Or maybe the cat was really hungry. Or Holt stumbled onto a nursing female who was protecting her cubs.'

Marge was unconvinced. 'You're rationalizing. He should have known better.'

'Then perhaps Holt wasn't the survivalist that Erin made him out to be. He lied about everything else. Why not that?'

Marge rubbed her forehead. 'But was he the computer genius that Erin made him out to be?'

'Since I'm not a computer maven, I don't know,' Decker answered.

Marge reached over his desk and drank up his lukewarm coffee. 'It's going to take the experts to break into all of Dee Baldwin's files. Her system has a ton of firewalls.'

'What about Merv Baldwin's files?'

'We haven't gone through all his, either. But hers are the ones having to do with the purloined tests.'

'So from what you and Scott were able to tap into, are we on the right track?'

She frowned. 'What's our track again?'

'Dee Baldwin acquiring advance copies of the achievement tests?'

'Yeah. Right. This is all we have so far. She was paying Holt money for something. I don't think it was because of his good looks or charm. Her computer has links to some systems, but we don't know what they are. She also has lots of test files that we opened with very little difficulty. Dr Estes said the tests in storage were just old achievement tests used for study purposes, not any different from SAT or SAT II or MCAT test books available for purchase.'

'We should go over the tests and find out when they were entered into the Baldwin computer. Then we'll try to find out when that particular test was given out to the students at large. *If* the computer date was earlier than the test date – or even the same day – it would tell us that Dee had insider's information.'

'Okay.' Marge wrote the assignment in her notepad. 'I'll see how Scotty's doing. Maybe we'll go back to the Beverly Hills office this afternoon.'

'And what about Merv?'

She shrugged haplessly.

'And Ernesto? Did you pull out the rest of his file?'

'Yes, we did. He seemed to be making progress. So their wee-hour tryst could have been just therapy.'

'Or if Ruby's letters are any indication, just maybe, *maybe* he was telling Mervin about his wife's illegal activities.'

'Why would he do that?'

'The kid had an attack of conscience. Maybe he thought Merv had one as well. Maybe that's why Holt popped both of them. He was tipped by Ruby, and Holt did the rest.'

'That's so depressing.'

'Yes, it is.'

Marge yawned, then swallowed back a sour taste.

'Go home,' Decker ordered.

Marge ignored him. 'You know, it would streamline things considerably if Ruby Ranger would wake up and explain everything to us in detail.'

'She is up . . . I mean conscious,' Decker explained. 'Well, she's not conscious at the moment, because she's in surgery. But at some point between going on the gurney and being prepped for the OR, she became conscious. What kind of evidence of wrongdoing do we have against her?'

'Nothing,' Marge said. 'She wasn't on the Baldwin payroll as far as Scott and I could tell.'

'Swell.'

'We didn't access all the files, so who knows? What about Erin?'

'She's out on bail.' Decker rolled his shoulders. 'Those two girls hate each other. And, while I can't swear that either was involved with the murders, I'm sure that both were into illegal activities. Erin has a nasty jones, and Ruby is a known hacker. I bet we can play one against the other.'

'Try to get Erin to turn State's?'

'Whoever rolls over first.'

'Erin's a juvenile. We can get her off easier.'

'But Ruby, being an adult, has much more to lose if she doesn't turn State's. We'll talk to the DA and see how it plays out. And maybe she can clear up what happened with Ernesto.'

No one spoke.

'Poor Ernesto,' Decker remarked. 'First, Ruby messed with his head. Then, when he starts getting it together, the bastard just cut him down.'

'Holt cut Dee down as well,' Marge said. 'Killed his own golden goose.'

'Holt was afraid that Dee would rat on him . . . that's my take.' Decker rubbed his eyes. 'I suppose we'll know more after we've talked to Ruby . . . if we can talk to Ruby. There are lots of things we don't know, and a scam of this magnitude with so many deaths . . . I hope we get everyone. More important, I pray that no more bodies pop up.'

'Amen.'

'Until we know everything, we need to be meticulous.

That means going over the crime scenes again to make sure we didn't overlook anything. We'll need to reinterview the witnesses . . . canvas the area again. Maybe someone saw Holt go in and out of Dee's beach condo even if the person didn't see him the day of the murder. Also, we'll need to question the boys at the nature camp again – one by one.'

'We questioned them one by one.'

'Notice I used the word "again". God is in the details. As far as I'm concerned, this is still an ongoing investigation. There could be dozens of people that we haven't unearthed.'

'I hear you, Lieutenant. But right now, I'm too tired to think.'

'Yeah, weren't you going to go home?'

'I was.' But Marge made no attempt to get up from the chair.

'Any reason you're dragging your heels?'

'Fatigue.'

'And?'

'And, actually . . . I feel more competent here than I do at home.' Marge sighed. 'At work, we've got some kind of method. You do an investigation, you follow a procedure. Sure, there's a kink here and there, but mostly it's . . .' She extended her right hand to mimic a beeline path. 'At home . . . I don't know . . . we make the rules up as we go along.'

Decker nodded.

Marge smiled. 'It's probably different when you've raised them since infancy.'

'No, not really.'

'C'mon,' Marge insisted. 'You got history together.'

'Good history and bad history. You don't think that Jacob has chinked some of Rina's armor?'

'Poor Rina. How does she deal with it?'

'Rina's low key. Not that she doesn't ache, but . . .' He threw his hands up. 'Outwardly, she's very calm. It bugs the crap out of me. She should get apoplectic like I do.' He threw a pencil across the room. 'Maybe she's had too many hard knocks to be bothered by an errant teenager.'

'You always said that Jacob was the easy one. What happened?'

'Things came up. Life is full of surprises, Marjorie.'

'He's a bright boy, Pete. He'll be okay.'

'That's what I tell myself.' He stacked up the papers. 'Well, I'm feeling pretty nonfunctional. Maybe we should both go home.'

'And feel nonfunctional there?'

'We've made our beds, Margie. We might as well sleep in them.'

Eight in the morning, and there were already visitors in the house. Maybe they were relatives, because Rina thought a few of the women resembled Jill. There were also about a dozen teenagers. Maybe cousins, maybe friends of Karl's, maybe kids from Ernesto's class. They were talking in hushed voices, the boys looking at their feet, the girls wiping their red eyes with tissues. Within moments, a Jill look-alike approached her, looked her up and down, then managed a courteous nod. 'I'm Brook Hart. May I help you?'

'Are you Jill's sister?' Rina asked.

'Yes, I am. What can I do for you, Ms . . .'

'I'm Rina Decker.'

'Oh.' Brook regarded her with suspicious eyes. 'The detective's wife.'

'Yes, but I'm not here on any police business.'

'So why are you here, holding a big briefcase?' Brook pinkened. 'I don't mean to sound rude, but this is a difficult time for the family. I'm sure you can appreciate that.'

'Yes, of course. Actually, I'm here to see Mr Golding. The contents of the briefcase are for him.'

'Oh.' Again the wary look. 'What's inside?'

'It's of a personal nature.'

'Oh . . . how personal?'

'Is he available?'

Brook frowned. 'Wait here a moment.'

'Thank you.'

The moment stretched into minutes. Rina busied herself by trying to look inconspicuous while she studied the people. There was one girl in particular who seemed to be focused in on her. Maybe it was Rina's clothes – the simple blue sweater, the midi-length jeans skirt that fell over her boots, the black tam that hid most of her hair. In this room, almost all the women were wearing pants.

The girl was still looking at her. Even with the nose pierce, the teen was a pretty little thing with dark hair, dark eyes, and dimples. Rina didn't recall meeting her. Still, when the girl smiled at her, Rina smiled back. The teen edged forward, slowly walking toward her. Then she stuck out her hand.

'I'm Lisa Halloway. You're Jacob's mother, aren't you?'

Rina held the thin fingers and gave them a light squeeze. 'Yes, I am. Have we met before?'

'No, but you look just like him . . . or I guess it's actually he looks like you.'

'It's nice to meet you, Lisa. Where do you know Jacob from?'

'Just from around.'

From the drug parties.

'How's he doing?' she asked.

'Right now, he's very saddened and upset by what happened to Ernesto Golding. I'm sure you feel the same way.'

Tears moistened her eyes. 'I was Ernesto's girlfriend . . . ex-girlfriend.' Droplets ran down her cheek. 'It's very . . . unreal.'

Without thinking, Rina reached out, and the girl fell into the embrace, crying with her entire body. Rina sighed as she smoothed the teen's bouncy curls. She was so young to be in so much pain.

'Life sucks!' Lisa choked out.

'Sometimes.'

'All the time.'

'No, not all the time.'

Lisa pulled away. 'Well, wake me up when I get to the non-sucky parts.'

'It won't be necessary.' Rina smiled at her. 'You'll know when you're there.'

Lisa broke away and took a step backward. 'Say hello to Jacob for me.'

'I will.'

'Tell him to drop by sometime.'

Sure, Rina thought. 'Sure,' Rina said. As she watched the girl melt in with her peers, Carter materialized by her side. They watched the kids together.

'Poor kids,' Golding said. 'What a thing to have to go through at such a young age.'

Rina turned to him. His face was drawn, his complexion wan. His beard seemed to have grayed overnight. He had been a short man. Now he was a small man as well. He wore a black turtleneck over black pants. His feet were covered with white crew socks, as if they'd been bandaged. She said, 'Did you get any sleep last night?'

'No. I don't think I'll ever sleep again.'

'I'm so sorry.'

'So am I.' He picked at his beard. 'Brook told me you were here.'

'Is there a place where we could talk in privacy?'

'All the bedrooms are being utilized by family members. Except for the master, but Jill's sleeping. I don't want to disturb her.'

'Of course not. Maybe we can talk in the kitchen or in a study?'

'This house doesn't have many interior doors. Except for the bedrooms, there are no other enclosed spaces with locks. I wanted everything out in the open. It's the type of people my wife and I are. Open . . . nothing hidden. What you see is what you get. See, I wanted that . . . because . . . my family was so hidden.' He faced her. 'I take it that's why you're here.'

'Yes.'

'What's the verdict?'

'Mr Golding, perhaps we could use a bathroom?'

'It's bad, huh?'

'No, it's complicated. How about an upstairs bathroom? I take it you have a lock on your bathrooms?'

'Of course we have locking bathrooms, we're not perverts!'

Rina felt heat in her face. 'Of course.'

Carter shook his head. 'I'm sorry I snapped—'

'It's fine, Mr Golding—'

'No, it's not fine! And call me Carter, damn it!'

'Of course.'

Golding stared at her, then looked away. 'I don't know what the hell is wrong with me. I can't control my temper . . . I can't . . .'

'Carter, I was a widow at twenty-four. It's not the same thing as your experience, but there are similarities. Don't apologize for your behavior. I never did.'

He regarded her. 'How did your husband die?'

'Brain tumor.'

'I'm so sorry.' His face filled with self-loathing as he shook his head. 'God, that was rude of me.'

'I don't feel bad about the question. You shouldn't, either. Can we go somewhere and talk?'

'Yes.' He nodded vigorously. 'Yes, of course. Upstairs. This way.'

She walked by his side as they climbed the stairs. Confessing her own baggage had humanized Rina in the man's eyes. She knew that. But it seemed like such a crass thing to do. Actually, it had slipped out.

Yitzchak had been dead for over a decade. She had been married longer to Peter than she had to him. He crossed her mind on occasion, but rarely when she was awake. In dreams . . . the dreams were always so real . . . his asking why she hadn't waited for him. The guilt was overwhelming when she awoke. It made no sense, but there it was anyway. Maybe she felt guilty because in her dreams he never, ever scolded. A sharp tongue wasn't Yitzchak's style. In her first marriage, she had been the volatile one. Funny how things change.

Carter led her into the upstairs powder room. It held just a toilet and a small pedestal sink topped with a round, beveled mirror. She found her reflection disconcerting because in Jewish homes, mirrors were covered during the first month of mourning. Carter locked the door, put down the toilet seat cover, and offered it to her.

'I'm fine,' Rina said. 'Why don't you sit?'

Golding didn't argue. 'I appreciate your coming here, Mrs Decker. And so early.'

'I've actually been up since five-thirty.'

'You should have called me. I was up.'

Rina smiled.

Golding said, 'Is that your normal time to get up?'

'It's early for me. But I had things to do. First, I went to the police station to badger my husband into releasing to me some more photographs from the evidence room—'

'What photographs?'

'Evidence left behind after the synagogue was

vandalized – and those from your son's room.'

'The pictures of the dead bodies?' Golding dropped his head between his knees. 'My father! What did he do?'

'Carter, I would never come here at a time like this and deliver bad news. Let me get this out, and then you can ask all the questions you want.'

Slowly, he straightened up. 'It's not bad?'

'No, it's not bad—'

'Just complicated.' Golding looked up. 'I'm sorry. Go on.'

There was a twist of the outside doorknob.

'I'm in here,' Golding shouted. 'Go away.' The sound of retreating footsteps. Carter let out a bitter chuckle. 'I'm too distraught to be polite. Go on.'

Rina cleared her throat. 'A lot of this is conjecture, but I think this may have happened. While looking through papers and old documents for research to write his family history assignment, Ernesto found these horrible snapshots—'

'Do you think I should see them?'

'They're graphic, but yes, after I finish my story, you might want to see them. May I finish first?'

'Of course.'

'Ernesto found these pictures among your father's effects. Then, he began to delve deeper, finding inconsistencies about his grandfather's emigration to America. He thought the worst . . . which is a terrible shame because I spoke to someone who might have had contact with your dad when your father was a boy – when they both were boys actually. I showed him the most recent picture you gave me – the one of you, your father, and your two sons. He didn't recognize your father. Instead, he thought that your son, Karl, resembled a man he had met in his youth.'

'Karl looked like my dad.' Carter was excited. 'It's true. Everyone thought they looked alike. Who is the man?'

'He's one of the handfuls of men who survived Treblinka.'

'So my father was in the camp?'

'I don't think so. I am telling you about a young boy of around sixteen – a Pole, not a Jew. This was around 1943, right before Treblinka was burned down by the Nazis. This young boy, the son of a Polish policeman, used to sneak up to the outside perimeter of the camp and go right up to the electrified gates. He used to take pictures of the inmates: some were living, some were dead. I don't know why he took the pictures. But I do know that by taking the pictures, the boy risked his own life. He was not a member of the SS, and if he had been caught, he would have been shot. Plus, the boy gave the inmates food – ersatz bread, bits of carrots and turnips . . . once even strawberries. All food was a luxury. At that time, food was very scarce, not only for the inmates but for all of Poland. So what he did was very, very generous. It's possible that this boy was your father.'

Carter's breathing was audible and shallow. He whispered, 'What was this boy's name?'

'I don't know. Neither did the man I spoke to.'

'So who is Isaac Golding?'

'I have no idea. Ernesto had information stating that Yitzchak Golding had died in Treblinka. But I don't know where that information came from.'

'If my father didn't do anything, why take on that name?'

'Maybe he didn't, but maybe his parents did because they needed the name of dead people to escape the tribunals and get false passports. I'm not saying that happened, but who knows? Or maybe your father took on the name because it was the name of a concentration camp inmate who made an impression on him. Maybe he did it to honor him. Perhaps you can find out. There are many records and lists. You know Yitzchak Golding was sent to Treblinka. If you search hard enough, maybe you'll find the history of Yitzchak Golding somewhere. It depends how far you want to take this.'

No one spoke for a moment. From the outside, someone was twisting the doorknob.

'It's occupied!'

'Sorry,' answered a muffled voice from behind the door.

Finally, Golding talked. 'This man that you spoke with. He's reliable?'

'As reliable as they come, considering that he's in the tenth decade of his life. He doesn't know the boy's name, and he doesn't know who Yitzchak Golding was. But he said the photographs were pictures of Treblinka. He could make out the wire fence.' Rina looked away, and wiped her wet eyes. 'It was excruciatingly hard for him to look at these pictures. But he did it to give you resolution, because he didn't want anyone to suffer. He called the boy photographer a minor hero. If that was your father, you should feel good about it.'

'And if it isn't?'

'As I said, it depends how far you want to take it.'

'He called my father a minor hero?'

'Yes. And my husband said that your son also might have died a minor hero . . . trying to do the right thing.'

Golding was silent.

Rina said, 'You know, most people never even get close to being any kind of a hero – major or minor. You have two of them.'

'You mean, I *had* two of them.' Carter's cheeks were tear-slicked. He stood up. 'Thank you for everything you've done, Mrs Decker. And so quickly.'

'It wasn't anything, Carter. And please, call me Rina. We've both bared enough pain to be on a first-name basis.'

38

There were cops outside Ruby's hospital room, their guns catching Jacob's eyes. Decker told him to hold on for a moment, leaving him about three doors away from hers. Jacob watched his stepfather talk to the uniforms and plainclothesmen assigned to the watch. It took about five minutes, then Decker stepped away and came to him, a concerned look on his face.

'She's still a mess. Not more than five minutes, all right?'

'You're bending a few rules?' Jacob asked.

'It's not a problem as long as you're quick.'

'I'll make you look good.' Jacob tossed him a smile. But he was nervous. The first step was the hardest. After that it was just a matter of placing one foot in front of the other. He stopped at the threshold. The bed nearest the door was empty: hers was on the right side, closest to the window. She was surrounded by medical apparatus – monitors, IV lines, and machines that bleeped.

He tiptoed over until he was in talking distance. She didn't notice him. How could she notice him? She seemed incapable of moving her head. The smell was strong and unpleasant. Jacob wiped his mouth with the back of his hand, staring as the seconds ticked on.

Her eyes were closed, her head a turban of bandages. What showed through was red and raw and swollen. A swath of gauze cut through the center of her face, hiding her nose and cheeks. He could see chipped teeth through her mangled lips.

She had been in the hospital for three days. Yesterday, she had asked for him. It had taken him a full twenty-four hours to shore up his courage.

The eyelids lifted, her brown orbs swimming in a sea of jaundice yellow and blood red. They glommed on to Jacob and looked him up and down. She muttered. He couldn't understand, so he stepped closer.

She whispered, 'You've grown.'

Jacob licked his lips. 'Couple of inches.'

'What are you?' she slurred out. 'Six, six-one?'

'A little under six, actually. The shortest male in my family.'

'Yeah . . .' Breathy voice. 'Your old man is real tall.'

'He doesn't count.' Jacob winced. 'I mean he doesn't count genetically. He's my stepfather.'

'That's right.' As Ruby moved her head, her eyes registered pain. 'So what'd you tell him?'

'Everything.'

The purple lids raised a fraction of an inch.

'I had to tell him about the place, so I had to tell him

everything.' Jacob forced himself to look at her. 'He felt your life was in danger.'

She closed her eyelids. 'Pretty good for a kike . . . never thought a prick like you . . . would do it.'

Jacob didn't respond, staring at her bandaged face. 'I guess the fantasy of rape is better than the reality.'

The lids snapped up, her expression ugly and angry. 'You shit!'

His voice rose. 'I became dirt in my father's eyes to save your life, and you have the gall to call me a kike and a prick?'

'Shut the fuck up, okay?' She was breathing heavily. She spoke softly and slowly. 'Worse things in life than being a kike and a prick.' She closed her eyes again. 'I'm going to jail. Not for the murders – I didn't know – but for computer stuff. I've got half of Quantico outside.' An attempt at a smile. 'Like I could go somewhere.'

Jacob didn't answer.

'I'm first . . . time felon with an . . . abusive father. I should get probation. No chance. Too many people dropped. I gotta do time.'

'I'm sorry,' Jacob lied.

'No you're not.'

'Yeah, you're right.'

The shredded lips formed something that approximated a smile. 'Whatever! I'll sell the movie rights for millions. Besides . . . dykes are okay. I like boys better, but . . . I can suck pussy better than any guy.'

'You rock, Ruby.'

'Fuck you, Lazarus!' She sneered. 'Self-righteous

asshole. Your God may have prevented you from putting on the uniform . . . but He couldn't stop you from rutting like a pig. You loved it, man.'

Jacob felt the stab down to the core. He tried to slough it off like dead skin. 'I'm sure I would have, had I been conscious.'

'Yeah? Rationalize it, baby! First, you were zonked, later . . . it wore off. You woulda nastied all night, *Yonkie*, if *I* hadn't stopped you!'

Slam dunk on that one! Jacob wilted. He couldn't look at her. 'So I liked it. So what?'

'So what? You hated me . . . but you still fucked me. What does that say about you?'

'It says I'm an idiot. Congratulations, Ruby. You humbled me.'

She managed to crank up a smug smile. But it didn't last long. Moments later, tears formed in her eyes. 'Write to me in prison?'

Such longing in her voice. It shocked him. But his hatred outweighed his compassion. 'No, I'm not going to write to you.'

'How about a birthday card? For your first girl?'

He turned to her and saw red, wet eyeballs . . . tears falling down the bandages. She was crying blood. Her voice had come out small and shaking . . . pleading with him just like she had done that night. Then the naked truth dawned on him. Through all the bravado, all the venomous words she had slung at him, she had actually liked him. He looked at her heart monitor, watching it record the *s* and *p* cardiac waves that he had learned about in biology. Yep, even

Ruby had a heart. 'When's your birthday?'

'August twenty-fifth.'

'Okay. I'll send you a birthday card.'

No one spoke.

Ruby closed her eyes. 'You were the number one hottie, Lazarus . . . the wet dream of every bitch at the raves. Which is why *I* got you. Once you figure out . . . what to do . . . I'm sure you'll make some nice *Jewish* girl very happy.'

The put-down sounded surprisingly good to Jacob's ear. 'I certainly hope so.'

That was his exit line. Wordlessly, he turned and left the room. His stepfather was down the hall, talking to some official, but he broke off the conversation when he saw Jacob approaching.

'Ready?' Decker asked.

Jacob nodded.

They walked without speaking, down the long corridors, passing a pink-clad orderly wheeling a cart of blood vials. When they were alone and out of earshot of anyone else, Decker said, 'You're not dirt.'

Jacob blushed. 'Exactly how much did you hear?'

'Overhear,' Decker corrected. 'Not much after that. You lowered your voice.'

'I was shouting?'

'You were expressing your displeasure at being called a kike and a prick. Also, I didn't want to hear any more, so I walked away.'

'That was nice of you.'

'Believe it or not, I try to respect your privacy.'

They walked a few moments in silence.

Decker said, 'I've been a disappointment to you, haven't I?'

Jacob stopped and stared. 'What?'

'When I married Eema, you thought you'd get a real hero of a dad. Someone to protect you and keep the bogey man away. And maybe I've done that. But you were also banking on a buddy – someone to ride horses with, to play ball with . . . maybe coach your team, a confidant to have long, meaningful talks with. Instead of a pal, you got saddled with a sullen adult male who not only works all the time, but who took your Eema away from you.'

Jacob swallowed hard, his eyes never leaving Decker's face. 'I don't think that at all.'

'Yes, you do. You're just being polite.' Decker headed toward the elevator with Jacob in tow. Arriving at the bank of lifts, he punched the down button and waited without talking. 'Take the other night. Even after I smacked your face, you came up to me to say good-bye. Instead of giving you my full attention for thirty seconds, I brushed you off because I was preoccupied—'

'It was understandable.'

'It was unnecessary. How long does a hug and kiss take? I'm sorry you got such a raw deal.'

The elevator chimed. Neither spoke as they rode the cage down to the parking lot.

When they stepped out, Jacob said, 'You've got it all wrong. I've been the big disappointment. I've caused you and Eema nothing but grief. I sometimes wonder why you put up with me. I know you have to because you're married to my mother, but it goes beyond that. I know you try hard. And I'm not even yours biologically. Or maybe that's why you can toss it off—'

Decker spun around and grabbed Jacob's shoulders. 'You and Sammy are as much my sons as Cynthia and Hannah are my daughters. Blood relationship or not, no matter what would happen to Eema – God forbid – you are stuck with *me* for the rest of your friggin' life.'

Jacob managed a wet smile. 'You make it sound like a death sentence.'

'Ask Cindy. I'm sure at times she feels that way.'

'It's fine with me, Dad. I love you.'

Decker hugged him so hard, he could hear the bones crack. 'I love you, too, Jacob. And I'm going to miss you terribly. All these years have passed . . . I can't get them back. I'm sorry—'

'Stop saying that!' Jacob lowered his voice. 'Just . . .' He broke away, then looped his arm around his stepfather's waist. 'Let's get out of here.'

'Good idea.'

They headed toward the car.

Jacob said, 'She said she's going to prison.'

'I'm not her lawyer, but I would say that's correct.'

'For computer hacking or for the murders?' He wiped his eyes. 'She claimed she didn't know what Holt was doing.'

'And you believe her?'

Jacob thought a moment, then shook his head.

Decker said, 'Do you like her?'

'No. I think she's detestable!'

'But you're still attracted to her.'

'If you like mummies.'

Silence.

Jacob sighed. 'Maybe.'

'It's understandable.' Arm in arm, they walked through the sea of vehicles, trying to find the car.

'You did a really good job the other night,' Jacob said. 'I was bowled over, how you just took command . . . had things all figured out in like no time. It made me proud to be your son.'

Decker allowed himself a slight smile. 'Thank you. You couldn't have said anything nicer.' He looked away. 'I still think you should let me tell your Eema about my dragging you down—'

'She'll only yell at both of us, Dad.'

'She should know about my stupidity.'

'Then she'll find out about my stupidity. Frankly, who needs the friction? Besides, it was neat . . . being on the edge like that. It had a certain pulse.'

'You talk as if you enjoyed it, Yonkeleh.'

'A little . . . a lot, actually.'

'Don't say that!' Decker cried out. 'You'll give your mother a heart attack.'

'So we won't tell my mother that, either. Another little secret.' He sighed. 'Lord knows we've had enough of them over the past couple of years.'

Decker threw his hand over his son's shoulder. Jacob was so young, yet weighted down. 'I know I have zero credibility with you, but you'll be all right. It'll work out, Yonkeleh.'

'Sure it will.'

'It will. All you need is a brilliant, stunningly beautiful, wonderful, Jewish, religious girl with a sexy body and an overactive libido.'

'Right!'

'They do exist.'

'No, Dad, they *don't* exist!'

'Oh, they do.' A slow smile spread across Decker's face. He raised his eyebrows. 'Believe me, they do.'

Jacob stared at him. 'Eeeuw!'

'Eeeuw?'

'Yes, eeeuw. Stop smiling like that! That's my mother!'

'We all come into the world the same way, Yonkel, both prince and bastard.'

'*Stop!* I love my mother!'

'I love your mother, too. Just a little bit . . . *differently* than you do—'

'Oh, gross!' He stalked off toward the car.

Decker smiled broadly, sticking his hands into his pants pockets. Poor Jacob. He thought he had invented sex.

Stalker

Faye Kellerman

Every move you make . . .

It began with a policewoman's sixth sense. Someone is watching her. Then, after the break-in and the midnight car pursuit, she knows. Someone wants to frighten her. Someone wants to hurt her.

But why?

As an inexperienced policewoman, daughter of one of the force's veterans, admitting what's happening feels like a confession of weakness. There seems no option for Cindy Decker but to go it alone, keeping her colleagues and family in the dark. And in a world in which someone is trying to kill you, alone is a very frightening place . . .

'Outstanding, suspense-packed . . . Wise and honest' *Publishers Weekly*

'The page-turner of a plot is fuelled by Kellerman's seemingly boundless knowledge of the psychological mind-set of both cops and criminals . . . Many compelling characters and asides on everything from religion to family dynamics . . . Another winner' *Booklist*

'Very exciting' *Mail on Sunday*

0 7472 5923 2

headline

Jupiter's Bones

Faye Kellerman

Dr Emil Ganz was always extraordinary, in death as well as in life. A physicist whose theories of Cosmology thrilled the world, he disappeared at the peak of his fame, to emerge years later as Jupiter, leader of a community that preached a bizarre blend of mathematics and mysticism, drawing the credulous, the unhappy and the utterly unscrupulous into their enclosed ranks.

And now Ganz's apparent suicide is threatening to destabilise this potentially explosive cult. As the battle to succeed Ganz commences, Lieutenant Peter Decker, working to uncover the scientist's precise fate, begins to fear that his death may simply be the start – and that innocents, the community's children amongst them, could be the first victims, as Jupiter's followers descend into their hellish vision of death and madness . . .

Praise for Faye Kellerman

'The most gripping of recent crime fiction' *Sunday Telegraph*

'Irresistibly plotted' *Financial Times*

'Kellerman succeeds brilliantly in making the search for understanding as compelling as the search for the murderer' *Publishers Weekly*

'Plotting as sumptuously as P. D. James' *Kirkus Review*

0 7472 5922 4

headline